Time for Eternity

By

Susan Squires

Time for Eternity

TIME TOR ETERNITY
Copyright © 2009 by Susan Squires.
All rights reserved.
ISBN: 978-0-312-94353-0
Printed in the United States of America
St. Martin's Paperbacks edition / September 2009
St. Martin's Paperbacks are published by St. Martin's Press, 175 Fifth Avenue, New York, NY 10010.

Republished by Susan Squires, 2015
ISBN-13: 978-1515316602

Susan Squires

To Harry, who chose These Old Shades *to read aloud when it was his turn, and to the wonderful woman who wrote it. They opened up a whole new world to me.*

I have been in love with them both ever since. (Technically, I was in love with Harry before the book.) Homage is due.

Time for Eternity

Praise for *New York Times* **Bestselling Author SUSAN SQUIRES**

ONE WITH THE DARKNESS "Superb writing, vivid narrative combined with complex plotting, and intricate characterization make each novel by Ms. Squires an absolute winner. Don't miss this exciting chapter in this unique and captivating vampire series." —*Romantic Times BOOKreviews*

"One With The Darkness is one of the finest, most innovative vampire novels I've read. "
--*Romance Junkies*

ONE WITH THE SHADOWS "Full of colorful characters, romantic locales, and vivid details of 1820s life, *[One with the Shadows]* has a delicious pace and plenty of thrills, and her vampire mythos is both mannered—almost Victorian—and intriguingly offbeat Bound to net a wide audience of paranormal fans, this *one* may even convert devotees of traditional historicals "
—*Publishers Weekly* (A Best Book of the Year)

ONE WITH THE NIGHT "Superb... captivating... With ho- usual dull and creativity, Ms. Squires has crafted a novel that is passionate, heartbreaking, suspenseful, and completely riveting." —*Romance Reviews Today*

"Few writers combine a sensual romance with a supernatural thriller as well as Susan Squires consistently does. Her latest is a terrific Regency vampire romantic suspense starring two courageous heroes battling one hell of a meanie." —*Midwest Book Review*

"This is an incredibly unusual take on historical vampire stories. Susan Squires delivers an exciting story."
—*Fallen Angel Reviews*

THE BURNING "A terrific tale ... the story line is action-packed."
—*Midwest Book Review*

"Blazingly hot and erotic." —*Romantic Times BOOKreviews*

"Marvelously rich, emotionally charged, imaginative, and beautifully written." —*BookLoons*

"A fantastic erotic vampire thriller." —*Fresh Fiction*

THE COMPANION
"A darkly compelling vampire romance... the plot keeps the reader turning the pages long into the night."
—*Affaire de Coeur*

"Bestseller Squires charts a new direction with this exotic, extremely erotic, and darkly dangerous Regency- set paranormal tale. With her ability to create powerful and tormented characters, Squires has developed a novel that is graphic, gripping, and unforgettable."
—*Romantic Times (4 ½ starred review)*

"Travel through Egypt's deserts and London's society with two of the most intriguing characters you will ever read about. You will encounter a dark world that is intense, scary, and sexy, and a love that will brighten it... powerful and passionate... captivating... Squires has a wonderful ability to keep her readers glued to the edge of their seat." —*Romance Junkies*

"A vibrant, riveting, and sometimes just plain scary novel that should satisfy anyone—including the man in your life—who enjoys paranormal tales ... Squires's saga is off to an intriguing start." —*All About Romance*

Time for Eternity

"Squires does a fantastic job of taking an old tale of vampirism, and she spins it into a new and fresh tale with characters who intrigue and captivate."

—*Fallen Angel Reviews*

"An unforgettable, sensual, and erotic novel that takes you places you've never gone before... will make you believe in the power of true love."

—*Romance Reader at Hear*
t

"*[The Companion]* delivers sensual love scenes, an intriguing plot fraught with danger, adventure, and the unexpected which will leave readers anxiously awaiting the next enthralling tale from this immensely talented author." — *Rendezvous*

"Squires has just taken the traditional vampire novel to a whole new level with *The Companion*. With her riveting and compelling writing, she has woven a tale of love amidst the most desperate of circumstances and created unforgettable characters... fans of the genre will be fascinated... *The Companion* will capture your interest from the first scene until the last... readers who like a strong historical novel as well as one with a definite bite should add *The Companion* to their wish list It will be a keeper for sure!"—aromancereview.com

"Squires has demonstrated a talent that few can surpass. Her descriptions and historical details are flawless. Her characters exceed their potential and the plot keeps you quickly turning the pages Squires has joined the company of authors whose books are classics. Look for this book to become a classic in its genre too. *The Companion* is a gem."

—*Coffee Time Romance*

"A totally absorbing novel... the characters are brilliantly conceived and perfect for the gripping plotline. The

Susan Squires

author gives the reader a unique twist on what vampires really are, a tortured hero to adore, the only heroine who could possibly be right for him, a truly horrific villain—and a fascinating story that carries the reader through one exciting adventure after another... Squires's prose grabs you from the beginning and gives you a relentless ride through this complex, beautifully written book." —*New and Used Books*

"A riveting story, the first of what I expect to become a fresh, unforgettable new vampire series." —*BookLoons*

"A book to be savored, not torn through at breakneck speed... Squires is a talented author and *The Companion* offers the promise of more beautifully, dark vampire novels to follow."

—*Romance Reader*

Time for Eternity

Also by Susan Squires

Companion Series:
Sacrament
The Companion
The Hunger (prequel to The Companion)
The Burning
One with the Night
One with the Shadows
One with the Darkness
Sacrilege (novella)

DaVinci Time Travel Series:
Time for Eternity
Twist in Time
Mists of Time

Magic Series:
Do You Believe in Magic?
He's a Magic Man
Waiting for Magic
Night Magic
The Magic's in the Music
Your Magic Touch (novella)

Body Electric
Danegeld
Danelaw
No More Lies

Find the latest by Susan Squires at <u>www.susansquires.com</u>

Susan Squires

Time for Eternity

Time for Eternity

One

Bartending wasn't a bad gig for a vampire. Night work. You could get a job anywhere. Especially if you looked not a day over twenty-five and exuded that vampire electric energy that made you seem more alive than anyone else around you.

Ozone was one of the trendiest gin joints in San Francisco. Frankie's shift had been attracting lots of tourists lately. See above, vampire attraction. That and the French accent she couldn't seem to quite shake. Americans loved accents. It might be time to move on. This city was too damned foggy anyway. She wiped down the brushed stainless steel bar. The bottles behind her on glass shelves were backlit by a huge glass panel that gradually changed colors, sliding along the rainbow. The stools were lighted blue disks that seemed to float in midair like the bottles. The neon sign O_2 outside in the murk cast a pale blue glow over the front tables.

The last of a birthday party was breaking up just before closing. The crowd milled around, collecting coats and umbrellas.

"See ya, Frankie." That one was a regular—Jason? Josh? He left a hundred on the bar. She'd been giving generous pours all night, no matter what kind of shit-ass drink they'd ordered. Chocolate schnapps and vodka was in no way a martini just because you put it in a martini glass.

She nodded to him and wiped her glass. Suzie, the waitress, saluted as the last of the crowd cleared out, letting Frankie know she was leaving half an hour early. She had a boyfriend waiting at home. Drove Frankie crazy sometimes, imagining what they'd be doing by the time she could close up and trudge back to her third-floor walk-up over on Holt. One (but only one) of the curses of having this thing in her blood was that it drove her crazy with wanting sex.

Time for Eternity

Great. She could blow outta here right at closing. Like she had somewhere to go or someone waiting for her. The weight that settled in her chest seemed natural after a couple of centuries. Eternity stretched ahead, empty of any real relationships. Couldn't let people close when you had something to hide. She couldn't even escape her fate. The thing in her blood loved life. A lot. It regenerated cells to keep its host body young, and once it got hold of you, you just couldn't bring yourself to commit suicide, no matter how hard you tried. And she had.

Maybe sex was an expression of its urge to life too. Maybe that's why she was so horny.

No escape and no solace. No friends, no lovers, not even God. She'd lost any interest in a God that let someone be made into a monster through no fault of her own.

For the millionth time she thought about the moment she'd been infected. A stupid little scrape. How could she know he was a vampire? Or that even one molecule of his blood could infect her? *He* knew what he was. He should have been more careful. But Henri didn't care about anything. Or anybody. It made her blood boil just to think about it

Damn you to hell, Henri Foucault....

She slid glasses into the racks over the sink at the end of the bar, hanging them by their stems.

If someone granted me one wish, I'd go back and do it over. I'd stop myself from touching Henri's bleeding hand.

It was a kind of game she played. How could you make one wish turn out the way you wanted when the universe was out to trick you? Wish to lose weight and you might lose a leg. Want money? What if people thought you stole it and locked you up? No, you had to wish for something in just the right way, with plenty of codicils. So not touching Henri's cut wouldn't be good enough. He might infect her some other time with the same result. She'd been living in his house and imagined herself in love with the "wicked duke." A young girl's foolish crush. The girl she'd been would never leave him. Henri was not only a gorgeous guy but he had that irresistible vampire vitality. Sooner or later, it would still have been vampire time for her.

She followed the twisted path she'd daydreamed about so many times before. The horrific conclusion didn't seem so horrific after you'd repeated it a million times.

The only way to prevent herself from being made vampire for certain was to kill Henri.

It had taken a while to accept that, rat though he was. She wasn't a killer by nature even now. Those people she'd killed before she knew how to take blood without damaging them still haunted her. For decades she tried to work out various ways of ensuring that her naïve former self wouldn't fall in love with Henri. But there was only one way to be sure. And what would it matter if he died? It wasn't as if Henri made any positive difference to the world. He didn't care about anything or anyone. He was a monster in the truest sense.

Glasses clinked as she dunked them two by two in soapy water, then in hot water laced with sanitizer, then set them out to dry on a wooden rack. The question was, how could a girl of twenty-one decapitate a vampire with more than human strength? They healed anything less drastic. She knew that personally. And she knew decapitation was the way to kill a vampire because that's the way two vampires had tried to kill her when they found she'd been made by another vampire, not born to the blood.

She'd found the answer to her problem during her addict phase in *fin de siècle* Paris. With enough fruit of the poppy, vampires could be drugged. It took a lot. Enough to kill a human. So if she could drug Henri, then…

The door opened. *Merde.* She glanced to the glowing blue clock at the rear. Twenty minutes to closing. Why couldn't these idiots stay home on such a raunchy night?

Then she felt the electric vibrations so powerful they existed just at the edge of consciousness and caught the scent of cinnamon and ambergris. Double *merde.*

The woman looked like she was about to walk a red carpet somewhere. Black hair done up in complicated, intertwining loops, eyes so dark they might be black, creamy shoulders wrapped in swathes of translucent coppery fabric shot through with gold threads. Her dress was copper satin, full-skirted. She might have been any age.

Literally.

Frankie's breath caught in her chest. Vampire. And that meant big trouble.

"I felt your vibrations on the street," the woman said. Her accent was vaguely…Italian. She slid onto a blue barstool.

"What do you want?" Frankie asked, her voice flat

"I'll have a Bombay Sapphire martini, straight up, two olives."

Like that was what Frankie meant.

The woman raised her brows. "And do use vermouth. So many bartenders these days don't. That makes it a shot of gin with an olive, not a martini."

The vampire might be preparing to kill her, but at least she knew how to drink. Frankie filled a martini glass with ice to buy time. Could she get past her to the door? She knew from experience that the vibrations meant that this one was very strong. Did Frankie even want to escape? Maybe death would be a relief, but the thing in her blood shuddered in revulsion. She grabbed the blue, square bottle and the Noilly Prat and scooped more ice into a stainless steel shaker.

"I can't place you. So you must be made."

Frankie stopped shaking the drink. "Look, if you're going to kill me just get on with it."

"Kill you because you're made?" The woman's chuckle was deep and throaty. "I'm the last to point fingers. I made my husband."

"You made him vampire?" *Whoa.* Probably some horrible divorce revenge.

The woman's smile could only be described as fond. "In A.D. 41. I hope he can get here before closing. He's hosting the after party for the opera. I find crowds difficult these days."

Frankie was shocked on so many levels. At how old the woman was. That she had been with one man for that long. That she still spoke of him fondly. "Didn't he hate you for making him…what he is?" How could he not?

She shook her head, still smiling. "It gave us forever. You were not made by a lover?"

Frankie snorted. "I thought I loved him." She set the martini on the bar. "But I was just a nuisance. He probably did it to punish me." She wanted to shock this woman who believed in love enough to stay with one man for almost two millennia.

The woman frowned. "You…you are French?"

Frankie nodded.

"How long ago were you made?"

Frankie shrugged. "Couple centuries and change."

"French, around the Revolution." The woman tapped her chin. "Not Henri Foucault?"

"The very one." Frankie's voice was light, as if she didn't care.

"He was a fine man," the woman murmured. "He would not have broken the Rules of our kind for petty revenge. It is the Cardinal Sin to make another vampire. One is outcast from vampire society if the Elders ever find out, never allowed the solace of others who understand one. It is a commitment to the one you make like no other. He must have loved you very much."

A fine man? Frankie snorted. "He loved no one. It might have been an accident. That's the best face I could put on it."

"Making a vampire is never accidental. The human needs repeated infusions of a vampire's blood to acquire immunity to the Companion and survive the infection."

The Companion. That's what Henri called the parasite too. "Oh, he made me drink his damned blood, all right. Then he abandoned me without a word."

The beautiful vampire thought about that for a moment. "You hate him."

"Bingo. And I hate what I am and I'd give anything to take back that instant when his blood got into that stupid little scrape on my palm." Frankie stared at her. "Anything."

"Ahhhh." The woman sighed. "Centuries of regret and anger can poison your soul."

Time for Eternity

"I try not to think about it." Frankie started putting the trays of limes, lemons, olives, and cherries into the refrigerator.

"But you think about it all the time." The woman's voice held pity.

Like she should be strong enough not to think about it? "Oh, only when I have to drink somebody's blood to stop the craving. Or when I have to hide my strength. When a wound heals instantaneously. Or when I can see in the dark, or hear the drip in the men's room sink from here, or smell that a woman wearing perfume walked by three days ago—that sort of thing." She sounded bitter, even to herself. "So, yeah. I think about it."

"I'm sorry." The woman took a long sip of her drink. "I know what regret is like."

Frankie shut the fridge door. "I just want to be normal. With normal relationships and a normal life span... You know...normal?" Frankie tried on a shrug. "Probably not. Anyway, I don't want to spend eternity serving the needs of this thing in my blood."

"Henri..." The woman's voice was hesitant. "Henri was guillotined. Did you know?"

Frankie jerked around. Henri, *dead?* Her parasite's reaction to the thought of decapitation sent another shudder through her. Or maybe it was something else. She'd thought he was out there somewhere, alive, callous, bored with the world but doing exactly as he wanted, always. She'd dreamed of confronting him, even searched for him a couple of times in Paris over the years. The thought that he had been dead all along just seemed...wrong. Then she started to chuckle. The damned, cruel good-for-nothing had escaped even being held accountable for his misdeeds.

She managed to suck in a breath and stop the laughing. It had gotten a little hysterical. The woman watched her, curious. It took a moment for Frankie to gather herself for another shrug. "The devil...the devil got his due."

The woman raised her brows as Frankie pointedly put the gin bottle away and wiped down the bar. *Merde.* Her hand was shaking. Then she started to think. How could a vampire be guillotined? Why not just disappear as she had seen Henri do? She glanced to the woman.

Who seemed to read her mind… "Too badly damaged to transport, perhaps. Or weakened by the sun…" Frankie stood immobile, thinking about that. Henri so wounded he couldn't escape, or blistered until he was almost unrecognizable by the sun… Did anyone deserve that?

"I am Donna Poliziano," the woman said quietly. "If ever my husband or I can do anything for you, you can find us at 430 Pine, up on Nob Hill."

Frankie stopped in mid-wipe. "Right. Like you'd do anything for me."

"But we would," the vampire insisted. "San Francisco is our city. We watch over it. We would know if you were killing for what you need. But the police have found no bodies drained of blood. So you have a soul. You haven't gone mad in spite of your difficulties. So it is a strong soul. Those are rare."

"Just leave me alone. That's what I want." Frankie wiped the same spot on the bar again.

"Ahhhh, but is it?" The woman twirled her glass, apparently thinking. Good thing she didn't expect an answer, because Frankie wasn't biting. Finally she reached into her evening bag and pulled out a tiny cell phone. Her face softened as she said, "Jergan, it's Donna. Change in plans. Meet me at home?" She smiled as she listened. "You too." She snapped it shut and stood. "*Ciao*, my vampire friend."

And with that she left.

Leaving Frankie feeling…angry. What right had Donna-whoever-she-was, vampire, to come waltzing in here, flaunting the fact that she liked being a monster so much she had made a monster of a man she obviously loved? And Henri had been dead for two hundred years and there was nothing Frankie could do about it. She'd never be able to tell him how much she hated him. She felt cheated. And…and he might have died, not quickly as the guillotine was meant to execute people, horrible as that death was, but slowly and painfully, damaged by sun or terribly wounded. Maybe she was angry at herself for the twinge of sympathy that evoked in her.

Time for Eternity

Frankie shook her head as though to banish all those thoughts. Time did *not* heal all wounds. But there was no way she was going to give up the callus she had grown to protect herself. It was the only thing keeping her sane.

She flipped up the portion of the bar that let her out and strode to the back room. To hell with cleaning up. Let Steve fire her.

*****

The next night Frankie pulled off her parka and tossed it onto the coat rack for employees at the back of the small kitchen that served Ozone. She hadn't slept all day, thinking about Henri and the vampire woman who loved her vampire husband and looked…wise and…happy. Bitch. And that brought her back to Henri. That the Donna person thought he was a fine man was puzzling. Maybe she was as twisted and evil as Henri. After all, she was a monster too.

Frankie was dressed, as usual, in black leather pants and heeled boots. Tonight she wore a sparkly silver sleeveless sweater, knit so loosely she had to wear an ivory-colored tank beneath it. To work at a trendy bar you had to look the part. Pale was good and who more pale than a vampire? Her blond hair curled softly so she spiked it out with some gel and streaked the spikes black. She was sleekly built and good-looking and her ice-blue eyes could stare down anyone. *De rigueur* for a bartender in a place like Ozone.

"Frankie. Someone left a package for you." Steve, manager-guy, dressed the part too. Expensive little suit covering his bony ass and a narrow black tie so unfashionable it was fashionable.

"Great." She pushed past him through the chaos of the kitchen. People parted for her as they always did—aura of vampires. That part came in handy.

Steve came up behind her. "Might want to let your friends know there's mail service in San Francisco these days."

"Yeah, yeah." Who could be leaving her a package at

Ozone? Or at all? She never got any mail other than catalogues and offers of free credit scores or Viagra substitutes.

She pushed into the din of the main room. The after-office-hours body exchange was already in full swing at six. The two guys who worked 'til eleven were really moving, in that economical way experienced bartenders acquired.

"Hey, Frankie. You got a package. It's under the bar." Ricardo had a body to die for. Too bad she didn't indulge at work. Or at all, these days.

"I heard." She began to set out her station, making sure her preps were just where she wanted them.

"You don't want to know what it is?"

"Not especially."

"Shit, Frankie, curiosity is killing me. It was delivered by *messenger.*

"Learn to live with it." Suzie brought up an order for a big table. The night was off and running. Cripes. Didn't people know how to order anything but Apple-tinis and Cosmos?

*****

The bar was empty. Frankie finished cleaning up. She did an extra good job to make up for last night to the day guys. Or maybe she was putting off opening the package. She had felt it waiting for her by the soda tanks all night, no matter what she told Ricardo. It was about the size of a thick photo album, wrapped in heavily waxed brown paper and tied with old-fashioned twine, labeled with her name in elaborate cursive script. She hesitated, then picked it up and set it on the bar. It was heavy. She poured herself a glass of Frank Family chardonnay and headed to a booth in the back, her package under her arm. Might as well relax and look at the pictures.

She settled in and tore open the wrapper. She could smell the leather binding. An envelope slid onto the table. "Open me first," it ordered in the same calligraphy. How coy. Okay, she'd bite (no pun intended). She turned up the little lamp on the table until it cast a pool of light over the letter. The envelope was made of heavy paper, the kind that felt like it was made of rags, like in the old days, not wood pulp. Expensive. She tore it open and spread out the sheets. It was

Time for Eternity

signed Donnatella di Poliziano. The woman from last night? Frankie frowned.

"My dear Ms. Suchet," it began. How did the woman know her name? Ominous.

> *I know you will not seek my help. So I leave this book to you instead, as a kind of a challenge. Please reserve judgment about what I tell you until you have read my note through and looked at the book. This is not a gift I give lightly. You are the first person with whom I have shared my secret in nearly two hundred years. What secret, you ask? Let us begin with the fact that time is not linear, but a vortex. It is possible to jump from one part of the vortex into another. (Remember; you are to reserve your judgment.) My friend Leonardo built me a machine. With a vampire's power and his genius, it is possible to go to another time. I went back and changed a decision I had regretted all my life.*
>
> *You can change what happened to you too, Ms. Suchet. The machine is in Florence under the Baptistery of Il Duomo. We should have destroyed it. But it would have been like destroying part of Leonardo. We simply couldn't bring ourselves to do it. On the attached sheet you will find directions.*
>
> *Be warned. There will be difficulties. This will be like no adventure you have ever embarked upon. But what choice have you? This is the only way to discover what you truly want and claim it.*
>
> *Do not let regret poison you, child. Have the courage to change your destiny as I changed mine. My heartfelt best wishes go with you.*
>
> *Donnatella di Poliziano*

Emotions chased one another through Frankie's belly and up into her throat. Time machine? The woman was a loon.

Yet the world held vampires. How many people would think that was crazy?

Her heart began to thump uncomfortably in her chest. What if you *could* change things, just as she had daydreamed for so many years? What if she didn't have to be vampire?

She opened the book. The leather was supple and cared for. The sheets were vellum. That had to mean it was really old. Her Latin was a little rusty, but there was a note to Donnatella and no one could miss the signature. Leonardo da Vinci. Donna's friend was da Vinci? Possible, if she had lived since ancient Rome. Of course the signature might not be real. The note said that time was a vortex. *Yeah, I got that part from Donna's letter.* She skimmed ahead. That you could think of another time and the machine would…would take you there. *Oh, right, and how was that?* And the machine couldn't stay in the new time forever. It would slip back to its point of origin. She flipped the pages. Lots of diagrams and scribbled notes, indecipherable. It looked like the notes were written right to left, as though to be read in a mirror.

This was bullshit, of course.

Her eyes slid back to the signature. Da Vinci. He'd invented a flying machine four hundred years before the Wright brothers… If anyone could have invented a time machine, wouldn't it be Leonardo da Vinci?

She sat in the dim blue glow of Ozone, the open book seeming to float in the circle of brighter light on the table. What was even more stupid than this obvious hoax was that somewhere inside she wanted desperately for it to be true. This was her chance to make that daydream real. The universe was granting her one wish.

Okay, authenticate the book. If the book was real...

She'd have a decision to make.

*****

Frankie looked up at the amazing green and white checkerboard marble of the cathedral called Il Duomo in Florence, glimmering in the streetlights. Vespers were just ending. Worshippers poured out the great bronze doors. In the streets to either side tourists were dining in the busy *trattorias*.

Time for Eternity

Frankie still couldn't believe she was in Italy. She'd taken the overnight flight from San Francisco to New York, and another to Paris the next night and then on to Florence on the third night. She still couldn't avoid some daylight, what with the time changes. Sunlight burned her, though the burns it induced couldn't kill her. So she bundled up as though she were a strict Muslim. That caused some stares. But at least her trip was only very uncomfortable, not actually shriek-inducing. She hated to admit she wanted this fantasy to be true that much.

You're just going to look and see if it's there.

There was no way she was going to find a time machine built by Leonardo da Vinci in the crypts under the Baptistery. So this whole journey was a stupid waste of effort.

The young woman in that tiny shop off Market Street hadn't looked much like an expert in old books. But the prof from Berkeley who frequented Ozone said she was. The girl confirmed the book was real and written by da Vinci. She almost didn't need to say it outright. The reverence in her voice after she compared the signature to known da Vinci autographs, examined the paper, tested a tiny spot of ink, said it for her. She said it was characteristic that he wrote from right to left. He was left-handed and eccentric. She'd translated passages more precisely for Frankie: the theory of how the machine worked, how he'd built it. And his note to Donna, like a kind of preface. The note said he'd never found enough power to operate the machine. But he thought that Donna could.

He knew what she was.

That still sent chills down Frankie's spine. Vampires could call on the power of the parasite in their blood. There was a lot of power. Frankie didn't know exactly how much. After some hesitant early experiments, she never used her power except to run out her fangs, and then she used as little as possible, at least until this week. But she'd seen Henri actually call power to create a whirling blackness and just…disappear. It was how vampires moved around without being seen. Handy for what she'd been up to in the last few days in Florence. And no doubt the source of the bat myth. Who knew the source of the other myths—silver and holy water, wolfs-bane? Thank God they were myths. She liked silver jewelry. And who wanted pizza without garlic?

So she left the book with the amazed girl expert as a gift, taking only Donna's note and directions with her. And here she was in Florence, just to see if this could possibly be true. Not that it could. Not that she'd do anything if it were.

Who was she kidding? If she didn't intend to use the machine, if she found one, then why had she used her power to disappear and reappear inside a hospital supply room to steal enough morphine to float a ship? She had never dared to use her power in that way before. And why had she bought clothes that might be mistaken for 1794? A waisted, full-length skirt in revolutionary blue, flat leather slippers, and an off-the-shoulder red blouse with a white scarf looking very much like a fichu. Let's not forget the fact that she'd gone back to her natural blond curls, sans spikes. They might very well be mistaken for hair arranged *a l'enfant,* as she'd worn it so long ago.

There should be no lying to herself. She'd bought a replica of a gladiator's sword and it was packed, along with a change of clothes, in a leather gym bag that had cost her a fortune at the Hermés store. The very concept of using it on Henri caused a shudder in her. Could she *do* this? She bit her lip. She wouldn't have to do anything. There was no time machine under the Baptistery.

Yet she'd bought Canadian maple leaves and South African Krugerrands at a precious metals exchange because she'd need currency good even in 1794, and nothing was easier to exchange than gold.

No, there was no question about what she was going to do if she found some kind of a machine under the Duomo's Baptistery. Or about how much she wanted it to be there.

She moved through the stream of worshippers to the cobbled pavement outside the cathedral. Across an open plaza the ornate octagonal Baptistery rose. She slipped inside the great bronze doors and slid into the shadows of one of the marble columns that marched around the perimeter in pairs. She hadn't been in a church in two hundred years. Priests moved quietly about, dousing lamps, signaling the visitors that it was time to leave. Soon only the many candles to the right of the altar shed their flickering light across the intricately tiled floor. To other visitors the amazing dome covered with mosaics in medieval glory and liberally doused with gilt would be lost in shadow. But Frankie could see it clearly, along with the statues lining the upper gallery whose bases held the relics of the saints they portrayed. The remaining priest looked around and, thinking the Baptistery empty, slipped out a side door.

Frankie exhaled. Okay. Okay, she could do this. She didn't even need to refer to Donna's note. She'd memorized it long ago. She crossed the marble mosaic floor to the altar at the far side and peered behind it.

Merde! Uh, maybe she shouldn't say that here. Or even think it, no matter how surprised she was at the gaping aperture at her feet. Donna was right. A stairway led down. Frankie was having difficulty getting enough air. It wasn't that the Baptistery was stuffy. Three breaths. Okay. She started down into the darkness. The air rising from below was cooler. A warm, if faint, glow increased as she descended. Bending to peer out before she took the last three steps, she saw a wide, empty room lit by a single lamp standing on a kind of altar in the middle. Donna said it always burned there. Marble coffins lined the edges, the profiles of their owners trapped in stone. The floor was made of heavy marble slabs with worn lettering. The place smelled like a basement. But there was also an aroma of dust and stone that somehow combined to convey age.

One slab was not inset. Frankie chewed on her lips. Just as Donna had said.

Below that slab were catacombs. She knew what that meant. Decaying bodies. Maybe rats. *Crap in a hat.* Could she do it? Just to see that a stupid machine wasn't there? Frankie should just turn right around and run up these stairs as fast as she could.

But she didn't.

It was impossible to undo what had happened to her. Even if the time machine was there (which it wasn't), even if it could take her back (which it couldn't), she might not be able to bring herself to kill Henri, or he might kill her instead. He was certainly stronger than she was. But if she didn't try, she would live forever half-drowned in a river of isolation and regret, hating what she was, with even escape into suicide impossible. She'd probably go mad, just as Donna had said.

So she had to try. And that meant lifting up the slab with the strength of a vampire and going down into the catacombs.

A nervous giggle escaped her and echoed against the sarcophagi. What was she afraid of? She was a vampire, for God's sake! She couldn't die. She'd heal a rat bite. Was she afraid she'd catch death from some moldering corpses? Not possible. But if it was, so what? She'd *welcome* death if she could escape eternity as a vampire. And the truth was, she herself was way worse than anything down in those crypts.

She strode across the floor to get the lamp and set it down next to the slab. She crouched and heaved the stone to the side. Echoes reverberated from the stone arches as she set it down. The angle of the hole revealed only darkness. Still she picked up the lantern and started down the worn stone steps. The walls of the stairwell were dry, surprisingly, and when she got to the bottom, the shadowy niches that surrounded her seemed to contain only dust. Not so bad. She held up the light, just to face her fears. Dust and some crumbly bones. Okay, there was one where the skull was pretty much intact. And here and there some primitive crucifixes, some scraps of leather were evident There was a feeling of fullness and…timelessness in the air.

She could deal. No sign of rats yet. *Save the best for last.*

She opened up the little map Donna had drawn. The catacombs formed a maze and she had to get to the other side. Kinda like the first computer games she'd played. Hope she didn't run into any gobbling ghosts. She muttered directions to herself as she turned corners. Left, right, right… Finally she came to a long straight corridor.

Bingo. She strode down between the niches stacked

Time for Eternity

four high to the wall at the end. She knelt. Tenth brick up from the bottorn. Push.

She wasn't sure if she was surprised or not when a portion of the wall swung open. Maybe this was an elaborate hoax to see just how far she'd go. Maybe someone in that darkness was waiting to pop up and make a funny home video.

It was a mark of her desperation that she didn't care. She stepped over the threshold.

Two

Her gasp sounded loud in the silence.

A huge machine towered over her. Giant gears and levers interlocked with smaller ones in some crazy pattern that was…well, beautiful. The metal gleamed golden, shiny with oil. Probably bronze. At points in the mechanism were set what looked like jewels the size of her fist, red and green and blue. Those couldn't be real. Could they? From the center of the machine thrust a three-foot rod topped by a glittering, clear stone.

Merde. That was a diamond.

She stood, transfixed. Slowly the whole thing began to sink in. She was in a secret room hidden in the catacombs beneath a cathedral in Florence looking at a time machine built by Leonardo da Vinci that could be powered only by his friend who was a vampire.

And Frankie. She could power it too. She just had to draw her power like she did to run out her fangs and feed, or like she did when she had appeared inside that hospital supply room. Only more power. Way more.

It was so unreal that it felt very real. She was a vampire who couldn't exist, but did. So why not a time machine to take her back and correct the very thing that had made her vampire?

Uh-oh. Bad thought. What if she changed the world by going back?

If she were never made vampire, the Frankie who had lived two hundred years would cease to be. But she'd never done anything important. She'd slinked along the shadows of life, trying not to be noticed. No one would miss her if she were successful and died after a single lifetime. And she'd probably only deprive Henri of a few weeks or months until he was guillotined. Who would miss a slimeball like that? Besides, Donna had gone back and corrected her mistake and the world

Time for Eternity

hadn't ended.

She stood there, breathing hard. Her life in the eighteenth century washed over her. Not great. The hooped skirts, the restrictions on women. Hated those. Hell, the head lice in those damned wigs everyone else wore or in their ratted natural hair were pretty horrible. Even the first time around, she'd refused that fashion. People didn't bathe often. Their clothes couldn't be sent to the dry cleaners either. A bastard daughter of the Vicomte d'Evron and his opera dancer, she'd never known her mother, and she didn't belong in her father's world. At twenty-one she'd had no prospects, living in genteel poverty in Paris, attendant and dependent upon a kind woman with no prospects herself. She'd been an outcast even before becoming a monster. Bread riots, starvation. And of course there was the Reign of Terror. People were denounced and guillotined for just thinking things that weren't sufficiently revolutionary. More than a hundred thousand died during those awful years. She and Madame LaFleur had lived in constant fear.

When Henri saved her from the mob, it had seemed a miracle. No wonder her childish crush had turned to a deeper feeling for him. He might have been callous and devil-may-care, but he was also fearless. That was awfully attractive to someone who felt powerless.

But she'd been naïve then. When she went back now she'd have two hundred years under her belt. The eighteenth century would be a piece of cake. She wouldn't think about the deed she was going to do. It was the price of saving her soul. Henri's death should make her mortal again. Then she wouldn't have the power to run the time machine. So the modern world would be lost forever unless she could just ride along when it returned to the present day. Eighteenth century or twenty-first? It didn't matter. She'd be human again.

She was already thinking about going back in time as if it were possible. Yeah. Well, no time like the present to find out. *Just do it, girl.* Frankie stepped forward and grabbed the diamond. She pulled.

Nothing happened.

Oh, the power part. She pushed the lever back up. *Companion!* she called, as though she needed it to run out her canines. Power surged up her veins like throbbing desire. Red film descended over her field of vision. To anyone watching, her eyes would have gone red. *Companion, more!* The throbbing became almost relentless. A whirl of darkness seeped up around her ankles. Uh-oh. She wanted her power directed to the machine, not to disappearing. She pushed down the darkness and concentrated on the machine. Her body tightened. She pulled the lever. Beyond the throb of power in her ears she heard the machine creak.

Still nothing happened.

This was going to take some doing. She called for more power, focusing all her attention on the machine. The giant gear in the center of the machine began to slowly grind, setting all the smaller wheels in frantic motion.

Bingo. *Companion!* Her body arched as the power sang in her veins and the song shrieked up the scale.

The gears whirred so fast they woe almost invisible. She should think about the instant she wanted to land in. Before the time Henri had cut himself on that stupid breaking glass. Just at the time she'd been taken into his household, so she'd have easy access...

God! A luminescent glow began to seep outward from her body, forming a blinding white corona. She'd never known she had so much power. The tension in her body, the shriek in her veins, were almost unbearable. Could she survive this?

Then the gears slowed. Everything slowed, even her thoughts. Had she failed?

Power still hummed in the air. It smelled like the ozone left in the atmosphere after lightning. She grimaced in a rictus smile. She couldn't escape ozone even here. She pushed for more power.

It didn't matter. The gears all stopped.

She'd failed. She strained toward the eighteenth century, trying to imagine it, the dirty streets, the roaming mobs of Paris. Poverty and ugliness. What a contrast with the luxury

Time for Eternity

of Versailles that Henri had showed her…

Everything snapped back into motion and she felt herself being flung like a stone in a slingshot into more and more and more speed. The jewels lit up. They magnified the power into colored beams that crisscrossed, swinging in arcs across the stone ceiling. Pain surged into every fiber of her body.

Then, blackness.

*****

Frankie raised her head and wished she hadn't "Shit howdy," she moaned. Vampires didn't get drunk. How could she have a hangover? Something hard poked into her shoulder. She wasn't where she expected to be. Unless she had rocks in her bed.

She cracked open an eye.

Merde. Merde. Merde. Above her in the dimness loomed the great golden machine, its gears still and silent against a ceiling of uneven rock. She was in some kind of a cave.

She pushed herself up on one elbow, groaning, and blinked to clear her vision. Reddish afternoon light filtered through the entrance to the cave. Outside, green trees fluttered leaves in the breeze. Was it a cave? Some of the walls merged into bricks. Where the hell was she? And when the hell was this?

She got to her hands and knees and pulled her skirts up around her thighs. She didn't trust herself to stand yet She half crawled toward the entrance. It was partially blocked by a huge marble statue. It appeared to be a naked man surrounded by six nymphs.

She gasped. She knew this place! It was the grotto built for the statue of Apollo in the gardens at Versailles, long gone in the twenty-first century.

Tears sprang to her eyes as she struggled for breath. The damned machine had actually worked! She blinked back the

Susan Squires

tears of shock and surprise. Could…could it really be? Was she really in 1794? It didn't seem possible.

The first time she saw this statue and its two companion pieces of Apollo's horses was when she'd been to Versailles with Henri. A flashing cascade of images from that night threatened to overwhelm her. The feel of his flesh, the gleam of passion in his eyes seemed so real, so near. That night had been her downfall. She must avoid it this time around.

She had meant to come back to Paris. The machine must have gotten lost somehow. Was it the summer of 1794? Or did the machine mistake that too?

But maybe the machine hadn't made a mistake. She ran her hands through her hair and tried to think. At the last minute, just when she'd given up hope that the machine would move, she'd thought about Versailles.

Okay, okay. This wasn't a disaster. Versailles was only twelve miles from Paris. And one of her gold coins would probably buy a hundred coach tickets to get there. The village of Versailles was used to supporting the court of Louis XVI. Surely she could change her gold coins there for sous she could actually spend in 1794.

She felt the sun set, as her kind always did. She must act quickly in the gloaming that would follow. She gathered up her leather bag. She pushed out into the grove around the grotto and down the little incline, past the marvelous marble horses that looked as though they might spring out into the intricate formal gardens of Versailles just ahead. The grand palace façade itself was far away to her right. Its creamy austere stone, and a fortune in glazed windows, caught the sun in the upper stories. Around the gardens, members of the Gendarmerie National in their blue uniforms herded people toward the main gates. Ever since the court had been forcibly moved back to Paris so that they might be accountable to the people, the grounds had been open to the public. The hoi polloi, dressed in the working-class fashions of 1794—the men in wide-legged trousers and clumsily made boots, the women in aprons and caps with coarse fichus thrown about their shoulders, roamed the grounds. But it wouldn't have taken the clothing to tell her

Time for Eternity

it wasn't the twenty-first century anymore. There was no smell of diesel from tour buses or hot asphalt from parking lots. The crowd chattered and laughed. Children screamed because they were tired but there were no ring tones insisting on attention, no angry car horns.

Frankie took a breath, blinking. She'd done it. Or rather Leonardo's machine had done it. She was in 1794.

A feeling of nausea cascaded over her. Her knees felt weak. She put her hand out to the marble basin of the fountain to steady herself and hung her head, breathing slowly and deeply. What was the matter with her? She almost chuckled. *I mean, besides just having traveled through time? Besides being in revolutionary France, where being an aristocrat is grounds for beheading'! Or that I've come here to kill Henri Foucault, vampire extraordinaire?*

She blinked and gathered herself. She couldn't fail, no matter how repugnant the task.

Frankie took a breath and started down the path around the pool that surrounded the great rock supporting the statue of Apollo. She made for the main gate, through hedges once neatly trimmed in fantastic shapes now going back to nature, shoots and errant leaves obscuring their design. The flowerbeds were clogged with discarded revolutionary tracts, and here and there some muddied piece of clothing. Public access was hard on the place. There must be no money for upkeep these days, and no desire to keep up the ultimate symbol of aristocracy.

Now for the village. There would be coaches leaving to take the picnickers back to Paris. And she'd be on one of them.

*****

Frankie stumbled from the *diligence* among a hail of other bodies and took a deep breath. The stench of Paris might be bad, but anything was better than the body odor inside that coach. Would she get used to this again? The coach held eight comfortably, but there had been twelve inside and about twenty clinging outside. Frankie had been crushed between a woman with a crying child and a man with roaming hands. Only when she gripped his wrist hard enough to leave bruises and deposited his hand back into his lap did he cease and desist with a sputtering protest. Respectable young women didn't travel alone. That thought made Frankie smile grimly. If the man only knew how unrespectable she really was, he would probably shit a brick.

She looked around the busy yard of the posting inn. Carriages clattered as they wheeled around, jockeying for position. Horses snorted and whinnied. The air smelled of soot and night soil. People shouted for coffee and toasted bread. She was close now. If only she knew exactly at what moment in her previous life she'd arrived. If she'd come too late—if even now, across town in the Marais district, he was infecting her then the whole thing had been for naught. If she was early enough, she might even save her employer and friend, Madame LaFleur, from arrest. She'd force the old lady to leave Paris before Robespierre and his bitch-mistress got to her.

Somehow she had to avoid her former self, the one that was living through this whole disorganized, dangerous mess for the first time. Time travel stories always said meeting yourself was a bad thing. If she succeeded in killing Henri, she would probably cease to exist as Frankie, vampire. Maybe she'd just blink out, leaving only the innocent girl she'd once been. She refused to get lost in the conundrums of whether, if her vampire self ceased to exist, she would be there in the twenty-first century to use Donna's time machine and come back to prevent herself from becoming vampire. That was what she hated about time travel stories. You couldn't avoid the inherent circular logic. All that hadn't seemed to bother Donna. Frankie held to that.

Frankie hefted her leather bag, tossed a sou to a vendor in return for a bun filled with unknown meat, and struck out into the sultry night, munching on dinner.

She hurried past cafes where men shouted their political views over the hum of laughing diners, and taverns where others drank their dinner. Paris had never gone to bed early.

As many times as she had imagined killing Henri, the

prospect of actually doing it was much different. She set her lips and hurried over the Pont Neuf across the Seine, striding down the Quai de l'Horloge toward the Marais, her heart pounding. Lord knows why Henri still lived in the Marais. In the seventeenth century it had been the height of fashion, but the aristocracy now lived across the Seine in the Faubourg St Germain. He was just contrary enough to avoid trends. Or maybe, being so old, he held to tradition. For whatever reason, she would find him in the faded grandeur of the Marais, the only place Madame LaFleur could afford.

She smelled the smoke. Her heart skipped. An orange glow over the Place Royale told her that she'd arrived on the exact night she joined the wicked duc's household. Some part of her was relieved. It was perhaps a week before the fatal moment when she had been made vampire. She had time to kill Henri. But was she in time to save Madame LaFleur? She turned into the huge open square. The beautiful façades of the houses across the park were in flames. Or rather one house. She broke into a run, her heavy leather bag banging on her hip. A shouting crowd threw rocks at the blaze not buckets of water.

She staggered to a halt. Madame LaFleur was already being loaded into a black beetle-like carriage, bars at its windows, by gendarmes of the Committee of Public Safety. She was too late! A woman stood on a box under one of the arches of the covered arcade that ran around the ground floor of the entire square, shouting the crowd into a frenzy. Madame Croûte. Frankie couldn't hear the words but she knew the sentiment. Aristocrats were an infection. They must be rooted out lest they poison the Revolution. Madame LaFleur was a devout Catholic, in spite of churches and priests being declared illegal. She could never bring herself to enter one of the new Deist churches the government had created. Maybe it was that which brought Madame Croûte and her rabble of *sansculottes,* the most rabid of the revolutionaries of the third estate who spied for Robespierre and his committee, to Madame LaFleur's house.

Robespierre, first member of the Committee of Public

Safety, looked on as the mob pushed over the stone urns on either side of the doorway under the arcade, shouting. A small smile lit his face. Flames flapped from the windows like orange bed sheets snapping in the wind.

As she approached the scene, she slowed. There had been nothing she could do the first time around and there was no way to change things now. Madame LaFleur's life was forfeit at the guillotine. It hit her harder than she would have expected. Somehow she thought that two hundred years of experience with the world's evils would make a single woman's death hurt less.

The gaoler's wagon moved off. That meant that in a moment...

She turned. Bingo. A carriage with elegant lines and a defiant crest on its doors trotted up the street toward the flames. Four matched black geldings sidled in the harness, made nervous by the smoke. A driver liveried in black and gold stopped the carriage well away from the crowd. A postillion, likewise liveried, jumped down and opened the carriage door.

Henri stepped out. He stood, surveying the chaos through a quizzing glass, his expression bored and disdainful as always.

The roaring mob, the crack of flames, the smoke all receded. Frankie stood, transfixed.

He was even more beautiful than she remembered him. He looked thirty-five or forty though she knew he was centuries older. His hair was black—he eschewed powder—and brushed back from his face in a long queue. He wore no wig. Who had need of a wig when you had thick, lustrous hair like that? His eyes were so dark as to almost be black. Their look, as they drifted over the crowd, was as contemptuous as ever. He was tall and powerfully built. He dressed in black, his only nod to the austere fashion of the Revolution. Or maybe he had dressed in black even when the fashion was for wild colors like yellow and magenta. It certainly suited him. His coat fitted his shoulders perfectly. The satin of his breeches hugged his muscled thighs. His cravat and cuffs sported lace, though lace was banned. He looked, and was, every inch the aristocrat.

Time for Eternity

How did he manage to flaunt the tyranny of the plebian so openly?

Perhaps by looking as though he didn't care.

She drifted closer to the edge of the crowd, drawn by him. *How are you dangerous to me, Henri? Let me count the ways…* She steeled herself. She must harden her heart to match his. She must commit a sin in the eyes of God and man. She must do unto him before he could do unto her and deprive him of no more than a few months of living that she might live again.

"What have we here?" he murmured. She heard him clearly with the vampire hearing he had bequeathed her. The curve of his lip was all insouciant condescension. He strolled forward, surveying the crowd of *sans-culottes.*

"Monsieur, surely you will help us!"

Frankie turned at the sound of her own voice. She gasped. There she stood, the she who had been, Françoise Suchet, not Frankie, her face a mask of innocence in distress, a gendarme holding each elbow. It was the face Frankie still saw in the mirror each day, just now streaked with soot. Her blonde hair glowed copper in the red light of the flames licking out the windows above her. Frankie knew intellectually she hadn't changed with all the years, but to know this face was not a mirror image but one that lived two hundred years ago shook her sanity.

Françoise stretched her arms as far as she could toward Henri in supplication. Foolish girl. The last thing she needed was Henri Foucault. That way lay vampirism.

Then the young Françoise stilled. Her head turned slowly. Her eyes locked with Frankie's. Frankie saw the eyes that were her eyes, blue and innocent, grow wide.

Frankie couldn't get her breath. Françoise seemed to grow nearer, even as the crowd behind her receded. Frankie dropped her bag, gasping, and bent over, grabbing her belly against the pain there. This was bad. *Really* bad. She should never have met herself. She felt like she was breaking up. A shriek escaped her. *All those time travel books were right,* she thought.

And then she was hurtling toward Françoise. She felt herself disintegrating into a mist.

Then nothing.

Three

Françoise shook her head to clear it. She had seen a woman at the edge of the crowd. The woman had looked like her, though dressed a little strangely.

But there was no one there now. Françoise felt...full. Her head felt tight and her chest almost burst with...with something. She looked around, dazed. There had been a woman...hadn't there? She couldn't quite remember. She must be mad to be daydreaming at a time like this. Everything she owned was in that burning house. The mob seemed bent on tearing down what was left brick by brick. Robespierre had ordered Madame LaFleur arrested and Françoise was about to follow her. That meant prison and the guillotine.

She glanced to the edge of the crowd. She had seen something there, hadn't she? Something that made her uneasy. But she didn't quite know what. She felt as though all her senses were dulled, somehow. She couldn't quite see as far as she expected, hear as much as she ought. Something inside her was vaguely...disappointed.

Enough. She turned to the Duc d'Avignon, crossing from his carriage, quizzing glass raised to survey the crowd and the burning house that shared a wall with his own, much larger dwelling. She must be mad to think of asking him for help. The wicked duc would do nothing for her. But no one could help her once she'd been arrested, so he was her only hope.

"Please help me, Monsieur." She hated that her voice was small and pleading.

His quizzing glass turned toward her and her two burly guards, magnifying his eye until he looked like a monster. This was the first time he had even noticed her in all the months he'd lived next door. She blushed, acutely aware that her skirts were torn and covered with soot.

"You mean to call him 'Citizen,' do you not?" Madame Croûte asked through gritted teeth. "We have no forms of respectful address for the nobility. France belongs to the people."

The quizzing glass was turned on Madame Croûte. The duc frowned then surveyed the burning building. "Really, this crosses the line." His voice was quiet, yet somehow the crowd around her subsided. Only the roar of the flames filled the night air. They must be reacting to that electric energy he always seemed to give off. She had watched him secretly as he went out every evening for months now. One could not help but be riveted by him. He was a handsome devil who seemed much more alive than everyone else. He flaunted his wealth and taste in the teeth of the revolutionary zealots as though he were fearless.

He cast his gaze over the crowd. "You'll burn down the Marais, and, more importantly, my house, with your nonsense." His dark eyes seemed to glow red in the light from the flames. "Put it out." His voice almost echoed in the night.

To her shock, the four men nearest him began exhorting the crowd to put the fire out. The crowd milled uncertainly, then gained purpose.

"To the mews! The stables'll have buckets."

"Take 'em to the fountain."

The crowd split into purposeful streams. This enraged Madame Croûte. "Citizens!" she screamed. "This refuge of antirevolutionary sentiment must come down!" But the crowd wasn't paying attention to her anymore. She turned on Robespierre. She was a handsome woman with a fine figure, albeit with a rather long face and slightly protuberant pale blue eyes. She was dressed in the style of a poor woman, with apron and cap, but the fabrics were rich and very clean, unlike those of her followers. "Citizen," she accosted Robespierre, "Do something."

The duc looked over her shoulder. "Ahhhh, dear Robespierre, what brings you to this sordid scene?" He glanced to Madame Croûte. "And your minion as well." Madame Croûte glared at him.

"Rooting out a traitor," the little man said primly. He was dressed with the greatest propriety in sober black, plain wool, his hair concealed by a modest wig with only two rolls over each ear. He wore a ribbon on his lapel with the revolutionary colors.

"I wonder"—the duc sighed—"that the Committee of Public Safety should be involved in starting fires. It seems such a contradiction."

The little man drew himself up, frowning. "You make light of our sacred charge, Citizen Foucault, but the cause of freedom must be protected at all costs."

"So I've been told." The dark eyes flicked back to Françoise and away. "And an old woman is certainly a worthy target of your wrath. I positively quake to think that I lived next door to such a dangerous character."

Was it her situation that caused Françoise's wobbly knees? Or was it whatever had disconcerted her at the edge of the crowd? She shook her head again. She couldn't remember what she had seen. But she had a feeling she had done all this before, in a dream perhaps.

"But what has my ward to do with all of this?" the duc drawled.

Had her attention wandered? What ward? The duc lived alone in the house next door, if one could call living with at least a score of servants living alone. She glanced around.

Robespierre frowned. "Who might you mean, Citizen?"

The duc gestured idly to Françoise. "This chit. Belongs to me. You'd hardly credit it, what with her appearance."

Françoise felt her mouth drop open. Only surprise kept her from protesting.

"She was found in the house with the old woman." Robespierre frowned.

"The citizens report she lives there," Madame Croûte added, as though delivering a coup de grace.

The duc raised one arched brow. "How strange that I should find the need to explain myself to you." He sighed in resignation. "She plays piquet with the old woman from time to time out of the goodness of her heart. I tried to warn her where it would lead, this having a heart. Personally, I gave it up long ago."

Robespierre would never believe she was the ward of the wicked duc. He couldn't be more than fifteen or twenty years older than she was. And what young man would adopt a girl child? Lying to the leader of the Committee of Public Safety would only land him in a tumbrel on the way to the guillotine right behind her. Robespierre and his committee had the power of life and death. They could condemn a person without trial, without witnesses, without evidence. And they did. Thousands had gone to the guillotine in the last months merely on suspicion of being antirevolutionary. Madame Croûte was perhaps even more dangerous. Though she could have no political power because she was a woman, she ruled the mob and they dispensed the committee's will. Not even the committee controlled them entirely. Robespierre and Madame Croûte would never allow themselves to be intimidated by an aristocrat who had no power at all.

And yet, before her eyes, the little man swallowed. Twice.

"Very well, Citizen Foucault." His smile was so bland as to be frightening. "I would not dream of threatening your...property." He nodded to the gendarmes. They released Françoise.

"What are you doing?" Madame Croûte hissed.

Robespierre did not answer her question. "Quiet, woman!"

"Might you feel the need to apologize?" The duc murmured his question.

Robespierre looked as though he would choke. He took a breath. "I apologize, Citizen."

The duc shook his head, smiling. "No, no, my good man. Not to me. To the lady."

Françoise felt a blush rising. Audacious!

Robespierre nodded curtly to her. "I apologize, mademoiselle."

"You allow this...his aristo to thwart the will of the

Time for Eternity
people?" Madame Croûte accused.

Robespierre did not answer, but turned on his heel and made his way through the line of people passing buckets of water from the fountain through the arcade to the open door of the house and got into a waiting carriage, Madame Croûte haranguing him all the way.

Françoise looked around, feeling not herself at all. What a surprising outcome. Why had Robespierre backed down? And yet it wasn't surprising at all. If she thought about it, she knew some part of her expected exactly what had happened. Blinking, she turned to the duc. Why had he saved her? There was something she should do, something tickling at her mind. She should be afraid of him. Of that she was certain.

The duc ignored her. He ordered his servants to help douse the flames. People poked their heads out of other houses along the elegant façade, offering buckets and help. The disordered mob turned into a rather efficient machine moving water from the fountain to the house.

The duc held a delicate handkerchief, embroidered and edged with lace, to his nose against the smoke. He seemed to have forgotten all about Françoise. The flames cast his face into satanic relief. Even with the excitement of a fire and the prospect of a mob lately engaged in tearing down the house next to his own, he looked bored, his eyes heavy-lidded, his full mouth curved in what was very nearly a sneer.

After some time, a dapper older man appeared out of the duc's house and presented a silver salver on which sat a crystal decanter filled with amber liquid and a glass. He bowed crisply at his master's side, but said nothing, just waited.

When at last he deigned to notice the servant, the duc seemed mildly surprised. "Gaston, you anticipate my need. But let us repair to the library. I do not care to imbibe on the street."

Gaston bowed again and the duc strolled down the arcade to his own door, Gaston in his wake. Françoise watched him go with dismay. She turned to look at the remains of the house she had lived in with Madame Lafleur for the last year. The façade was still intact, but most was a smoking, wet ruin.

Susan Squires

The door out to the arcade hung at a crazy angle, and people were tramping about inside, dousing the remaining flames. The windows held only broken shards of glazing, the brick above them stained with blackened tongues of soot. The roof had fallen in places.

Where was she to stay?

A liveried footman opened the door for the duc. Light spilled into the street. Before the duc could pass inside he paused and looked back. He had obviously forgotten her. But he covered well. "Are you not coming in, my dear?"

Françoise froze. She was not the duc's ward. No man with the reputation of being the devil himself would ever have a ward. Entering that portal would put her entirely in his power. All her upbringing told her that her very soul was in danger if she set foot inside that house. And yet part of her felt that there was something she must do, and that doing it required that she be near the duc. What was the matter with her tonight?

None of her scruples mattered. She had no choice. The old lady's rheumatism had made getting her out of the flaming house slow work. There had been no time to grab any belongings. Françoise had no money, no friends to take her in tonight. No respectable inn would take her without money and looking like she did.

The duc waited, amusement lurking in his eyes. When he saw that she had fully comprehended her dilemma, he raised one brow.

Françoise bit her lip. Something inside her whispered that she must go with him.

The duc did not wait longer but turned into the house, knowing she would follow.

She trailed after him, under the impassive gaze of the footman.

She might be confused, but she did not doubt that entering this house was dangerous.

Françoise passed into an elegant foyer. The duc's house was impeccable on the inside. The central houses on the grand façade of the Place Royale were much larger than Madame LaFleur's, which was the first in the line of smaller residences beside them. The Hotel d'Avignon was almost a palace. Black and white tiles stretched away on the floor of the foyer and twin staircases joined halfway up to the first story, where she knew for a fact there was a huge ballroom. She had seen the duc's decadent revelries from the street on many a night as she came home late from the market. Several delicately carved chairs and tiny tables were set about the foyer for the convenience of visitors seeking admittance. The chandelier that hung from the high ceiling held fifty candles at the least and dripped sparkling crystals. Françoise had never felt so out of place, with her cheap, dowdy clothes, soiled with soot, the hem of her dress muddied with runoff from the burning house. Most absurdly, she wished she had used some of her small salary from Madame LaFleur to buy one modish dress.

Her host seemed to have forgotten her again. He was strolling through the hall under the stairs, Gaston in his wake.

Very well. She might have to stay here tonight but tomorrow she would seek out another position. And she'd tell Monsieur le Duc just that. She set off across the foyer, shoes clicking on the marble tile, and pushed her way in behind Gaston before the door could close. This room was much cozier than she imagined. It was lined, floor to ceiling on two sides, with bookcases. Two comfortable-looking wing chairs sat facing a grate with a small table between them. A low fire burned and, even though it was summer, the crackle was not unwelcome. These old houses were always a little damp in the evening. At one end was a large desk, inexplicably covered with papers. She couldn't imagine the duc doing anything that required a desk. Surely his minions paid his tailor's bills and household accounts.

The duc collapsed into a wing chair, one slippered foot negligently out in front of him. Gaston set down the brandy, murmuring, "Dinner at the usual time, your grace?" The duc could afford brandy, even taxed as it was these days. No one drank brandy anymore.

"But of course. And see that another place is set."

Well, at least he remembered her existence, not that she

could touch a bite of food while in the devil's lair. As Gaston left, said devil peered around the wing of his chair. "Well, are you going to sit down or stand there like a pillar of salt?"

Stung, she started forward and stood next to the other chair. "Which would make this house Sodom and Gomorrah?" *Where* had that come from? She would never have thought she had the courage to retort to the devil that way...

He apparently didn't either. His brows lifted. "Many think so." He motioned to the chair.

She cleared her throat. "I...I thank you for your thoughtful gesture and...and assure you that I shall not trespass upon your hospitality for more than one night."

"I *am* relieved." He poured a brandy as he glanced up at her. "You have relatives in Paris other than the old woman?"

"She was no relative. She employed me as a companion." He would despise Françoise for that. She raised her chin.

"Ahhhh." He examined her critically. She detected a faint scent of...cinnamon. And something else. Something sweet. Unusual scent for a man. They always chose sandalwood or some such in her experience, limited as that might be. And in spite of his languid manner there was that sense that he was more alive than anyone around him. That, added to his other not inconsiderable charms of person, combined into a package nearly lethal to a young girl. It was to her. She'd daydreamed about the wicked duc since he had moved into the house next door.

"You're not of the servant class," he remarked.

How did he know that? It wasn't by her dress. She was not about to tell him that she was the bastard daughter of the Marquis d'Evron and an opera chorus girl. "I might as well be." She couldn't keep a hint of defiance from her tone. "I shall seek another position tomorrow."

After you've done what you must.

What? Where had that thought come from? What was she supposed to do?

"You can have no family if they allowed you to so demean yourself."

Time for Eternity

The duc was obviously not one to mince words. "I do not," she said, lifting her chin.

"Distressing situation." There was no sympathy in his voice.

What had she expected? If she couldn't find a place immediately... Well, she wouldn't think about that.

A knock sounded and, without waiting to be invited in, Gaston entered the room. He bore a heavy silver tray on which was balanced a single stemmed glass and another cut-glass decanter filled with some kind of light red wine.

The duc raised his very black and mobile brows. "I do not recall asking for anything, Gaston." His deep voice was silky, yet a threat of power hummed under it.

"I felt sure, your grace, in all the excitement, that you had forgotten to order ratafia for the young person." Françoise, who was still standing, saw the duc's mouth tighten.

"Thank you for reminding me of my manners." He was probably a horrible master. She hoped he didn't take revenge on Gaston later.

But Gaston seemed unperturbed. He set down the decanter and the glass, poured a goodly portion of ratafia into it, bowed and withdrew.

"Since my servants will no doubt take me to task if you are still standing when next they enter, I beg you to seat yourself, for my sake if not for your own."

She would not have thought him capable of that wry, even self- deprecating tone. She sat on the edge of the wing chair. He gestured vaguely to the glass.

The wine would be welcome after all that had happened. He waited, sipping his own brandy, until she had taken several sips. She watched the glow of the coals and the random flicker that remained of the fire. Strange that fire could feel like the end of the world one moment and comforting the next.

"I cannot help but feel that your efforts to find a position may not meet with success."

She looked up to find he had been watching her, his

dark eyes heavy-lidded. He wasn't telling her anything new but she didn't care for his tone. "I'm sure to find something suitable."

"Most of the aristocracy has left France to escape the Terror. Of those that remain a goodly portion are in prison or likely to be so shortly. For those few that remain free and happen to be in the market for household help, you can hardly be suitable."

She found herself flushing. He was right. Madame's other three servants had planned to go back to their relatives in the country if ever Madame could not keep them. That's probably where they were even now, turned into farmers or working in small taverns in the countryside.

He continued, not heeding her discomfiture. "You are too young for a governess or a housekeeper, too refined for a chambermaid…" Here he seemed to consider. His brows drew together. "And how did you come by your education? Your diction and your demeanor do not fit with your clothing or your situation."

Ahhh. That was how he knew she wasn't of the servant class. Perceptive. She was willing to wager he would smell a lie at thirty paces. She decided not to answer at all. "That is hardly your concern, your grace."

"You might repay my efforts to keep you out of gaol by reassuring me that I am not harboring a murderer or a thief."

"I hardly think your grace is afraid of a girl like me."

His mouth twitched. "You feel you owe me nothing in the way of explanation?"

Oh, dear. She *was* beholden to him. She swallowed once then decided that another sip of ratafia was in order. The sip turned to a gulp. He was right. She would repay him by telling him what she never admitted. She was a castoff. "I am the bastard daughter of the Marquis d'Evron and an opera singer, I am told." She lifted her chin again. He might as well have the whole sordid story. Something told her it wouldn't matter whether he knew her story, at least not for very long. "My mother left me on the doorstep of my father's ancestral home. He never acknowledged me, but his maiden sister raised

Time for Eternity

me and educated me on her estates in Provence." She glanced again to the fire. She had loved Lady Toumoult. "She died of consumption."

"Your father did not provide for you?" His voice was sharp. "If his sister raised you, your birth must have been common knowledge."

She wished it weren't. "I'm sure he had other things on his mind."

The duc poured himself another brandy, frowning. "I remember d'Evron now. He didn't even try to speak for moderation in the Assembly. He just packed up his household and emigrated."

"Since I was not a regular member of his household I was left behind." How frightened she had been at being left on her own in the midst of a country in chaos. She had no right to go with him, she reminded herself. She was not legitimate. She wasn't even his servant. She had no claim on anyone. "I...was seventeen. I made my own way. Madame LaFleur hired me." Her eyes filled. The old lady who had treated her more like a friend than a servant would be on her way to the guillotine shortly. The two women she'd cared for and who had cared for her in return would both be dead. Maybe it was her fault somehow. Maybe she was bad luck...

"Well," Avignon said as though something was decided. "There is nothing for it. You must go to England."

"With no money, no acquaintance, no references? Even if I had money for the passage, my situation would be even worse in England." When families emigrated, they took their support system with them. Even if all you had was a title, at least it was an entrée to society, an autornatic calling card. She had neither family nor birth.

That took him aback. He studied his brandy. When he next glanced her way, he looked disgusted. "We will speak more of this. In the meantime, you had better stay here as my ward."

What was he saying? And then she had a very good idea what he was saying. She straightened her back. "If you think

Susan Squires

that because I am a bastard I was born with loose morals you are wrong. I'll find a position."

His eyes met hers and steadied. "No, I do not think that. But everyone else does. So you will not find a position. No woman would have you in a household with her husband or her sons. You were lucky to find an old lady who still had money to hire a companion, but no family, no desire to live the remainder of her life on foreign soil, and who obviously had no idea of your situation. Lightning will not strike twice."

She felt her breath coming quickly. "I'll hire myself out to a shop or a factory."

He chuffed a laugh. "Shops aren't hiring. The whole fabric of the economy is coming apart, in case you haven't noticed. The National Assembly gave the factories to the people. The men who owned them and knew how to run them picked up and went where the government couldn't nationalize a lifetime of hard work. The aristocrats who owned land that was confiscated took their money with them when they left. Which leaves—bread riots."

"There must be some way I can earn my keep." She hated that her voice sounded small.

He sat forward, grabbed her hands, and held them palm up. His warm touch to her bare skin sent shocks of something through her. She tried to pull away, but she couldn't. For having hands that looked so elegant he was strong. "Who will hire you for hard work with these hands?" Abruptly, he let her go. "Where are your *brains,* girl?" His voice was hard. "You don't belong in a factory, even if you could talk someone into giving you work. You'll say you can act like them, blend in. But you'd betray yourself. And they'd have you out on your ear or arrested for concealing your aristocratic background before you could blink. Only a brothel would take you."

She blinked rapidly, trying to contain the tears. "I know my chances," she choked. "No matter what you think, I'm not stupid."

He took a swig of brandy. "Then stop acting like it," he muttered. "You'll stay here."

He didn't say it as though he wanted her here. But that

50

Time for Eternity

didn't lessen the danger. She swallowed around the lump in her throat. "I can't stay here." Somewhere she found courage she didn't know she had. She sat up and put her empty glass back on the tray. "Whether you serve one man or many, a whore is a whore. And I'm not a whore." She rose.

"I'm not assaulting your virtue, for God's sake. I said you could stay as my ward."

"And who would believe *that*, your grace?" She surely didn't. "You are what, thirty-five, forty? I am twenty- one. You're not old enough for me to be your ward."

To her surprise, his shook his head wearily. "Oh, I am more than old enough to be your guardian." He seemed to muster his resolve. "At any rate, you have no choice. And whatever they think, they will accept you because I demand it."

She didn't want to stay under this roof for more than one night. One night. Even that could be dangerous. She had this dreadful feeling she shouldn't be anywhere near him or she'd end up doing something dreadful. And yet another part of her wanted her to do that very dreadful thing, whatever it was. Was she afraid she would succumb to the wicked duc's wiles? A sense of urgency and dread crept over her that was almost overwhelming. Tonight. She'd get through tonight, do what she must and then be away. Because a man so attractive, so *dangerous* somehow, could break her heart in the worst possible way if she let him.

Where were these thoughts *coming* from? Françoise shook her head to clear it.

She might have had a schoolgirl's crush, but she was in no danger of actually falling in love with Monsieur le Duc. He was nobility of the first consequence, just the type who always looked down on her, and wild to a fault, irresponsible. He lived his life as though there were no Terror, no slow dying of the hope that the ideals of the Revolution would save man from himself. He didn't use his influence to push France back into the right course. He cared for no one, not even the prime articles he mounted as his mistresses. Françoise may have daydreamed about the handsome devil next door worshipping at her feet, but in the cold light of reality, the devil was much more stubborn and despicable than her daydreams. Not someone she could care for.

And not someone who would have the slightest interest in a dull and virtuous girl, of no birth, whose looks were well enough but who was not a beauty, inexperienced and unfashionably dressed. He must be positively laughing at her fear that he would take advantage of her virtue.

She sighed. In some ways that was…depressing. But… in another way it was a relief. What interest would he have in her? Which made his offer of sanctuary most puzzling. But one she need not fear to take advantage of for a few hours.

She looked up and found him watching her. She realized she had been staring at the Aubusson carpet. She sat down again in the wing chair. "Very well. I accept your kind offer."

"I am never kind." The duc unfolded himself from the chair and pulled the bell rope.

Gaston materialized as though from thin air. "Your grace?"

"Show Mademoiselle…" He realized he did not know her name and looked to her.

"Suchet," she supplied.

"Ah, yes. Show Mademoiselle Suchet to a suitable room so she may refresh herself before dinner. A room off the *west* hall, Gaston, if you please." He gave Gaston a sharp glance. "I suppose you could not procure a female attendant upon short notice?"

Gaston showed not the slightest dismay at this odd command. In fact he looked confident and…pleased. "Of course I can, your grace."

"Ahhh. Not something beyond your powers." His grace seemed disappointed.

"No, your grace." Gaston bowed. "If Mademoiselle will come with me…"

How would he pass her off as his ward when his servants knew he was ignorant of even her name, she had no idea. Perhaps they were forced to discretion through fear.

Time for Eternity

"And Gaston, see that Fanchon is here tomorrow afternoon for fittings for the girl."

Gaston blanched.

"Ahhh. Finally a task worthy of your talents, I see." Avignon turned away as though she and Gaston didn't exist and downed his brandy in a single gulp.

Fran^oise followed the stiff-backed majordomo out the door. He stopped and whispered to the young footman who had let them in. The handsome lad with a red queue of hair, unpowdered like his master's, nodded and scurried to the back of the house.

Gaston bowed, his face neutral. "Mademoiselle?" Then he turned and walked sedately up the grand staircase. Françoise followed. She had no choices here. She was about to become, at least for tonight, the Duc d'Avignon's ward. May God protect her soul.

*****

Henri Foucault, Duc d'Avignon, stared at the closed door. What the hell was he thinking? She was an innocent, for God's sake. And that was a recipe for disaster. She'd fall in love with him. They always did. Attractive as she was, he didn't dally with innocents. He looked up at the painting over the fireplace, an old hunting scene. Fifteenth century. It had been about the time the paint was still wet on that canvas that he'd learned his lesson about innocents...

The tower room was round, its windows narrow slits in the stone that looked out across the valley. Now they revealed only darkness and winking lights from the windows of the village far below. A huge bed laid with brocades and velvet dominated the space. He turned to the girl he had desired since the moment he saw her at her father's side. She was everything he was not; innocent, hopeful. Perhaps for a few years she could give him back his faith that life was worth living. At least until she grew old and died.

Susan Squires

Just now her blue eyes were wide with fright. How much was the normal apprehension of a virgin on her wedding night? He knew she coveted him. He had felt her eyes on him in her father's feast hall for many nights, and after the battle, when he had fought like the demon he was against the invading hordes of Saarland, she had welcomed him back to the castle with tears of relief. And now, for saving her father's realm, she had been given to him in matrimony. He smiled to reassure her. "You must be tired after that long banquet. May I order a bath for you?"

He enjoyed bathing far more than his hosts here in the Alsace. He had been an itinerant mercenary for nearly a century and a half now, wielding his strength for civilizations from the North of Africa to the Yangtze River, picking up bits of their cultures along the way. He was a skilled general. And he fought his battles at night, often taking the enemy by surprise. It was an effective strategy. Kingdoms vied for his services. He fought for anyone who paid his price, having long ago ceased to care who won and who lost. Life stretched ahead, and he felt insanity lurking in wait for him if he did not find some meaning in it. She could give that to him. Perhaps.

She shook her head. Her breath was coming in little gasps.

He turned away lest the intensity of his gaze upset her. He would show her pleasure tonight. Once he had bedded her, all would be fine. He unbuckled his scabbard and chain mail, shined bright for the wedding ceremony, and laid them on a carved bench. Perhaps a look at what was in store would steady her. He pulled his shirt over his head.

When he turned to face her, naked to the waist, there were beads of sweat on her forehead and she alternately flushed and paled.

"What is it, Lady Cerise?" he asked, concerned. "Are you well?"

Her eyes were dilated pools of midnight blue. They matched the voluminous folds of her velvet dress. "They say you are the devil," she whispered.

Had she discovered his secrets? "They always say that

Time for Eternity

about a strong man."

"You fought like twenty men, stronger than a man can be."

Which is why he always moved on after getting his gold. Not this time. He was sick unto death, if death were possible for one such as he, of roaming the world. He couldn't have family. He at least wanted love. "The better to protect you, now you are mine."

"They say..." Her voice was distant now. Not a good sign. "They say that when the battle was done, you returned to the field strewn with slain bodies and while everyone did celebrate in the camp, you...you drank the blood of the dead under the full moon."

Very bad. "What old woman has been filling your ears with lies?" He moved in toward her, to comfort her, let her feel the warmth of his body.

That was when he saw the dagger in the hand she hid in the folds of her skirts. She couldn't kill him, but he didn't want to let her see him heal either.

"Give me that," he said, imbuing his voice with calm.

"My father has given me unto the devil," she said, panting. "In return for victory."

"I thought you wanted this..."

"Before I knew you for a monster." Her voice cycled up into a wail. "I must save my immortal soul."

He'd have to take the knife. Her eyes grew even bigger. And suddenly the knife was not aimed at him, but turned inward, toward her own lush breasts. He grabbed for her arm.

Too late. She pulled the knife in with both hands. Black bloomed on her midnight dress.

"No!" he breathed as she sank to her knees. He cradled her in his arms. He daren't pull the knife out. The innocent creature had somehow dealt herself the perfect killing blow, up, under her ribs to her heart.

"May God forgive me..." The last word burbled with blood that leaked from her mouth.

"Cerise," he choked. The light died in her eyes, leaving

them flat and dull. "Cerise…"

The very act of breathing was an effort. What had he expected? He was a monster. She was right about him. And he had no right to try to use her hope and innocence to save his soul.

He gathered her in his arms and laid her on the great bed.

He'd poisoned an innocent with his foul nature. She had taken her own life rather than spend even one night with him. His head sank on his breast. There was nothing for him here now. He drew his power. Companion! *It shushed up his veins. The world went red. The whirling blackness rose up around his knees.*

He'd sought salvation in a young girl's arms. What he'd gotten was certain damnation.

Henri closed his eyes, slowly, against the memory. Now he never bedded innocents. Or stayed with any one woman long enough for her to know his secrets. A stable life of love and mutual respect was a dream that could never be real for him. His kind was not meant for the ties that bind. His own vampire mother had abandoned him at puberty when he came into his powers. Children were so rare for his kind as to be almost a miracle, and yet as soon as the children were full vampires their parents obeyed the Rule laid down by the Elders that vampires live rally one to a city and essentially abandoned their children. That Rule was second in importance only to the Rule that forbade making a human into a vampire by sharing the Companion. After all, if vampires crowded into a city, or made other vampires, soon humans would discover them, and the tenuous balance between those who drink blood and those who give it would be broken. So, no connections for his kind were possible, human or vampire, ever.

Not that he didn't satisfy his needs. But he stuck to worldly creatures; widows, actresses who expected no more than what he was likely to give them—money, pleasure, and the illusion that their beauty would never fade. And he did give them pleasure. He knew how to do that. His own releases couldn't really be called pleasure anymore but they kept his sexual demons at bay. And always, it was he that left them. In his nature he supposed. Or maybe he took revenge on the distaff world for his mother abandoning him. It was the way of his kind. He couldn't break that most harsh Rule of vampire nature, no matter his occasional longing for something stable to anchor his long years.

It didn't matter.

What mattered was that he not pollute the world more than was absolutely necessary. He could not help showing some his nature. It was how he did his work, after all. But he could refuse to defile innocence. Now he had an innocent in his very house. He could hear her talking to the maid Gaston had remarkably procured. He'd have to think of some way to get rid of her. Quickly.

Susan Squires

Four

As Gaston bowed himself out, Françoise found herself not in the lurid boudoir with gold-flocked fleur-de-lis wallpaper on a black background and red carpets she expected but in a very comfortable and stylish chamber. Gold leaf highlighted the intricate curves of delicate, white-painted furniture. A dressing table sat in one corner, a large wardrobe in the other. The bed was hung with sheer blue bed curtains and covered with a very becoming brocaded and embroidered quilt. Dozens of pillows were piled high against the headboard. The draperies were light blue, and the thick carpets were swirls of blue and taupe. The whole thing looked…feminine.

Françoise felt like such an interloper. What must they all think of her? She wandered from bed to dressing table, touching silver-backed brushes and tiny colored glass bottles that smelled of expensive perfume. Her senses were a little dulled with all the momentous events tonight. She felt as though the world had lost color, somehow, or taste.

A knock sounded at the door.

Françoise almost looked around to see who had the right to allow entry to this lovely room. "Come in." A young woman hurried in and bobbed a curtsy.

"Annette, if you please, my lady," she said, slightly out of breath. "I'm to help you dress for dinner." She had red hair, a plain, round face with light eyelashes, and a dumpling of a chin.

Françoise smiled ruefully. "I'm afraid that will be quick work. My other clothing was destroyed in the fire." The servants would know she lived next door.

The girl smiled, almost kindly. "Do not worry your head, your ladyship. Gaston, he has ordered the bath, and before you can dry yourself, I will have just what you need all laid out and waiting. Mind you, I'm not a lady's dresser, so I hope I'll do for your ladyship."

"I'm not a lady, Annette." *Just someone with nowhere else to go.* Annette opened the wardrobe. It seemed folly stocked. "I'm sure you will be just fine. Are you normally a housemaid here?" That seemed the most plausible explanation for her sudden appearance.

"La, no, mademoiselle. The duc has no female servants. I'm housemaid three doors down. Or was until ten minutes ago."

Françoise blinked, not sure which part of this speech to question first. "So you just... quit without notice?"

Annette chuckled. "Don't expect Madame even knows I'm gone. But when my brother tells me that my salary just tripled if I'm here within five minutes, I don't ask questions."

"Your brother?"

"Footman here," Annette said proudly. "Name is Jean. He's been with the duc near on three years, and everyone knows the duc only takes the best."

So that's how Gaston had provided a maid on short notice, and why Annette's red hair seemed familiar. No wonder Avignon had thought it a hard task to procure a female attendant—he employed no females himself. She would have expected a man of Avignon's morals to keep a host of girl-servants he could take advantage of at a moment's notice whenever the latest in his string of paramours was unavailable. That was the lot of young women. It might be her lot when Avignon ended his charade. If she was lucky. If not, it might be the brothel. "You're not afraid to serve here?"

"Well..." Annette looked dubious for a moment, then she shrugged. "Jean says the devil...his grace, I mean, won't bother about me as long as you're here."

Oh, well, that made Françoise feel better all around. Her grim thoughts were interrupted when the door opened and two footmen brought in a bath three times larger than any she had ever used and set it by the fire. They were followed by a line of servants all carrying buckets. The room overflowed with activity, then emptied. Before she knew it the room held only

Annette and a steaming bath, lavender-scented soaps, and thick towels, all looking more inviting than she would have imagined. The water didn't even smell. Wasn't it from the Seine? But water from the system of wells that sold water privately was horrendously expensive. Could Avignon be rich enough to use it for *bathing*?

"Now just you let me help you out of that nasty dress," Annette fussed, unbuttoning and unhooking and untying.

Françoise stepped into the steaming tub. "Thank you," she breathed, sinking in to the nape of her neck. Heaven. Her hair would still smell like smoke, she was sure, but the rest of her would be clean, cleaner than a bath with river water could ever make her.

And Madame LaFleur was spending the night in who knew what horrible cell? Guilt slapped her. Conditions in the Conciergerie were rumored to be deplorable. But even imprisonment would be better than Madame's plight as soon as she had stood before the committee. If only the duc could have saved Madame as well. She had no idea why Robespierre had backed down, even offered Françoise an apology, instead of arresting her.

What hold could the duc have over the chairman of the Committee of Public Safety? Whatever it was kept him out of the clutches of the mob, no matter how blatantly he flaunted his aristocracy. He hadn't even been wearing a ribbon with the French colors on it to show his support of the Revolution. She should be grateful for whatever his influence was, or she would be sharing Madame's lot tonight. Poor Madame.

Françoise stepped out of the cooling bath and wrapped herself in a towel. Annette was sorting through a heap of clothing on the bed. "This looks like it might fit you, little thing that you are." She held up a frothy cerulean-blue confection with actual lace at the neckline.

Françoise blinked. She had never had such an expensive dress in her life. It was not made in the severe revolutionary style. If it wasn't au courant, neither was it left over from the prerevolutionary excess. There were no hooped panniers or elbow-length sleeves with ruffles. It had a square décolletage

Time for Eternity

and long, translucent sleeves that ended in narrow cuffs at the wrist. It was an altogether original look, much too beautiful to be worn except if one wanted to be riding in a tumbrel to the Place de Revolution surrounded by a mob shouting for your blood. She had never seen anything like it.

Yet it was totally familiar. She reached out to touch it.

"Oh, my." Stupid. But it was all she could think to say. The fabric was silk.

What was a dress like this doing in the house of an unattached man?

She snatched back her hand. There could be but one answer to that. She looked around at the feminine furniture and the cut-glass bottles of perfume. How stupid she was.

"My dress is good enough." It cost her something to say that.

Annette's eyes went wide. "You're never going to wear that sooty thing to dinner!"

"I…I don't care to wear the clothes he keeps for his…his companions." She sounded stuffy even to herself.

"Me, I'd give my eyeteeth to wear a dress like this, don't matter where it comes from." Annette's hands were absently stroking the almost transparent sleeves. "And his grace has taste that's nice to a fault," she continued briskly, coming to herself. "Won't do to spoil his dinner looking at that nasty dress."

"I… I shall take a tray in my room." Oh, but the dress was lovely.

Annette's eyes opened wide. Then she set her lips. "Yes, mademoiselle." She was clearly miffed. "I'll tell his grace that you chose not to take advantage of his kind offer to dine with him—him that Jean says dines alone so often. Still, I expect he's used to it."

The wicked duc, dining alone? Not one night in twenty, she wagered. Still, it was rude to refuse his offer, even if, as he said, he hadn't made it to be kind. He had saved her from Robespierre and Madame Croute, after all.

Can he do the same for Madame LaFleur? The thought

popped into her head. Why not? There was no one else who could help her. But would he? She doubted it. He didn't extend himself for anyone. And yet, he had extended himself for her...

But she must go carefully. She must find out why he had bothered himself with her plight. If she knew that, maybe she could convince him to do the same for her friend.

"Annette," she called as the young woman was pulling open the door. "You're right. It's not the first time I've had hand-me-down clothes and it won't be the last."

The girl turned, all smiles over teeth that weren't quite straight. "That's the way, mademoiselle. And I'm not much of a hand at dressing hair, but I expect I can manage yours."

*****

Henri put one foot up on the andirons of the fireplace in the smaller dining room. He'd pack her off to England. That's what he'd do. But he must wait until the end of the week and ship her off with the others. He didn't trust Robespierre not to have her arrested on the way to Le Havre just to spite him if he sent her ahead on her own.

She was right about England though. Without connections or position, emigrating was a dicey business, and for a woman alone...

He sipped his wine, annoyed. The ornate water clock on the mantel had chimed the hour five minutes ago. He liked to dine sharply at nine. And tonight he had much to do.

Well, he'd give the girl some money at least. What else could he do? He'd saved her from losing her head at the Place de Revolution. The rest was up to her.

He tapped his finger on the mantel. A dull dinner this was likely to be, though she had surprised him with a sharp tongue. She'd lose her wit and her tongue soon enough when she fell under the spell of his magnetism. They always did.

The hell of it was that with her around, not even dining alone would be a refuge. Over the years, alone as he felt inside, he had grown to like his privacy at dinner. It was a nice contrast to feeling alone in the crowds of bored revelers and ne'er-do-wells. The servants thought him mad for serving himself. Let them.

It occurred to him that he had lost heart. Not courage. A creature such as he was beyond fear. He would keep to his chosen course. It was a matter of will and he still had resolve. But hope had vanished centuries ago. He had seen too much and it all ended the same way no matter what one did. So he had ceased putting his heart into it. Still, he continued. What else could one do except go mad?

The doors to his right opened.

One of the servants ushered in the most surprising creature. How long since he had been surprised?

*****

It was only a few minutes after nine when Françoise came down the curved stairway to the ground floor, following Jean, of the red hair and the sister. She felt like someone else entirely in this dress, not least because Annette could find no fichu to cover her breast. At least none that matched. She wore no jewelry, of course. But the dress itself felt like a jewel. The slippers Annette had produced might not be a perfect fit, but a little tissue stuffed into the soft white satin made them serviceable. Her hair had been coaxed into its usual soft curls, a little longer at her nape. Annette had offered rouge and lip color and something to darken her lashes, but she had refused. She did *not* want to look like a loose woman.

He has no interest in someone like you, she recited to herself. *You're just here to see if there is any chance he'll help Madame.* She was about to beard the lion in his den.

The footman opened the door. "The smaller dining room, mademoiselle."

Again the room was not what she expected. She'd thought the duc would prefer a grandiose setting to match his consequence. But this was cozy like the library. The ceiling was of carved wood. A round table gleamed with polish in the candlelight. It sat six rather than the twenty or thirty she'd imagined. A sideboard was heaped with covered silver trays. Crystal sparkled. The china set for two was Sevres, figured in blue and gilt to match the blue and red of the carpet and the midnight blue of the draperies, closed now against the night. The whole was warm and cheery.

And leaning against the mantel, his booted foot on the andirons of the flickering grate, stood the duc, wine glass in hand. He wasn't a lion. More like a black panther, sleek and powerful. Dangerous. The room fairly…quivered with his presence.

Be careful. Don't let his handsome person befuddle you. She would think of tonight as research. She'd discover why he saved her and use that information to get him to save Madame.

All the time she'd been dressing, she'd had a most uneasy feeling. That the duc was a threat was obvious. It wasn't that. All of this seemed…familiar somehow. That strange sensation of déjà vu one got sometimes usually lasted only for an instant. But she just couldn't shake the feeling that she knew this man and she'd done all this before.

And that it hadn't turned out well.

He glanced up at her entrance. He blinked once, twice. "Well, that is an improvement."

She blushed. How *could* she? She had to appear strong, not naïve and vulnerable. "Anything would have been an improvement."

Another footman joined Jean to take the covers from the dishes on the sideboard.

"I hope you don't mind an informal dinner. I like to dispense with servants whenever possible." He was looking at her quite strangely, no doubt comparing her unfavorably with the last wearer of this marvelous dress.

She set her teeth. *Be polite. Get him talking.* "I trespass on your hospitality. However you choose to be served can only please."

He looked faintly…pained. Well, perhaps that had struck a false note. "Oh, very well. I actually like informality." She breathed and smiled. "It was one of the nicest things about

Time for Eternity

living with Madame LaFleur. She treated me quite like a friend. Cook and her girl and Robert were our only servants. So we often dined informally. I find it comfortable." *Liar.* How could one be comfortable with an attractive devil like Avignon ready to steal your soul?

Now who was being dramatic? Stealing souls. These thoughts seemed entirely foreign.

He kept his own counsel, but the pained look had been replaced by one of...speculation. The footmen took away the covers after pouring white wine in two glasses and red in two others, and leaving the decanters. The duc picked up a plate and began putting tidbits on it. She picked up another.

He frowned at her, took her plate, and set it back down. "Allow me," he said firmly.

He was going to serve her? How odd for a wicked duc. He didn't ask what she'd like to eat, but chose for her. *That* seemed entirely in character. The sideboard held platters of oysters on the half shell with mignonette vinegar, chicken Dijon, beefsteak, a ragout of sweetbreads, spinach in a cream sauce, *haricots verts,* a platter of buttered lobster tails among a dozen others—the largesse was embarrassing. She hadn't seen so much food in one place for several years. And there was a whole shallow dish full of salt.

"You...you set a fine table," she murmured, at a loss for words. Salt was precious these days; taxed by the government until it was too dear for almost all households.

Her mouth began to water in earnest. This food would have been cooked with salt.

"Ahhhh, I see you are admiring my little import. One likes to command the elegancies."

"Salt. Brandy. Well water. Wherever do you get such luxuries?"

"Well, the water is easy. I own the system of wells, at least until they are nationalized."

Really? That was surprising. Had he bought them, had them dug? "God forbid the wealthy should drink water from the Seine like everyone else."

Susan Squires

He glanced at her, his eyes unreadable. "Those who pay for it finance wells for those who cannot. The latest is going in upriver, near the slaughterhouses."

She bit her lip. "I would not have thought you so generous."

"Generous? No. It keeps my wells from being vandalized."

She should have known. When her plate was full, he set it on the table and drew out a chair for her. She seated herself. "Thank you."

His bare hand brushed her shoulder as she sat back and she felt it through to her bones, as though he had been rubbing his shoes on a carpet. Goose pimples rose on her neck and coursed down one side of her body. She had never felt anything quite like it.

He walked back to the sideboard, rubbing the hand that had touched her shoulder surreptitiously on his coat. Had he felt the touch as she had? The coat was of satin, blue so dark it was almost black. He was strongly built. It was hard not to think about his body moving under his clothing as he filled his plate. His muscles were not ropy, stringy things. They bulged. She would be able to see the veins that fed his biceps... The image made her...tingle.

Where had she gotten thoughts like that? The only times she had ever even seen men without their shirts was from a distance during haying time on her aunt's estates. Yet she could imagine just how Avignon's muscles would look if she could see him naked...

Stop it, she told herself. It was as if she already knew what he looked like naked.

He sat down next to her with his own plate. That was too close. His suppressed energy hummed and echoed in her veins. He had brought the shallow bowl of salt with its tiny silver spoon. "Feel free, " he murmured, "but Pierre would be desolate if you didn't taste first." He didn't seem to be the type to say grace. The devil wouldn't thank God, would he? So she murmured her own thanks under her breath and turned her attention to her plate. How had she not realized she was

Time for Eternity

famished? Everything tasted wonderful. There was no need to add salt. After some time she slowed enough to realize her companion was only toying with his food. She must look like some starving urchin to him.

She cleared her throat "My compliments to your chef."

"I should have Pierre in to see your enjoyment."

She shrugged. "With the Revolution, things have not been so easy. Madame LaFleur has had to watch her sous carefully since her husband died."

"Things are never easy when the common man runs wild. All descend to the lowest common denominator."

"I had such hope at first," she murmured. "Things were so bad, the taxes so hard, the priests so venal... I thought that if one but followed the principles of Rousseau and Voltaire..."

He grimaced and shook his head. "It never works."

"You are a royalist, of course." He would be, with huge estates no doubt confiscated in the name of the people without a king to protect them.

"The royalists are as stupid and greedy as our fine new 'citizens.' Fear and greed are the only truths." He sipped his wine, looking to see if he had shocked her.

"A man like you would believe so." Strange, but some part of her believed that too.

"Ahhhh, and what does your...experience tell you about men like me?"

She felt herself coloring. He was baiting her because she was young and inexperienced. In truth she had never known anyone faintly like him. She was not going to give him the satisfaction of admitting that. "Your reputation is generally known."

"But what a unique opportunity," he observed, cutting a beefsteak that bled onto his plate it was so rare. "Do tell me what the general populace thinks of me."

"It... it is not my place to say." Her oysters consumed her attention.

"Surely you can satisfy my curiosity in return for my hospitality this evening?"

Susan Squires

Did he have to keep reminding her of her obligation? Well, there were some things she could deduce. And Madame LaFleur had gossiped. "You cannot blame the messenger then."

"Fair enough."

"Well...well, you are thought to be ruthless."

"True." That did not seem to faze him.

"And a libertine of course." He said nothing. "Because of the women," she felt obliged to explain. She had seen those for herself in the grand ballroom.

"Of course. Because of the women."

"And the gambling."

"That too."

"The fact that you never return from your debaucheries until dawn."

"Dear me, do people notice that? I'm flattered."

Well, really! If he admitted everything so blithely, she'd have to reach deeper to make him feel his faults. She bought time by taking a bite of the creamed spinach.

"You are called the 'wicked duc.' " That was weak. It was only she who called him that.

"So I've heard." He couldn't have heard that. He was just toying with her. The expression in his eyes was almost a kind of laughter.

"Mammas keep their daughters from you." Madame had certainly warned Françoise.

"A relief."

"Even men are, I think, a little afraid of you." Robespierre seemed to be, after all.

"Convenient, really."

She was getting angry. "So I ask myself, why do people fear you so?" She tapped her empty fork against her lips. "It could be something you have done in the past so horrible that people will not speak of it." He watched her, wary now. "Or...it could be because you seem to have secrets. Secrets both attract people and make them afraid."

He blinked, twice. She considered that an achievement. Then he took a sip of wine. "I think boring people so want there to be secrets they will make them up if they don't exist."

Time for Eternity

That wasn't *exactly* a denial. "Are you saying you don't have secrets?"

"We all have secrets, child." He examined her from under those lush lashes. "Everyone lies. Everyone tries to get what they want, without revealing how much they want it."

Françoise sucked in a breath. Did he know what she wanted of him? Would such a cynic extend himself to help Madame? She must not go too fast. A man like Avignon would resent any attempt to push him. She changed the subject. "I wonder you stay in France. Why not abandon the country to her foolishness? Especially when you are in danger by your very birth?" He had that in common with Madame. Could she play upon his sympathies for one like himself?

He set down his glass. "Don't make me a romantic figure. I am in no danger."

He certainly acted as though the committee and the mob posed no threat. "How is that when you make not the slightest accommodation to the rules of the committee?"

He raised his brows in surprise, whether because she dared to ask the question or because she did not know the answer, she couldn't tell. "Why should I make accommodation?"

"How can you not, and stay out of a tumbrel?"

"Ahhh." He studied her. "Perhaps *that* is my secret."

"I'll wager it's not your only one," she grumbled, stabbing a piece of lobster.

"It seems to *me* you should be grateful that my standing…let us say, 'encouraged' Robespierre to lose interest in you today."

"Why? Why did he let me go?"

"Oh, perhaps because he and I are old friends."

Not likely. The little lawyer, precise to a fault, had never let anyone close in his life, even Marta Croûte, who was rumored to be his mistress. He lived for the Revolution and guarded its integrity to the point of insanity. He had started sending the earliest proponents of revolution to the guillotine themselves a few months ago, just because they were no longer zealous enough for him. Even Danton had lost his head. Françoise didn't believe Robespierre let her go out of any feeling for Monsieur le Duc. But in some ways it didn't matter why. He had. That meant the duc could help Madame. She took a breath, about to broach the subject, but thought better of it. Best she approach obliquely.

"Why did you bother yourself about me, today?" That would tell her much about him.

"I thought it might be diverting to flaunt you in Robespierre's teeth when he knows you are not my ward." He smiled. The effect was not what one would call warm. "I must invite him and that woman who is such a rabble- rouser... What is her name?"

"Marta Croûte." He had saved her only to spite Robespierre and Madame Croûte?

"Yes... I shall invite them to my little soirée on Wednesday, where I shall present you to what is left of society." His eyes crinkled in anticipation. He wasn't looking at her at all. "My acquaintances will be scandalized by them, not unamusing in itself."

The man was totally unfeeling. Françoise had never felt so small. She was saved from the guillotine by this dreadful man only for his own amusement. He would never try to help Madame. She felt tears well in her eyes.

That sense of urgency washed over her. There was something dreadful she must do. Pain pierced her head. She put her fingers to her temple, unable to think.

What was there to think about? She couldn't ask the wicked duc to save Madame. He'd just end up throwing Françoise out of his house in the middle of the night for daring to importune him. And yet, she must. What other way was there to help her friend?

"You are not well, mademoiselle?"

She glanced up to feel his eyes boring into her. That only made her headache worse. "I... I have the headache."

He sighed, and looked...bored. "Then perhaps you'd better retire to your room." He snapped his fingers, and even without pulling on the bell rope, the door opened.

Time for Eternity

Jean stuck his head in. "Your grace?"

"Escort Mademoiselle to her room. Perhaps her dresser can find a vinaigrette."

All he wanted was to get rid of her. He would never help Madame. She rose, gave a brief curtsy, and stumbled from the room.

"I put your valise in your room, mademoiselle," Jean called after her. "I'm afraid the rabble stole your purse." She hurried up the stairs, wiping her cheeks, wanting only the refuge of her room.

*****

Henri pushed back from the table. In one moment of weakness he had saved her and now he was stuck with the chit until he could rid himself of her. Let that be a lesson to him. A headache. The oldest excuse in the book. He took his glass and the decanter to the window. The dining room looked out on a little garden with a pear tree in the center, surrounded by geraniums.

Though he had to admit, she'd had quite a day. The house she was living in burned down. She might even have considered it home. Her friend arrested. She'd almost been arrested herself. Which was tantamount to a death sentence. And then she'd been claimed as a ward by someone she knew very well was not the benevolent type. Perhaps there was some excuse for her retreat into that old favorite of women who didn't want to deal with life.

Actually, he had expected only the annoying timidity of a very young girl who knew nothing of the world. She *was* innocent. It amused him to watch her struggle to shock him with his own reputation. But her comment about secrecy being attractive was surprisingly perceptive.

Too bad it would be at least a week until he had an opportunity to pack her off on a barge to meet the *Maiden Voyage* in Le Havre. He could just hand her over to Jennings now and let him keep her in the warehouse down by the Seine.

Susan Squires

But...Jennings and the crew, for all their loyalty, were rough company for a virgin girl of twenty-one. They'd probably frighten her to death. She had enough spirit to try to escape what she would believe was a kidnapping. Would he give orders she was to be locked up for as much as a fortnight?

He sighed.

That meant he was stuck with her. All this drama made his own head ache.

Sacredieu. He was stuck with a crying female in the house. He could hear her even now with his preternatural hearing. Well, he had no time for Mademoiselle Suchet. He had work to do. And it must be done before three so he could put in an appearance at a gaming house or two before dawn. Lord, but she had put him on edge. Maybe what he needed was to feed tonight.

Drummond waited with his cape and his tricorn, his cane and his gloves. His valet took one look at his face and his own countenance went blank. Wise man. Henri made sure his pace was leisurely as he crossed the chessboard floor and the servants shut the door behind him.

Five

Annette was waiting for her in her room as Françoise stormed in. The girl's eyes went wide. "Why, whatever's wrong, mademoiselle?"

"Nothing."

"Would Mademoiselle like to get into a dressing gown, or is she planning to go out?"

"I'm going to bed. I have a headache." Tomorrow morning she'd visit Madame then spend the rest of the day at placement agencies for household help. There had to be something she could do to earn her bread that didn't involve lying on her back.

But she had to find a way to help Madame LaFleur too. If the duc wouldn't help, it was up to her. An image flashed through her head of the great, evil machine that stood in the northwest corner of the Place de Revolution, looking like a mouth open wide with its blade hanging at the ready to devour its next victim. And it did devour many victims every day, to the intense enjoyment of the crowd.

She put her hand to her mouth to steady herself.

Her eyes fell on an oddly shaped valise lying by her dressing table. "What is that?"

"Ooooh, mademoiselle, did Jean not tell you? He saw you drop this at the edge of the park, so he brought it in for you. He snatched it from the crowd. Shall I unpack it?"

She was just about to say that it was nothing of hers, when a strange frisson of familiarity rippled down her spine. Maybe it *was* hers. "No. No, thank you. I'll take care of that." She turned around. Annette unbuttoned her dress and unlaced her stays. What was in that valise? She almost knew. It was just at the edge of her mind... Like a word you couldn't quite remember.

Susan Squires

Annette handed her a lovely night rail, delicate and embroidered, an almost sheer peach color. Exactly the garment the kind of women Avignon entertained would own. At any other time she would have refused it. But now she just wanted Annette out of the room so she could examine the contents of that valise.

Annette laid out the luscious robe that went with the ensemble and bowed herself out. Somewhere downstairs a door thudded shut. Françoise went to the window and drew aside the draperies. Outside, the Place Royale was quiet. The mob had moved on for the night. She couldn't see the sidewalk under the arcade from here. But she could hear the click of heels. And then a figure strode from beneath the arcade at an angle into the darkness of the square, twirling a cane as though he didn't have a care in the world.

Hateful man. At least he was out of the house, probably until dawn.

She picked up a candelabrum and took it to the dressing table. The valise was very strangely constructed. It was not closed with a metal clasp. Instead it had a long line of what looked like interlocking metal teeth that ran across the top. At one end was a metal pull tab. She had never seen anything like it. Still, the implications were clear. She took hold of the tab and pulled it a few inches down the line of metal. The little teeth unlocked. Amazing. She pulled it back. They closed. It seemed almost diabolically clever. The leather was soft and buttery. It was the same color as a well-worn saddle, deep chocolate. Gingerly, she pulled the tab again—this time all the way across the top.

She peered inside. Hmmm. She pulled the gaping mouth apart and held up the candelabrum. Metal glinted. Goodness! Was it...? She reached inside and pulled out a leather scabbard. From one end a hilt protruded. The grip was blunt, made to fit a man's hand, and covered in strips of new leather. It was very clearly a sword, though unlike any she knew. Men carried rapiers—thin and deadly. She drew it out. This was perhaps two feet in length, wide, gleaming. It had a . . . brawny feel to it. Obviously it had never been used.

Time for Eternity

I am meant to use it.

The thought made her gasp. The very idea of cleaving flesh with an instrument so heavy and sharp made her stomach turn. And whom was she meant to use it on? She gave a nervous chuckle. She wasn't strong enough to cleave and hack with the sword anyway. A wave of disappointment shot through her at that—almost tristesse for lost strength. That was strange. She'd never be strong enough to use a weapon like this.

An image flashed through her mind of herself, raising the sword high.

The duc came out of the shadows and, her heart in her mouth, she brought the sword down at an angle. The thud of the blade into flesh reverberated up her arm. Blood bloomed on the duc's white cravat.

She gasped and shook off the image. Her stomach rolled. What was she thinking? Was she mad? She would never try to kill the duc, or any man, no matter how despicable. She shoved the sword back in its scabbard, shaken. Her imagination was getting the better of her.

Steady yourself, she admonished. *Think of something else.*

She reached inside the bag and pulled out… clothing? She held a scrap up to the light. It was shiny and black and…stretchy. Leg holes. Oh, dear. Could this be an undergarment? She blushed just to think of it. Why, it would hardly cover anything. There was no slit between the leg holes. You'd have to take it entirely off to use a chamber pot. She stretched the fabric again. Like a stocking. Was it…knitted? Impossible. The fabric was fine and silky.

The bag held other stretchy undergarments. Another, also black, was obviously meant to hold one's breasts. It would leave your midriff entirely bare. Who would ever wear this?

The duc's mistresses, of course. This was clothing for a prostitute.

She rummaged around and found two more sets of…well, whatever they were. One in off white, and one in pale pink. She also found a shapeless shirt, knitted but not nearly so fine, that would come to mid-thigh. She looked at it closely. It had, for some reason, tiny pictures of sheep jumping over a moon, each with a nightcap on. Underneath were containers. She took one out. It was shaped rather like a bottle, but it wasn't made of glass. Whatever it was made of was opaque, colored a bilious shade of lavender, with writing on it. It gave to her touch and smelled strange. That made her start. "Pureology," it said on one side. What did that mean? "Serious colour care. Anti-fade complex. Pure volume shampooing." She turned it over. Tiny writing covered the other side. The first paragraph was English but her eyes were drawn to the French one below it.

"This unique moisture-rich formula is free of harsh colour-stripping sulfates and salts. It pumps up your fine, limp hair and keeps the colour fresh. To use, wet hair. Lather, Rinse. Repeat."

It was soap! Whoever heard of a liquid soap? Handy though, for hair.

She peered into the bag again and saw lots of other containers made of roughly the same material—maybe ten of them. She pulled out several. There was another Pureology-lavender one, but this sloshed in a very different way. The liquid inside was more the consistency of water. There was no cork or stopper. How did one get into it? Wait. A little half-moon on the top of the bottle looked like it could be pressed. The top popped up, revealing a small hole. She sniffed. It smelled almost like alcohol, medicinal.

She shook several other containers. They all sloshed like the second one, no matter what was written on their outside. Experimenting, she found that some had tops that twisted off. The medicinal smell of the liquid inside was overwhelming. She quickly capped them up. Medicine? Someone must be very sick.

What a strange valise. Prostitute's clothes, a sword, hair soap, and lots of...medicine?

Who would use this motley collection? And such odd things in themselves: bottles that gave to the touch, clothes that

Time for Eternity

stretched without appearing to be knitted. They seemed the accoutrements of a lewd sorceress of some kind. She heaped the contents back inside.

Why hadn't the servants brought the valise to the wicked duc? How had the footman thought she had dropped it? She had never seen this strange case in her life.

Yes you have.

The feeling was so strong it washed over her in waves. Nausea swept over her. She hung her head for a moment until the feeling passed.

This was ridiculous. She *was* in dire straits. A kind old lady was in prison and likely to be executed. She had lost her livelihood and might end in a brothel, if she didn't fall prey to the wicked duc first, or anger him so that he abandoned her to the tender mercies of Robespierre and his supporters. She had no friends in a world gone mad with suspicion and bloodlust. Things were bad. But she had to get hold of herself.

She stared at the bag. It seemed squat and almost evil sitting there, its contents spilling out. She cocked her head. Her hand reached for the sword handle. The leather strips were rough.

Use it.

She dropped the sword as though it were a coal from the grate. What was happening here? It was almost as though she had heard the words inside her mind. Shaking, she pushed the sword into the bag with the very tip of one finger and pulled the little tab. The metal teeth closed together, sealing it. She should march down right now and return this valise to the footman.

That would be a mistake that would change everything from now until forever.

She felt the knowledge in her bones. It was the strangest feeling. How would it change things? Was the dreadful thing she'd been worried she'd have to do tonight all about this valise and its contents? She wasn't going to use a sword on anybody, least of all the duc who was the only thing standing between her and the guillotine.

This thing was evil. She should get rid of it.

Susan Squires

A stab of pain shot through her head. She couldn't do it. She couldn't get rid of the valise when she wasn't sure about the consequences. Mother Mary, she wasn't sure of anything.

Maybe your purpose can wait until you try to save Madame...

The pain eased. She looked around. If she couldn't get rid if it, she still didn't want anyone else finding it. The wardrobe? Annette would look in there. Her dressing room?

In the end, she stuck with the tried and true and shoved the valise under the bed, right under the headboard. Then she doused the candles and crawled up under the duvet. She was sure she wouldn't sleep a wink tonight in a house like this, waiting for its owner to come back from whatever debaucheries he was indulging, with such a thing stuffed under her bed.

Thoughts whirled in her head. The fire and Madame Croûte shouting for her death. The full feeling she'd had all evening. The feeling of déjà vu that wouldn't go away. And then the image of her cleaving the wicked duc's neck with the sword. Was that a vision? It had seemed so real. But she would never do something like that. She hoped. Was she going mad? And now she must get Madame out of prison, or her friend would go to the guillotine. How, if the wicked duc wouldn't help? And who would hire her?

She couldn't think...

She was talking to Avignon. Just talking. And it was the most frightening experience she'd ever had. Her soul trembled as she watched his mouth. She couldn't hear what he was saying. The cut-glass tumbler he held caught the light and gleamed. The glass was evil. She knew it, and the man who held it even more so. And then he stared at her and deliberately dropped the glass. It shattered in a thousand evil pieces. One separated from the others, and defied gravity to bounce back up and cut his hand. Blood, bright red, bloomed on his wrist. She reached out...

Françoise started up, clutching her hand to her chest as though to trap it. She gasped for breath as fear washed through her. What kind of nightmare was that? She was afraid of a glass?

She shook herself back to reality. She was in the wicked duc's house. Dark shapes of the furniture huddled in the corners. It was so stuffy in here. No wonder she couldn't catch her breath. She rose and went to the window where a lighter sky peeked through the draperies. She pulled them back. The trees in the wide park across the street were alive with birds. Their sleepy calls foretold the sun. Already servants scurried to be first at the market. Wagons rumbled through the side streets. Horses were being exercised on the tracks in the huge park. The city exploded with noise and smells though the day had hardly begun. This was the Paris she knew. And loved. Paris had been so foreign and so overwhelming when she had first come from Lady Toumoult's estate in Provence. But now being here seemed right and true.

Then she saw him below her. One figure that stood out among the others, if only by its insouciant, strolling gait as it moved out of the darkness across the park.

Her lips drew together in a thin line. It could only be the wicked duc. She had risen early many times to watch for his return and dream that he gave up his depraved ways for the simple girl he loved more than life itself. How stupid that felt now. She didn't even like him.

Well, she needn't like him. What she needed was for him to intercede on behalf of Madame LaFleur. She was afraid to ask him. He might just throw her out. But what choice did she have? She watched him disappear into the arcade below her window.

There was no time to dress. Avignon would be on his way to bed. She pulled on a scandalous cherry-red dressing gown. Hurrying down the hall, she tried to think of some argument that would weigh with him.

There he was, just coming up the stairs. Even now, with her mind fully on Madame and her plight, the coruscating energy around him made her feel a bit light in the head.

"Your grace." She dropped a hurried curtsy.

Susan Squires

He looked resigned. "You're up early."

She stepped to the top of the stairs, blocking his path. She could look him in the eye from here. Those eyes were impossibly dark. Yet, they were not flat black as one would suppose if one only saw them from a distance. Silver-gold flecks floated in them. Really, they were quite the oddest eyes she'd ever encountered. They looked like the night sky, gleaming with stars. No one would ever suspect that his eyes held such depths unless they were close enough to see them as she did now. A lover perhaps, an enemy. And she, what was she? She should have been surprised at his eyes, but she was not. She knew those eyes, had always known them.

She almost forgot herself. It was that easy to get lost in those eyes. "I... I wanted to talk to you about Madame."

He raised a black eyebrow. She'd never seen an expression so disdainful. "Another time."

"You helped me—"

He grasped her upper arms and set her firmly aside. His touch burned her even through her dressing gown. He froze, his hands locked about her arms. She looked into those dark eyes and saw a flame ignite there. Did that touch affect him as it did her? She felt again that she had always known him. Or that she had never known him at all.

"Your grace, will you take some refreshment before you retire?"

Both Avignon and Françoise jerked toward the sound of Gaston's voice. The servant glanced from one to the other. A look of surprise crossed his face before it went blank.

"I am going directly to bed." And with that, Avignon set Françoise aside and pushed past her. Her breasts brushed his right arm. He jerked his head around to look at her, as though arrested by the effect of that touch. She could say nothing. Her tongue seemed cloven to the roof of her mouth. The man could make her womanly parts ache with just a touch.

He pulled his gaze away and strode down the hall in the opposite direction of her own bedroom. He opened the last door on the right. That must be his bedroom. A dapper gentleman in a well-cut coat hurried up from what must be a back stairs for

Time for Eternity

the servants.

"Your grace?" he asked as he followed Avignon in. "May I assist...?"

The door closed. Françoise felt as though a light had been doused. She looked around in a daze. How was she ever to ask Avignon to save Madame, when he wouldn't even speak to her? And she had to move quickly. She had the worst feeling that Madame did not have much time.

"Be ready at a moment's notice today, mademoiselle." Gaston bowed.

"For what?" she asked, a little dazed still.

"For your appointment with La Fanchon, of course." Gaston smiled under his prim mustache. "I feel sure I shall achieve success in arranging one." He retreated down the stairs.

She turned back to her own room. Madame couldn't be condemned immediately. It took weeks to be brought before the Committee of Public Safety. And more time still to join the parade of tumbrels on the way to the Place de Revolution and the hungry Madame Guillotine.

But knowing all that didn't remove the sense of urgency. She must help Madame before it was too late. And something inside told her it would be too late very, very soon.

*****

Françoise, dressed in her charred morning dress, stood near the front of the long, sweating line that twisted up to the gatehouse of the Conciergerie under the Tour d'Argent. It had taken her all day to get this far. The fourteenth-century palace was now the largest prison in Paris and the least savory. The fumes off the Seine added to the stench from the twenty-four hundred or so prisoners inside at any given time. Madame LaFleur was here, or so said the guard after he consulted a long scroll brimming with names. It was the fourth prison she'd tried. She'd hoped Madame would have been taken to one of the converted monasteries. Conditions were better there. If she didn't get in before they closed the gates at sunset, she'd have to start all over again tomorrow. If only she'd had money for a bribe she could have seen Madame at noon.

Some in line had been coming here for months. They carried packets of food, clothing, pillows, bottles of wine, small children, anything that could be a comfort to those within. Françoise wished she had thought to bring something for Madame. The garrulous woman in front of her was finally let in the gate. It must be after seven.

As she drew closer to the guardhouse, she'd heard them talking.

"But how is it done? How?"

"Me, I would like to see that captain do any better job than we have done preventing it."

"They just disappear... *Alors,* one cannot prevent that."

"And the prisoners, they will not say how this thing is done no matter our persuasion."

"Me, I think they do not know," one said almost under his breath. Françoise strained to hear. Were people escaping from prison? Hope thrilled in her breast. At least someone got out of here other than in a tumbrel or a casket. But maybe the guards just miscounted.

"And now we count, and count. What good? The numbers, they only get smaller."

She wasn't the only one to think they'd miscounted. "Always it is families or children. It is strange, *n'est- ce pas?'*

"Perhaps it is over. It has been, what, three days?"

"Your money is mine if you care to wager on that." This was said with disgust.

She might have heard more, but it was her turn. A youngish guard in a blue and red uniform that had seen better days and needed a good cleaning jerked a thumb in Françoise's direction. She hurried forward, through a small side gate. She hurried past guards playing cards, guffawing loudly, and contributing to the general aroma of sweating human bodies.

"Come quickly, girl," her guard said impatiently. "I am nearly off my shift."

She hurried behind him. He led her down narrow stone

stairs into a huge, windowless room. It must be belowground. The stone ceiling was supported by Romanesque arches disappearing into the shadows above. The click of their boots echoed in the immensity. At least it was cool down here. But then he opened a heavy wooden door strapped with metal fittings and led her down a corridor lined with cells. Huge bolts secured the grated doors. The cells themselves were packed with people. Each cell must have more than fifty prisoners in it. Old, young, women, men—they were all packed in together. The noise in the stone corridor was deafening from conversation, shouting, even laughter, as out of place as that seemed. With a start, she saw that some cells held children. She had heard that the committee had taken to condemning whole families just to make sure the anti-revolutionary fervor was rooted out, not only of this generation, but of generations to come. To see children in such surroundings brought home that these policies were lunacy.

Hands stretched out to her as she walked by, but other prisoners just stared, vacant-eyed. They were by far more frightening.

At last the guard stopped in front of a cell no different than the others. "In here," he said.

She could see nothing behind the first row of prisoners pushed up against the bars. "Madame?" she called. "Madame LaFleur?"

"She is in the back," a sad-eyed man of perhaps thirty said. He carried a towheaded boy of about four in grimy short pants in one arm, pressed up against the bars. Perhaps the air was better toward the front. "She will never be able to push her way to the fore."

"Oh, dear." Françoise's eyes welled. Was Madame even alive back there?

The sad-eyed man pursed his lips as though making a decision. He set down the child in the crush against the bars. "Watch my boy," he said to Françoise and began to shove his way back into the throng. "Make way there! Make way." The little boy began to cry.

Françoise knelt. "And what is your name, brave boy?"

"Emile," the child snuffled. He turned up a dirty face streaked with tears. "Is Papa coming back?" The throng had swallowed his father but his continued progress was betrayed by the wave of angry protests.

"Of course he'll come back," she said briskly. "Where is your mama?" Tears welled again in the child's eyes. Françoise had a horrible feeling she shouldn't have asked.

"They took her. Papa says she isn't coming back." Françoise stuck her arms through the bars and held the child, shushing softly. What villainy was this that could tear families apart? A woman pressed above them murmured soft encouragement. They stayed like that, aching, until Emile's father reemerged, a breathless Madame LaFleur in tow.

"Oh, madame, how glad I am to see you," Françoise said. "Thank you, monsieur. May I know your name?"

The sad-eyed man picked up his clinging boy and smiled. "I *was* the Comte d'Ambroney. In these troubled times, call me Christophe St. Navarre."

"You have a brave boy, Comte."

The man smiled at his son, but the smile was wistful. "He is the best of me."

Madame pushed the last few feet through to bars. She reached through the grating and grabbed Françoise's hand, her expression clouded. "You should not have come here." She glanced to the guard. "It is too dangerous to be seen with me."

"And could I let you languish here alone? Not likely." She leaned in. It was not as if their conversation could be private what with people pressed in on either side of them. "My benefactor will secure your release, I'm sure," she whispered.

Madame's old eyes held pity in them. That surprised Françoise. It was she who should pity her friend. Madame was about to say something, then thought better of it. "Of course," she said lightly. "Your benefactor, he is good to you?"

"I had lobster for dinner last night with a salt cellar on the table."

Madame frowned. "I'm sure you did. But is he good to you?"

84

Françoise snorted. "Good? Avignon? The two words cannot exist in the same sentence."

Madame shook her head. "I mean…is he a gentleman?" she whispered.

Françoise smiled ruefully. "What would a man like him want with a girl like me?"

Madame grimaced. "If I need to tell you that, you are in more danger than I thought."

Françoise blushed. "You needn't worry. He thinks me a nuisance. But he will intercede on your behalf and then we will be comfortable again."

Again the look of pity. Françoise was about to protest that look when the guard interrupted. "You there, girl. Enough. You come back tomorrow if you want to chat." He prodded Françoise away. She stretched her hand back to Madame, who reached out through the bars to prolong the human contact.

"Thank you for coming, child. But don't come again."

Françoise's eyes filled.

"Au revoir," the comte said. Emile waved a still-chubby hand.

"Get along, now. My wine waits for me." The guard pushed her back down the corridor.

She *had* to get Avignon to intercede for Madame.

*****

Françoise trudged up to the front doors of number sixteen, intending to knock. The door opened as she raised her hand to the knocker.

"Mademoiselle," Jean said. "Come in, come in."

Gaston hurried up as she entered. "But where have you been, mademoiselle?" He didn't give her a chance to answer. "You crept out without letting anyone know. La Fanchon waited for three quarters of an hour before she stormed out. After I had arranged at great personal cost that she do your fitting here. And now you are in that dreadful, smoking dress." His hands fluttered in distress. "What will his grace say?"

Susan Squires

"Oh, dear." She had forgotten. Gaston had said something about an appointment when she was so distressed this morning. "Who is Fanchon?" Françoise hardly felt up to all the emotional energy in the foyer. Another footman was busy closing all the draperies. Why did they keep the house so dreary and dim?

"A dressmaker," Jean explained.

"Dressmaker?" Gaston rolled his eyes. "That is like calling…calling Michelangelo a stone cutter." Gaston was about to go on, but he peered at Françoise and abruptly shut his mouth. "Well, never mind all that. Jean, get ratafia and bring it to the library." When Jean did not move fast enough he added, *"Rapidement, s'il vous plaît?"*

He gestured Françoise down the ground-floor hallway. "Or perhaps Mademoiselle would like some cakes to sustain Mademoiselle until supper?" He opened the doorway to the library in which she had first met Avignon last night.

Françoise sat gratefully in one of the wing chairs flanking the fireplace. Today no fire burned there. "I am just a little tired." In truth the visit to Madame was the perfectly dreadful cap to a very long day. She ran her fingers through her curls.

"Where is that lazy Jean? Oh, here you are. Bring that tray here." He took it from the footman. "Now go tell Pierre we need sustenance for Mademoiselle."

Jean took himself off. Gaston poured ratafia. "And what has so fatigued Mademoiselle?"

"I went to see Madame LaFleur in the Conciergerie." Her eyes filled again.

"Quel horreur! But that is no place for a young person." He handed her the wine.

"It isn't a place for anyone but there are hundreds there. Children too." She sipped. Gaston motioned for her to take another drink. She did.

"There, that is bettor, no?"

She did feel a little better.

"We will not speak to his grace of this visit to a place it is not at all *comme il faut* to go, will we, Mademoiselle?"

Time for Eternity

"That would offend the duc's sensibilities, would it?" She shook her head. "I might have known. It must be horrible to work for such a man."

"Horrible?" Gaston seemed surprised.

"Does he throw things? He would be just the type. "I'll wager he has a dreadful temper."

Gaston gave a very tiny smile. "When his grace is displeased he becomes very quiet and polite. His voice is like silk." He shuddered. "A terrible thing to experience, I assure you."

Not what Françoise expected. Still... "Why do you stay?"

Gaston drew himself up. "Does Mademoiselle know how difficult it is to find a patron worthy of my skills in this time of rabble and cowards? Nor would I deign to leave France for some barbaric outpost like London or Rome or...dear God save me, Vienna." He shook his head sadly. "No, when one must work for the best, there is little choice. The duc is far above the competition in the best of times...the nicety of his taste, the demanding trust he puts in one to accomplish the impossible on a moment's notice, and of course, the fact that he recognizes my superior skills. What is a little silken tone to those accomplishments?"

Interesting perspective. She was about to ask more when the double doors to the library were flung open. A large man filled the doorway. He wore a starched white coat, an apron smudged with various sauces over his ample girth, and a hat that bloused over one ear. He was followed by a bevy of other servants, all male, carrying trays.

"Never fear, my little *pâte à choux*. I, Pierre, have come with sustenance." He waved the servants forward and pulled a low table in front of Françoise. The footmen put three trays down. Jean brought up the rear with a silver coffee service. Pierre pulled the cover off the first tray. "Voilà, quenelles. Salmon with a dill sauce, chicken with a curry sauce, and a light white fish with the lemon. A bite of each?" He did not pause for her consent but dished her up three of the delicate little pillows and covered them with sauces from silver gravy boats.

"You... You should not have troubled yourself."

"Trouble? I made these for your luncheon. Should such brilliant food go to waste? I think not!" He poured some wine. "Here, a little white bordeaux to wash them down. And then I think you will not disdain this small soufflé with the cheese? He pulled up another cover and added it to her dish. "And you may finish with the candied quinces and the buttered nuts. Just a little soupçon of pleasure to tide you over until you can eat properly with his grace tonight."

Françoise had to laugh. "If this is a soupçon, I am afraid to see what an entire meal would be." Wait, might that not be an insult? "Actually, I have had an entire meal of yours. Last night was supremely satisfying. The ragout of sweetbreads was extraordinary."

The large man's florid face lit up like a lighthouse. "Ah, the duc, he demands the best. But he provides the best ingredients. A fair trade, I think. And of course, I never disappoint."

She tasted the chicken quenelle. It melted in her mouth. "Monsieur, this is heaven."

"But of course." He bustled out, followed by footmen like a mother quail by her chicks.

Gaston bowed crisply. "I must leave you also, mademoiselle. His grace will soon be rising, and he will require a bath."

"Thank you," she murmured. "You have all been so very kind."

She was alone. Her wits came back slowly. The wine helped and the food. But nothing could erase the feeling that Madame was doomed unless Françoise could free her.

And no one could do that but Avignon. He *must* help Madame. He just must.

She couldn't let him put her off. He might throw her out of the house if she importuned him. Without anywhere else to go... It didn't matter. She had no choice. She was going to ask him and she wouldn't take no for an answer. She had to do it

Time for Eternity

now while she had her courage in her hands. And she knew where he was at this moment. Somewhere he couldn't avoid her. He was about to take a bath.

Susan Squires

Six

If only his servants weren't all hovering about him when he bathed. Françoise wanted him alone, no servants there to throw her out, and he unable to leave because he was naked. Oh, dear. That caused the most distressing cascade of images.

How did she *know* these things?

She mustn't think of that. She should think only of Madame. She stole up the stairway, her blood starting to pool in her center. Avignon naked. Shoulders, chest, belly, and...

She shook her head to banish thought—at least those thoughts. She knew which room was his. He had shown her only this morning. Now she was glad the house was so dim. The lamp at the top of the stairs cast wavering shadows from its candle, but the light did not reach down the hall. She sidled up to the far side of the door to listen.

He wasn't alone. She could hear him giving orders to someone. His valet, Drummond? Whoever it was responded, "Very good, your grace," to every command. How Avignon must love that clear, competent acquiescence. He was never challenged, was he?

She heard footsteps approaching the door from inside the room and melted into the shadows at the end of the hall. A dapper man dressed with immaculate precision appeared and trotted down the main stairway. She crept up again and pressed her ear against the door. She could hear him moving in there, but he seemed to be alone. Perfect.

She was almost shaking. *Think of Madame LaFleur.* She cracked the door and slid inside.

The room was lit by candelabrum everywhere. She was aware of a massive bed off to the right a dressing table holding gleaming silver brushes and a small knife for paring nails, a fireplace, several comfortable chairs. The impression was of red and black masculinity. But her gaze was captured by the figure in front of the large porcelain bath. His dressing gown was laid over a chair. At least he had his back to her. Golden light played over the muscles moving in his broad back, the gleaming roundness of his buttocks, the thick bands of muscle in his thighs. A coruscating vibration shouted that he was more alive than anyone she had ever known.

He stilled under her gaze. "To what do I owe this honor?"

She hated that insolent assurance. How did he know it was she? But she had no right to hate it. That insolent assurance was what could free Madame if he applied it to Robespierre. "For my friend, I would dare anything." She felt herself blushing from head to toe.

He turned. Dear God. Shocking. Yet not shocking at all. More…intriguing. A throbbing began between her thighs.

"Was this what you wanted?" His tone was calm, bored even. Well, it wasn't as if he needed to be embarrassed by his body. That seemed a very fine specimen. As if she knew anything about men's bodies. And yet she did know this man's body. The black hair on his broad chest, the small dark nipples, peaked just now, the veins that fed his biceps, the bands of muscle over his abdomen, the bulge of his upper arm, all seemed incredibly familiar. She resolved not to stare at the most interesting part of all. At least not for long. But she didn't have to. She knew that the vee of hair pointing downward led to an organ that was most impressive. And it wasn't even roused. She could picture it erect. Mother of Jesus. She'd never had thoughts as graphic as these. She was getting wet.

She tore her gaze away from him. But it only landed on the bed. And she thought of that naked body lying in that bed, tangled in the sheets, with a woman. With her. Kissing her, stroking her, gently, as though she were a treasured possession to be cared for…loved…

She shook her head, took a breath, and turned back to him. He didn't care for anyone, least of all her. She wanted to tell him that he must use his influence with Robespierre to save Madame. But she couldn't make her throat move. He was

Susan Squires

becoming aroused, that much was evident. She wanted to run from the room. But she also wanted to stay. He was dangerous. Not only to her virginity, but also to her soul. She felt it. Part of her knew everything and was screaming to her to protect herself. And part of her knew nothing, and was just rebellious enough to want to know everything.

*****

Well, it hadn't taken her long to throw herself at him. He couldn't quite figure her out. The blush had certainly been maidenly. But then there was her frank appraisal of his endowments. As though she were most familiar with men and their parts. Still, she had grown uncomfortable and turned away. But as she stared at his bed he could see her considering all the games one might play in bed together. And he started thinking about that too. Mistake. She might be wearing that sooty, tawdry dress but he could still see the curves she had displayed last night in that blue dress he'd had made for…for whatever her name was. This girl's body was petite but lush. He could feel himself growing tight and heavy, the ache beginning that signaled some desire that would never be fulfilled, no matter that he spent himself in a woman. He smelled the musk of her own desire on her. He could always smell when they lusted after him.

She turned back. And he thought her reaction to his coming erection would tell him whether she was bawd or innocent. It didn't. Her eyes were the strangest mixture of naïve shock and experienced appreciation. He stared in fascination. Some part of her might almost be as cynical, as damaged, as he was himself. And yet there was a halo of hopefulness that still believed in new possibilities hanging around the edges of her eyes. Innocent? Or worldlier than anyone else he had ever known? Which was she? *What* was she?

Sacredieu, she was his ward. What was he thinking? *"Vous permettez?"* He glanced to his robe pooled over a chair.

She came to herself and nodded convulsively.

He reached for his dressing gown and shrugged into it.

He pulled the belt ruthlessly around his waist to cover his erection, which might not be increasing since he had realized she was his ward, but was not exactly subsiding either.

The girl was trying to find her voice. To his surprise, he wondered exactly what she would say. He had long ago ceased to find humanity a surprise.

"I went to visit Madame LaFleur today. I finally found her in the Conciergerie." She said it as though it were a challenge.

"You what?" Surprise indeed. She'd combed the prisons for her friend? That took courage. She might also have ruined his efforts to save her by associating with the old woman.

"The conditions are appalling."

As he knew only too well. "I am aware."

"Illness may take her before she can be guillotined." Her eyes welled with tears again.

Spare me tears, he thought, grimacing. He'd seen enough tears, both crocodile and real, such that he never wanted to see more in his lifetime.

"You could help her. I know you could."

The damnable part was that he was probably the only person in Paris besides Robespierre or his hell-spawned bitch who could, though not the way the girl thought. "You think I am someone I am not." He made his voice hold finality and a hint of derision.

"Someone who has influence, or someone who will care enough to try?" she challenged.

She was persistent. "Your choice," he murmured. He made his eyes bore into hers, telling her his heart was stone, making her believe his refusal as no protestation could. That would stop her.

"You can sit by with your salt and well water and your brandy and lift not even a finger to relieve the suffering around you?"

"I lifted a finger to save you," he reminded her gently. "Don't make me regret it."

She swallowed. She'd heard the threat in what he said.

That would do it. "And me, I am grateful. But you could do more. What kind of a man are you, that you will not even try?"

He retreated behind a mask. She challenged him after he'd threatened her? "No kind of man at all." He let his voice drip boredom. A monster, maybe, a freak, but not a man.

"You have influence with Robespierre. I saw it. The most he can say is no."

She didn't understand. The old woman was long past anyone's influence. Robespierre would never let her go once she was in prison. That would give the other prisoners hope. The only way she could be saved was the way he saved the others. But the old woman didn't fit the pattern. That would draw attention to her. And she was his neighbor. They would connect him to her. Trying to save her would jeopardize all his work for the others. He half wanted to explain to the girl. Surprising. He couldn't of course. "The cost would be too great."

"What cost?" she pressed. "To your pride? A small price on the whole."

"What do you know of cost?"

That expression of lurking pain that said she knew...everything, just as he did, crossed her face. And then the innocence prevailed. "I am not experienced, as you are." She was embarrassed by her innocence. He saw her gather herself and resolve to press her case. "But I know the cost of Madame's life. Your soul may have many stains on it, Monsieur le Duc, but that only means it cannot stand another."

A perspective that could only be held by someone young. "You know nothing of stained souls."

"But I do." She looked surprised at herself and then her eyes unfocused as she looked within. "You become disconnected from humanity. You believe you are different, a monster even, and then, because you cannot change anything you have done, or felt, or been, your only choice is to become numb to others' pain. Because if you can't become numb to their pain, you will never be numb to your own, and that, in the end is the best you can hope for."

He blinked. Then he cleared his throat. "If that is what

94

you think, how…how could you believe that I would trouble myself over someone else's pain?"

She frowned, puzzling over it.

Yes, my pretty one, that is your problem in convincing me, is it not? And mine in finding a way to live with this burden I have become to myself.

"Because," she said slowly, "I think the only way you can overcome what you have done to yourself, and to others, is to resolve to leave yourself open to yet more damage. Yes. Resolve. That is the only cure."

He frowned. Resolve was what he had used to banish his own demons for centuries.

She looked up at him. "Can that be right?" She was innocent enough to admit she wasn't sure. And experienced enough to know everything. How was that possible?

"No. It can't." He couldn't take any more of this. "Now, will you leave me to my bath?"

She was still musing to herself. "But I think it can." She glanced up at him and shrugged a smile. "You must see that if I believe one must resolve to overcome cynicism and be open to the world and all it can do to one, then I must believe you will help me in spite of your nature, and resolve to see that you do. Which means I'm not going anywhere without your promise."

He sighed in exasperation. "I shall discuss this with you over dinner. Not while I'm taking a bath. Is that enough of a promise?"

She curtsied, the corners of her mouth hinting at a smile, and slid out the door.

Hell and damnation. What kind of a chameleon had he brought into his house? And how the hell did she know him so well?

*****

He strode downstairs half an hour later. He could take no pleasure in his bath. Not when he kept remembering how she had looked at the bed. Or replaying in his mind her tenuous exposition of the exact mental process he had been going through in the last years as he tried to find meaning in his life. The fact that touching her the other night had raised a cockstand on the spot was only because he had not assuaged his Companion's need for sex of late. Nothing more. His hair was now ruthlessly brushed into a simple queue. Drummond had worked his magic on the coat and he had tied his own cravat in record time.

The amazing thing was that he was going to do something very stupid tonight. It might cut short his usefulness and make Paris impossible for him.

And if he lost his purpose, he might just lose his soul. So why was he going to do it? Because she challenged him? Or was it because she seemed to think one could find hope in spite of how much damage years, and alienation, could inflict on one?

He squeezed his eyes shut. He knew better. And yet he was going to get the old woman out for her. He was *not* going to tell the girl what he was doing. That would only add to the danger. She'd not have to know his part in the thing at all. So, he'd just put the girl off tonight and avoid her until the thing was done. He'd have to spend all his time away from home. *Merde.*

He pushed into the library. She was already there, reading a book, still wearing that awful dress. Which reminded him…

"Gaston tells me you missed an appointment with La Fanchon today."

She looked guilty. "I apologize for that. I was distracted when Gaston told me the time, and it took me all afternoon to get into the prison to visit Madame once I'd found her."

"You have no idea how large my order will have to be to smooth her ruffled feathers." He strode to the sideboard where the brandy was set out and poured a glass. Gaston had set out ratafia as well. He lifted the decanter and offered it to the girl. She shook her head.

"No, thank you."

"You will perhaps deign to let her attend you

96

Time for Eternity

tomorrow?" He raised his brows pointedly.

She was positively pretty when she was embarrassed. "I...I had hoped to visit Madame again and take her something more useful than my comfort." She squared her shoulders. "I don't need clothing. If your grace could perhaps loan me a small amount of the money that would have gone to dresses, I could bribe the guards to get in with some food and perhaps a blanket for her."

He set his lips. "I'll not have you looking like...like a street urchin."

She looked down at her dress and swallowed hard. "Well, perhaps one new dress."

"One?" The girl was impossible. "You really must think of my reputation." He lifted one hand to forestall her protestations. "You will be given an allowance which is yours to spend as you will, on bribes and blankets even. But tomorrow you will wait on La Fanchon." He could see she wanted to protest. It was killing her not to tell him she would do as she liked and his priorities were topsy-turvy. But she couldn't be ungrateful, and he wasn't asking much. The dialogue with herself was clearly going on in her eyes. Finally she bit her lip. "Of course, your grace."

He nodded approval. "Wise decision." He downed his brandy. "Now, I find I must go out for the evening."

"But you promised that you would discuss helping Madame with me over dinner."

"Did I? I can't recall. Well, we will talk about it sometime very soon."

She surprised him by rising and striding over to stand much too close to him, her eyes snapping in anger. "Don't you dare try to wriggle out of a promise by pretending to forget."

Caught. But he couldn't tell her his plan. When she made it to the Conciergerie and found Madame escaped, she'd best think it had nothing to do with one Henri Foucault.

"I'll talk about it when I choose to talk about it, dear girl." That would madden her. It couldn't be helped. "And right now I choose to have a peaceful dinner far away from talk of

Madame LaFleur and Robespierre and prisons and executions."
He sighed with what he hoped was long-suffering boredom.

"You are absolutely…hopeless."

True. Hope had gone out of his life a long time ago.
And he was mad to even think she could bring it back.
"Agreed," he murmured as he set his glass down. "I shall
discuss this with you when you are dressed in a way that does
not offend my every sensibility." And with that, he walked out,
leaving her sputtering. Not kind, but necessary.

*****

The stone walls of the Conciergerie loomed over him in
the darkness. A little after one in the morning. The guards
would be bored and getting drowsy. The better to think they'd
been dreaming if one chanced to see the act itself. He sidled up
to the guardhouse. He could hear them playing cards. Hell, he
could smell them, even over the stink of the place. Everything
smelled like a republic rotting from within to him these days.

"Who has drawn making the next round?" one asked.

"Denny."

"Me? You jest, cur. I just did it last hour."

"And lost the last hand at piquet, no?"

"I was sure we said it was to be the one who lost the
next hand."

"Mes amies? Next hand?"

"Last hand." This from several voices.

Grumbling. Denny would be Henri's mark. Keys
clinked being removed from the wall. Peering through the great
iron grate that served the old palace as a portcullis Henri saw
him start out the back of the guardhouse. He headed down
some stairs.

Henri drew his power and watched the red film pour
down over his field of vision. The whirling blackness swept up
to engulf him. Then the familiar pain seared through him and
he was through the portcullis. He made no sound at the pain
transporting caused. He had grown inured to pain after all these
centuries. He moved silently down the stone staircase,

following the glow of the guard's lantern, but well back, in the shadows.

The stairs opened out into the huge Romanesque crypts. He remembered when they had housed the stables for Henri IV's army back in the 1500s. Bobbing ahead was the circle of light. He could hear the guard's noisy breathing and the echoing clip of his boot heels. The faint noise of the cells began to grow. He quickened his pace into a narrow corridor.

Denny whistled, perhaps to keep away the dark, so he was caught unawares when Henri pulled him around. He stared straight into Henri's red eyes. Fear bloomed in his expression then faded as Henri held him immobile by the force of his will and the power of his Companion.

"Madame LaFleur. An old woman. You know her? She was brought in yesterday."

The man nodded, all expression absent from his eyes.

"Take me to her cell."

The guard turned back down the hall. They passed several cells emitting the stench of human bodies not recently washed, piss, defecation, vomit, and the subtle sweetness of infection and death. He knew it well. He had been to these cells many times. So he ignored the supplicating hands, some holding letters they wished to get to loved ones on the outside, and the faces, some tearful, some stony and still, the eyes dead.

The guard paused in front of the third cell and pointed. "In the back."

"Let me in."

The guard opened the small doorway in the larger iron grating without thought for whether anyone inside could overpower him and get out. The guard locked the door. Henri turned to him and whispered, "You will remember nothing."

Then he let him go. He watched Denny shake his head as though to clear the cobwebs from it then shrug and continue on his rounds.

Henri turned into the cell and swept his crimson gaze around the dazed prisoners. "I am not here. You will remember nothing."

Susan Squires

They took no notice of him, but went on with whatever they had been doing. They parted as crowds always parted for his kind. He strode to Madame LaFleur, letting his power slide back down his veins. So it was an ordinary duc she saw inside her cell.

She raised eyes that were very wise for one who had lived only a single lifetime and smiled. "Françoise sent you."

It wasn't a question. And it was the truth. He wouldn't be here without the girl's prodding. "I've come to get you out of here."

"How?" she asked.

He wouldn't answer that. He examined her carefully. She might be old, but she looked healthy enough, if a little drawn about the mouth and eyes. Spending a night and a day in the Conciergerie would do that to one. "It will involve a little pain." He smiled. "Can you bear it?"

She nodded and a roguish twinkle came into her eyes. "The alternative has a little pain involved as well." She looked around. "The others…"

"No." He cut her speculation short. "Only you."

She drew herself up. "There is a man with a child here. Take them instead of me."

A family? He hadn't noticed. He looked around now. No one paid attention to him. There they were. A man in his early thirties and a boy of perhaps three.

He turned back to the old woman. "I'll come back for them. But first you, or Françoise will never forgive me." As if he cared for her forgiveness. But the old woman didn't need to know he was lying.

"You are not who we thought you were."

He put his arm around her shoulders and drew his power. The world went red again. She lifted her face to his in question as the blackness began to whirl around them both. She would feel the thrumming energy racing through her. As she saw his red eyes, her own opened wide in astonishment. The blackness engulfed them. Pain struck through him. He heard her scream.

What appeared around him was his warehouse down at

Time for Eternity

the quay off the Seine. Dark barrels and crates were stacked in regular heaps. He still gripped Madame's shoulders. That was why he felt her legs give out. He lifted her into his arms before she could fall. She weighed almost nothing. She had probably just fainted from the shock of transporting. It was even more painful for humans than it was for him.

He strode through the maze of cargo to a desk illuminated by a cone of light from a lamp sitting on it The desk was empty now. Jennings should be about somewhere. His crew and his warehouse manager were all English, though they spoke excellent French and could pass when necessary. A long table to the side of the desk was covered with inventory ledgers. Henri swept them aside and laid the old woman across the table.

Her right hand grabbed her left arm. She moaned, blinking to consciousness. Her left hand curled into a claw. That was bad. He lifted her shoulders. Her face was paper-white.

Jennings hurried up. "My lord, what are you doing here?"

"Get me some water, man, or better yet brandy." He turned to Madame. "Your heart?"

"It has always been weak," she whispered.

"Damnation. I would not have taken the chance had I known."

Again her eyes crinkled at the edges. "I'd rather die this way than on the guillotine."

"People survive such incidents." Not many. Jennings poured from the jug on the desk.

She shook her head, ever so slightly. "I am old. I have no regrets." She looked up at him. "One. One regret."

"What is it?" He shouldn't ask. She'd make him promise to take care of an aged cat or some task equally distasteful.

"I should like to see Françoise once more."

He chewed his lip. His night was complete. Why not take another dreadful chance? He nodded. "Jennings, stay with

Susan Squires

her." He laid her down and walked into the shadows.

"Just you drink this," Jennings was saying in French as Henri drew the darkness. "Finest French brandy. Set you up all right and tight."

Seven

Françoise couldn't sleep. Instead she stood at the open window of her room and looked out over the dark Place Royale watching the shadowy trees dance in the hot wind. The experience of seeing the duc at his bath had been deeply disquieting, as much because she had known how he would look as for the overwhelming desire she'd felt. It seemed as though everything she experienced were just a memory. The dreams she'd been having (she'd decided not to call them visions) only made her feel more on edge. Was it the edge of madness?

And then there was the terrible sense of danger she felt all around her. It wasn't just the danger to Madame. She still had hope that she could convince Avignon to help her friend. It was some danger to herself. And it had to do with Avignon. She felt beleaguered, assaulted by her feelings for him. And she'd had all evening to think about that. Dinner had been a lonely affair. The evening stretched and even books from the duc's library could not distract her.

A shower of rain flapped over the park. Drops splattered her face but Françoise didn't move. The air cooled with the shower, and that cooled the hot blood that pumped in her veins.

Lust. That's what she felt for him. Just lust. Not something she was proud of. But who would not lust after a man possessed of such dark beauty and a body made for sin? That was not to mention that feeling of being exquisitely alive, and totally dangerous. The package was almost irresistible. He played upon that beauty, that vitality, to get women into his bed.

She was not going to be one of them. Her life and soul depended on it somehow. She'd just resist his siren call. The protection of thinking he wouldn't be interested in a girl like

Susan Squires

her was gone. She'd seen the evidence of his desire tonight in the bath. Men like that wanted everything, no matter if it was worthy prey or not.

But a man like that would have lots of female servants around for easy access to those powerless to stop him. He didn't. Perhaps he knew what he was and wanted to avoid succumbing to his worst inclinations. That would mean he had a conscience about seducing women, at least women who were powerless. And she was very sure he had no shred of conscience.

That was why she had to protect herself against him.

Her thoughts flew to the strange bag concealed under her bed. The sharp-edged sword, the many bottles filled with what had to be medicine. The bag wasn't hers, was it?

The time will come when you must use the contents of that bag.

The thought was almost like a voice inside her. Françoise shook her head to clear it. What could you use a sword for except killing? Françoise was no killer, in spite of the images that had flashed through her mind the other night.

You didn't kill a man for being attractive. Or even unprincipled. She almost had to laugh as she imagined how awkwardly she would hold that Roman short-sword.

He would certainly laugh at her. And then he'd bat the sword away and...

She turned into the room as she heard movement. Her heart stuttered.

"Come." She'd recognize that baritone anywhere. "You must hurry."

"What are you doing here?" Her hand went to her throat. This wasn't supposed to happen. She didn't have that sense of déjà vu at all. And that was shocking.

"Madame is ill." He moved toward her. She heard a clatter in the street below. "She asked for you."

He had been with Madame? In prison? "Her heart?" He nodded even as he went to her wardrobe.

"I'll dress," she protested.

"No time." He pulled out an evening cloak and whirled

Time for Eternity

it around her shoulders.

She tied the silken cord with shaky fingers as he hurried her from the room.

By the time they got to the front door, Jean was there to open it. Outside, it had stopped raining. A groom held a great black gelding prancing at the end of his lead. "No carriage?" She couldn't ride such a horse.

"No time." Was that all he could say? He mounted. The groom unhooked the lead and Avignon collected the reins, murmuring, "Easy boy." The horse settled. It was really quite amazing. Avignon reached down a hand. It was ungloved. So was hers. She took a breath. Madame needed her. Still his firm clasp on her hand shot sensation straight to her core. Would she ever get over the effect of his touch? He pulled his foot from the stirrup. "Put your right foot in the stirrup and I'll pull you up." And he did. Effortlessly, turning her to sit in front of him. He had the reins in one hand and the other around her waist. She should have felt insecure sitting sideways like this, but she didn't. What she felt was his body pressed to hers, all hard planes and muscle. She had never been this close to a man before. Yet the sensation was totally familiar. His scent wafted over her, spicy, uniquely his, and the electric life that glowed from him seemed to light her from within. The horse clattered over the stones. The night was shiny black and wet. The streets were filling again after the rain shower. Faces flashed past as they thundered through the Marais. They did not turn north toward the Conciergerie, but down to the river through empty streets lined with darkened warehouses. How had Madame gotten here? She must have escaped prison. But how?

At last Avignon drew the horse up in front of an immense stone building with impressive wooden doors twice the height of a man and a crane protruding from the upper story to load freight into wagons. He slid her to the ground and swung down. He cast the reins around a post set for the purpose and grabbed her hand. She ran to keep up with his stride. He pushed open the doors onto an immense darkness. Huge wooden crates and dusty barrels loomed in piles. The place smelled like dust and tar and raw wood and spirits of some kind. Maybe brandy?

Avignon pulled her toward a glow, wending his way between stacks of big spools filled with what looked like lace. They emerged into a clearing in the forest of crates and barrels. A weathered man stood looking down at Madame, who lay on a table next to a desk with a lamp.

Françoise darted to her side. "Madame, are you well?" That was stupid. Her face was like old parchment, her lips so colorless they were blue. Someone had pillowed her head on some sacking. Her eyes looked cloudy rather than their usual piercing blue. Françoise took her hand. It was cold.

"Glad he brought you, child," she murmured. She glanced behind Françoise to where Avignon stood. "Thank you, your grace. A kind act."

"Nothing of the sort," he said.

Madame's eyes crinkled. "He won't admit to being kind, will he?"

"The wicked duc? I should think not." The blurring of Françoise's eyes belied her light tone. "Did...did you escape? But how? And what has happened to you?"

"My heart..." the old woman murmured.

"You will get better, Madame, I know you will." She pressed Madame's hand.

"I fade, child. I haven't long." Acceptance filled her voice.

Françoise did not accept. It was all *his* fault. "How could he expose you to the danger of an escape? He was just to speak on your behalf to Robespierre, use his influence." The wicked duc had killed her friend.

A faint smile touched Madame's lips. "No one comes out of that prison through influence, dear. Robespierre and Madame Croûte could not afford to give prisoners hope, now could they?" This effort seemed to tire her. She closed her eyes. "I didn't tell him about my heart," she managed.

"But you can't go..."

Madame opened her eyes. "I can't decline God's invitation, I'm afraid."

Time for Eternity

Tears coursed down Françoise's cheeks. She buried her face in Madame's shoulder.

"Promise me one thing." Madame's voice was fading.

Françoise sat up. "Anything." But Madame's gaze was fastened upon Avignon. Françoise turned in time to see him nod once, curtly.

"Take care of her."

Avignon's lips formed a grim line. He didn't like his hand being forced. And obviously Fransoise was an unwelcome burden. But he nodded once again.

Madame's eyes drifted to Françoise. "And you, *ma petite dindon.* Look deep. Don't be fooled by what is on the surface, even in yourself."

"I won't," Françoise promised. What did Madame mean? What a strange promise she exacted on her deathbed. Françoise glanced back to Avignon. "Can't we make her more comfortable? A blanket perhaps?"

Avignon stared at Madame. "Only God can make her comfortable now."

Horrified, Françoise turned back. Madame's eyes were open but Madame was no longer there. She had died in the moment Françoise turned away. Could a life be extinguished so… casually? Françoise groped for breath around the sobs that choked her. Not fair. Not fair at all.

*****

Lord, what did one do with a mere child experiencing her first taste of death? Avignon glanced to Jennings, who rolled his eyes. Avignon folded his arms across his chest to suppress the impulse to take her in his arms and make soothing sounds while he kissed her blond curls. He didn't have time to comfort her. He had to get back to Lacaune's before he was missed. He had planned to be gone only long enough to transport into the prison and back out to the warehouse with the old woman, a moment more to blink back to the gentlemen's retiring room at the gaming hell. Twenty minutes at the outside.

Susan Squires

How long before the guards noticed the old woman's escape? She was not part of a family. She was his neighbor. People would have seen Avignon, his ward up in front of him, galloping through the Marais to the river tonight. All were things to draw attention to him. Henri hoped Robespierre was not as smart as he thought himself.

Henri cleared his throat. Best move this along. "Jennings, do we have an empty crate? I'm certain Mademoiselle would like to see her friend laid out respectfully." Jennings nodded, showing by the gleam in his eyes that he appreciated Henri's ploy. He disappeared into the shadows. The girl was trying to compose herself.

"Thank you for bringing me."

"It was nothing," he lied.

Jennings returned, dragging an empty crate shaped pretty nearly like a coffin. Françoise rose and whirled off the expensive evening cape he'd had made for that opera singer and spread it, red silk lining side up in the crate. Henri picked up the frail old body and laid it in the crate. He pulled the edges of the cape in to cover her. The physical husk looked peaceful. He hoped her soul was likewise.

The girl stared down at what remained of her friend. She was so young and looked so fragile, clad only in the sleeveless night shift of finest linen. The fair, blushing skin of her upper arm made him want to touch it. The nape of her neck as she bowed her head was…vulnerable. He could see the outline of her spine where it disappeared beneath the cloth to join the delicate wings of her shoulder blades.

"Jennings, why don't you take one or two of the men and…find Madame LaFleur a place of rest in the *Cimetière du Père Lachaise?*"

"Right ho, your grace." Jennings lowered the top of the crate over the dead woman.

"Without a priest or a funeral?" the girl gasped. "Madame would be horrified."

Henri took a breath before he spoke so his words would not be sharp. He laid a hand on her shoulder to steady her. But his words disappeared in his throat at the feel of her flesh on his

108

Time for Eternity

palm. It sent shock waves straight to his loins. He tried to keep some semblance of pride as he jerked his hand from her shoulder. She was looking at him very strangely. He swallowed once and cleared his throat. "Priests are illegal, and any kind of a ceremony will draw attention to her, and through her, to us."

She looked at him with those big, innocent and experienced blue eyes and managed to look both disappointed and accepting of his refusal. Goaded, he turned to the makeshift coffin and bowed his head. He glanced pointedly at the girl and she did the same.

"Lead me from the unreal to the real. Lead me from darkness to light. Lead me from death to immortality." He took a breath. "Earth to earth, ashes to ashes, dust to dust; in sure and certain hope of the Resurrection unto eternal life. I am the resurrection and the life: he that believeth in me, though he were dead, yet shall he live: And whosoever liveth and believeth in me shall never die. We commend the body of thy servant into thy care. In the name of the Father, the Son, and the Holy Ghost. Amen."

She looked up at him, studying his face. "What was that first part from?"

"The Upanishads."

She nodded thoughtfully, as if she knew what the Upanishads were. Of course no good Catholic girl knew the Upanishads. "I wouldn't have thought you'd know the benediction."

He wouldn't tell her he'd been a monk for forty years or so in the thirteenth century. He could still recite big swatches of the Bible. "Even Satan knew the Scripture. I know several."

And then because she made him uncomfortable, he said, just to have something to say, "Can you get this place cleared out, Jennings? We must make room for another shipment."

Jennings gave a mock salute to make sure Henri knew the question was unnecessary. "Absolutely, your grace. It's all spoken for."

When the girl began to peer around her into the shadows, examining the crates and barrels, Henri realized he had drawn attention to something he had no desire for her to know.

"Are all these things yours?" she asked. She rose from where she knelt beside the makeshift coffin and went to finger a bolt of lace. She looked to a barrel clearly labeled SALT.

Well, this was it. No use denying when he'd all but admitted it by giving Jennings orders. Much of elite Paris knew this secret. "They are."

She turned to him, blinking. "You're a smuggler, aren't you?"

"I'd describe it as being a dealer who doesn't require taxes to be paid on his goods."

He saw her processing that. "That's why you have influence with the new government."

"The new villains like luxury as much as the priests and nobility who were the old villains."

Her nose wrinkled in distaste. That's why dealing in contraband was such a perfect cover. Everyone disdained his activities, even if they craved the results. It wasn't usually so painful to be despised. "Why would you need to break the law? Avignon is the richest property in France."

"Avignon is confiscated." True. True also that he didn't need its income. But his tenants, now, they were likely to starve if he weren't sharing the gains from his trade and his wells with them to keep the land in good heart. The chaos the Revolution had created meant that seed and farm implements had become exorbitant. And of course, there was the real reason he smuggled. The ships running back and forth from England. She mustn't discover how he used those ships. Or the rooms at the back of this very warehouse, concealed behind a brick façade. So let her think he was a callous lout, making hay while the country went hungry.

"But smuggling?"

"Robespierre's dependence on my various... endeavors kept you out of prison, my dear *ward*. And it gives you lovely dinners like you had last night. You might show more respect."

She swallowed. Then she glanced away. "You are right,

Time for Eternity

of course. How stupid of me."

"Now, I must get you back to the house. Come." He turned and strode out through the shadowy warehouse.

*****

Françoise followed Avignon's echoing steps. Some part of her noted that he was almost running from her. She felt strangely empty. She ought to be sobbing. Her only friend in the world had just died. But after the first tearing sorrow, it seemed inevitable that Madame should die, as though Françoise had experienced and grieved this death before. Madame was *fated* to die. If she escaped the guillotine she must be felled by some apoplexy, robbed of life no matter the means.

Was there no hope to change one's fate? Françoise felt her purpose for living tremble.

When Françoise emerged Avignon was untying his horse. The heat was back. The cool after the rain shower had been only a momentary diversion.

Avignon swung into the saddle and held out his hand. She knew what would happen if she grasped it. Even his comforting touch on her shoulder in the warehouse just now had sent a shiver of energy down her spine. He took his foot out of the stirrup. She lifted the hem of her shift with one hand, acutely aware that her breasts were moving freely under the fine linen. Her nipples tightened. Then she put a slippered foot into the stirrup and clasped his hand. Warm, smooth, strong— its electric sensation of life struck her harder even than she had imagined.

She wanted that life. After the death she'd witnessed tonight, his feeling of intense life called to her as never before. He swung her into the saddle. Her hip was pressed into his groin, her shoulder to his chest, as she sat sideways on the pommel of the saddle. The rise of it rubbed right against her most private parts. Her arm just naturally slid around his taut waist to steady herself, even as he held her close and gave the horse the office to start.

They said nothing. He probably felt nothing. But for the second time tonight she felt… everything. She was full to overflowing with the strange and the familiar all mixed up together; the feeling of impending doom, the inevitability of it all.

"Look deep," Madame had said. Why? Did she think Françoise saw people only on the surface, even Françoise herself?

Maybe Madame was talking about Avignon. Françoise had always thought of him simply as the wicked duc. But he had actually tried to rescue Madame. Not the way Francçoise had intended. But neither he nor Madame thought using influence would take the trick. So he'd engineered an escape from the Conciergerie. That took far more energy and frankly, probably put him in more danger than she intended. Would she have pressed him if she'd known she was asking him to risk his life? It had all turned out badly, but after her first shock, she couldn't blame him. She could only marvel that he had attempted it at all.

She'd been surprised too when he pulled the cloak so tenderly about Madame's body. But the real shock had been the benediction he'd said to spare Françoise's feelings. He might have just hustled her away without any solace. He might have told Jennings to dump the coffin in the river, instead of sneaking into *Cimetière du Père Lachaise* and burying Madame. His actions tonight were…kindness. There was no other explanation.

Had she been wrong about the wicked duc? That question echoed through every part of the fullness inside her. It wasn't supposed to happen this way. Things had gone off track, perhaps dreadfully wrong.

Something hard pressed into her hip. It was his erection. Part of her was not quite so appalled that he might desire her. Part of her was depressed that she was not appalled. It seemed as though she were drifting toward him and there was nothing she could do about it.

This time the trek up through the Marais was slow. The movement of the saddle with the stallion's rolling gait rocked against her woman parts. How far to the Place Royale? She'd be moaning and begging him to use her if she couldn't get out of this dreadful position soon.

At first she hardly noticed that they were attracting attention. Yet, late as it was, there were loud jests and guffaws along their course. People didn't see a duc and a half-naked woman on a horse every day. Avignon saluted the hecklers as though everything they were thinking was true. How could he?

When they finally arrived at the house, she slid down and dashed through the door Jean held ajar while Avignon dismounted and tossed the reins to a groom. She was fairly humming with need. It was almost as if she were humming with life.

Something inside her roused itself. Avignon was still a horrible danger to her, regardless of his kindness tonight. Bad things would happen if she allowed herself to care about him. It would ruin her entire life. She *had* to take action.

Yet if one couldn't change fate, what use to resist? Madame's death proved that what would happen would happen. She found that so depressing, it started the tears again.

She shot a glance back to Avignon and saw a look of…consternation on his face. He did not enter the house, but simply nodded to Jean and said, "See that Mademoiselle has a brandy. She has had a shock."

And then he turned on his heel and left.

Just like that.

He must be going back to his evening of gaming as though Madame had not died or was going to be buried by an Englishman who was probably a Protestant in the dead of night without a priest. Just as though he had not said a benediction over Madame's body.

The man was impossible, and she'd best realize that and get hold of herself.

*****

Henri materialized in the recesses of the cloakroom at

Susan Squires

Lacaune's. Tonight had been a disaster. Nothing had gone according to plan. Not only with the escape, but also with the girl. He'd nearly spilled his seed in his breeches during that ride from the Seine to the Place Royale. Her hip ground against his groin with every step Dauphin took. The feel of her body underneath that ridiculously thin night shift was pure torture. He'd *had* to hold her in place, hadn't he? Did she realize her breast bounced on his forearm when Dauphin broke into a jog? He must not let her close. He more than anyone knew what would happen if she found out his real secrets.

She'd hate him on sight and scream his secrets to the world. She was an innocent, for God's sake.

He really had to make a visit to the Rue Lesparre tonight. He'd spend himself in some woman he didn't care about and that would make him proof against the girl. In his very house! There would be no respite from her. He'd journey down to Avignon for a week or two if he didn't need to be filling up his warehouse with "cargo" again. The next best thing was to spend some time in brothels. And he'd better do it quickly. He'd take a cup of blood into the bargain just to make sure it wasn't hunger that itched in his veins. If only it were that simple.

As for the rest of the disaster, he'd repair what he could. He had already tried to confirm the gawkers' opinion that he was just out on a sexual lark with her by saluting them and smirking. He could also give himself an alibi for his absence from the gaming rooms. Perhaps no one would even notice Madame LaFleur's escape. The guards were notoriously bad at counting prisoners in the crowded cells. Still...

He stepped through the rows of cloaks and shelves of hats carefully. The pretty, buxom cloakroom attendant hummed to herself as she brushed a tricorn hat. Lacaune's was the most popular gaming hell in Paris because of two simple house strategies. The play was honest and the staff was composed of comely females.

He called his power. *Companion,* he thought. Power surged up his veins. A magenta stain dripped over his field of vision. He didn't need much power to accomplish this task. He reached out and touched the attendant on the shoulder. The girl squeaked in surprise and turned…

And he caught her in his gaze. Her eyes went blank. He slid an arm around her to support her and kissed her thoroughly so that her lips would be slightly swollen if anyone cared to look. He liked kissing, but he took no pleasure in such a one-sided application of the process. When he finished, he mussed the curls escaping from her exaggerated coiffure and pulled several strands free from the tiny mock-tricorn she wore (in red and blue, of course) to mollify the new gentry. They liked to lose their money to one another and to the house here, just as the old nobility had.

"I have been here for the past hour," he whispered. "We dallied together. You had the most pleasure you have ever experienced." He might as well let *her* add to his reputation, unearned though it might be. If anyone ever asked her, which he hoped they would not. He crumpled the satin of her dress, and tore a corner of the lace at her bodice—lace Lacaune's had probably bought from him. Just enough that it would be noticeable if someone were looking for it. Then he let her go.

The reddish tint faded from the room.

"La," she said, blinking. "You take a girl's breath away, milord."

He raised her hand to his lips. "Until we meet again."

She gave a slow seductive smile. "Anytime you like, milord."

He gave a smile he hoped was not a grimace. Another female mooning over him. One he would never let close to who he really was. Then he slipped out to the gentlemen's retiring room to adjust his appearance before entering the main gaming salon. People expected to see him without a hair out of place.

He strolled into the large, comfortably appointed room. Chandeliers dripped glittering light on red and gilt. The women, clad in low-cut gowns and those silly little tricorns, moved among the tables with food and drink and new cards. Men crowded round the baize-covered tables in the center, playing faro and baccarat. Every card table was filled. Only the place he had vacated an hour and a half ago was still empty.

"Avignon, old beast" General Digne called. "Where have you been?"

"Er…busy, General."

"How will we win our money back if you keep disappearing?" The general had grown more interested in gaming than in leading armies since soldiers now felt they could vote on the general's strategy before each battle. Equality made for poor military outcomes, and the French armies were beleaguered on all sides. Which made the general want to spend his time in Paris and leave the actual fighting to his lieutenants. One in particular, a Corsican nobody named Bonaparte, seemed able to inspire the recruits as the general could not.

The others around the table were equally keen to take their revenge on Avignon. Rustau was a minor dignitary in the new government. St. Martine was a remnant of the old nobility so ancient he could not bring himself to emigrate. Romaine? Now what did Romaine do? Ahhh, yes, he ran some of the less savory coffeehouses that fleeced the *sans-culottes* of their coins in games of chance while giving the new poets of the Revolution a stage to read tracts and dogmatic poetry. Normally Avignon struggled to lose to his fellow gamblers. People thought much more kindly of people who lost money to them. But it was hard work. Vampires were notoriously lucky at any game of chance. It had something to do with the positive energy of the Companion. And then of course, he had some skill. He'd had hundreds of years to develop it.

But tonight he was in no mood to lose. He sat at the table in front of the pile of chips he'd left. "Well, gentlemen, let's see what you can do."

*****

She was in a dark place that had no walls, no ceiling. Even the floor was obscured by rising mist. Every direction was like every other, so there was no place to run.

And she must run somewhere. There was something

Time for Eternity

very frightening in this space with her, something that would do more than rend her limb from limb. It would damn her for eternity. She started to run, not knowing whether she was running away or toward her deepest fear. She ran until her heart was pounding in her chest and her breath wouldn't come. She wouldn't be able to run forever, but the monster would pursue her unto death and beyond. Even now she knew it was behind her. She fell, and struggled up ...

And there! A gladiator's short-sword gleamed in the light like pure salvation.

Or damnation.

She stood, slowly, unable to turn away from the gleaming sword. And then she heard boot heels clicking across a surface she couldn't see. Terror gripped her. Grab the sword, *she thought.* It's your only protection.

But she didn't. She couldn't. Because she wasn't sure the sword would save her. Using it might change her beyond recognition. She turned to face her nemesis.

Avignon walked out of the darkness, looking as Satanic as ever. His hand was bleeding.

Françoise woke, gasping. She couldn't even scream. Slowly the room resolved around her. The darkness wasn't featureless. The wardrobe loomed. The chair sat next to the dressing table. She cowered in her bed in the room she had been given in number sixteen Place Royale.

Slowly she became aware that she was drenched in sweat.

Then another feeling began to creep over her.

The sword. She could feel that sword in the bag under her bed like a squat and evil presence in the room. Something inside her wanted her to use it for the worst of purposes.

She scrambled out of bed, breathing hard. She couldn't sleep with that thing beneath her. She stood there, chest heaving. She couldn't imagine crawling under the bed to retrieve that leather bag in the dark. She'd sleep in another bedroom.

Susan Squires

But what would the servants think? She didn't want to advertise her... Well, the kind word would be "whims," but some might call them something else. Incipient madness, maybe.

Was she going mad? That feeling of fullness and impending disaster, the certainty that everything she did she'd done before... was that why she imagined she already knew what the naked duc would look like even before she saw him?

There were no answers to her questions. No way out.

She crawled up into the wing chair that crouched before the cold grate and curled up to make herself as small as she could. There were forces at work here she didn't understand. And they might just tear her apart.

Eight

"Too lucky by half tonight, Avignon." St. Martine tossed back a brandy, too many for the evening. "No one has luck like that."

Henri ignored the implication. "Why, I thought it was skill." One of the girl attendants scraped his winnings into a pile with a small rake.

"A kind of skill," St. Martine muttered.

"You're drunk, man." General Digne was, surprisingly, always the peacemaker. "Don't say things you'll regret. Avignon loses often enough. And he doesn't need the money."

"If you object to being fleeced, stop buying his goods," Rustau remarked. "Playing cards with him is the least of our problems."

"Ahhh, but we all like what he provides too much for that," Romaine remarked. "Tonight is just is the way of the tables. Some are up, some are down. We will soon be up again." He was the philosopher of the group.

St. Martine was about to respond in an unfortunate fashion when the double doors to the grand salon burst open with a bang. Soldiers marched in and spread out.

A hush fell over the room. Henri glanced to the door to see Robespierre, the tidy martinet of a man, marching in behind his henchmen. Henri continued putting the coins into equal stacks that could be wrapped into roulades.

"The declaration that gaming is an antirevolutionary activity was clearly posted." Robespierre glared at those members of his own government salted around the room. Some colored, some stuck their chins out in defiance. Someday, Robespierre would not be able to keep his own in line. You couldn't suppress everything without having something give way.

"Where is the owner of this establishment?"

"Here, sir." Lacaune stepped forward.

"Arrest this man," Robespierre ordered. Soldiers moved in to do his bidding. *Damnation.* Lacaune was an honorable man, and there were too few of those, no matter their trade.

Henri felt a spring inside him coiling. *Uncoil it,* he told himself. *You can do nothing here.*

"I am certain you citizens want to contribute your winnings to the revolutionary cause." Robespierre had such a prim voice. Was he really so tightly controlled? Or was he afraid that the violence and sexual urges within would unleash themselves and destroy him in the eyes of the world? Perhaps both. Henri wondered what Robespierre's sex with his mistress was like.

Murmurs of protest broke out around the room. Henri retrieved some roulade papers left on the table and started wrapping his gold. When each man had "contributed" he was allowed to go, though Robespierre dispensed lectures liberally during the proceedings.

Henri lounged in his chair, his winnings now stacked in neat roulades before him. At last Henri was the only guest remaining besides the soldiers. The little man came and stood in front of him. The employees gathered in a nervous clump near the baccarat table.

"Foucault, I might have expected you to be here."

"But you did not? How odd."

"Report has it that you were absent for some time in the middle of the evening."

"I come. I go. Even I can't keep track of me." He was going to brazen it out of course, but the man had a purpose for asking. Not good.

"Well, there were some other surprising events tonight."

"I am agog to know," Henri murmured in his most bored voice.

That goaded Robespierre. "Well, you should be. Because there aren't enough prisoners in the Conciergerie tonight."

Time for Eternity

"Are there ever enough prisoners for your taste?" Henri inquired politely.

"I mean that one escaped."

"However would you know in all that crush?"

"Because we heard a scream." Robespierre smiled like the proverbial cat. "And screams always portend an escape."

"I take it you have made a study." Henri let his tone imply that he could care less about screams. But if they had jumped to that, it would make his job harder. He often had to return to the same cell twice or three times to get an entire family.

"And this particular escape was most interesting. It wasn't like the others."

"The others? Dear me. I didn't know you were so careless with prisoners."

Robespierre frowned. "The others were families. This was an old woman. Your neighbor in fact."

"Madame LaFleur?" Henri put up his quizzing glass to examine the little man. He had the satisfaction of seeing him squirm a bit. "You let her escape your clutches?" He shook his head in dismay. "Hardened criminal that one. I hardly feel safe knowing she's at large."

Robespierre's lips tightened. "I'd like to know where you were during the time you left the premises tonight, Foucault."

"Left? But I never left." The quizzing glass came down.

"Then where were you for the period between... He referred to a small notebook. "Ah, approximately one and two-thirty A.M.?"

Henri glanced to the huddled employees and smiled. One girl smiled back. "Ask her."

Robespierre stared at him. "You... Right on the premises?"

"In the cloakroom." Henri began loading roulades into his pockets.

"Those winnings belong to the state."

Henri glanced up. "Oh, surely not. What would

Madame Croûte do for lace?" He disposed of the last roulade. "By the way, why ever did you tax salt and brandy? No one can afford them now. And you know how French like good brandy and good food. And of course there's the clean water you and Madame Croûte both love so much."

Robespierre flushed. "I could confiscate your wells."

"Probably with the same result as the other enterprises you've confiscated. Factories are not exactly humming. Whatever would your revolutionary friends do if the water ceased to flow? As for procuring the niceties of life—you just don't have my contacts."

"I'll talk to the girl. Don't think I won't."

"Ahhh. I would never doubt that." Henri lounged back in his chair as Robespierre stalked over to the girl, who answered his questions tearfully but with what she believed was the truth. When Robespierre turned away in disgust, all the other girl attendants crowded round her asking very particular questions about Henri's anatomy and technique. Robespierre must have heard them, for his face grew grim.

Henri raised his brows as Robespierre approached. "I take it I'm free to go."

"Yes." The word was torn from the man's gut.

Henri rose. "It would be an honor to have you and Madame Croute attend my small soirée on Wednesday. You'll be quite the toast of the party. Celebrities of the Revolution and all."

"I would *never* attend one of your dissolute gatherings."

"Never say never, Citizen." Henri lounged toward the doors, pockets bulging.

He was in no immediate danger, but Robespierre and his cronies would be watching him a little too closely from now on. Damn. And he had a shipment to deliver next week.

*****

Henri shut the door to the house in Rue Lespasse in the Faubourg St. Germain with a slam. What was he thinking? That would only draw attention. That was the last thing he wanted.

Time for Eternity

He'd thought to make his sexual urges stand down by spending himself at Madame Fontaine's exclusive establishment. Yet when it came to the point, so to speak, he couldn't manage. The girl had been willing enough and beautiful. He provided her pleasure and care, as always. She would have only wonderful memories of tonight. But his nerve failed him (among other things) when it came to his own satisfaction.

He strode down the street, glowering. It was nearly dawn. His cane tapped on the cobblestone with an irritated sound. As well it might.

Maybe it was because the prostitute fawned over him. They had no choice, did they? Maybe it was because she only went through the motions of pleasing a man. It all seemed pathetic somehow. He only accentuated his loneliness, not alleviated it by stopping in a brothel. What had he expected? He'd been alone since his mother left him. He'd never known his father. And craving love for one such as he was always a disaster.

In any case, tonight he couldn't do it. Mother Mary and Joseph, what was he coming to?

*****

Insistent tapping. Françoise lifted her head and groaned. She uncoiled herself from the wing chair, stiff in every part of her body. A bright channel of light cut across the carpet. It must be late in the day. She'd fallen asleep after many hours in fear of... something.

"Come in."

Annette bustled into the room. "Mademoiselle," she said breathlessly, "Make haste. La Fanchon will be here at any moment."

Françoise rose and tried to stretch the kinks out of her body. The last thing she wanted was to see a dressmaker. She caught sight of herself in the mirror over the dressing table. *Alors,* but there were circles under her eyes from not sleeping.

Or maybe from crying over Madame.

The events of yesterday poured over her. She bit her lip. She had to get out of this house. Now that she couldn't help Madame, she must leave this place. Except there was something she had to do before she could go. She couldn't think what. But it made her shiver.

In any case, before she could go, she must find another situation. "I… I need to go out today, Annette."

"Ayyyyy!" Annette practically wailed. "The duc, I cannot vouch for his temper if La Fanchon is kept waiting for even an instant."

But she wasn't kept waiting, because the door burst open and the lady herself swept into the room. "Me, I do not wait downstairs, for the *jeune fille* may escape by the servants' entrance for all I know."

The woman before her was petite but bursting with energy. Her impossibly high coiffure, studded with real flowers and various feathers, only contributed to the impression that she was exploding with personality. She had been a beauty once and she was still a handsome woman. And her dress…Françoise had to admire how the military epaulets enhanced the shoulders, and the decreasing bands of gold between the frogs made a vee down her bodice that only emphasized her tiny waist. She wore the colors of the Revolution in a way no revolutionary would ever consider, and that was in itself a triumph.

"I am so sorry I missed you yesterday," Françoise apologized. "Please don't blame his grace. It was my fault entirely."

"Of that I was sure, mademoiselle. The duc he would not dare to keep me waiting." She spoiled the effect of this announcement by winking. "I know too many of his secrets."

Françoise did not like to think what secrets this woman might know about Avignon.

"And what was so important that you offended me?"

Françoise swallowed. "I…I visited a friend who was arrested."

"In prison?" La Fanchon gasped.

124

Time for Eternity

Well, if she thought it not fashionable to visit one's friends, no matter how unfortunate they were, then she could just *be* offended. "Yes. The Conciergerie, though I had to visit several prisons to find her." All her outrage left her. Madame was dead. She felt her eyes fill.

"You combed the prisons for your friend?" Madame sighed. "Well, at least I am not thrown over for less than friendship in the most trying of circumstances." She peered at Françoise. "I am sorry for your friend's fate."

Fate. That word again. Françoise shook her head slowly. "But is it? Is it fate, Mademoiselle Fanchon, which takes one and leaves another? And who decides? Robespierre could have chosen a hundred others to arrest."

"I don't know, child."

"Maybe no one decides," Françoise whispered. "Perhaps it is… random." She looked up. The little lady had gone still. "We would not like to believe that, would we?"

The room froze for a moment. "No, we would not." La Fanchon's eyes were sympathetic. Then the dressmaker clapped her hands. "But who can know? In which case, all we can do is dress well. Now, a dressing gown for Mademoiselle? We have much to do." She did not wait for Annette but threw open the wardrobe and began tossing peignoirs and elegant dresses out onto the floor. *"Non. Non.* Definitely not." She came to the charred dress. *"Quel horreur!* Woman, throw this on the rag heap." The offending dress landed in Annette's arms.

"With pleasure," the maid said.

"But…that is my only dress. Everything else I own was burned."

"So his grace intimated. Fanchon will provide." She tossed Annette a silk dressing gown.

And she whooshed out of the room, saying over her shoulder, "The yellow salon. The light is good there."

"Dear me," Françoise murmured, looking after her. "A force of nature."

Annette had the dressing gown on in no time. The maid practically shoved her out the door and hissed, "Third door on the right."

Françoise tiptoed down the hall, listening to the bustle coming from behind the half-open door to the yellow salon and feeling trapped. She should be looking for a position, not being fitted for dresses. Yet, one did need to dress well to hunt for a job. One dress? Well, two dresses. Two dresses only. Françoise pushed the door open.

The room was a hive of activity. Half a dozen assistants swarmed about, setting up a long table, opening the draperies to bathe the room in light, carrying bolts of heavy pattern cloth and stacks of fabric swatches. One set out a low platform, and another carried in a cloth dummy on a metal stand. At the center La Fanchon directed the whole like a symphony.

"Here, here." She motioned to the low platform. "Stand here."

She swept the robe off Françoise, leaving her to stand in her undergarments. No one seemed to notice her at all.

"Measurements," Fanchon called. Assistants rallied round with tapes, pulling Françoise this way and that, measuring every conceivable part of her.

Françoise was merely the object here. That freed her to look around. The room was lovely, with mirrors and big windows out to the park from the first floor of the great house. It was full of lightness and promise somehow. It seemed a long time since she had been in a room like this. Some part of her was nervous. Darkness seemed more comfortable.

But she needed a dress before she could find a situation. Was that what she must do before she could leave this house? Or was it something else? Something worse? She pushed down the image of the sword in the evil leather bag.

*****

The assistants were packing up at last, having measured every part of her, held up swatches, prepared a stuffed mannequin that matched her figure.

"I shall send over a dress until we can put together the"—here Fanchon smiled sweetly—"two day dresses you

Time for Eternity

require." Fanchon waved a hand. "My customer lost her head before she could claim it." She glanced to Françoise's look of horror. *"Je m'excuse,* mademoiselle. I do not guarantee a perfect fit, you understand, but you must have something on your back, and what is in the wardrobe in your room is hardly suitable."

Françoise gathered her courage. "I am not sure some of the fabrics you chose would be suitable for everyday dresses..." She faltered under Fanchon's raised brow.

"You question Fanchon?" The little lady raised her brows.

"I should never do that, child." The baritone drawl came from the shadows in the hall.

"Your grace, what a pleasant surprise." Fanchon motioned for the assistants to close the draperies. All Françoise could think about was that he was seeing her in her chemise. She didn't reach for the dressing gown. The room dimmed. She could feel his eyes on her. Part of her was horrified at her boldness, and part of her was...was challenging him. And she didn't know which part was which.

He sauntered into the room, his dress the height of fashion except that he didn't powder his hair or wear any patches. His eyes were glued to hers. They seemed to burn. Then they jerked away. "One may count on La Fanchon without reservation for her taste." His tone was insouciant, in contrast to his recent expression.

Fanchon looked from one to the other then bent to retrieve Françoise's dressing gown. "That is one thing we have in common, Avignon. I've always thought Satan probably had much better style than all those angels in that dreary white."

Françoise took the dressing gown and, as she slid into it, a blush crept up her throat. A little late, that blush.

"Alors, what are you waiting for?" Fanchon swept the assistants, who were standing as if transfixed by Avignon, out of the room. "We have much to do."

"I should like to consult with you on your way out," Avignon murmured. He slid a glance at Françoise, who stepped off the platform so the last assistant could carry it away. Then he took Fanchon's arm and they walked out of the room. Françoise didn't like the stir of anger that took her as she watched Fanchon lay her other hand over the duc's arm and look up into his eyes.

Belatedly, it occurred to her that he had come into the room only after Mademoiselle Fanchon had ordered the draperies closed. That was odd and... interesting.

Nine

Henri shook himself. It was almost as if the girl had put a spell on him. Her eyes, as she stared at him, had held both ancient wisdom and…and innocence. Her limbs had been just as white, as finely formed as he'd imagined. And curse it all, he *had* been imagining. He should make her leave this house. He was in danger of courting disaster once again if she did not.

But he had come away as much to speak to La Fanchon as to escape the girl.

"Mademoiselle…"

She raised her brows in question. "Your grace?"

"At her first presentation tomorrow night, I want the world to be very certain that she is my ward—and nothing else. Do we understand each other?"

Fanchon cast down her eyes, but not before he saw the speculation in them. "But of course, your grace."

He gestured ahead and they continued walking to the staircase. "She is an innocent, and I want her to dress that way."

They reached the head of the staircase. Fanchon looked up at him. The speculation was back. "How old is she, your grace?"

Startled, Henri said, "Twenty-one, I think. Why do you ask?"

"No reason." She stared past his shoulder down the corridor. "Only, sometimes I catch a look about her…a feeling that she is much older and more experienced. More…world-weary. No girl of twenty-one looks like that."

He wasn't imagining it. The dressmaker saw it too. "One strives to capture the spirit of the woman in the dress one makes for her." She tapped one finger against her lips as she thought "Can one ignore that strange duality of innocence and experience?"

"Mademoiselle Fanchon," he said firmly. "*À la jeune fille.*"

Fanchon seemed to come to herself. "I know. I know. It will be as you desire. And yet, would it not be a test of skill to express that complexity of character in a wardrobe?" She sighed and glanced up to Henri. "Be careful, your grace."

Henri waved a languid hand. What did she mean? "I? I am never careful, Fanchon."

She looked him over. "But I think you are. Very careful. You cultivate the bored façade. You never let any of your women near to the center of you. And you *do* have a center, your grace, however hard you try to conceal it. But this one…"

He led the way down the stairs into the foyer. "This one is a charity case, nothing more. She is gently born and fallen upon hard times. I took her in with the purest of intentions."

Fanchon laughed. "If you want people to believe that, I suggest you stop looking at her as if she were a life preserver and you were a drowning man."

She did not give him a chance to retort but strode to the cluster of assistants at the door. Fanchon did not enter or leave by the servants' entrance. At the last moment she turned. "By the way, she has given me very strict instructions to make for her only two everyday dresses. They are what she requires to make her way in the world and she does not desire to be beholden to you for more."

"I hope you know from whom you take your orders."

"Of course." Fanchon laughed. "And I leave it to you to explain to her. Good day, your grace." Jean opened the door and the gaggle streamed into the darkening street.

He did *not* look at the girl that way. The woman was mad. Was she? Or was she too perceptive by half? She had seen the way the girl flashed between experience and innocence. Henri knew what experience could do to one only too well. What he could not remember was any feeling that the world held promise, the eagerness for experience that was the essence of innocence, and if one obtained that experience, its demise. And he knew for certain that he was death to all

Time for Eternity

innocence. So all he had was his work, and that was like lighting a candle against the darkness in the pits of hell.

Best he get to it then.

He glanced up the stairs. How did she get that world-weary look of experience? He thought of her life as she described it. Growing up with an aunt who treated her well even if her father did not acknowledge her. That aunt dying and the girl cast upon her own resources. The life of a paid companion. Belonging neither among the other servants nor among those she served, no doubt dodging advances on all sides. Bleak prospects now that her friend had died.

But those experiences were only a glimpse of the horrors of the world he had seen over the centuries. And they did not begin to touch the things one did, the things one became... Not enough to turn one so young into a cynic like he was, nor to grind down one's spirit, as the world had been grinding on his spirit for nearly five hundred years.

And yet enough so that the mere fact that she had any duality at all was remarkable. Perhaps it was her innocence that was the miracle. Oh, that he could learn to retrieve some eagerness for the world. Even his work could not give him that.

He found himself climbing the stairs again, almost against his will.

He should stay away from her. *Mon Dieu,* but she raised a need again in him at the mere thought of her. Why was she so different from the pathetic creature in the brothel? They were both human. By nature that made them both pathetic, doomed to die in only a few years, subject to the ravages of illness and time. He couldn't bring himself to feel any desire in the brothel. Yet even now, his loins were heavy, thinking of the girl. His testicles tightened as he strode down the hall to the yellow salon. He hesitated, then threw open the door.

The room was empty, dim.

She'd taken the opportunity to escape. Was he so fearsome?

Of course he was. He could drive a girl to suicide. He took a breath; let it out. Well, then. He'd use that image to his advantage. It would keep her away from him. He strode out of the yellow salon and down the hall. He'd go back to his room.

And do what? Think about her? Try to ignore the erection thinking about her brought? Even now he swelled. Why did she draw him so?

He found himself unable to pass her room. He hovered, indecisive, in front of her door.

Damn.

He did not knock, but opened the girl's door unannounced.

It was a good thing the sun was low in the sky. The draperies were open to the light. But the trees in the park across the street cast long shadows into the room. It was just bearable. Still, he squinted. The girl stood in front of the wardrobe. She whirled to face him, her eyes big.

"What are you doing?" It was the only thing he could think to say.

She looked puzzled. "Trying to find something to wear, your grace. Annette took away my only dress. And these others are... hardly suitable for afternoon."

She wore the silk dressing gown. He could see the swell of her breast where the fabric gaped. This was not helping. He pushed past her and rifled the closet.

"Wear this." He handed her a dress at random. It was some pale orange color. Fanchon would call it peach, or spring sunset or some such silly name. It was one shade away from rose. She would look well in rose. "Join me in the library in a quarter hour. For drinks." He sounded inane. What excuse could he give for his command? But then he didn't need an excuse. He was the wicked duc. She had told him so. He grimaced to think he had been afraid she would fall in love with him.

For once he wished he were as immune to emotion as he pretended. Then he'd just seduce her as coldly as he seduced the others, have his way with her and get her out of his system. But she was under his protection. She was an innocent. Maybe. And he never seduced innocents anymore.

So he simply turned on his heel and left.

132

Time for Eternity

*****

My. Whatever was the matter with him? He had looked so fierce. And he had squinted against the light in her room. There must be something wrong with him. Had he been sick? Sometimes she felt that way about light after she'd had a bad cold. She'd heard that gentlemen were sensitive to light if they had drunk too much the night before. That must be it. Avignon no doubt drank too much every night. But he had invited her to join him in the library. She still tingled from his nearness when he'd reached past her to grab a dress from the wardrobe. This throbbing she experienced whenever she was near him was strange and yet not strange.

She wanted him. She wanted him sexually.

Oh, dear. That brought images flashing through her brain of him standing in the bath, nude and rising. She could practically feel how silken his skin would be against the palms of her hands if she ran them over his back. And down to his hips. And over the swell of his buttocks, cupping them. And if she were close enough to do that, then he would be holding her against his bare chest. Would she be naked too? Her nipples would be tickled to a luscious awareness by the hair on his chest.

How did she *know* that? Her nipples tightened at the thought. She felt them brush against the silk of her dressing gown.

She would *not* think about what else she would be able to feel against her belly if he were that close. She'd want to grasp it. Oh, *mon Dieu.*

"Annette!"

Annette came hurrying through the door. *"Alors,* but I was on my way, mademoiselle. One doesn't have to yell like a fishwife." The girl looked around. "I passed the devil in the hall, looking like he had just been thrown out of heaven." Annette appeared to be a devout Catholic. Françoise had no doubt the serving girl never thought about Avignon, nude and erect, or wanted to feel his erection...

"Stop that," she muttered.

"But what, mademoiselle?" Annette wore an aggrieved expression.

"I'm only talking to myself," Françoise apologized. "Pay no heed."

Annette bustled over and took the peach dress from Françoise's hands. "No need to crumple it like that." She shook it out. "Looks like it's never been worn." Franchise shook herself back to reality. "He wants me in the library in a quarter hour."

"Not possible."

"You are too nice in your idea of how I should look, dear girl. It's only Avignon."

In the end, it took her seventeen minutes before Jean was showing her into the library. Her hair was brushed into soft curls. Her lashes were darkened ever so slightly, though she refused powder or rouge or patches. She did not want to think why she had allowed Annette to do even so much. The dress was another matter. It was entirely more scandalous than even the cerulean blue she'd worn the first night. It was cut so low that her aureoles were in danger of showing. The fichu that went with the ensemble was entirely transparent. Tucked into the space between her breasts and covering her shoulders, it really concealed nothing. The bodice was laced so tightly she could barely breathe. That pushed her breasts up, of course. The underskirt, revealed by a wide vee, was one shade darker than the silk of the overskirt above it. The vee itself was edged in gold embroidery as were the sleeves that ended in a wide flounce at her wrist. That she wore no jewelry only contributed to the feeling that she was nearly naked.

You're going to bowl him over. Just control your own feelings and you can make him suffer for the little time he has left.

Where had that come from? It was almost like a voice inside her head talking to her.

Still, she did appreciate his expression when he turned to greet her. He looked stunned.

Time for Eternity

"Do you like your choice of dress?" she asked.

He cleared his throat. "Perhaps not entirely suitable."

"Well, none of them are, really, since you had them made for your mistresses. And I'm not your mistress."

He swallowed. "Well. Fanchon said she would send over something more suitable."

"Perhaps I should have waited." She was enjoying this. She had herself well in hand now.

He motioned her to a wing chair. This was her favorite of the rooms at number sixteen. Cozy and masculine. It smelled of old leather and furniture polish, and the duc's subtle scent of cinnamon with that sweet undertone. She sat and he handed her a glass.

"Ratafia again?" She shrugged. "I prefer a good brandy." She suppressed her surprise. Ladies did not drink brandy. Had she even ever had brandy?

He drew back the proffered drink, studying her. "Where did you learn to drink brandy?"

"Oh, I don't know." And she didn't.

He went to the desk where a tray held two decanters and poured her out a brandy to match his own. She took it with what she hoped looked like a practiced hand and sipped.

It was all she could do not to choke. The stuff burned like fire. She could feel it sliding all the way down to her stomach. She pressed her lips together firmly. His eyes were laughing at her. He didn't think she had ever had brandy in her life. Which she hadn't. "This is good," she said. Then added, "Aged twenty years, I'd say, in new French oak." Where had that come from? "Is it made by the Rèmy Martin family?"

His eyes widened ever so slightly. She counted it a victory. "You are a puzzle box of extraordinary complexity, Mademoiselle Suchet."

Perhaps even to herself these days. She changed the subject. "Do you dine in before you set out for your clubs tonight?"

He lounged over to the mantel of the fireplace, and put one foot on the cold andiron, one elbow on the marble mantelpiece. "I think I shall eschew gambling tonight. Last night Robespierre appeared at one of the clubs I frequent and arrested the owner. He seemed very interested in the disappearance of Madame LaFleur from his prison."

"Oh, no." This was her fault. "I have gotten you in trouble."

He looked at her strangely. "I hardly think you care about that."

She didn't. And yet she did. She felt herself blushing. It was to keep her from badgering him that he had saved Madame. And it had come to nothing in the end. She felt a weight descend upon her shoulders.

"Well, Robespierre can sniff about all he wants," Avignon went on. "He daren't touch me. I'm too important to his friends."

"Because of the…" She lowered her voice. "Smuggling."

"Just so." He tossed back his glass of brandy. "Still, I think I shall keep a lower profile in the next week."

She took another sip of her brandy. This time it didn't burn so badly. One might say it was…a warming feeling. She heaved a breath. Avignon's eyes never left her face, but she knew he was acutely aware of her bosom. "Do you believe in fate?" she asked.

Again he looked taken aback. She would not have been able to identify that expression two days ago, but right now she felt as if she had known him a long time. "Individual fate or collective fate?"

She raised her brows. "Is there a difference?"

"Yes." He sipped his drink. "Man is brutish, greedy, cruel, and unable to moderate his impulses for the greater good. Societies always crumble. We are witnessing that in France." He glanced over to her. "So I believe there is a collective fate."

That sounded so grim. But when she searched for some example to confound him, she faltered. Greece? Conquered and disintegrated from a grand achievement to a simple agricultural society under the thumb of the Ottoman Empire. Rome? Fallen into debauchery and sacked by the Goths. The Holy Roman

Empire? Not a shining example. European states? Centuries of petty bickering for supremacy.

"Wise girl." She actually saw one corner of his mouth curve up.

"What about individual fate?"

His expression softened. He thought he knew why she asked that. "Ahhh. That is harder. I want to believe you can change an individual's fate. Is it enough that I want to believe it?"

"Maybe Madame was destined to die—if she didn't die at the guillotine her heart had to give out. Or what if she wouldn't have been guillotined at all, and I caused her death by badgering you to rescue her?" But some part of her said that Madame had been doomed.

He didn't answer either question. "The real question is—how will we act when we don't know that answer? Because we won't know it. We can't."

She sipped her brandy. He was the one who was wise. There was only one answer to his question. "We'll keep trying to change bad things. What else can we do?"

He didn't make fun of her. There was no smile, even in his eyes. In fact, they were looking inward. "Exactly," he said softly. "What else can we do?"

In some strange way, that made her feel better, whether about Madame's death or her own future, she wasn't sure. And the duc was not what she had thought him. She had been in love with the picture of him as a bad but infinitely attractive man. And he was. But he was more. She was feeling quite relaxed now, warm, almost... comforted. If she had known brandy could make you feel that way, she would have started drinking it sooner.

She rose and put her hand on his shoulder. The feel of the thick muscle under his coat was shocking. His energy seemed to rush all around her, making her feel alive, aware of each part of her body in a way that was suddenly uncomfortable. She shouldn't have done that. "Thank you," she murmured. But she didn't take her hand away. She was playing with fire. Somewhere inside she knew it was dangerous to her in ways she could not comprehend. Maybe it was the brandy. Or maybe she was tired of being frightened. She was feeling rebellious about what she should or shouldn't do. Her hand moved over his shoulder.

*****

"Don't thank me." Henri frowned. He wished she wouldn't touch him like that. It sent blood rushing to his damned cock, and his balls were almost painful. And then he saw it in her eyes, the wanting. He'd been wrong about her. She wasn't going to be one of those silly girls who fell in love with him. But she wanted him sexually. There had been many of those women as well... the ones who didn't love him, but just wanted their pleasure of him. Was she so hardened as to be one of those? He didn't think so. She still seemed frightened of what she was creating here. Or maybe he just didn't want to think she was so callous. There was only one way to find out. He shouldn't. He didn't want to.

But he did anyway.

He lowered his head to hers. Her eyes got big. She knew what was going to happen. She wasn't an innocent, after all. Was she? He didn't know. She had needed comforting just now, and he had given her what truth he could. And now her eyes said she wanted a different truth from him, even though it frightened her. Her lips parted. He had never seen lips just like those. Full, soft- looking...

God help him, he was going to kiss her.

*****

Françoise felt what was almost pain between her legs. She was swollen and wet and it felt as if her pelvis were being slowly pulled open. That should have been unpleasant but it wasn't. It made her realize she was a void at the center that wanted nothing so much as to be filled.

He lowered his head. She parted her lips. He slid one

138

arm behind her back and pulled her to him. His body was hard beneath the satin and she could feel the rigid swell between his legs. His lips were soft as they brushed over hers. His tongue— welcome intruder—skimmed over the inside of her lips. She captured it and sucked, gently, then touched his with her own. How intimate! She'd never felt anything like it. And yet she had. Maybe it was the inborn knowledge of a woman, but she knew exactly what pleasures lay ahead, and what to do to bring them on, even though some part of her warned her against it. She nibbled his lip and was rewarded with a growl of growing desire. She wanted this and what would follow, no matter the consequence.

A knock sounded discreetly at the library door.

Françoise started and Avignon pulled away. "What is it?" he barked.

The door cracked open and Jean slid in apologetically. "A…female to see you, your grace." He presented a card on a silver salver.

Françoise smoothed her dress and wondered whether Jean could tell that she had been kissing Avignon. She still felt almost faint. Who knew that a kiss could be such a powerful force that it seemed to shake you, inside and out?

Avignon strode over and snatched up the card. He glanced to Françoise. "I'll see her in the green salon."

"Very good, your grace." Jean bowed and was gone.

Françoise pursed her lips. After a kiss, he could just go directly to entertaining one of his paramours? She felt small and insignificant. The kiss hadn't meant anything to him. It had meant too much to her. She had thought she had hold of herself. She didn't.

"Bring Mademoiselle Suchet a bowl of summer fruit, Jean." He glanced again to Françoise. "I shan't be long."

And he was gone. She was likely to be here for at least an hour, dancing attendance on him while he ... he made love to the next in line of his liaisons.

She was totally disgusted with herself. But she had nowhere else to go. She scanned the shelves for a book. At least she'd show him that she didn't care how long he took to return.

*****

Marta Croûte paced the salon of number sixteen, a nervous energy enveloping her. Foucault. She might have known it was him. The fellow dripped disdain. Sinfully good-looking. And he knew it. He'd use that to get innocent young girls with child. She knew his kind. Only too well. A shudder of revulsion rippled through her and her empty womb. They thought the rules did not apply to them. And in truth, for most of Marta's life, they hadn't applied to the aristocracy. They did as they pleased no matter who they hurt. Foucault was just that kind. But no more. Now they were getting back their own. And she would enjoy grinding that handsome face under her thumb.

Look at this place. Probably furnished from his estates before the committee could take them in the name of the citizens. It was a strange mixture of old and new. The painting over the mantel was dark with age, a bucolic scene with a river. If it had been her room, she would have replaced it instantly. But the clock on the mantel was the latest innovation. It had a gold mechanism clearly visible under its glass case. The draperies were new, but the furniture was heavy, from before Louis XIV. And here…she went to the mantel and fingered the porcelain figurine of two little boys and a dog. Probably cost an arm and a leg. Someone else's limbs, not Foucault's of course. The innocent faces of the little boys… She touched the cold porcelain. Not real. Not real children. Not the kind that would suckle at your breasts and laugh when they brought you frogs from the river. She wanted to smash it.

But that wasn't done.

So she'd have to smash Foucault instead.

*****

Henri opened the door to the green salon to find Madame Croûte turning over in her hands a figurine of two shepherd boys and their dog. The room was closed to the fading

Time for Eternity

sunlight, lit by chandeliers and candelabra.

She glanced up at his entrance. Her gray eyes were cold and acquisitive. "You probably paid more for this than my family made in a year."

Henri bowed. "My apologies, Madame Croûte." He was not going to justify himself to this harpy. He glanced to her clothing. Of course she wore red and blue, the Revolution's colors. But the red was too orange for her complexion. She would have been better off with cherry. And she had chosen the rougher, peasant style of fichu, which could only make a woman's figure look lumpy, no matter that it was the height of fashion. Still, he noticed that she had some familiar lace at her cuffs. It didn't go with the rest of her ensemble, as though it was an afterthought. "May I offer you refreshment?"

She shook her head without thanking him for the offer and put the figurine back in its place on the marble mantel. Her hand trembled slightly.

"How may I be of service to so illustrious a member of the new guard?"

She didn't answer, just walked around the room, feeling the heavy brocade of the draperies, trailing her hand over the carved wood of the chair backs. "I've never been inside a house on the Place Royale. I wonder that you live at such an unfashionable address."

Henri remained impassive.

"Perhaps we should change its name now the king and his whore of a wife are dead." She took up a clock whose golden mechanism was visible behind the glass case, clicking away. "The Revolution changes all, Citizen. We can remake even the landscape in our own image."

"You can change the name of a park." What was she getting at and why did she come to a bachelor's house, alone? He felt the sun set as his kind always did. But then, of course, rules of the old society wouldn't apply to Madame Croûte in her view.

"Oh, more than that. We changed the name of another square to the Place de Revolution."

Susan Squires

Henri smiled grimly. "I see what you mean. Madame Guillotine sits there. And she changes everything, doesn't she?"

"Exactly." She arranged herself on a settee. "It was really very altruistic of Monsieur Guillotine to invent a way to execute criminals that is so humane. Hanging was so unreliable and sometimes took so long. And of course one really cannot trust an executioner's axe. The blow may be insufficient, or go awry. But the guillotine is so…trustworthy."

Henri chuffed a bitter laugh. "He did mean it as a kindness, delusion as that was. But any new invention can be put to ill use."

She looked up at him. Her gray eyes were flat. "Do you despise us?"

Henri walked to the delicate table that held one of his snuffboxes and picked it up. "No more than I despise most of humankind. Does that insult you?"

Madame Croûte looked at him with speculation in her eyes. "You certainly meant it that way." Her eyes hardened again. "Do you know why I am here?"

He raised his brows. "A social call?"

Madame Croûte looked smug. She folded her hands. Her knuckles were large. She had done work in her life. "Let us say, a warning. I have many friends among the citizenry, and perhaps some little influence," she said.

"So I have been given to understand."

"My friends are able to ferret out those who do not hold the Revolution in their hearts."

Everyone knew she was the one who fed the names to Robespierre's committee. "And have your friends discerned that I am no friend of the Revolution? Not a revelation. You could have asked anyone. I am no friend to any but myself."

"That is the only reason you provide small luxuries for the new leaders of the citizenry."

"Yes." They wanted a piece of the pie as much as they wanted to change things. And a woman like this, with ambition, from a poor family, wanted all the influence and luxury that had been denied her in the old world. They were all the same. Just a new name for an old cancer.

142

Time for Eternity

"There will come a time when we don't need you, when the engine of France's economic might makes her the most powerful country on the Continent," she continued.

He doubted that France's economic engine would be cranking anytime soon. When things got too bad these petty tyrants would fall. It might take a tyrant to displace them though. "But until that time?"

"Your...services make you useful." She rearranged her skirts. "As long as you do not actively work against our cause." She looked up at him. "But do you? There is the matter of this...ward...of yours." She said the word with as much disdain as she could. "I have it on authority she was not so before you claimed her."

Better brazen it through. "What matter when I claimed her? She is my ward now."

"Whatever she is, she is not your ward." Madame Croûte's mouth drew down.

Henri smiled. "A ward is one under the protection of another. And she is that." He made his voice deliberately kind. These vile creatures wouldn't be allowed to threaten the girl.

"I know a whore when I see one."

Henri carefully unclenched the fist his left hand had made. "I'm sure you have seen many, Madame Croûte. They are all over Paris, serving your 'citizens.' But I would not refer to my ward in that fashion if I were you."

"What else would you call a woman who rides out on the same horse with a man after midnight, with her bottom pressed up against him on the saddle?"

She thought she had him. *Not yet,* he thought, *not yet.* "She had a fancy to see my warehouse down at the Quai de St. Paul."

"In the middle of the night? In her shift?" Madame was outraged.

"Unconventional, but not a crime." Henri shrugged. Would the other shoe drop?

"On the very night when her former employer escaped from the Conciergerie?" Madame's eyes lighted with grim triumph.

The shoe dropped with a chink. He feigned only a mild interest "An old woman like that—I wonder how?"

There was a long pause. Madame Croûte didn't want to admit she didn't know. "Never mind that. The important thing is that all the other escapees have been families. Only this one old woman is different. The woman who lived next door to you, whose servant you claimed as your ward. And you were seen just after the escape careering down to your warehouse."

Henri shrugged. "I've no idea. But you're welcome to inspect my warehouse. Bring as many men as you like. Take as long as you like."

"They're down there now." Madame smiled in satisfaction.

Henri thought he'd be one step ahead of her by volunteering. He'd have to watch this one. They couldn't find the quarters behind the brick in the back that housed the freed prisoners until the barge took them to the ship docked at Le Havre. At least he didn't think so. The quarters were empty just now at any rate. It was his job to fill them in the next days. He hoped to God Jennings hadn't been so foolish as to let his men resist, or they'd be arrested.

"Of course, your goods will not be confiscated."

They didn't want to kill the goose that laid the golden egg.

"Shall we go down and see what they've uncovered?"

Henri feigned boredom. "Jennings will clean up whatever mess you've made. I've better things to do."

Madame Croûte showed her shock. "What could be more important?"

Henri let go a slow smile. "You don't really want to know that, do you, madame?"

He had the satisfaction of seeing a flush creep up her throat into her face. Her eyes narrowed in hatred. Then it occurred to him that she thought he was going to swive his ward. He sobered. He didn't want her thinking that. Though why what she thought should mean anything he didn't quite know. "The cards call again tonight And I would be glad if you

Time for Eternity

could convince your so-dear friend not to spoil my game."

"Let's see what your ward has to say about her midnight ride."

This woman appointed herself chief inquisitor? What gall. What lack of manners. "Not possible tonight. She has the headache and is keeping to her room." Besides, he couldn't let this shrew see the girl in that dress she was wearing. "But you and your friend are coming on Wednesday, are you not?"

"I've no idea," the shrew said, obviously disgruntled but unsure how to demand what she wanted in the face of Henri's denial.

"Well, then, best get down and supervise the search, don't you think?" He ushered her firmly to the door. "Jean," he said to the waiting footman. "Do show Madame Croûte out."

She'd be back on Wednesday, he'd wager long odds. Just to prove she belonged there.

When the door closed he turned to call for Gaston and found him standing by the stairway. "Get down to the warehouse. Don't take a direct route. See Jennings and find out if anyone has been hurt or arrested." Gaston nodded and turned to go immediately.

"And Gaston?" The man turned back. "Be discreet."

"Of course, your grace."

They wouldn't find anything. Once they'd searched the warehouse, it would actually keep them from thinking they had to search again. And he'd keep the girl safe from the likes of Gargoyle Croûte. But the kettle of Paris was getting hotter.

Susan Squires

Ten

It was just as well that Avignon had left to see his mistress. It gave Françoise time to get her balance and let the effect of the brandy wear off. She flipped a page of the book she was reading, though she had no idea what it said. What had she been thinking to let him kiss her like that? That way lay madness and destruction. She mustn't fall in love with the wicked duc who smuggled luxuries to corrupt the leaders of the Revolution and had a new mistress every month. He was loyal to no one but himself. The image of the squat sword cutting into his neck throbbed through her brain. *No!* she thought *Don't think of that.* He had been so good to rescue Madame. And to comfort Françoise by saying the benediction over her friend. was that the action of a soulless man?

He's evil, at least as far as you're concerned.

The thought popped into her head as though it came from someone else, just like that vision of the sword across Avignon's neck. Lord, but that felt strange. The full feeling came over her again, as though her dress were too small or her shoes too tight. She rubbed her temples. There was something she must do. And there was not much time. And whatever happened, she mustn't be seduced by Avignon.

The door opened. "Apologies," the man himself murmured. He seemed distracted.

She hadn't been expecting him so soon. "What, did your mistress spurn your advances?"

He seemed to find that funny. "The day I take to keeping Madame Croûte is the day you can clap me up in a madhouse."

Françoise went wary. "She was here? Why?"

He sat beside her in the wing chair and took up a peach from the bowl of fruit she hadn't touched and one of the linen napkins Jean had brought. "Oh, something to do with a

Time for Eternity

midnight ride to the warehouse on the night your friend escaped from prison."

Françoise gasped and sat up straight. The Revolution had spies everywhere. How could the man sit there calmly eating a peach when he might be arrested at any moment? And it would be all her fault for goading him into trying to save Madame LaFleur when she was doomed to death anyway. "What did you tell her?"

"I invited her to search the warehouse." He shrugged. "She'd already done it." He saw her look of horror. "She already knows about the contraband. She was wearing my lace today." He took a bite of the peach. Did he know how distracting it was to see that bit of juice drip down his lips? It made her think of… Well, she wasn't going to think about those things.

Avignon frowned. "I only hope none of my men resisted. I don't want them hurt."

He wasn't putting himself out about it. "Shouldn't you go down there to see?"

"And give Croûte the idea I cared? I sent Gaston. Much less conspicuous."

What if they arrested Avignon? They didn't need any real evidence to send him to the guillotine. Who would she get to rescue him? And what would happen to her?

Avignon tossed the peach pit into the bowl Jean had provided, and rose. He took her chin between thumb and forefinger and raised it. She searched his face. The electric connection of touching shuddered through her. "They won't arrest the source of their luxuries."

"What if they come for you? What will you do?"

"I'll hie myself off to hide at Versailles." He was making fun of her.

Something niggled at her brain. Something important was at Versailles. "I've never been to Versailles." There was so much she hadn't done. "And now it's too late."

"Now is the perfect time," he said, still holding her chin and looking into her eyes. "You'd never credit how crowded it was with the court and the government there. Now we'd have the place to ourselves. Are you game?"

"Game for what?" She really couldn't think with him touching her like that.

"For Versailles."

"At night?"

"Tonight. Now."

Now? "I…" But he was already turning away. He rang the bell, and Jean appeared.

"Your grace?"

"Have Courson get the carriage out, and Pierre convert our dinner to a picnic."

"Right away, your grace." Jean didn't even look surprised. She no longer thought Avignon beat his servants or threw things at them, but they liked to please him. In some ways they might even like him. That thought startled her. It was as though she should have seen it before, though when she didn't know, since she had only been in the house three days.

Don't go to Versailles. The thought was almost a shout in her mind. It made her blink.

"We can't go to Versailles tonight,"she began.

"Why not? Twelve miles. Less than an hour after you get out of the city."

An hour each way alone in the carriage with the delectable duc? How would she survive it? "I have nothing to wear." What a stupid excuse.

"Wear what you have on."

"This? It isn't even respectable."

"You'll fit right in at Versailles," he said dryly. "You can borrow one of my cloaks."

"I couldn't take your cloak." Now she was grasping at straws.

"I'm not giving it to you," he noted. "I'd like to have it back."

"Well, of course. I didn't mean—"

Gaston burst through the door, gasping. Avignon strode across the room to him.

"Get your breath, boy." Avignon led him to a chair and

poured him out a brandy. When Gaston had taken a gulp, Avignon asked, "Were any hurt?" She was surprised to see real concern in his expression.

Gaston shook his head. "One hothead got his cork drawn, but Jennings kept them in check on the whole."

"They didn't arrest anyone, just for spite?"

Again, Gaston shook his head, his chest still heaving.

Avignon relaxed. "Good work. See that Jennings gets an extra something to distribute for their courage tonight and take a gold piece for yourself."

Ahhh, the old French aristocratic custom of the *douceur.* Madame Croûte would despise it, but Avignon knew how to keep his help loyal. He thanked them in a very practical way. It probably wasn't kindness, but it would pass for kindness. No wonder they liked him. She watched Avignon as Gaston caught his breath enough to tell the whole story. Avignon listened carefully. Then he patted the man on the shoulder.

"Get down and see if Pierre has something to restore your strength."

Gaston nodded. "Thank you, your grace." He disappeared.

Avignon excused himself and she could hear him issuing languid orders in the hall. All became quiet. Was she really going to go to Versailles with the wicked duc? Everything inside her screamed that she shouldn't.

And that was just the rub. A rebellious part of her *wanted* to go to Versailles with the duc, wicked or not. She wouldn't even mind if he kissed her again. In fact, she might as well admit it right here. She wanted him to kiss her again.

You'll get your heart broken. He'll ruin your life. Don't fall in love with him.

There it was again, that feeling that there was a voice inside her she didn't control. A bit of fear cycled inside her. She pushed it down. She had to get hold of herself. The voice was just the teachings of her aunt coming through as admonitions. And of *course* the Duc d' Avignon would break her heart if she let herself fall in love with him, if he used her and abandoned her, which he would if given the chance. Any fool could figure that out.

But... What if she went her whole life without finding anyone who made her want him the way she couldn't deny she wanted Avignon? Very likely, given her prospects. Wasn't it better to have experienced that thrill once than never to have known it at all? Yes, she might mourn when it was gone. But to refuse it would cause even more regret. And she had a strategy. The only way not to get your heart broken was to never offer it. She'd go, and enjoy, and not let her heart engage at all.

You don't know what regret can do to you.

She lifted her chin. Lady Toumoult had been trying to protect her. One couldn't fault her for that. She had been kind to a fault to take Françoise in and raise her when everyone knew she was Lady Toumoult's brother's by-blow. But Lady Toumoult had died a maiden, never having dared to know a worldly love. Could that be better than having had the courage to ignore the world's admonitions and experience a carnal knowledge of a man?

Frightening thoughts.

Exciting thoughts.

I can't stop you, can I?

Fear trickled down her spine. That voice was getting stronger, more separate from her. What did it mean? Was she going mad? She mastered her breathing. No. She wasn't going mad. These thoughts were born of anxiety about what she'd decided to do.

Still, Françoise was in a dither by the time Avignon returned with two cloaks, not knowing whether what she was about to do would free her or condemn her. Avignon had dressed for evening in black satin breeches with small silver buckles at the knees and shoes that sported large silver Artois buckles. His stockings were black as well and his tightly fitted, skirted coat was black brocade. Only his white waistcoat, embroidered with black clocks of all things, broke his silhouette, that and the white foaming lace at his throat and wrists. He swung one cape round her shoulders as she stood to greet him. It was black silk with a rosy lining just heavy enough to keep the night chill off in a moving carriage. On him it was probably three-quarter length, on her, it swirled about her heels, just off the ground.

"Do try not to shred it," he said as he tied the silken cord at her neck. His knuckles brushed the notch in her throat where her heart beat. "I remind you that I want it back."

She never knew when he was serious about being rude, or whether it was all some kind of game to him. He was really quite a mystery, and in spite of the fact that she had discovered how he made his living, she didn't think smuggling was the only secret he kept.

As in a dream, she followed him. She was going to Versailles, with all that might mean. He handed her down the steps of number sixteen and into a shining black carriage drawn by four snorting horses. He nodded to the coachman, a capable-looking man who held the reins of the demanding team as though they had been part of his hands since birth. Pierre bustled out from the doorway with a large basket that smelled wonderful. He shoved it up to the coachman. "Only I, Pierre Dufond, could have contrived on a moment's notice to provide such a repast a full hour before dinner was to be delivered."

"But you contrived?" Avignon asked, as though he were in doubt.

Pierre drew himself up. "How not? I am Pierre Dufond."

"Ah, yes. I remember now. That is why I hired you. I have only the best, you know." Avignon acted as though he were sharing a secret. He swung up into the carriage and closed the door with the crest on it. Only Avignon dared have a carriage that still sported a crest.

Pierre fairly beamed as they pulled away.

Françoise scooted over the red velvet squabs of the seat to look out the carriage window. She was very conscious of Avignon's body sprawled out on the opposite bench, his long legs crossed at the ankles. She could hardly see his face in the shadows of the coach. The driver was wending his way skillfully through the crowded city streets.

"What do you find so interesting?" The baritone was even more seductive in the dark.

"Paris. I didn't get about much," she said. "Madame needed me to attend to her."

"You were allowed days off, weren't you?"

"Not really. A companion is a companion all the time. Sometimes I went to pick up small items for Madame at Savoirs, or we went together to choose a book. But it wasn't safe to be out alone. That meant taking Robert away from his other work." Françoise felt her eyes fill and turned back to gaze out at the busy cacophony. "My ignorance of Paris made my search for Madame difficult."

"Well, there can't have been much of interest in the bookstalls for you," he said, effectively changing the subject "All tracts and philosophy these days. How boring."

She managed a smile. "Sometimes we longed for a good novel or even a batch of poetry that wasn't filled with homilies. Thank goodness for the English."

"Hmmm. So you read English?"

"Yes. And German and Italian, of course. Lady Toumoult thought languages essential to a woman of the world." She could practically feel his doubtful smile. "Well, I might not be so much of the world as you are, but I'm not *ignorant.*" She was going to do something about her ignorance and her innocence tonight. Rebellion coursed through her. Frightening. Exciting.

"I have copies of some of Mr. Fielding's novels in my library. You might enjoy them, though they've caused a bit of a scandal. I'm afraid I don't have Richardson's *Clarissa,* if that style is more to your taste, but I have Rousseau's *Julie.* It is much the same."

"Not my style," she said firmly. "Lady Toumoult told me about them. Neither heroine takes the slightest action to avert her fate. They always just slide into a decline and die. I mean, you have to *do* something. You can't just wish things were different." That sentiment resonated inside her in a way she couldn't explain, like a violin string vibrating in sympathy

Time for Eternity

with a cello. "Even if it's difficult."

"Yes."

That word was weighted somehow, fraught with as much emotion as he ever let himself display. Suddenly, she thought that a carriage ride to Versailles with the duc held many possibilities. She resolved to embrace them, regardless of consequences. She was not going to become Lady Toumoult, no matter how dear her aunt had been to her.

*****

They talked about Rousseau and Voltaire and how the Revolution had twisted their ideas into zealotry. Henri was surprised. They discussed the line between individualism and the needs of society. She was intelligent. Her opinions were surprisingly sophisticated for one who'd seen so little of the world.

In short, Henri found her an enigma. He couldn't think of the last time he didn't know instantly who someone was and what they would say next. That was the curse of living as long as he had. Especially fascinating were those times when she seemed to surprise herself by what she said. He'd first noticed it that afternoon when she had obviously never had brandy burning down her throat and yet correctly guessed that it was twenty-year-old Rèmy. Where did she get that knowledge of spirits if she'd never actually drunk any?

They clattered up to the back gates of Versailles, the ones that gave entrance to the park. He wanted her first view of the palace to be from the park, not through the village across the court in front of the stables where all was obscured by that crowd of government buildings. Two guards stood just outside the old stone gatehouse, dressed not in the red and blue of the revolutionary guard, but in plain brown and gray coats. Locals pressed into service and glad for the job. Henri leaned out the carriage window.

"My good man, are we too late for a tour?" Henri's query was greeted by a guffaw that was quickly swallowed when he let the light from their lantern glint over the gold in his hand.

"Just in time." The older of the two men grinned. His coat was buttoned over a swelling belly. There was a coin for each, probably more than they made in six months. The guards caught the largesse he flipped to them in midair.

The younger one, his hair like errant straw, scrambled for the gate. "Just this way, Citizen." The wrought-iron gates topped with spikes made of fleur-de-lis creaked open. Henri sighed. They were rusted. What had Versailles come to? But it didn't matter. The girl had never been here. And everyone should go to Versailles once in her life.

The coach rolled smoothly down the graveled drive through the winding park. The girl slid over the seat to crane her neck out the window on his side.

"I can't see very much," she said. "But those gardens look very inviting."

"They are in the English style, less formal, full of meandering paths used for trysts, formerly by members of the court, and now by the citizenry that comes to picnic here."

"Is that a village?" she asked in astonishment "How very quaint."

"Of sorts. The late queen had a hamlet built so that she could play at being a milkmaid."

She looked at him with big eyes. "How sad that she needed to escape her real life."

"We all want to escape our real life." But there was never any escape.

"Is that the palace?" He could hear the excitement in her voice. She was on the wrong side for it to be the palace. He peered out. "Good God, no. That is one of the smaller palaces Louis XV built for trysting with Madame de Pompadour."

She turned to him. Her smile was mischievous. "A smaller palace. A nice distinction I shall strive to remember."

They turned left on the Avenue de Trianon, which allowed a plain view of the grand canal and its terminus in a gigantic fountain surrounding a statue of Apollo. They could hear the water flowing even over the crunch of the gravel under

Time for Eternity

the wheels. What would she think of that?

"Oh, my." Her tone was reverent, astonished. He would hear that a lot tonight. It should portend frightening boredom. But he wasn't sure he would be bored. How odd. He wanted to be the one to show her what she had longed to see. He wanted to see it through her eyes as a wonder of the world, and not the den of silly iniquity and excess it had always been in his experience. Now, where would he take her to eat Pierre's picnic? The formal gardens? It was warm enough tonight. But a heaviness in the air and some electric sense of anticipation said they might get wet.

"Where is the Grotto of Apollo?" she asked suddenly.

"The Bassin d'Apollon is that big fountain at the end of the Grand Canal. I didn't know there was a grotto. Who told you about it?"

"N-no one. I mean... I don't know who told me." She looked profoundly disturbed at that. "It has three statues that were displaced when a building was torn down. They put them in...in a man-made cave of some sort." She looked a bit appalled at what she'd said.

"Well, I'm sure we can explore if you're up to it. You had a late night last night."

"Oh, I slept into the afternoon today, really." She looked up at him, examining his face. "I'm starting to keep your hours."

"Depraved indeed," he murmured.

"I wonder." She sat back in the squabs of the upholstered bench. "I think you're sensitive to sunlight. That's why you keep the house dark all the time. I definitely saw you squinting when you came into my room as though even the late afternoon sun were painful."

Too bright by half. "Guilty as charged."

She frowned. "Is it a medical condition?"

"Yes." He glanced out the window of the coach. "And if you are any more inquisitive about my illnesses, you will miss the palace entirely."

She craned forward. "Oh... *My!*

Susan Squires

"Precisely."

They swept up the center drive. The façade was so long it faded into the night. Faint light glowed in the rooms behind the great portico but most of the gigantic palace was dark and cold. The ornate symmetry of the last century looked…hard. At least she would probably think it so.

Henri stepped out of the coach almost before it had stopped rolling. He handed the girl down and reached for the basket Philippe lowered. "Take the carriage round to the stables and get yourself some dinner in the village. We won't need you until a couple of hours before dawn."

"Very good, your grace." The carriage rolled away. "Well, where would you like to have our dinner? We could explore the park and look for your grotto." If indeed there was a grotto.

The question was answered by several large drops of rain, rapidly multiplying into a downpour. He grabbed her hand and they ran to the grand portico. She was laughing. Laughing at something so simple as rain. He couldn't help but smile.

"Oh, dear, all your finery wet." She giggled as the rain thundered down in a curtain just beyond the grand marble columns of the portico.

He took off his tricorn and shook the drops from it. The silk of his breeches would be ruined, unless you liked watered silk. "You're not exactly dry yourself." As a matter of fact, her pale rosy-orange dress was almost transparent over her breasts where her cloak, flapping as they ran, had allowed it to get soaked. He could clearly see her nipples, just at the edge of her décolletage. He cleared his throat and tried to ignore his wakening interest. The last thing he wanted to do was to frighten her with a cockstand. Though he might not have much choice about that. "Let's see if we can get someone to let us in."

It was an excuse to turn away, concealing his rising problem. He was about to rap the great ceremonial knocker when the door swung open on hinges that creaked. He remembered when these doors had been better tended and when the place had blazed with light, when the crush of courtly

Time for Eternity

bodies had made passage impossible. Those days were gone. Perhaps just as well.

The dour man who opened the door must have been eighty. Wisps of white hair wafted round his head like pulled Egyptian cotton. He peered out at them from rheumy eyes, holding high a candelabrum.

"What do you want?"

"To give ourselves a tour, with your permission," Henri said, polite this time. This was a remnant of the old guard, beleaguered as he might be in these troubled times.

The man's gaze roved over them, sharpened, then he bowed. "Please forgive my lack of manners, your grace. There is so little use for them these days." He opened the door wide. Henri hadn't expected to be recognized. Was it the electric feel of his Companion that stamped him?

"And you are?"

"Brendal, your grace, the last permanent remnant of the palace."

"You have a hard but important job, Brendal. My sympathy and my gratitude." Henri looked around. He hadn't been to Versailles in ages. It had been too silly and too dangerous a place when the unbalanced king and his overmatched queen had been in residence. The entrance hall was much the same, if bare of furniture. "Have they stripped the place?"

"Not all of it," the caretaker said, his mouth a grim line.

The girl was staring about her with big eyes. As well she might. The huge, dim hall was really just a grand foyer, but the carved ceiling was twenty feet above them and the chandelier that hung in the darkness was a good ten feet in diameter. The paintings, the gilt wood carving everywhere, the marble expanse of floor, even the echo of emptiness spoke of a grandeur lost or never realized. The building might be grand, but the people who used to reside here were not.

"I'd like to show my young guest about with your permission. We've brought a picnic dinner. I'm sure there is enough to share."

"Your grace is kind, but my *chère* wife made a nice pullet for dinner. A tour perhaps?"

The girl wandered into the center of the hall, staring up at the chandelier. How he wished she could have seen it lighted. "No need," he said to the caretaker. "I know my way."

The old man glanced to the girl with a small smile. "Very good, your grace." He turned to another candelabrum sitting on a small table and lighted each candle from one of his own.

Who did not smile when they saw her? Her beauty was fresh. But it was that light of intelligence in her eyes, her emotional resonance that moved her from the ordinary into the extraordinary. Henri had barely noticed her, though she'd lived next door for nearly a year. And now he could hardly take his eyes off her. What had changed? And now she was off-limits because she was his ward.

"One can hardly imagine living in such luxury," she murmured.

He, of course, could hear her clearly. "The public rooms are very grand, and of course the king's and queen's suites. But the courtiers lived in tiny boxes, three thousand of them crowded into a veritable rabbit warren."

"Really?"

"Oh, quite, my lady," Brendal confirmed. "Almost squalid conditions."

Henri picked up the candelabrum, nodding his thanks to the old man, and slipped the expected gold into a discreet hand. "So we shan't bother with them." He motioned her ahead. "The Hall of Mirrors, however, is definitely on the tour." With his flickering light in one hand, and their dinner basket in the other, he trailed after her as the old man drifted away. The sway of her dress shushed across his senses. The aroma of wet hair and fresh female flesh wafted behind her. None but he could have caught the scent. He found it more erotic than the perfumed elegance of the women who usually filled his bed. All that perfume was meant to mask long hair rarely washed, just powdered and ratted, and bodies that bathed once a week at best.

Time for Eternity

Who would have guessed that the simple scent of a woman could rouse him so?

*****

"Who are all these people?" Françoise asked as they came to a salon with portraits hung in dizzying profusion from the wainscoting to the ceiling on red padded wall covering.

Her companion obligingly held up his candelabrum. "I've no idea," he said after a moment. "I'm afraid the painters are more recognizable than the subjects."

"What do you mean?"

"Well…" His eyes searched the wall. "Third down and five over from the doorway. Dutch school. Vermeer. And two over from that, Rembrandt without doubt." She went to look closer at the Rembrandt.

"Why, it says it's a self-portrait. How odd that he wouldn't make himself more attractive. It's very alive-feeling though, isn't it?"

Avignon followed and held up the light. She was acutely aware of his body standing so close to hers. The power of his muscled frame was only enhanced by his electric sense of aliveness. A thrum started inside her. "He was more interested in light and truth than in conventional notions of beauty. Not good for business, I'm afraid."

She couldn't help but chuckle. She turned back to the face that glowed out of the dark canvas. "Memorable, though."

They wandered on, through salons sometimes stripped of carpets, always stripped of anything small enough to be carried away, like clocks and lamps. Often only the huge rococo chests were left. "I wonder what this would have looked like when it was fully furnished."

"Overwhelming. That's the effect they wanted. Austere on the outside, and over-ornamented on the inside. They thought it made them grander themselves."

He pointed out the pastel pastorals of Fragonard, populated by chubby women and cherubs, and the romantic myths of Poussin in huge canvases that dominated the walls.

"I wonder how much gilt they used in here?"

"Ah, you are coming to the best, the Grands Appartements." He led the way into a huge room. "This is the Hercules Salon." He pointed up. "Each is named for the painting in the ceiling. Lemoyne, if I remember."

She peered up into the dimness. The immense painting was only partially illuminated by Avignon's flickering candles. Hercules was apparently being welcomed into heaven. "Imagine having that stare down at one."

"Remember, not for living, but for overwhelming. Louis wanted everyone to feel small."

"He achieved his aim," she murmured, touching the gilt carving of the fireplace set with the faces of Hercules.

Avignon led her through room after room, each with another painting on the ceiling. It all began to run together. "You're looking a little peaked. Are you ready to dine?" Avignon asked.

"I don't suppose there's an intimate little dining room around here anywhere."

"No." He smiled. She liked that smile, roguish and always a little rueful. She understood the rueful part on some level. "But it wouldn't be a picnic then, would it?" He led the way into…

A wonderland. Avignon stepped into a vast long hall and the candles in his holder seemed to multiply. Floor- to-ceiling mirrors along one side faced windows equally large on the other. Just now those windows were black, only hinting at the waves of rain outside. Françoise stood and stared, imagining dancers whirling in panniered dresses and skirted coats of magenta and yellow under the glittering chandeliers whose light was cast back by the mirrors. Golden statues held crystal lights that would have echoed the chandeliers in a long line.

Avignon set down his burdens in the center of the room then spread his cloak on the parquet floor. "Voilà," he announced. "We picnic in the wild wasteland of Versailles."

She smiled. He took off his coat and knelt on the cloak

in his shirtsleeves and waistcoat to begin digging through the hamper. She shrugged off her own cloak, still damp, and sat on his, tucking her feet under her. He produced a bottle of wine and cut-crystal glasses, knives to carve a cold duck with cherry sauce on a platter. The dishes kept emerging. He served her, talking lightly of life at Versailles and telling tales of the outrages the kings of France had perpetrated on their unruly and possibly subversive followers. Whenever she laughed she was rewarded with that elusive smile. The circle of candlelight created an intimate space inside that grand hall. The wine was a marvelous burgundy. He cut her meat and poured her wine. She felt…cared for, perhaps for the first time in many years.

With a start she realized she was utterly comfortable with him.

No, no, no. One shouldn't be comfortable with the devil. Panic seeped in. She should never have come. At the least she should keep him at arm's length rather than laughing at his ridiculous stories. The intensity of that feeling was more overwhelming than the Hall of Mirrors.

That must be the girl surfacing that Lady Toumoult had warned and frightened into believing that experience was dangerous. She'd already made her choice tonight. She wanted to come to Versailles. She even wanted Avignon to kiss her. She watched him pack up the hamper.

"Anything else you'd like to see?"

She swallowed. "The king's apartments? Or the queen's. I'd like to see how they lived, where they slept."

He examined her face, her eyes. He wanted to know what she meant by that. She felt a slow flush creep from her breasts to her throat and into her cheeks. Unfortunately, that would tell him exactly what she meant.

"Very well." He rose, and helped her to her feet. Why did touching his hand always seem to shock her right between her legs? She'd never felt anything like that. He swung her cloak around her, and picked his up along with his coat and carried them over his arm. He grabbed the candelabrum. "Let's go."

Susan Squires

"Are you going to leave the hamper?"

"Think of it as a gift for Brendal and his *cherè* wife."

He took her hand and led her onward. Her hand in his felt small, protected. *Danger!* a voice shouted inside her. *Don't do this.* She pressed it down and followed Avignon. "We will eschew his public apartments. He didn't live there, at least not for very long."

He led her up the stairs into a cozy room lined with cupboards of some dark wood, a porcelain bath painted with scenes, a bed with a brocaded coverlet. It was really rather comfortable. Not what she expected.

"This is rather nice."

"As the dressing room of a king should be."

This was a dressing room? It was three times as big as her bedroom at Madame LaFleur's house had been. He opened a door onto a huge room that looked like a receiving salon, then thought better of it and tried another door.

"Yes, here it is."

She stopped, stock-still.

"Oh, my."

This room was gigantic. The ceiling was carved and adorned with painting. Red and gold brocade hangings lined the walls. There was an ornate dressing table, several wardrobes in the rococo style, a gaping fireplace with an ornately carved marble mantel and great golden andirons. Chairs lined the walls as though the king held audiences here. Dominating the room, a huge bed, ornately carved and heavy, sat on a raised dais hung with so much gold braiding and red-fringed draperies it looked as though it were a room in itself. Everywhere rich carpets, gold-threaded brocades, shiny satins, and the rich gleam of wood gave the room a kind of heavy magnificence that was enough to weigh one down.

"This is the king's bedroom." Avignon came to stand behind her as she stared at the bed. He held the candelabrum high. His voice was deep and bittersweet, like the cup of chocolate she'd had with *petit dejeuner* the first morning in his house.

She knew what might happen there. And she ruthlessly

suppressed the fear that threatened to close her throat. She was not dear Lady Toumoult. She would not die having never experienced anything. Having never experienced *this*. It was an adventure and she would have it. It needn't be more.

Susan Squires

Eleven

Henri looked down at that wondrous combination of innocence and experience in her eyes, shocked that what she wanted was so clearly writ there. Her breasts rose and fell against her bodice—so near to escape it made him unaccountably nervous. He'd been holding her hand as he led her up the stairs. He should never have done that. His Companion screamed for life, sending blood careering from around his body to the one place that didn't need more. His body wanted her. He'd had a thousand women want him. Why was this one any different?

Maybe because the women had all fallen into one of two categories. Either they were attracted by his power and his money alone—grasping creatures out to get what they could from him. Or they were innocents ensorcelled by his attractive vampire sense of life, only to be frightened by what they had unleashed, even if they never realized truly what he was.

An image of an innocent girl, driven to suicide by horror of him, blood blooming on her breast, made him swallow hard. He pushed it down. He didn't dally with innocents.

But this one was not innocent. He had seen her experience in her eyes when she caught him at his bath, when she so accurately described the failure of heart that long life engendered in one. And yet she still had hope. He could see it almost glowing around her at times. She'd searched the prison for her friend, refusing to give up. She was determined to look for a situation when it was hopeless and anyone else would have cast herself as a courtesan or worse long ago.

He searched her face. He saw no young coquette seducing him without a notion of what that meant. She knew. He could see it in her eyes. They were filled with a hot eagerness, laced with world-weariness. He found it infinitely

Time for Eternity

attractive. So much so that if she looked down right now, instead of so boldly into his eyes, she would see something he was now quite sure would not surprise her. How long had it been since he had wanted a woman like this? He couldn't count the years. Just the resurgence of interest made him feel as though the world still held possibilities for him. She need never know what he was. It could be a liaison like any of his others, and not that emotionally charged disaster so long ago that had ended in death for a girl who would rather end her life than spend another instant of it with a monster.

Except it couldn't be a liaison like his others.

He tore his gaze from hers. "You are my ward, have you forgotten?" Jesus and his Mother, how could he have thought to seduce her? He was her protector, even from himself.

"No, your grace."

Was she playing games of ambiguity? "No, you haven't forgotten?"

"No, I'm not your ward, your grace." She took the candelabrum and set it on an inlaid chest next to the great bed.

"Don't call me that." He couldn't help but snap with his balls so tight and his cock straining at his breeches. "There is nothing of grace about me."

She smiled. It was a knowing smile. "Henri, then, if you prefer."

He did not. But she'd trapped him. He found himself grinding his teeth. "You are my ward, whether you acknowledge it or not." He should put his coat on again. What was he doing in his shirtsleeves? And why had he let her set down the candelabrum as though they were going to stay here? In a bedroom? That smile again, damn her. He would have been ready to swear she was a virgin yesterday, but now...

"A fiction and you know it. I am more than of age. Almost a spinster. With no prospects but that a very dull shopkeeper might one day offer for me. Not an exciting future."

He turned away and ran his hand over his mouth, which had suddenly gone dry. "I am your protector. You have a right

Susan Squires

to rely on me, and that means…certain things."

"You shock me. The devil has a sense of honor." He felt her hand on his arm. The shock they were both really talking about went straight to his loins. She turned him toward her. *Did he have a sense of honor? He cultivated the image of Satan. How long until one became a devil in truth? He gambled and whored and…* But not with this girl.

She ran her hands over his chest. "Your honor is misplaced. I'm of age. You would be doing me a great service."

What was she saying? He couldn't think when she touched him like that. He could only feel her palms burning his chest even through his waistcoat. He'd been alone so long, regardless of his liaisons. She offered a moment of intimacy with someone who might be a kindred spirit in some small way, and that moment, like a fragile candle flame flickering against the darkness, might give him heart enough to go on. If his liaisons had not been satisfying lately, it might be because the women all seemed sly and greedy. This girl was neither. She was dangerous. She would fall in love with his vampire attraction. No one knew him for himself. Neither would she.

But that was good, wasn't it? That would make it a liaison like any other, after all.

She stepped into him, where he stood rigid with indecision, and turned her face up, expectant. "Tomorrow it will all be over. I will expect nothing of you. Tonight I want to know what it is like to have the wicked duc make love to me. Is that so wrong?"

She wouldn't love him. She was cynical enough to know that. In some ways that freed him. She stood on tiptoe and brushed her lips across his. He was lost.

He ran his hands around her and pulled her in against his body. The feel of the length of her pressed against him sent anticipation through him that seemed tremulous with hope. He had just enough restraint to avoid taking her mouth like some kind of pirate. He kissed her forehead. An achievement. And her nose. That wouldn't frighten her. Her heart beat against his chest. It wasn't in fear. She raised her lips and he couldn't help but kiss them. She opened to him immediately, soft as his

Time for Eternity

approach was, and her tongue came seeking into his mouth.

God in His heaven, she was not new to kissing. He'd almost forgotten his discovery in the library. He twined his tongue with his. Kissing had never felt so intimate. Their bodies shared precious moisture and warmth. More than warmth, heat. Her slender body in his arms felt so fragile. He could crush her without thinking, so he was careful, so careful. With difficulty, he pulled away. This was the last question a man should ask. But he asked it anyway. "Where did you learn to kiss like that?"

She blinked in surprise. It was a very direct question. But then her look turned puzzled. "I…I really don't know."

Was that puzzlement feigned? It didn't seem so. Just like she knew about brandy, she knew about kissing.

She smiled at him. "But I suspect you are just the man to show me more."

God help him. Holding her in his arms like this, feeling her fragile body throbbing against his, his experience making love to women seemed irrelevant. Could making love ever be new again for him? That would be a gift beyond price. He mustn't expect it. He felt almost awed, a little frightened of what might happen here.

She raised her brows at him, her breath warm over his lips. "Show me?"

He felt a growl coming up from his belly. He was on fire. He was frightened. And he was helpless. He brought his lips to hers and let his growl into her mouth. Then he was consumed.

*****

Françoise wondered for an instant what beast she had unleashed here. Henri kissed her with a ferocity that sent a thrill of fear through her. That fear was delightful, so different than all the other fears that had consumed her lately. She was about to experience all Lady Toumoult never had. She wouldn't think about tomorrow. After tonight, the deluge. She didn't care.

Susan Squires

Her hands slid up his arms as his tongue searched her mouth. The bunched muscles in his upper arms under the fine-gauge linen shirt were a revelation. She pressed herself to the hardness of his body, enveloped by the scent of cinnamon and...ambergris—that's what that sweet smell was—and the male musk of need. The vibrating life she always felt emanating from him seemed to cycle up some scale until she could hardly think. She was carried away by the force of him and by her own desire.

A hard ridge pressed against her abdomen as he ravished her mouth. Oh, the duc was delightfully wicked. And she wanted to experience all of him.

He was kissing down her throat now. She felt vulnerable as she tilted her chin up. He kissed her collarbone, the rise of her breast. Her heart knocked about inside her without any rhythm at all. "I want to see you naked again," she murmured into his hair. Its scent was redolent of night and sensuality. Maybe that was why she had been bold enough to say such a thing.

"And so you shall," he said. He bent and let his lips pull at the edge of her neckline. Her nipple popped free and he sent his tongue swirling around it. She sucked in a breath. How did he create such sensation? He freed her other breast with one hand and caressed its nipple too. The place between her legs swelled almost painfully.

She had almost forgotten her demand when he raised his head and said with a sinful grin, "But only if you're naked too."

Naked? With this complicated dress?

"Don't worry. I know something about women's clothing." He had read her mind, or her expression. And before she could say more, he was feeling for the ties on her skirts. She was soon stepping out of them, even as he untied her sleeves. The feel of his hands kept her humming inside. She kicked off her slippers and stood in chemise and her bodice.

"I'm ahead of you," she said with mock severity, trying to mask her uncertainty. What if he was disappointed in her? What if her ignorance let him down? "And...and I asked first."

Time for Eternity

He suppressed a smile. "You're right. Turnabout is fair play." Stepping back, he unbuttoned his embroidered waistcoat and pulled out his shirt. He untied his cravat and tossed it away as he too kicked off his buckled shoes. He pulled his shirt over his head.

She bit her lips. Oh, she did like to see his naked chest; the muscles, the curling dark hair. She had wanted to touch him that day in his bath and had been horrified by her desire. She wasn't horrified now. She found herself moving toward him without ever having decided to do so. Her hand reached out of its own accord. She felt him staring at her but her own eyes were only for his body. She placed her palm over his right breast, smoothing the crinkly hair, feeling the soft nipple peak. She rubbed the nipple with her thumb. He had kissed her nipples, and as he said, "turnabout." She only had to lean in a little bit to let her tongue dart out and lick them. Slightly salty, pebbly to the touch.

He cleared his throat. She didn't think it was because he had anything to say. She ran both hands down over the ribs of muscle to his belly, then over the hard rod of flesh under his breeches.

He took her shoulders, breathing raggedly. Without a word he turned her about to unlace her bodice. It dropped to the floor and he turned her again to pull her chemise over her head.

She was naked before him, except for her stockings and garters. She had never been naked in a man's presence before. She'd always been self-conscious about her appearance. Her breasts were perhaps less fulsome than was fashionable. One could only call her short. But suddenly that didn't make any difference. Her hesitancy melted away. Some part of her now *knew* she was desirable. Let him look his fill. He was looking, even as he bent to unbuckle his breeches at the knee. He looked as he worked the buttons at the waistband. His black, wicked eyes were burning. In a moment she would see his naked manhood, fully aroused. Once that prospect would have been frightening. Not now.

She felt her eyes widen as he pushed his breeches, his

smalls, and his stockings down in one motion and stepped out of them. Well, *that* was impressive.

His eyes narrowed. "Have you ever seen a man...in this state before?"

"No." She shook her head. Had she? "Yes."

He didn't ask her which it was, which was good since she couldn't have explained it. Instead he turned his back, revealing round, muscled buttocks and broad shoulders. His skin was the same pale marble perfection all over his body as though he had never seen the sun. She swallowed. He went to the king's great bed and pulled back the red gilt brocade in great swaths. The bed was just as it had been left, with clean white linen on it He took the pillows from their elaborate covers. When he turned back to her, a pillow cover, casually held, covered his erection. Now he was the one who seemed hesitant. Had she ever seen the wicked duc hesitant?

If he thought he'd frightened her he'd never go through with it. She was suddenly certain he had that much honor and that much self-control, though she never would have believed it a week ago. She walked over to him as calmly as she could, her eyes never leaving his, and tossed the glittering pillow sham on the floor.

"Don't you dare have second thoughts," she whispered, cupping the nape of his neck. Her breasts brushed his chest. "Because I don't." She turned her face up to be kissed. She floated along with the gleaming silver specks floating in the blackness of his eyes.

He let out a breath he had apparently been holding. Then he smiled. That smile was so sad, so careworn. She stood on her tiptoes to kiss it away. What good was it to be the wicked duc if you couldn't be fierce and devil-may-care? It was as if he had been wearing the mask of a wicked duc all along and only now had she glimpsed the man behind the façade.

Slowly, his arms came around her. But instead of holding her to his body, he lifted her up and turned to place her on the high bed behind him. "You won't be sorry," he breathed. "I'll make sure you're never sorry."

He couldn't do that of course. Some little voice inside

Time for Eternity

Françoise said that she was likely to be sorry indeed for all this. But she shut the door on the little voice. Henri crawled up into the gigantic bed beside her.

*****

He settled in beside her, his brain engaged once again. He had made love to women so many times in his life that repetition made the experience fade into gray history. For the first time in countless years, he wanted to make this special. For her. But how experienced was she? Dare he use his mouth on her? Or had she merely kissed Robert, the servant next door?

He would go slowly, feeling his way, so to speak. As long as he could hold himself. Lord, he was like a schoolboy, the pressure inside him ready to make him spurt. What good was all his experience if it didn't make him capable of controlling his body?

He leaned in to kiss her, his hand sliding over her delicate shoulders. She ran her palm over his back and down to cup his buttocks. She squeezed. Not shy. And then, while he kissed his way down her throat to her breasts, she ran her small hand over his hip and found his cock. She grasped the throbbing shaft and slid her thumb along the vein on the underside to the sensitive crown. He groaned over the breast he was suckling, struggling for control. She found the drop of moisture at the opening unerringly and smoothed it over the head. "Françoise, you'll end it too soon," he gasped.

She opened her eyes wide. "You wouldn't let that happen, would you?"

Thank the heavens, she let go of his cock as he pushed her gently onto her back and suckled at her breast. At least he knew his way. This woman was as experienced as the most hardened courtesan he had ever tumbled. He could employ his entire repertoire to please her.

*****

Françoise could hardly think as he turned his attention to the other breast. But why would one want to think when one could feel all that sensation driving straight from her nipple to the center of her body? His mouth, wet and sensuous on her breast, was a revelation. She could feel the slickness on her thighs. Henri parted them gently with one hand, and then put his palm over her mound. She couldn't help but grind against it. Wasn't one supposed to lie passive as a man had his way? Lady Toumoult had intimated as much when she talked about "the marriage act." But Françoise couldn't control her hips when Henri slipped one finger inside her folds. He rubbed along some spot that suddenly sent shocks of the most intense pleasure through her. That was the most exquisite feeling she'd ever known. And he kept doing it. Her hips moved in counterpoint of their own volition. She found her hands wound into hair that had somehow come loose from its queue and now spread out over his shoulders. It gleamed in the flickering light from the candelabrum set on the ornate chest behind him. The feeling in her woman parts was relentless—a promise or a threat of something yet to come. She couldn't get her breath.

But she wasn't relieved when he removed his hand. She longed for that exquisite torture. He slid down her body, kissing and licking as he went until he lay with his shoulders between her thighs, and she was open to him. The feeling subsided to a tingle. She writhed on the sheets, not sure what she wanted, but knowing that she wanted more.

"God, but you're beautiful, Françoise," he said. He said it reluctantly, as though he didn't have a choice. And that made her feel powerful. So she didn't mind being open to him when he parted her nether lips with his fingers. She might be open, but that openness commanded him.

What he did next made her gasp in surprise. What was he doing with...with his mouth? Ohhhhhh. She craned to see. Should she be letting him do this? But she didn't want it to stop.

God, but he's good, isn't he?

The voice inside her was so clear, so wistful. But she

didn't have time to answer because Henri was licking and...and, dear Lord, now he was sucking. And sliding his tongue right into her. Lady Toumoult had no idea about this kind of thing, Françoise was sure. She was also fairly certain it was a sin. It felt too good to be anything less. And then that promise of even more to come got stronger and stronger. What Henri was doing became less important than that all-encompassing sensation washing over her, making her hips lift in supplication for whatever was to come. She could hear herself moaning as from a distance.

And then something else entirely happened. The sensation was suddenly so intense it seemed unrelated to the earlier pleasure. She gasped and squeezed her eyes shut. She might have moaned or even shouted. Her head buzzed.

Breathe!

Everything in her body shattered.

The sensation slowly subsided, like a tidal wave being sucked back into an ocean. She'd just had an orgasm. How did she know that? Were they always like that?

No, they aren't. The voice was almost a sigh of resignation.

But she didn't feel resigned at all. That was *wonderful.*

Henri slid up beside her and held her. She opened her eyes. She couldn't help but grin. She must look like a loon to him.

He smiled in return. It was smug. "Did you like that?"

She nodded, trying to control her mouth. "Pretty much." Where had that come from? It was a strange turn of phrase. Though that experience might indeed be called "pretty." "I mean yes, very much." She was so glad she'd decided to push for what she wanted tonight. And kisses had turned out to be only the beginning. "But what about you?" she asked, feeling suddenly shy. His shaft still lay, hard and throbbing, along her thigh.

"We're getting to that." He turned her chin up with one finger and kissed her again, deeply. She felt warm and wet and even more sensitive and open to his kisses. She tasted something slightly salty in his kiss and realized that must be what she tasted like. Not...not a bad taste. It spoke of men and women together.

She reached to touch him again. This time she just held the sac filled with his stones, gently, and rubbed a little with her middle finger just at the base. That made him growl again. She played with him, using instincts she didn't know she had. The throbbing was back.

"You drive me mad, woman." His breath was truly ragged.

"I want to drive you mad." How bold she was! She threw one thigh over his hip, which put his manhood right against that place he'd been kissing. Could he fit inside her? Were all men that large?

No, they aren't, came the voice, almost disgusted. *Or that skillful with it.*

The tip was almost at her entrance as he rolled her over on her back once more. He continued to kiss her as he leaned on one elbow and held his shaft with the other hand. It slid along her slick flesh until it found her opening. She was about to lose her virginity and she was glad. She wanted to lose it with the wicked duc and not some dull apothecary's assistant. Let the future be damned.

She wrapped her legs around his hips. He pressed inside her. She was tight around him. She felt filled. That wasn't so bad. She looked down. His loins were still separated from hers. She could see his shaft disappearing inside her.

He bent to kiss her neck, now balanced on both elbows above her, and he thrust in fully.

She gave a little shriek as a stab of pain shot through her. Like she'd cut herself, but not deeply. He went still.

"You're a virgin." It sounded like an accusation. He dropped his head, his face curtained by his hair. "I...I didn't know. I thought...I would never have just..."

"It's better now." How embarrassing that she'd shrieked. Now he felt warm inside her. Satisfying. This was where she belonged, joined to Henri Foucault. How had she thought she was filled before? "This is nice."

174

Time for Eternity

"I... I can make it nicer if you'll let me. I promise it won't hurt like that again."

He looked so contrite. But more than that, he looked a little...frightened? Not like the wicked duc at all. She couldn't have that. "That kissing before...down there...was nice."

"Have you...never had an orgasm?"

She shook her head. "I would have known, I'm sure."

He took a breath and squeezed his eyes shut. Then he opened them as though he had decided something. "You can get the same feeling again, only by a different means, if you'll bear with me." The small smile was back, but it was very rueful now.

"I'd like that."

He began to move inside her, gently at first. As he moved in and out, the friction pulled a little at the lips of her mound and the spot that felt so good there. The feeling of wanting more returned. She began to move in counterpoint, even twisting a little at the end each time to get more of that delightful friction. And then his shaft inside her seemed to rub on some most fulfilling place deep inside her. She wanted to be crushed, filled with him, covered by him. So she thrust up her breasts to his chest and let the hair there rub against her nipples. His thrusts came faster. Her hands on his hips wanted to help him press inside her. His skin was gloriously damp. In no time the wave came crashing in again as he thrust in and out and she bucked against him. Her moan spiraled up into a wail and she found herself gripping his hips and holding on as though she needed to tether her soul or be blasted away to some place of wind and light.

Just after her peak, he stilled and she felt a throbbing pulse inside her as he loosed his seed. She opened her eyes. The look on his face was inward and she knew his own wave was crashing over him. She waited, fascinated, as the moment went on and on.

He collapsed and rolled to the side, cradling her in his arms to keep them joined. He kissed her hair softly. "Françoise. Françoise." She realized he had never called her by her first

Susan Squires

name until tonight. She liked to hear her name on his lips.

He reached for her hand and kissed her palm. "Are you all right?"

What did he mean? Oh. "Yes. It was nothing."

"It was *not* nothing. It was inexcusable of me to assume… I should have asked, or checked first, or… Well, I'm sorry it had to be that way for you."

"I thought it was wonderful."

He cleared his throat "You were very…skillful."

"Was I? I didn't feel skillful."

"You know things about a man's body…"

Ah. He wanted to know how she knew how to please him. "Uh ... woman's intuition."

He raised a brow at her, but apparently decided not to pursue the issue. "You needn't worry about any issue from our bed-sport."

Bed-sport. That was sobering. Because that's what it was to him. She had known it, of course, but just for a while she had thought…

Remember that. The strange voice again. Her and yet not her.

Wait. Issue? "You mean a child?" Lady Toumoult had warned it could happen if you strayed even once, but Françoise had always thought that was just exaggeration meant to frighten her into good behavior. She'd known women who tried for years to conceive.

"My kind… I mean, children are very rare for men like me." His voice was tight.

"Oh." How sad for him. Perhaps it was related to the illness that made him so sensitive to sunlight. What could she say? A man like him wouldn't want a child. Like her father hadn't wanted her. She swallowed past a lump in her throat. Bed-sport. He didn't want her either. She hadn't expected more, she reminded herself. She'd wanted a night, one night, of glorious bed-sport because she was never likely to have another.

Then that's what she would embrace. "In that case, perhaps we can do it again?"

Time for Eternity

He looked down at her. What was that in his eyes? Softness? "Perhaps. When you're feeling better."

She didn't try to control the behavior of her mouth. "I feel better now."

Susan Squires

Twelve

Françoise blinked. Someone was kissing her hair.

Ahhh. Henri. The scent of him surrounded her. Life seemed to throb in lazy luxury around him, rather than thrumming in the air. She lay in his arms. The weight of his thigh over hers was delicious. She felt warm and safe from anything here.

"Wake, Françoise," Henri whispered in that husky baritone. She smiled. She had made the panther truly growl this night. She opened her eyes.

It was dark. The candles had long ago sputtered out. Did he want to make love yet again? She ran her hand down his ribs to his hip. She'd like that. She was a little sore, but it was a good kind of sore. And she didn't want the night to end. She looked up into his eyes and their expression was soft.

Some part of her was startled. *I don't remember him ever looking at me like that.* A stupid thought on the whole, since of course he'd never looked at her like that before.

"It's time to go." He looked sorry. "I let it get too late. It's almost sunrise."

She sighed and nodded. "I have no idea how I'll dress in the dark," she said, pushing herself up to one elbow.

"I'll dress you. I see well in the dark."

And he did. He didn't fumble or grope. He knew just how to lace and tie. She didn't like to think about how he knew that.

"Now if only you dressed hair."

He ran his fingers through her curls. "This is all you need."

She touched her neckline to make certain nothing was showing that shouldn't. Dear me but this was a sensual dress, just made to drive a man wild. A dress he hadn't bought for her.

Time for Eternity

You fell for him. You've only made it harder. The voice *must* be only her own thoughts but it came out so distinctly, as though it were a different person altogether. It sounded accusatory. Fell for him. Did the voice mean she'd fallen in love?

She wasn't in love with him, she told herself firmly. Love a man who cared for nothing but his own pleasure and made money off the weaknesses of others? He took their coin and their ideals in one gesture. One couldn't fall in love with a man like that.

She watched him dress. A shame to cover a body like that. She'd like to go for days or weeks, never leaving the king's apartments, never covering that beautiful body, so hard, so different from her own. But soon he was most proper again. Wordlessly, they made up the great bed as best they could. He swung his cloak around her shoulders and they slipped out into the broad hallway, down the grand stairs, through the salons to the portico overlooking the gardens.

The coach waited in the gray light. It was almost sunrise. Françoise looked around, an insistent itching in her brain. There was something she had forgotten. What was it? The feeling was so strong it was almost physical.

She looked around at the immense palace, standing so dark and severe, her mind casting about frantically. She looked down at her clothes. She had her reticule, her cloak. It wasn't that Henri trotted down the stairs, but she hesitated. Between the wings that flanked the west façade the gardens stretched serenely. Wait! The grotto with the statues of Apollo and his horses—it was terribly important she go there. *Terribly* important.

"Wait," she called. "We never got to see the grotto. The one with the statue of Apollo."

He turned. "Too late, now." He cast a glance at the sky. The indigo was paling to the east.

She stood, frozen at the top of the stairs. That grotto held the key to all she wanted to know about herself, all the feelings and dreams she'd been having lately. Going there would fix everything.

How stupid. A grotto? Dear God, but she was letting her imagination run wild. She trudged down the stairway, trying to suppress the feeling of urgency inside her.

Henri handed her into the coach and climbed in beside her.

The carriage crunched down the gravel drive. Françoise leaned out as the façade of the palace, in all its severe grandeur, receded. It was as if the place were enchanted, sleeping under some kind of a spell. Once they left, it would disappear and no one would ever find it again. It was the perfect place for one glorious night of bed-sport that would never be repeated.

*****

Henri watched her leaning out the carriage window, staring at the palace, as they rolled away. What had he been thinking? Deflowering a virgin? Strictly against his code of conduct, even if she wanted it. He had vowed never to involve himself with an innocent again. And one who was living in his house, for God's sake, under his protection? A double violation. Could he be any more stupid? She'd either fall in love with him or hate him. Either way he'd ruin yet another life. And if she found out what he really was? It would change her forever.

The damnable thing was, he was incredibly attracted to her om so many levels it was rather startling. How long was it since he'd been startled by life? It made the whole thing seem…well, new, if he had to put a word on it. He found her sweet and cynical, courageous and naïve, full of hope and world-weary with experience. He could spend a long time unraveling those contradictions. He didn't want to think what that might mean.

If life could seem fresh, it might mean there was some hope for his soul.

He closed his eyes. Did vampires become senile? If so, he undoubtedly was. He knew very well what life held for him. And his work was his only hope to stave off madness. He

180

Time for Eternity

meant to continue that work as long as he could, in spite of Robespierre and his bitch dog Croûte sniffing about.

So he could afford no entanglements. The girl pretended she wanted only dalliance, but he'd seen the look he knew too well in her eyes last night. How many hearts had he broken? A thousand? And that was without them even knowing he was a monster, spoken of in nurseries in hushed, childish voices to provoke shrieking giggles of fear. If they knew that, then...

He'd keep her at a distance. That way he wouldn't be tempted again by her lithe, young body or her contradictions.

He still couldn't believe she was a virgin. She knew exactly how to drive him wild. When she'd rolled on top of him the last time and ridden him like he was an unbroken horse, her breasts thrusting and bouncing...

He wouldn't think about that.

Suffice it to say it wasn't the behavior of a virgin. Yet she'd stained the king's sheets with virgin blood. An enigma, this one. One he was *not* going to try to solve.

He'd present her to society tonight to give her countenance and make sure everyone was very clear that she enjoyed his protection. That would keep her safe from Robespierre and the Croûte woman. Then he'd pack her off to England next week with the others.

He closed his eyes. He didn't want to see her expression just now.

*****

She stood looking at the curious leather bag, knowing that her life, her soul, depended upon its contents. The house was dark. The rooms seemed alive, whispering of hellish fates in words she couldn't quite hear. Something bad was going to happen to her, something worse than she could imagine, and only the contents of this bag could save her. The sword and the vials. She knew what those strange vials were. They were drugs.

She was in the yellow salon, though all was black and

Susan Squires

shadows. Outside a warm, summer wind blew. Even the wind felt evil.

Henri stepped out of the shadows. His eyes were glowing red, like coals. He was the source of all the evil in the house. She realized that now. And he was coming toward her. He opened his mouth to snarl like a black leopard. His fangs dripped saliva. If he caught her he would rip her throat out with those fangs and she would be damned to the pits of fire for eternity. She groped in the bag behind her and found one of the strange soft bottles colored in innocent pastels. He was strong, this devil, but she must fight him if she was going to save her soul. She sprang on him and grabbed for his throat. He tottered backward, snarling. It was Henri, but not Henri, and that was most frightening of all.

Somehow she had his neck in one hand and she was squeezing the bottle that wasn't made of glass. Liquid squirted past the snarling fangs and into the evil creature's throat.

He went limp under her hands.

She raised herself and stood, panting. The creature that was Henri but not Henri lay sprawled before her, his chest heaving. But he would wake soon. And then her soul would be more in danger than ever, and the monster before her would be angry. Very angry.

Slowly, she turned to the bag. The Roman short-sword gleamed there with its own internal radiance. Images flashed through her mind of lifting the sword high, bringing it down, and the metal cleaving through flesh, and the bloo....the blood was everywhere.

*****

Françoise gasped. Somewhere a wail still echoed in the air. She looked around wildly. Where was she? Frantic knocking reverberated through the room.

"Mademoiselle. Mademoiselle, are you all right?" Annette's voice.

She breathed. This was only the luxurious, feminine room that wasn't really hers.

Time for Eternity

"Coming, Annette." She threw back the bedclothes and got up. Her knees were shaky. She started for the door, then paused and looked back. Underneath the bed, right about where her pillows were, that strange leather case squatted like some interloper. And in it were bottles that weren't glass, filled with what she was now sure were drugs, and a gleaming sharp-edged sword. A sword that something inside her was urging her to use... Dear God, was she going insane?

She put a hand to her mouth as bile rose in her throat. Nonsense. She wasn't strong enough to use a sword to decapitate anyone. That...*that* was what the dream exhorted her to do? Decapitation. A shudder of revulsion rushed through her. She *was* going mad. She must be.

"Mademoiselle?"

"Coming." Her hands shook as she used the key in the door to let Annette into the room.

"And are we locking our doors these days?" Annette scolded.

"Apparently so." She didn't remember locking her door.

Annette peered at her. "Are you ill?"

"A bad dream." She managed a smile. "No more." It wasn't more, was it?

"The noise! How could it not wake you? Such preparations! Everybody's relatives are here, and still there are not enough hours in the day. A dozen bottles of champagne already have burst their corks. Like a battlefield it is."

The noise of distant bustle came from downstairs. Was that Pierre shouting something about butter? "What is everyone preparing for?" Françoise felt dislocated, as though she and Annette spoke different languages.

"Why, for the soirée this evening." Annette peered at her, waiting for a reaction. When Françoise looked blank, she said, "It's Wednesday," by way of a prompt.

"Oh. Oh, yes." The party where Henri was going to present her.

Henri. Last night washed over her. She was still a little sore from their lovemaking. The dream seemed to stand between today and that enchanted night. Well, she wouldn't let it. She was glad she had spent one night with Henri Foucault, Duc d'Avignon. That he had made love to her still seemed miraculous. She wouldn't let some dream make it anything else.

But today was reality.

And reality was that she was only bed-sport to him.

Best she find a way to get on with her life. She'd put her application in at the placement services today.

"What time is it, Annette?"

"*Alors*, it is nearly four of the afternoon."

"Four? Oh, dear, did I sleep so long?" It was too late to go to the agencies today.

"When one doesn't get to bed until eight in the morning, to sleep until after three is not unexpected." She glanced up at Françoise slyly. "Would Mademoiselle like a bath?"

Françoise cleared her throat. "Yes. Yes, that would be nice." Did Annette know?

Françoise bathed and dressed *en déshabillé*. Footmen appeared with boxes. Mademoiselle Fanchon had disobeyed Françoise's express order for two dresses only. She couldn't accept more, of course. Still, she might as well just look. Who could blame her for that?

Opening the boxes felt like she was Cinderella. Each held a new delight; a riding costume of green with gold braid *à la militaire, a* walking dress of navy meant to be worn with…yes, a red waistcoat. It was outrageous, and yet the good citizens could not complain because it was done in the colors of the French flag. Dress after dress, for morning, afternoon, or evening, outrageous, gorgeous, sinful delights all. Fanchon had forgotten nothing. There were stockings and chemises, and more than a dozen pairs of shoes; evening slippers, walking shoes, riding boots. Then there were the reticules, an evening cape, even a sun parasol.

Guilt washed over her. She would leave all but two behind. Perhaps they could be adjusted for Henri's next mistress. She swallowed hard. Mentally, she chose the walking

Time for Eternity

dress (without the waistcoat) and a morning dress with crisp black stripes on a cream ground. Those would do for making applications. She'd pay Henri back for them, somehow.

Annette cooed and exclaimed as she hung each dress. "Which will you wear tonight?"

Oh, dear. She couldn't wear a morning dress tonight. Well, one of the evening dresses then. Worn just once. She didn't know which one until she opened the last box.

It was white. But that was nearly the only thing virginal about it. It eschewed the fashionable hooped silhouette for a more natural line, and an abundance of bleached white lace in the overskirt. The underskirt was of satin, deep and lustrous. And it was hardly more discreet than last night's dress. An almost transparent scrap of fichu was meant to be tucked into the deep décolletage. Tight, elbow-length sleeves with lace cascades finished the look. White on white. Her gold hair and her blue eyes would provide the only color.

She stared at Annette.

"I'll just hang the creases out, shall I?" Annette murmured, her voice reverent. "Perhaps just touch up the lace with the lightest of irons."

"Yes." That would keep her busy. Just what Françoise needed, because she had work to do. She would not sleep another night with that dreadful leather case beneath her pillow. No wonder she was having bad dreams. She'd take that case and...

And what? She wanted to throw it away, burn it. But... a shudder coursed through her.

Damned, that's what you'll be.

She couldn't bring herself to do it. She'd put it somewhere safe instead.

Safe from what? From whom? Maybe from herself...

She reached under the bed and retrieved the case, checked its contents. She'd put it in the stables where it wouldn't disturb her sleep at least. She slipped out the back stairs to the mews while everyone was in a frenzy of preparation and put the bag behind a pile of straw bales.

Susan Squires

As she walked away she felt as though a weight had been lifted, even though uneasiness circled in her stomach. She was in a tangle somehow and she couldn't quite put her finger on what it was. True, she'd made love to the man who was her protector. And no one could protect her from being alone in the world. Certainly Henri had no intentions of doing that. That would take marriage, or him offering a carte blanche. One he'd never dream of doing. The other she'd never dream of accepting. Making love to Henri was an adventure. She believed that. Truly. That meant she was in no more of a tangle than she had been yesterday.

She'd just get through tonight and tomorrow she'd make her application at the agencies.

She felt lost that afternoon. There was nothing anyone would let her do to help. Henri was nowhere to be seen, though Jean was kept scurrying with letters issuing from his master's room to be delivered posthaste. So she retreated to the library. The duc had not only Mr. Fielding's works in English but the scandalous Choderlos de Laclos's *Les Liaisons Dangereuses,* in French. Françoise didn't dare address the latter. It would only remind her of her own situation or get her remembering the fevers of last night. So she chose *Tom Jones* instead.

It was nearly seven when Annette bustled into the room, her hair flying in wisps around her head. Françoise had forgot herself enough to be laughing softy at Mr. Fielding's wry prose. That had apparently given away her location.

"Mademoiselle, I have been looking all over for you. *Mon Dieu,* but who knew you would be reading?" Annette appeared to think that was akin to eating worms. "Your dress, your hair…" She snatched the book, snapped it shut, and tossed it onto a table. "But hurry."

"There is no need of haste." She had heard Henri's parties from the tiny room under the rafters of the house next door often enough to know that they started late and ran until morning.

"His grace has called for dinner an hour early, which leaves…oh, dear…less than an hour." She gave a kind of wail.

"More than enough time," Françoise soothed as she

Time for Eternity

followed her into the back hall.

As they passed into the central entry, who should be coming down the stairs but Henri, wearing the most delightful burgundy silk dressing jacket? If possible, he looked even more the wicked duc in dark red. He surveyed the scene as the great central chandelier was raised in heaving gasps by three footmen pulling on a rope. The candles had all been lit. The crystal glittered. Annette froze, eyes downcast apparently eager to avoid the duc's attention.

Henri raised his quizzing glass and surveyed Françoise. "I wondered where you were."

How unlike him! "I was reading. You were right about *Tom Jones.*"

His eyes crinkled at the corners. "Amazing. I was correct about something."

"Do…do you think we'll be ready?" she asked, just to have something to say.

"I have no idea."

Gaston chose that moment to hurry into the foyer, carrying a stack of silver serving trays that gleamed. He was obviously frazzled. He stopped at Henri's comment. "When have we not been ready to entertain, your grace?" His voice was more an accusation than a question.

"Never, else you would not still be in my employ."

Gaston hurried off, muttering to himself about ducs who had no faith in the talents of their staff. He was wrong. Françoise knew Henri had ultimate faith in Gaston.

The chandelier was duly tied off and the footmen scurried away. Henri turned his glass back on her. "Are you well?"

Françoise flushed. "Yes." Last night was best forgotten. But of course he didn't mention it. Not in front of Annette and the scurrying servants.

"You do intend to dress for dinner?"

Oh, dear. "I was just on my way."

"Ah." He reached into the breast pocket of his jacket and withdrew a little upholstered box. "In that case, you will

Susan Squires

need these."

Françoise blinked. The box was long, padded with red velvet.

"Aren't you even going to look?"

She cleared her throat. "Of course." This could be bad.

She flicked open the little clasp and took a breath. This was very bad. Gleaming softly in the box was a necklace of delicate pearls. A larger pearl drop hung from the strand in the center from a short link of diamonds. A matching bracelet of two strings of small pearls was fastened with a diamond clasp. Small pearl drop earrings and some hairpins attached to pearls completed the set. The pearls glowed with a satin luster. The tiny diamonds glittered. She had never touched such expensive jewelry. He couldn't buy her these.

Henri cleared his throat. "I...I noticed that you had pierced ears."

Françoise tried to say something. She had noticed that he had silver specks in his eyes. But she couldn't say that.

"I...I trust they go with the dress Fanchon provided for tonight?"

Françoise tore her gaze from the pearls. "How did you know? The dress was just delivered this afternoon."

He shrugged. "She has taste. She would choose white for you on such an occasion. With your hair, your eyes, your skin...well, she would choose white."

"She did," Françoise whispered. She shook her head.

"Don't say you won't accept them," Henri interrupted. "I want everyone to know tonight that...that I value you. They must not question that you are under my protection."

Françoise bowed her head. "Thank you." He might have declared her his ward on a whim, but he didn't have to give her pearls. To refuse them would be churlish. But she would be certain to leave them behind when she left.

"Trumpery things. Not even diamonds enough to mention." He cleared his throat again. "Dine at eight?"

A small, strangled sound came from Annette. Françoise smiled. "I'd better go."

Henri nodded and turned on his heel, heading back up

Time for Eternity
the stairs without another word.

Susan Squires

Thirteen

Annette was a miracle worker. Françoise descended the stairway to the small dining room no more than five minutes after eight. She was nervous. The people who would be here tonight were so far above her in station. And she was inherently an imposter. It was some comfort that this was the best she had ever looked. The dress was perfect. The pearls were not ostentatious in comparison to what other women of Henri's set would be wearing, yet obviously expensive.

Avignon was staring into the grate in the dining room, even though it held no fire. She had resolved to give up his first name. She had no right to use it. And it recalled an intimacy she must forget. He looked up at her entrance. He blinked. Twice. And then he seemed to find himself and smiled. She liked the fact that he blinked.

"Fanchon has outdone herself." He gestured to a seat at the table and held out her chair.

"So have you. The pearls are lovely. I wonder how you managed to procure them in daylight, and when?" He seated her and moved to the sideboard. "I patronize Coulet. He opens his establishment at night for me. I saw them a few weeks ago. It occurred to me today that they would be perfect for you. So I sent a footman for them."

He'd seen them when he was buying jewels for someone else. Someone who was not his ward. She wouldn't think about that. "You trust a footman with so much money?" He was choosing food for her plate.

"Coulet trusts me to address his invoice when it is presented."

He lived a different life than she did.

He set her plate in front of her. It was such an intimate gesture, serving her without the aid of servants. And this was the third time he'd done it. He poured her some claret and

Time for Eternity

turned to his own plate. "I have been thinking. I must insist you go abroad—at least while revolutionary fervor rules France. One of my ships is leaving at the end of the week for England."

"We've been through that. Without friends or money, England is no better than France."

"You would have money."

There it was. She swallowed. Her mouth was dry. "I won't be kept by you."

He stilled. His back was to her. She saw his shoulders sag, ever so slightly. But when he turned, his plate full, his voice was light. "What kind of a protector would I be if I let my ward live in such a dangerous place as France or in England without resources?"

That's what she was, his ward. Was he denying what had happened between them last night? Evidently. That was what she wanted. Wasn't it?

"We'll talk again at the end of the week," he said, realizing apparently that pressing her would not bring results. He was preparing to move on to more innocuous topics.

She couldn't let him. "I w-want you to know that last night, while a fine adventure, won't be repeated." She had to get it straight between them.

"A sad lapse." He shrugged. "For both of us. You needn't fear I'll importune you further."

And that was that. He whiled away dinner talking about the people she would see tonight and what they were to France then or France now.

"At least Monsieur Robespierre and Madame Croûte will not be here," she managed. "I find those two frightening."

"I'd wager a set of sapphires to match those pearls they will arrive early and stay late."

"At one of your soirées? It's contrary to everything they believe in."

"When beliefs are in conflict with one's emotions, emotions always win."

"But why would they want to come?"

"Ahhh. Robespierre would not. But Madame Croûte? I

think she craves what has been denied her. She is stronger than Robespierre. And more emotional, therefore more dangerous."

Françoise widened her eyes. She felt so young. And yet another part of her, the part that recognized the truth of what he said, didn't feel young at all. "You're right. They'll come. I wonder what she'll wear?"

Avignon smiled and raised his eyes to the ceiling. "Let's see. Aubergine, I think. Just dustier than royal purple, which is what she'd like to wear. Too much jewelry, too much lace."

"You are severe. I'd better look to my lace." She cast a glance to her dress.

"Your lace is where lace ought to be. Hers won't be. You'll see what I mean." He examined her. "Are you nervous?"

"No. Yes."

"You needn't be."

"I am an imposter." She couldn't seem to raise her voice above a whisper.

He chuckled. "It doesn't matter. They don't dare question because they want what I can give them."

"That doesn't change what I am. They'll talk."

"Let them." His dark eyes burned. "You are of aristocratic blood. Half in the room respect that, misguided as that may be. The other half knows that blood is blood and yours is as red as anyone else's. Either way, you'll be fine." He lifted his glass of wine and held it, waiting.

She looked into those eyes for a moment, wondering if she knew him, if she had ever really known him. He was just like his eyes, a flat surface with hidden depths. He had more secrets than just being a smuggler, she was sure of it. Was everything she'd ever thought about him even remotely true? The feeling flooding her was just the opposite of déjà vu. She'd done all this before, but it seemed different now. She saw it with new eyes.

Am I the fool, or you, Françoise?

The voice. It was unnatural. The fear of madness flashed through her again. She shook herself. This whole situation was ridiculous. Of course she'd never known him. She'd met him four days ago. If she ignored the voice it would go away. She lifted her glass.

He clinked his glass with hers. "Enjoy tonight, *ma petite*."

Her mind darted between Robespierre and Madame Croûte, Madame LaFleur's death that seemed fated, the dreadful bag with its even more dreadful contents, and the feeling of urgency inside her. How could she enjoy a party?

*****

"May I present my ward, Mademoiselle Suchet?" Avignon's baritone introduced her for what seemed the hundredth time. The gentleman bowing over her hand was portly and avuncular. His wig smelled of rancid oil mixed with powder under the perfume.

"My dear, do say you will save me a dance this evening." He was…a general, Avignon had said. Still, dancing with him might be bad for her toes.

She mustered a smile. "It would be my pleasure."

"A treasure, Avignon," the florid-faced general said, *sotto voce*, as though she weren't standing right in front of him.

"One I hold close, Digne. Remember that." Avignon's voice sounded bored, but Digne shot him a piercing glance. He wasn't fooled any more than Françoise was. Avignon was much less bored than he pretended. The general moved into the room beyond.

The orchestra sat in the little balcony provided for musicians that hung over the hall. It wasn't as grand as the Hall of Mirrors at Versailles but it held a hundred easily. A very young man came up and bowed. She extended her hand and he kissed it, a trifle too fervently.

"My eyes, they are smitten. My heart, it bleeds." He tore his smitten eyes away. "Monsieur le Duc, I must know this angel's name."

Avignon steadied his lips. "Mademoiselle Françoise

Suchet. My ward."

"Oh, that I should be allowed to offer her my protection."

Patently absurd, since he was so young. Of course, Avignon was really too young to be her protector either. A fact she'd seen registered on several faces tonight.

"Mademoiselle, may I present Monsieur Besset? Monsieur is one of the Revolution's most potent orators. He will want a dance, I'm sure."

"But yes! That I should be so smiled upon by fortune—"

"Yes, yes, of course," Françoise interrupted. For there, coming through the doorway were Monsieur Robespierre and Madame Croûte. It was still early.

Avignon had been right—about everything. They'd come. And Madame Croûte had sought to dazzle. Cascades of off-white lace over aubergine silk, lace flounces, lace ruffles in the neckline, a lace fichu. She even affected a lace mantilla in the Spanish style over a tortoiseshell comb set in her ridiculously high, powdered wig. The cream and aubergine was unfortunate with her ruddy complexion. Her neck was practically weighed down with amethysts. Her expression reminded Françoise of a vulture trying to be regal. Surely Avignon was wrong about her being stronger and more dangerous than Robespierre.

*****

Marta Croûte surveyed the crowd that talked and laughed and clinked their glasses under the magnificent chandeliers in number sixteen's ballroom. They had found nothing at the warehouse. But that didn't mean it wasn't Foucault who was carrying out these blatant escapes. It was their duty to be here tonight, to catch him out. That's what she had told Robespierre. It wasn't that she had a fancy to see a ball given by Foucault. She had, in truth, felt a bit intimidated by the occasion. But the house was only in the Marais. All the real aristocrats lived in the Faubourg St. Germain. Foucault had nothing to brag about with his address.

The crowd was half old aristocracy and half stalwarts of the Revolution. Only Foucault could have drawn such a *mélange* together. She saw several glance toward her and her dourly dressed and diminutive lawyer companion. The eyes of the aristocrats disdained her. But she saw fear bloom there too. A little thrill shot down her spine. They'd better be afraid.

She had made sure she had nothing to be ashamed of tonight. She tugged surreptitiously on the lace at her sleeves. She had more lace than any of them and more jewels—only amethysts, to be sure, but that was what matched her dress. She assessed the crystal, the gold plate, well enough to be sure. But the furniture was old, like it was in the salon in which she had met Foucault before. Not in the latest style at all, and the woven and embroidered hangings portraying some battle or other in the room where she had laid her evening cape were positively threadbare in spots. She smiled, a little smugly. Perhaps Foucault had to smuggle to support his gambling and his whores.

"Ahhh, my so dear representatives of the very spirit of the Revolution," the man himself greeted them. He was dressed exquisitely. There could be no <u>mistaking</u> that. And he was beautiful. More handsome by far than Robespierre. His newest whore was by his side. "You know my ward, of course. Mademoiselle Suchet." He gestured languidly to the girl, who dipped her curtsy. "How delightful that you could honor this humble abode. Perhaps you'd like to search for escaped prisoners? I open my house to your hunt, of course."

Robespierre flushed. "These escapes are a damned serious business, Foucault."

"Dear me. Do they continue? How...lax of the army."

"Not for a week or so, except for the old woman. They are spirited out," the little man said, watching Avignon. "By the time we hear the screams, it is too late."

"Screams. Dear me." Avignon's shudder was feigned, Marta was sure. "But my so dear Madame said that it is families who escape. Surely after the first member is taken you can watch the rest of the family and prevent their following."

"The guards are incompetent," Marta interjected. "They must be incompetent because even under torture they do not admit to taking bribes. And torture breaks everyone." She knew that well by now.

Robespierre glared at her then clamped his mouth shut. What was he on about? That she talked of torture at a party?

"It sounds supernatural to me," Avignon confided. "Ghosts, perhaps. The ghosts of Danton and Desmoulins." Robespierre flushed again. He'd never been secure about weeding out the first leaders of the Revolution, but they had not been nearly resolute enough to take it forward. Marta knew they had had to go. "I don't believe in the supernatural, Citizen," Marta said firmly. "There is an explanation and we will find it, *and* the one or ones who are flaunting justice."

"Justice..." Avignon mused. "One must serve justice. Being a devotee of Voltaire requires no less."

"Strange that we agree, Foucault." Robespierre's eyes narrowed.

"Enough of Voltaire. I have come to see this...ward...of yours." Marta examined Françoise. She couldn't help but frown. The girl was...lovely. It galled Marta to say so. The dress had less lace than Marta's own, but there was something about it...the drape of the fabric... Marta wasn't sure what. All she knew was that Foucault's whore insulted them all by wearing white. "Well, she's dressed better than she was the other day."

"My ward dresses like a woman of the people when the occasion allows, as she did the day of the fire. Surely you cannot quibble with that, Madame." Foucault raised his quizzing glass. "As your own dress proclaims your admiration of the Citizen style."

Shock washed over Marta. He...he was insulting her taste. She had no desire at all to look like an ordinary citizen tonight and he knew it. The hate that welled up from her belly sent bile into her throat She stood there, speechless, unable to think of a retort, getting angrier. The blasted man looked only bored and that just enraged her the more.

196

Time for Eternity

"Marta, come," Robespierre said. "I see St Denis." He took her arm and she shook him off. But she stomped away, her lips grim.

*****

"You shouldn't have done that," Françoise whispered to Henri.

"What I should do is claim the first dance with my ward before I lose you to the bevy of fools to whom you've promised yourself." Actually, Henri wondered if she knew how to dance. Had that spinster aunt thought to provide for her social education? He should have asked earlier. Perhaps that was why she seemed to dread this evening. But she didn't demur as he raised his hand to the musicians. They struck up a minuet and couples began to form sets. He took her hand. The shock of touching her had not diminished. He must make the assemblage believe her his ward, no more, in spite of the feelings she raised in him, no matter his resolve. Dancing with her must look like an obligation.

That was onerous, when all he wanted was to take her in his arms and ravish her mouth with kisses. For all her dress was white, Fanchon had captured the fact that she was not quite an innocent. Would anyone notice? What they couldn't miss was that she was by far the most beautiful woman in the room. Françoise was right. There would be talk. He schooled his face as he led her to the head of the line of couples. He wouldn't make it worse.

As it turned out, she was a lovely dancer, graceful, her movement slightly sinuous. *Mon Dieu* but she fascinated him. The very reason she was off to England as soon as the ship came in. He'd start filling up the warehouse with families this very night if he could get his guests out before dawn. His cargo would be safe now that the Croûte woman had searched the warehouse.

He'd think about his work and not those blue eyes looking up at him. He saw her searching his face as they came together in the figure of the dance. She was uncertain of him. Afraid? Yes. No. He wasn't sure. All he knew was that she was holding herself away from him inside. He'd felt it ever since the ride home in the carriage from Versailles.

That was good. It was what he wanted too.

So why did it feel so damned bad?

The dance drew to a close. Couples parted. He was about to escort her for refreshments when their progress was blocked by one of the young men hovering about the edge of the room.

"M-mademoiselle," the young cub stuttered. "M-may I have this d-dance?"

"Go," he said, shushing her away. "This is the last I'll see of you tonight."

And it was, nearly. Henri drank old burgundy from his cellars and talked with his guests, all the while watching her out of the corner of his eye as she made conquest after conquest. He couldn't even take refuge in the card room since he must be seen to chaperone her.

It put him in a foul mood.

He resolved that he was *not* going to watch her. He deliberately turned his back. No one would dare make love to her in the house of her protector when that protector was Satan.

Unfortunately, the conversation group he had turned into contained the general, Madame Croûte, and Robespierre, among others.

They were talking politics, the "spirit of the Revolution." What an ordeal. The only positive was that they were all too engrossed in making their points to take notice of him.

All except Madame Croûte. She changed places with the general to stand beside him.

"I am surprised, Citizen, to see that you watch your 'ward' so closely tonight. It is almost as if you could not take your eyes off her." Croûte's eyes were worthy of a basilisk.

"This social situation is new to her. Someone might take advantage of her inexperience."

"I'd wager you're the only one to do that."

Henri made his face a mask. "Even the devil has limits." But she was right. That was just what he had done.

"I suspect the only thing beyond you is being her protector. As if she needed one. The creature is twenty if she's a day."

"I consider that very young." She didn't know how young that seemed to one of his kind.

Madame Croûte gave a chuckle worthy of a devil herself. "She's got you in thrall, Citizen, the conniving creature. She'll be your downfall." She turned away before he could respond. "You are wrong, Citizens," she said to the group at large. "Voltaire is more relevant than ever."

*****

"No, no, monsieur," Françoise gasped, laughing. "I cannot, I assure you."

"Then let me take you for some air." The lovely man was not as young as the others. What had Avignon said about him? Yes, he was impoverished aristocracy of some kind. A vicomte? Yes. That was it. She liked him. But still he seemed very young.

"I think I should not go out on the balcony with you, Monsieur le Vicomte."

"So proper." He sighed. With apparent reluctance, he handed her to a chair in an out-of-the-way corner. "Then let me be your slave, and procure you some refreshment." Françoise watched him walk away. Flirting with him felt strangely flat.

"So this is why Henri has been too busy to see me." Françoise jerked her attention to the woman who had suddenly appeared at her elbow. She was tiny, exquisitely dressed in red satin, with a chandelier's worth of diamonds nestling in her ample cleavage. Not in the first blush of youth, she was like a rose still beautiful but just past its prime, its petals beginning to curl.

"I'm s-sorry?" Françoise stuttered.

"Marianne Vercheroux. And no, Henri did not introduce

us." She flipped open a delicately painted fan with ivory sticks and slowly waved it back and forth as she studied Françoise. "In fact, I doubt he knows I'm here."

"I'm certain he would welcome you if he knew." Françoise took refuge in politeness.

The woman laughed, a throaty contralto. "A man never welcomes a former mistress." She raked her gaze over Françoise. "I wasn't quite certain I was 'former' until now."

Françoise blushed. "Whatever you think, Madame, you are wrong."

"I saw the way he looked at you. He hasn't taken his eyes off you all night."

Françoise glanced over to where Avignon stood in a group, his back to her. "He isn't looking now."

"He knew he was making a fool of himself and had to force himself to look away."

"I am his ward. He has been very kind to me." But even as Françoise said it, she felt the flush coming on again. She couldn't hide from the sharp brown eyes examining her so critically.

"I'm sure." Madame Vercheroux looked over at Avignon and pursed her lips. When she looked back, her eyes were hard. "I'll wager you think that's love. But it's your youth he craves. With him, it's never love, only lust. He's thrown over a dozen women to my knowledge and moved on without a backward glance. There's a reason they call him the devil. No one gets close to his heart." She laughed again. "I'd love to think you were a calculating latch, but you're not. More's the pity. He'll hurt you, the callous bastard, if you let him. So here's advice from one who knows. Don't let him. Take him for all he's worth. But don't let him take your heart."

Without waiting for a reply, she turned and sauntered toward the door.

Françoise stood staring after her for a long moment. Then she turned to where she'd last seen Avignon. He was looking right at her. He strode across the room, overtaking the vicomte who was wending his way through the crowd with two cups of champagne punch. Avignon took the cups with a murmured dismissal and bore down on Françoise.

He handed her a cup. "And what did the so *chère* Madame Vercheroux have to say?"

"She says you're the devil," Françoise whispered. Avignon's lips took a rueful turn. "Ahhh. Then nothing you didn't already know."

*****

The last of the guests included Robespierre and Madame Croûte, as well as the vicomte and several others. Henri ushered them out the door at near dawn.

Françoise was asleep in a chair in the hall near the ladies' retiring room. Poor chit. She'd done well. It had been an exhausting evening for her, but she was gracious and witty, and had captivated almost everyone but Madame Croûte, Robespierre, and Vercheroux. He'd give a good deal to know what that woman had really said to Françoise. It didn't matter of course. He had no business trying to get the girl's good opinion. And she'd be off to England within the week.

"Françoise." She showed no signs of waking. He took her shoulder. She waved him away with a little moan but without opening her eyes.

So he lifted her into his arms and carried her upstairs. Her head dropped onto his shoulder. Cradling her against his chest, he wanted to keep her safe from the world and what it could do to one's soul. But his desire to protect her did not dampen his desire for her. The heat of her body against his made his genitals tighten. Dear God. Did he have no control at all? And he'd made love to her to the point of satiation just last night.

But apparently he wasn't satiated. Maybe he'd never be able to get enough of her.

Which was why she had to go.

He pushed open the door to her room with his foot and laid her on the turned-down bed. Her maid peeped in from the dressing room, rubbing sleep from her eyes.

Susan Squires

"See to her," he ordered, his voice rougher than he planned.

And he made his escape. He had lists to make and plans to lay if he was going to fill a ship with families before the week was out.

Fourteen

"You're keeping his nighttime hours and falling in love with him," the voice accused. "Yet you won't let me out to take control and protect you."

The voice was so clear. Where was it coming from?

The stable in the mews behind the house.

She tiptoed through the deserted house and out into the bright sun. How long since she had seen the sun? She darted across the carriageway and slid through the doors into the dimness beyond. No one was about here either. She could hardly see after the bright morning outside. The stable was lit only by the thin channel of light from the door behind her. But beyond that knife blade of sunshine, all was darkness. Horses moved in their stalls, blowing softly. The stables smelled of hay and oiled leather.

Someone was in the stable with her. It would be the owner of the voice.

Fear rushed through her. But she had to know who owned that voice and what made it so clear inside her head. It was all she could do to stand there, waiting.

Slowly, her eyes adjusted to the darkness. A figure moved out from behind the last stall. From the place where Françoise had hidden the leather bag full of sharp shiny steel and strange-smelling liquid in soft bottles. It was a small figure. A woman?

"You are in terrible danger," the voice said. It was clear the voice came from the figure for she could see the shadowy lips moving, but it echoed inside her brain as well. "Let me help you," the voice said. "You must do as I say."

The figure walked forward. Françoise began to tremble.

"I've lived what will happen if you don't." The figure was still in shadows. The outline of the woman was…familiar.

"What will happen?" Françoise breathed.
"You'll lose your soul and burn in hell for eternity."
That sounded melodramatic.

"But true," the woman said as if she could read Françoise's thoughts. The figure walked forward. "You know what you must do. I know you do. You must kill him."

And the figure walked into a channel of light. The face was hers.

*****

Françoise jerked upright with a gasp, emotions making her heart pound in her chest. What kind of a dream was that? She felt full to overflowing. There wasn't room in her chest to breathe. The voice telling her to kill Henri was her own.

A nightmare. Just a nightmare. Nightmares didn't make sense. So it was not a problem that a voice she'd been hearing quite clearly lately turned out to be herself. Better she talk to herself than that she hear other people inside her head. It made her less mad, didn't it? But she was telling herself to kill Henri? How could that be? She would never kill anybody. Especially not Henri. And never with drugs and decapitation with a sword, for goodness' sake.

Nothing about this was real. She had to cling to that.

Except the leather bag and its ominous contents. That was real.

She was *not* going to kill Henri. The only way he could damn her soul was if love for him festered in her, knowing he didn't love her back. But she wasn't going to fall in love with him. She'd made love to him. That was different. A lark, an adventure. She wouldn't take back that night at Versailles for the world. But how could she love a care-for-nothing smuggler? The voice was wrong about that.

But *was* he a care-for-nothing? He had tried to save Madame LaFleur. He had said the benediction over her. That had been kind. Or maybe it had just been expedient, to get Françoise to stop importuning him. In that case why didn't he just throw Françoise out on her ear? Why did he buy her

204

clothes and jewels and introduce her to his friends to make certain all knew she had his protection? Why did he bother?

Maybe because he wanted to give her a carte blanche.

Well, she wasn't going to accept a carte blanche from Henri. No, Avignon. She wasn't going to call him Henri anymore, even in her mind. And she wasn't going to kill him with that sword either. She'd just leave. As she'd planned. She'd find a situation and go.

She got up and went to the window. The sun was high. It must be early afternoon. Plenty of time to present herself at the agencies. She had to believe she'd find a suitable situation.

But somewhere inside she felt that it was useless to hope. She'd done all this before and it had been useless.

*****

"You've forgotten to complete the section on references." The dour-faced woman sitting behind the desk adjusted her spectacles and frowned at Françoise over them.

Well, there was the problem, wasn't it? There were really only three reputable placement agencies left in Paris, and the other two had already refused to even accept an application without references. Françoise swallowed. All she could do was try to explain a third time.

"I did not forget. I…I have good references. But they are not available for consultation."

"What do you mean…not available?" The interviewer frowned.

Françoise gathered her wits. "Well, Lady Toumoult, sister of the Marquis d'Evron, has unfortunately passed on. The marquis and his remaining family emigrated." Let this woman think she had served the family. "And my latest employer, Madame LaFleur, died just Sunday. That's why I'm applying for another position."

"Well, we really don't have a call for ladies' companions these days." The woman looked pointedly at Françoise's walking dress. Françoise blushed. She had realized

Susan Squires

at the first agency that Fanchon's creation was much too stylish for a servant. But Fanchon's dresses were all she had. "You are too young to teach children. Obviously not a maid. And with no references, I can hardly…"

Françoise felt a little swirl of panic in her throat. Avignon had been right. But if she couldn't find a situation, she couldn't support herself. She'd be dependent upon Avignon. And if she couldn't escape Avignon, something dire would happen to her. Or maybe she would go mad entirely and do something dire to him instead.

She took a breath and plunged ahead with the only piece of information that might sway her interlocutor, for better or for worse. "I…I have been working in the Duc d'Avignon's household since Sunday." Well, maybe not working, but it was only a small lie. "He lives next door to Madame LaFleur's house, and kindly took me in when Madame died. Of course, it's a bachelor's household, so I can't remain there." She dared not offer him directly as a reference.

The woman chewed her lip. "A bachelor's household. Hardly suitable. Still…the Duc d'Avignon is extremely…"

Françoise would never know what the woman would have said.

At her back a familiar voice said, "Excuse me, mademoiselle, but his grace is waiting for you in the carriage."

She turned to see Jean bowing, his face totally impassive.

Avignon had found her.

"I'll just conclude my business here, Jean, and be right out. Thank you." It was amazing she could make her voice sound calm.

Jean took a breath as if to say something, thought better of it, and turned on his heel. "Very good, mademoiselle."

Françoise watched him retreat, his black uniform trimmed with gold braid causing quite a stir among the motley throng crowded into the applications room. Anyone there would have killed to be a paid member of Avignon's household. Anyone but Françoise.

She turned back to the representative of the agency.

"I'm sorry for the interruption."

"Well," the woman said, raising her brows, "if you are important enough that the duc sends his carriage…" She glanced to Françoise. "Did he say the duc was *waiting* in the carriage for you?"

"He did." This time the voice was baritone.

Oh, dear. The smell of cinnamon and ambergris wafted over the room. She turned. Avignon was squinting against the light from the open door, and his face was turning pink. But his appearance was, as always, impeccable, dressed in black from head to foot except for the white froth of linen and lace at his throat and wrists. The gold of a signet ring and a quizzing glass hanging from an enormous black button on his coat were the only color on his person.

He lifted the quizzing glass to his eye and surveyed the low-ceilinged room. Everyone in it stepped back a pace. "What, may I ask, is my ward doing in such an establishment?"

"Your ward?" the woman behind the desk squeaked. "Oh, excuse me, your grace. I did not know she was your ward. She was looking for a position as a companion to an older lady."

"Ahhh. A lark no doubt on her part." He turned his glass on Françoise. She couldn't help but squirm. "But entirely inappropriate." He turned back to the woman taking applications. "I'm certain you would not insult my ward by actually offering her such a position." He did not wait for an answer but stepped to the side and motioned Françoise ahead of him. "Come, child."

This was uttered so firmly Françoise found herself obeying whether she would or no. And it didn't matter. The woman behind her believed Avignon a powerful person, Revolution or not. She would never chance offending him. *If* she believed Françoise was only his ward. And if she believed Françoise was something more (or less) than his ward, she would never place her in a respectable household.

Françoise sighed. Avignon put a hand on the small of her back (protectively? possessively?) and guided her to the door.

As they pushed out into the afternoon sunshine, she heard his breath hiss. He hurried her to the carriage. Jean had no time to leap down from where he sat beside the coachman. Avignon ripped open the door and practically pushed her up into the carriage. He climbed in after her, banging the door shut. The shades were down. She could hardly make him out in the gloom. Was his face blistered? He was *that* sensitive to light? A stab of guilt shot through her. He'd come out in the afternoon sunlight to look for her.

His own fault. Your affairs are none of his business. Listen to me. You must—

The voice again. She shook her head to shut it out.

Avignon pushed himself into the opposite corner where he was obscured in shadows. "What did you think you were doing in there?" His voice was thick.

"Trying to find a position. And now you've prevented me from ever getting a situation by telling them I'm your ward. Which no one believed." She knew her tone was huffy.

"I'm sure that wasn't the only agency you visited."

"It was not." She took a breath and let it out. There was no use lying to him. "They found my lack of references a problem."

"I expect they would. Just as well." He sounded better now.

Her eyes were growing used to the darkness. She peered at him. She must have been mistaken about the blisters. His face wasn't blistered at all. Just pink, a little. No, it wasn't even pink. It must have been the lighting in the employment agency that made her think so.

She resolved not to speak to him again. How would she get through dinner?

What was she thinking? Her problem wasn't dinner, but how in the world she would support herself. With no friends, no references… And if she didn't take his money, it would be the same in England. But if she did take it he would never be out of her life. And something very bad would happen to her.

The feeling of urgency inside her was almost painful.

208

Time for Eternity

That something was about to happen. She mustn't let it. But she knew very well that the voice (the voice that absolutely wasn't her—was it?) wanted her to… to try to kill him. She couldn't do that of course. What did that leave? She *had* to get him out of her life.

A bleak feeling descended on her. She wanted him gone. Didn't she?

*****

As it turned out she didn't have to get through dinner. She came down, dressed in one of Fanchon's evening dresses, at nine sharp, and found him at the street door. He carried a snuffbox and a large black silk handkerchief.

"*Au revoir,* my aggrieved one. You will have to save any choice words you have planned until later. I am promised to Revientot for dinner this evening. Then it's on to the tables."

All the man apparently did was gamble. Or consort with women like Madame Vercheroux. What did that say about him? He waved languidly as he went out the door.

*****

Four families in one night. Twenty people including that baby. Quite a haul. He'd almost been caught. But what could he do? With babies, he had to take extra care, bring them under his power, prevent them, through the power of suggestions, from feeling the pain of translocation. It took time. They'd barely made it out. But now the whole lot of them were secreted in the rooms behind the back wall of the warehouse. Jennings would take care of them for the next few days. He'd visit when he could to reassure them.

Henri walked across the park in the center of the Place Royale toward number sixteen under a lightening sky as the city began to wake. He was tired. Transporting himself, and one and sometimes two, others so many times in one night sapped his Companion's strength. The days ahead would be a

Susan Squires

strain. He had not much time to fill the warehouse.

The *Maiden Voyage* would arrive in Le Havre from Portsmouth on Sunday. A day to unload. He must have everyone he'd managed to rescue on the barge and ready to float down the Seine to meet her on Saturday night. They could be away Monday.

The girl wouldn't want to go. She wouldn't take his money. He'd arrange with Jennings to set her up.

Why not go with her? An image flashed through his head of an English country manor in Kent, a cozy fire burning in the grate, her head in his lap as he read to her.

Get hold of yourself, man. He was vampire, for God's sake. She was not. The minute she found out what he was, she'd leave him. If she didn't commit suicide, that is.

I haven't been bored lately.

The thought occurred unbidden, unanticipated. Since she'd come into his life he'd seen the world in a new light. Through her eyes. The trip to Versailles was a revelation; her wonder, the freshness of picnicking in the Hall of Mirrors, making love in the king's bedchamber.

Merde. He'd fallen in love with her.

He stopped at the edge of the park and leaned against a tree. Was he insane? How long since he had been in love? Four hundred years? No wonder he hadn't recognized it. But now that he considered, he could see all the telltale signs. Wanting to be with her. Wanting to protect her. A small trickle of belief that she might be able to save his soul by making his life seem bearable.

Well, this had to be nipped in the bud. She must never know. She would be appalled. She considered him the wicked duc. Making love with him was an adventure to her. Nothing more.

Good. That was good. He pushed himself off the tree and started across the street.

All this meant was another chip in the carapace that he had built around his soul. It would hold. He had his work. He could probably avoid her until Saturday. Then he would bundle her aboard the barge that would take her to the *Maiden Voyage* and get back to work.

He managed a saunter as he approached number sixteen. The door opened and the day footman ushered him in. He went straight to his room, banished Drummond by saying, to that gentleman's amazement, that he would change himself, and bolted the door.

****

Last batch tonight. Good thing. It was perhaps four in the morning. Henri's strength was seriously depleted, even though he'd slept like the dead all today, eaten like a horse at a tavern, and taken a cup of blood from a tavern wench. He slid along the familiar corridors of the Con- ciergerie, a black silk scarf tied about his neck and up over his nose to hide his white lace cravat and his face, the white lace at his wrists tucked up his sleeves. The place was swarming with guards since the screams that indicated an escape had been echoing through the corridors all night. He was forced to draw his power quickly and master many minds at once. And of course there was the extra time he had to take with the children. The whole thing was getting difficult.

He slid up behind the guard outside the cell that held the Rideaux family. The captain had taken to putting families in private cells to better guard them. He motioned to the man holding the bars, for silence, and watched hope bloom in the gaunt face. Rideaux's wife, two boys early in their second decade and an older girl, were huddled in the corner, their eyes big.

The guard heard Henri at the last second and turned to face him. Henri called his Companion. The world was washed with crimson. "You will remember nothing," he whispered.

"Watch out!" Rideaux hissed.

It was too late. A sword found Henri's shoulder as he whirled. Where had this one come from? Henri didn't draw his sword. He just locked his gaze into the man's eyes. The guard's sword clanked to the stone floor as the man stood there, wavering.

Henri put a hand to his shoulder. The wound was deep. It would heal, but he couldn't chance infecting the Rideaux family with his blood.

"Fear not," he said to Rideaux, his eyes still red. "I'll be back tomorrow night for you."

The man's face went blank. He nodded.

Henri heard the gallop of many feet. *Companion!* he called silently. Darkness whirled up and engulfed him. The familiar pain swept through him.

He materialized in the mews behind number sixteen and staggered in through the servant's entrance to avoid leaving a trail of blood to his front door. At the back door that blood might have come from a beefsteak or a chicken. Stumbling through the kitchen, he surprised the cook's boy lighting fires for the coming day. Did his kitchen staff rise so early? Henri leaned on the butcher block and grinned conspiratorially. "Little the worse for wear tonight." As if that would explain the master of the house using the servants' entrance. The lad's eyes widened, but he pulled his forelock in the ancient gesture of obeisance.

Henri pushed through, up the stairs, into his rooms.

Drummond would not be expecting him so early. That was good. He stripped off his coat. Blood had soaked through the waistcoat. His shirt was drenched with it. The wound would cost him strength. He'd need to feed again before he tried for the Rideaux family tomorrow. He unbuttoned his waistcoat and pulled off his shirt. Striding to the dressing table mirror, he examined his shoulder. Hurt like the devil, but it was already healing. He poured a basin of water and ran a washcloth over his chest to clean off the blood. Then he dumped the basin out the window.

A knock sounded at the door.

"Not now," he barked.

He pulled on a silk dressing jacket from the wardrobe. The knock was not repeated, but he hadn't heard steps retreating down the corridor.

The door opened, and Gaston presented himself with a

Time for Eternity

bow. He had dressed hastily.

Henri froze. "Well. This is interesting. You've disobeyed a direct order."

Gaston's eyes slipped to the pile of bloody clothes. "The cook's boy got me out of bed to tell me your grace left a bloody handprint on the butcher block. I dismissed him for the day and came to see if your grace needed assistance."

He could turn this to advantage. "Duels," he sighed. "But what can you do with a challenge direct? Especially when the man is in the right. Since you are here regardless of my wishes, you may dispose of those." He sighed and pointed to the bloody shirt and waistcoat.

Gaston blanched. "Shall I summon a physician?"

He frowned as though Gaston could not be that stupid. "Not *my* blood. What could one do but lift his head in spite of the danger to one's toilette? The man was gurgling." He did not need to ask for Gaston's discretion. Dueling was a capital crime. It was considered an aristocratic way of settling disputes.

Gaston bowed crisply and retrieved the ruined clothing. "I shall burn them."

"Excellent." Gaston turned to go. "And Gaston?"

"Your grace?"

"I will pass on this disobedience. I shall not pass on another."

"Very good, your grace."

By the time Henri had had two glasses of brandy and was ready to retire, the wound in his shoulder was only a pink weal. Soon even that would be gone. The sun would be up in another hour. He needed rest. He rose from the wing chair. He'd go to bed a little early.

A commotion downstairs was followed by hurried steps in the hallway. One set, followed immediately by several others. This was not propitious.

A brief knock sounded. "Come in." Poor Gaston. He'd taken the rebuke to heart. Those behind him would not have knocked.

Susan Squires

Gaston poked his head in. "Your grace ..."

The door was shoved open and Robespierre, Madame Croûte, and several uniformed soldiers pushed into the room. "Where were you last night?" Robespierre barked.

"Here, there...the usual haunts." Henri sipped his brandy.

Françoise scooted up through the guards. Damn. Was this going to be a public trial?

"What is the matter?" she asked. He could see fear in her eyes. She was afraid he would be arrested just like her former employer.

"We're apparently receiving visitors at a very odd hour." He smiled to reassure her. "Perhaps you could ask Pierre to supply some refreshments? He will no doubt know what one is to serve at...er...five in the morning."

"No refreshments," Robespierre said through gritted teeth. "Where were you?"

"I am astounded, Citizen. How can my poor wanderings interest you?"

"Because your cook's boy was down at the greengrocers saying you left a bloody handprint when you stumbled in through the servant's entrance at four this morning." Madame Croûte smiled in satisfaction. "And coincidentally, that's just after an intruder was stabbed in the shoulder at the Conciergerie while trying to free a family named Rideaux."

"My, you are busy," Henri drawled. "Questioning my cook's boy at this early hour?"

TThe people are everywhere," Madame Croûte said. Her smile was unwholesome.

"And you think I was involved?" He gave a chuckle. "Have I become an idealist now who rescues prisoners, risking my person? Quite a reformation in fact."

"There is the matter of your neighbor and her escape." Robespierre held firm.

Very well, it was time to take a chance. "Well, well. So you suspect me. And you think I stand before you with a wound in my shoulder." He shrugged. And hoped to God that

Time for Eternity

the last pink of new skin had disappeared.

"Strip off his jacket," Robespierre ordered the soldiers. Henri raised his hands.

"Hardly necessary, gentlemen. If the lady doesn't mind?"

"The lady insists," Madame Croûte snorted, ignoring Françoise.

Henri untied the silk rope at his waist, and slid the jacket down his shoulders.

Madame Croûte peered at his shoulder. "Is there...?"

She stepped closer. "No." She sounded very disappointed. Henri heard Françoise let out the breath she had been holding. Robespierre looked...annoyed. Madame Croûte had made him seem ridiculous. Good. Let their black union strain and crack. He had a feeling that if Robespierre tried to throw off Croûte, she would be the winner, and find a new member of the Committee of Public Safety to support.

"Perhaps the intruder wasn't wounded? There must be some way you can lay this at my door," Henri said as he shrugged his jacket back on.

"There was a good five inches of blood on the guard's sword," Robespierre said thoughtfully. "He remembered black eyes."

Henri should have taken time to plant a suggestion. That was what came of being tired. But that the man remembered black eyes was a lie. He'd seen only red eyes. Robespierre wasn't willing to discredit his witness by admitting that. Or maybe the guard was afraid to admit he'd seen something impossible. "Dark eyes are so uncommon, too..."

Madame Croûte steamed. Robespierre too, but he concealed it better.

"Now, if you all will excuse me? I find my bed much more attractive than entertaining visitors at such an ungodly hour."

Gaston woke to his duty and herded them all out the door. He would think Henri was concealing his duel. Françoise would put the whole down to the First Citizen's paranoia and enmity. The better to convince her to leave the country next week.

Henri found the whole exercise depressing. It was now clear there would come a time when he could not continue his work. When Françoise was gone. When life would stretch ahead with maddening familiarity. The door to his room closed. The whispered recriminations retreated down the main staircase. He looked at the bed and knew he wouldn't sleep for a long time today.

Fifteen

What a strange morning. Avignon was hiding something. Françoise was sure of it. He'd been avoiding her for two days. And Robespierre and Madame Croute thought Avignon, of all people, was helping prisoners escape.

Was that so strange? Françoise knew of at least one prisoner for whom that was true.

That's not his secret, the voice said. *If you'd listen to me—*

"I'm not listening to you," she whispered to herself. She had to know if it what Robespierre thought was true. So she questioned the cook's boy. Shy, hesitant, he told her about the bloody palm print. He also reported that someone had burned clothes in the kitchen fire, for there were still charred scraps when he'd returned from the greengrocer's. Fine linen and black brocade.

Pierre said Paris was buzzing. Another fourteen people had escaped from the Conciergerie last night. The guards were a laughingstock. One guard had been swearing in a coffeehouse that whoever was getting them out had blood-red eyes and disappeared into thin air. They were making up ghost stories to account for their incompetence.

Françoise didn't know what to think. If the intruder had been wounded it couldn't have been Avignon. But what about the bloody palm print? She couldn't see her way.

Maybe he wasn't risking himself directly. Someone else got them out of prison, and he transported them out of the country with his smuggling network. The nobility would pay an extravagant sum for transport. The wicked duc wouldn't be doing it for anything less.

She watched from the top of the stairs as he left for the evening. The affectation of his trailing black silk scarf and his quizzing glass would have made any other man look ridiculous.

She ate dinner, alone again, and sent her compliments to Pierre.

Then she went to her room. Annette helped her to undress and was dismissed. The household kept an odd timetable. Half the staff tidied his room and prepared for his return near dawn with food and drink and slept as Avignon did, during the day. Those who slept now did his business during the day. They all seemed to have adapted to it, almost cheerfully.

Still, by slightly after midnight, the house was quiet. She realized that she wanted to know what secrets Avignon kept, whether or not they related to prisoners escaping from the Conciergerie. The obvious choice for a record of his doings was his desk downstairs. But Avignon was not ordinary. She'd be surprised if his secrets were kept in his desk. So she slid down the hall to his bedroom and slipped inside, her heart in her mouth. Perhaps because the room still smelled of him, spicy and sweet. *Don't be silly.* She went through his dressing table drawers. But there was nothing there that any man would not have; a knife for paring nails, a boar's bristle brush with a silver back, a silver comb, and a selection of black ribbons to tie back his hair. They were only remarkable for what they did not hold. No powder, no patches, no rouge or other affectations. And no bottle of perfume. Where did he keep that? The whole room smelled faintly of his signature scent. The drawer under the stand that held the washbasin contained only tooth powder and brush and extra bars of soap. The night table held only flints and strikers for the candelabrum set upon it, the other only a copy of Voltaire's *Candide*. A little odd for a man who had no ideals at all, let alone those of the people's Revolution.

Very well. She'd been wrong. It must be in his desk. She tiptoed down the stairs, past the nodding footman in the foyer, and down the back hall to the library. Would his desk be locked? She'd not stop at prying locks, though she'd have to go up and get the knife for paring her own nails to do it. But none of the drawers were locked. Trusting man. There was even a roulade of gold pieces in the center drawer. Were all his

218

servants as trustworthy as Gaston, Drummond, Pierre, and Jean? The other drawers held papers. She carefully went through them. They seemed to be invoices from a variety of vendors, including ... Fanchon.

Dear mother Mary! Her wardrobe had cost six thousand francs? That was almost enough to keep her for life. Oh, this was dreadful. To be so indebted to him! Even though she would only take two dresses with her, she had worn the evening dress because she was vain and it was pretty and... Could he give them back? Maybe not. Oh, she was just a horrible person. He had been generous to her. And here she was rifling through his personal things, looking for secrets.

But maybe he had been generous to Madame Vercheroux as well. The woman had fingered those diamonds the whole time she was in the ballroom upstairs. That hurt.

It shouldn't. Money apparently meant nothing to him. He used it to get what he wanted. At least Vercheroux gave him fair value for money. Françoise had told him she wouldn't be kept by him, wouldn't make love with him. He'd wasted six thousand francs.

Maybe he went every night to Madame Vercheroux. Maybe he wanted to put Françoise on his ship to England to get rid of her. Or maybe, when she was alone and powerless in England, he would have his way with her and he needn't be generous anymore.

She realized she was very naïve in matters of men and women. In which case, finding his secret would give her leverage with him.

The kind of secret he has isn't found in a desk. The voice seemed annoyed. Françoise continued her search; breeding papers for his horses, records of what he paid his servants. That was interesting. He was surprisingly generous. One day Pierre, Drummond, Gaston, Jean, and the others would retire with a good amount of money. At last she came to bills of lading for his cargos, and examined each one carefully. There was no sign of human cargo. What had she expected? Him to leave a paper in his desk saying, "Ten escapees from the

Susan Squires

Conciergerie on 10 June, in exchange for fifty thousand francs?"

Would the wicked duc rescue anybody?

"Maybe. For enough money." She sat back in the great red leather chair. Bookshelves ran from floor to ceiling all along three walls, with breaks for the fireplace and doors. The fourth wall held windows. There were so many books she couldn't imagine trying to look through all of them for some hidden piece of paper. And a paper that said... What? What would he have that would reveal that he was making money off someone else's altruistic impulse and the impossible risk they were taking?

She closed the desk drawers, retrieved her candle, and trudged back up the stairs. If whatever she was looking for were hidden in a book, she'd never find it in that huge library. If it were up to her, she'd keep anything to do with illicit doings somewhere more personal anyway.

So if he were going to hide something in a book, it would be in the one in his nightstand.

She almost gasped.

Stupid. Ridiculous. But once the thought had popped into her head, she had to check. So she let herself back into his room and placed her candle on the nightstand. She pulled open the drawer. The red leather binding of Voltaire's masterpiece gleamed in the candlelight.

She picked up the book and held it by the two covers. The pages fanned out. And a folded paper wafted to the floor.

She was so surprised she couldn't move for a moment. Finally she picked it up, unfolded it, and held it to the light.

It was a long list of names in careful script. Family names or titles, and then indented, given names. After the first given names, father or mother was notated, implying that the others were children. Twenty groups were crossed off. The first name not crossed off was Rideaux.

The implications washed over her in waves. He wasn't just accepting for transport whomever someone else brought to him. This list said he planned whom to rescue, crossing off specific names as the job was completed. Was he the one

Time for Eternity

actually rescuing them?

Not hardly. The voice spoke so strangely. But she knew what it meant.

"The man who tried to rescue Madame LaFleur and read the benediction over her could be doing this," she whispered to herself. "And not just for money. You just refuse to see it."

In which case, she'd been entirely wrong about Avignon, along with everyone else in Paris. The man who had served her food, the man who had carried her to bed after the party, the man who had made passionate love to her—that man could risk his life to rescue families from the guillotine.

But the rescuer had been stabbed in the shoulder, and Avignon's shoulder was whole.

It's not him. He's transporting them to England on his ships. Maybe. That's all.

She *had* to know which part of her was right about Avignon. Henri. The only way was to catch him in action. That meant the Conciergerie.

At night.

Impossible.

Why? Guards could be bribed. She knew that for a fact. And there was a roulade ready-made for the purpose in the center drawer of the desk in the library. That's probably how he was doing it, bribing guards. If it was he actually rescuing them, then she knew where he would be tonight. He was taking the list of families in order. He'd left off with Rideaux. She'd copy the list and return his original to *Candide.*

She was going to do it.

Be my guest. You're wasting your time, though.

*****

"Ye can't see the Rideaux family."

The young guard with the luxuriant mustachios and the limp hair was avaricious. She could see it in his eyes. Still he refused nearly a third of Avignon's roulade.

Susan Squires

"Why not?" she asked.

"They was sent to the hungry Madame this morning. First Citizen figured they'd be next to escape, since someone was almost caught in front of their cell—before he disappeared, right in front of Colbert's eyes."

"The...the whole family... guillotined? There were...three children."

The young guard chewed his lip. "I know... But sins of the fathers and all that... They'd be a breeding ground for the counterrevolution." The young guard looked away in shame in spite of the excuses he was giving. Françoise could barely control her stomach. To think of those children, laying their heads on the block in front of the jeering crowds...

She had to get hold of herself. One family was lost, but there were fifteen or twenty others on the list with names not yet crossed off. There was still hope for them. "Well, then, I... I want to see the... the St. Navarre family." The next names on the list. Wait. Wasn't that the name of the sad-eyed man who had helped her find Madame LaFleur? He had a son, Emile. Panic blossomed in her like a blood-red rose.

The guard looked at her queerly.

"They knew my aunt." A lame explanation at best. She held out the coins.

She saw him decide as he fingered the coins. He marched her past cells full to overflowing with prisoners trying to find enough room to sleep. Loud snores, quiet voices, groans and sobs echoed through the stone passageway. "We put the families in cells around the courtyard, so we can keep an eye on 'em. Montmorency will let you in, if you grease his palm."

Françoise hurried to keep up with his long steps. They came out into an open court, probably designed for prisoners' exercise. It was a bleak place made of stone, not a plant in sight, with cells around the perimeter. Guards patrolled along the cells and crisscrossed the yard, some carrying lamps held high. Françoise heard several babies crying. She was finding it hard to swallow. The very thought of Emile and his father being sent to the guillotine made her ill.

"There." The guard pointed to a cell on the same side as

they had entered the square about three cells down. He waved to a guard with epaulets and a burgeoning paunch. Françoise felt for her roulade.

"Lady wants to see St. Navarre." Her guard spoke low so others couldn't hear.

Françoise knew her cue. She pressed half of what remained of Avignon's coins into Montmorency's hand. "Please, sir, if you will."

Montmorency held a coin to the light and chuffed a laugh. "This way."

Françoise felt as though she were one of the wires in a harpsichord tightened to the breaking point as she clicked down the stones. What would she see? A family in distress or something more?

As the little procession of Montmorency, her, and her young guard drew near the cell, they saw another guard standing, frozen, looking inside.

"Devereaux," Montmorency called. But the guard did not answer. Montmorency broke into a trot, her guard right behind him. Françoise hurried to keep up. All three saw a figure dressed entirely in black, a silk scarf up over the lower half of his face under his tricorn inside the cell. He had a man in a ragged shirt clutched to one side and a young boy in the crook of his left arm. The eyes of the man in black glowed an unearthly red.

"Quiet now if you can, though this will hurt you. Not your boy. He will feel nothing." The voice was a whispered baritone.

Henri.

"You there," Montmorency cried and fumbled for keys.

In the dim cell Françoise saw what seemed to be a blackness so black it was the essence of nothingness gather around the three figures. It whirled like a vortex. Her guard held his lamp high. Françoise gasped. The blackness didn't dissipate. It surged up. The sad-eyed man and the boy in Henri's embrace were wide-eyed with fear. Henri's red eyes pulsed and glowed.

And then the vortex ate them up. There was a strangled cry from the man, and…

And they were gone.

Françoise gasped and clamped her hand over her own mouth to prevent her scream. Her brain refused to function. Her gaze bounced around the cell as though the figures were still there somehow, if she only looked harder.

What? He's actually doing this? The voice sounded as stunned as Françoise felt.

Montmorency found himself first and, with shaking hands, unlocked the door. The frozen guard, Devereaux, came to himself, looking around as if dazed.

"What… what happened here?" her young guard whispered.

"Nothing," Devereaux said, smiling. "Just making my rounds."

"What was that?" Her young guard seemed to be asking himself more than anyone else. "It wasn't human."

Françoise's mouth was so dry she couldn't swallow. Not human.

Listen to them. Not human. The voice pressed her. Her head began to ache. Yet she could feel some uncertainty. The voice didn't want to believe Henri was rescuing prisoners.

"They've escaped," Montmorency announced. He too looked around the empty cell as though an entire family might somehow still be hidden there.

Devereaux blanched. "No!" He rushed into the cell, and was dumbfounded to see it empty. Other guards descended on the vacant cell from around the courtyard.

Françoise began to back away. She couldn't be seen here.

"How could you just stand and watch it?" Montmorency shouted.

"Watch what?" Devereaux was genuinely puzzled. "Did you move them?"

"You fool!"

Françoise looked around. A guard stood frozen before another cell across the courtyard. From here all she could see

Time for Eternity

were two glowing red coals inside the cell. Red eyes.

She didn't point out what was happening. She didn't want Henri caught. Whatever he was. She couldn't think about that now. She wouldn't think. She backed toward the archway where she and her guard had entered.

And smack into a large, florid-faced man. A huge ham-like fist locked around her upper arm.

"And what are you doing here, eh, mademoiselle?" Montmorency shouted, "Another escape, Captain." Just then a wail echoed from across the way. But the guards didn't consider that out of the ordinary. Avignon was using the chaos in the courtyard to cover an escape in that cell with the frozen guard. And that was good— however he was doing it.

I never knew. The voice inside her was thoughtful. The florid-faced captain dragged her with him as he surveyed the empty cell. His face was grim as he turned to her. "Why were you here, girl?" He looked around. "Who let her in?"

Her young guard shrugged and got a hard stare from Montmorency. He swallowed. "She give good money for a visit, Captain."

The captain was holding her arm so tightly he would leave bruises. "I'll wager she did." He jerked her around. "What have you to do with all this?"

"Nothing," she managed.

"We'll see about that." He pushed her ahead of him. She stumbled, and put out her hands to break her fall.

Everything slowed. On her hands and knees, she brought her palm up. It was scraped. Blood welled.

It's only a scrape, she thought.

It's the damning of your soul, the voice shrieked. *The beginning of the end that has no end. Listen to me, you little shit. Now you have no choice. You have to kill him, or...or run away this very night and never see him again as long as you live.*

Was the voice changing its mind about killing Henri?

The world started moving again. The captain was jerking her up. He dragged her back down through the archway to the guardhouse. The prisoners, wakened by the brouhaha, pressed against the bars. This was what a madhouse must be, though she had never seen one.

"Just you sit here," the captain said, pushing her into a chair.

A shriek echoed down the corridors.

"Damn," the captain muttered. The guards dashed back the way she and the captain had come, leaving Françoise, quite surprisingly...alone.

She blinked, looked around at the card game left scattered on a table, the remains of a meat pie, several flagons of ale, some coats and cloaks, and two pairs of boots standing forlornly in the corner of the guardroom.

Then she got up and ran into the street. Where to go? She had nowhere else besides number sixteen.

If he isn't what I thought...if he has honor and courage... The voice paused as though mulling over this new situation. *Then he'll never let you go. If you escape him he'll come after you in some misguided act of kindness and responsibility. And then he'll make you something you can't live with, even if it's accidental. So there's nothing for it. Get back to number sixteen and kill him.*

"I'm not killing anyone." And she couldn't leave number sixteen. She had nowhere else to go. She put her hands over her ears as she ran but it didn't help. Her head ached so that she could hardly see her way.

No choice, girlfriend.

She ran until she was exhausted, then walked and ran again. She was running to the house of a man who could raise the darkness and disappear, who had red eyes, who was not human.

She wouldn't kill Henri. Of course she wouldn't. But he wasn't human and he was a danger to her in a way that would change her forever, somehow. So she *had* to kill him.

Either way, her only path was to the Place Royale.

Sixteen

Jean opened the door. Françoise stumbled into the house, gasping for breath.

"Mademoiselle," Jean said anxiously, leading her to a chair. "What is wrong?"

What wasn't wrong?

Get the leather bag, the voice ordered. *You must save yourself. There's not much time.*

She pushed herself off the chair, trembling in every limb. Jean looked horrified. She ran her hands through her curls. "When the duc arrives—"

"But his grace is already here." Jean looked surprised. "He is in the library."

She blinked at the footman. How could he have gotten here ahead of her? He wouldn't dare to use his carriage.

Get the leather bag! the voice shouted inside her.

She gathered herself and pushed the voice down. She wasn't going to kill anybody. No. She should confront him. He had a right to defend himself. She'd tell him she knew he'd been at the prison. With red eyes. And whirling darkness.

Fear threatened to close her throat.

She pushed it down again. There was an explanation. There had to be. A monster wouldn't be rescuing families from the guillotine. And you couldn't kill a person just to prevent some imagined future misdeed.

Even the voice's resolution wavered.

She gulped and stilled her breathing.

"May I bring you something?" Jean was concerned.

She shook her head. "I'll join his grace in the library." Her head began to pound.

Don't go in there. This must be it. It happened in the library, even though last time I never went to the Conciergerie

Susan Squires

tonight. Let me control!

For pity's sake, the voice wasn't even making sense. Something inside her was struggling to get out. It was almost as frightening as seeing Henri tonight with red eyes as he was engulfed in whirling darkness. It felt as though she were two people in one body. Pain shot through her temples as she trembled before the library door. She *must* be going mad.

"I'm stronger than that," she whispered. "I'm in control."

She pushed open the door.

He swirled brandy in a delicate crystal snifter. This time the grate he was staring into was lighted. It was cool tonight. The threatening feeling in the air might have been from that feeling of electric energy that presaged a storm. Or it might have been from Henri, or the fact that something inside her might want her to commit murder.

He glanced up. As usual, he was impeccable, not a hair out of place. His eyes were black, unfathomable. She couldn't see the silver flecks that floated in them from here. She realized how little she knew of him. He must be a pampered son in a long line of pampered sons. Then why was there such pain behind his insouciance?

She shook herself, trying to make the headache subside. "You were at the prison tonight."

He gave no sign of consternation or surprise. He just waited.

"You've been rescuing them."

He managed a chuckle. "I don't know what you thought you saw—"

"I heard your voice. It was you. Or are you referring to the red eyes and the whirling blackness? What was that?"

"Your imagination, obviously."

"I didn't imagine anything. You are either going to explain who, or, or what you are, or…"

"Or what?" His shoulders sagged.

Threatening a man who wasn't human? Ridiculous.

Get out of this room. Right now! The pain in her head became excruciating.

Time for Eternity

He strode across the room, glass in hand. "I think you should join the others at the warehouse for the next few days until I can get you out of here."

"I wouldn't tell Robespierre and Madame Croûte who is behind the escapes, if that's what you think. They're vile, and whatever you are, you're at least trying to save people's lives."

"Go and pack. I'll send Gaston——"

"I want to know what you are." She took his wrist in one hand and felt the electric jolt.

No, Françoise, no!

"You don't want to know anything about me." His face went hard. He looked down at her hand on his wrist.

And then it began. Everything started moving very slowly. His other hand on his glass was clenched too hard, as though he didn't know his own strength. The glass shattered, sending tinkling shards to the carpet. His palm was cut in several places. Blood welled. Instinctively she reached out to him.

"No!" he shouted at the same time as that voice inside her screamed, *No!*

She snatched back her hand as he pushed her away. Falling, she stared at the blood welling in his palm.

Relief coursed through her. She didn't understand why. The pain in her head subsided. She was still bursting full. Something writhed and struggled within her. She felt herself dividing inside as though she'd broken, just like the glass.

One became truly two.

We did it! It didn't happen the way it did before.

Françoise tried to breathe. The voice was stronger than ever, and more separate. It wasn't hers. She felt that now. And that was shocking.

"I'm sorry," he said. Then he frowned. "Is that a scrape on your palm?"

"I fell at the prison tonight."

He stared at her abraded skin and blanched. "My God, girl, you might have…"

She couldn't take her eyes from his hand for some

reason. As she watched, the cuts sealed themselves. She gasped. "W-what is that?"

We still aren't safe from infection. We just bought time.

He glanced to his palm. The cuts turned to red weals. He took a breath. "That is part of my disease," he said. His voice was shaky. "And you were very nearly infected."

He used the same word as the voice inside her head. Infection. Was everyone going mad?

Do you want to be like him, you little shit? Leave the room. Now. He's a monster.

A monster? Truly? When he saved children from the guillotine? She felt a waver of uncertainty in that other inside her. Françoise didn't talk like that. "Buying time." "You little shit." That proved the voice wasn't her. No one else talked like that either. She struggled to her feet. He made no move to help her, but went to the bell pull and rang for a servant.

In some part of her, certainty locked back down. *It doesn't matter that his character isn't what I thought. You must still protect yourself. He'll infect you, if not today, then tomorrow. I don't like it any better than you do, but it's self-defense. You've got to kill him. He'll probably infect others too, if that makes you feel better about what you have to do.*

Kill him? She couldn't kill *anyone.* Especially not Henri.

Her head began to ache again.

Jean appeared at the door.

"Please bring a basin of water, some soap, and some rags."

Jean's eyes widened. But all he said was, "Very good, your grace."

Françoise sat in one of the wing chairs, a war going on inside her with stabbing pains that made her want to shriek out loud.

Go out to the stable. The bag. You need the bag.

Her throat was closing. She was so full. She had to stop this—whatever was happening to her. She held her head. "I won't kill," she whispered as she rocked back and forth.

"What did you say? Are you all right?"

"I…" She choked. "I must go." She pushed up and out the door, leaving him frowning after her. She couldn't think anything except that she wanted the pain to stop.

*****

Dear God, he'd nearly infected her. Henri rubbed his mouth. What would he have done? Watched her die as her body rejected the Companion? He stared at his face in the mirror above the fireplace. A vampire's face. Only when he called the power to translocate and the field grew too dense to allow light to escape did his reflection disappear.

He could not have let her die. He would have given her his blood to grant her immunity.

The realization struck him like a physical blow.

That would violate the prime Rule of his kind. If one made vampires and they made vampires, where would it end except in a war with humanity and not enough blood for too many vampires?

But he would have done it, Rules or no.

He…cared for her as he had not cared for anyone in centuries, no matter that he saved them from the guillotine, or dug wells to keep them from sickening from bad water.

He would have committed the ultimate sin for her.

Did that mean he loved her?

He was never going to find out. It would also have been the ultimate sin against her. No woman wanted to be a monster. She would have reviled him for it. He couldn't risk another accident. Already she knew too much about him. So he'd keep her at a distance, insist the whole was her imagination, send her off at the end of the week. He was not to be trusted.

*****

Go to the stable. The voice rode the pain, inexorable. It was stronger than she was now. She began to run, back through the kitchen where Jean was getting rags, and out into the warm night, across the stones of the mews to the stables. Pull open the stable door.

Gasping, Françoise stumbled to her knees in front of the hay bale behind which she had hidden the leather satchel.

We haven't any choice. The voice sounded as though it were panting too. Françoise could hear the desperation, the doubt underneath the order. But the stabbing pains didn't stop.

Françoise moaned and fumbled at the strange, toothed-metal closure. The mouth of the satchel gaped like a hungry beast. Inside the sword gleamed. The soft purple and pink bottles lurked beneath it. "No. In the name of God, no," she gasped as tears streamed down her face. She must find a way to refuse this wicked voice. "I'm not strong enough to decapitate him anyway."

That took the voice aback. There was a pause. *True. I'd forgotten how weak and deaf and blind I was.* Another pause. *Okay, okay. There must be another way. I don't want to kill him either. But we can't have him coming after you if you walk away.*

The pain eased up a tiny bit. "He doesn't love me. He won't come after me."

Don't bet eternity on it now that it turns out he's got some morals. The voice was grim. *All right. You'll drug him and leave him. Right now. Tonight. And he'll hate you for it, so he won't let you near him ever again. Deal?*

The pain eased down so she could think again. Yes. She had to leave Henri. He'd never love her. She wouldn't be kept as a mistress. She had no future with him, much as that sent despair washing over her.

What she would do without a position or a way to earn her living, she didn't know. But what did it matter, without Henri? "You have a bargain."

Hide it in your skirts. Run!

Choking and coughing as though her throat were full, Françoise stumbled back to the house. She made it all the way to the library without meeting anyone.

In front of the door, the voice said, *Stop. Now calm yourself. Breathe.*

232

Time for Eternity

She managed to swallow. A breath. Two. Three. Slower. She wiped at her eyes.

Better.

The door to the library opened. Jean came out with a wooden box from the desk.

From inside the room Avignon called, "Bury it in the park. No one touches the glass."

"Yes, your grace."

She entered the room. Avignon looked up from his hands and knees. A very unduclike position. He was scrubbing the carpet with a rag and a basin. Françoise blinked in surprise.

Even the voice seemed taken aback. *He's trying not to infect anyone... Shit. I really was wrong about him.*

Avignon got to his feet and wiped his hands on the rag, frowning. "Are you all right?" He tried on a tiny, tentative smile. "It was just a little blood." He seemed shaken, though.

Right. A little blood. And a little parasite inside it that changes you forever.

"I'm better," she said. Her voice seemed far away. The pain in her head was gone, but she knew the voice could bring it back at any moment. She fingered the soft bottle she held at her side in the folds of her skirts. She was listening to a voice in her head as though it were a separate person altogether. She was truly mad.

Or maybe you're Joan of Arc. Get him talking. Pour him a drink.

"Do...do you want to explain?" Françoise asked Henri. She wanted an explanation.

He'll never tell you. It's a big, bad secret.

"And don't try telling me it's my imagination," Françoise added.

He stared down at the rag in his hand, apparently torn. He took a slow breath and looked up at her, his eyes still questioning himself. "I have a disease in my blood."

One way of putting it.

"And the healing?" She realized she'd seen it earlier when his face was blistered.

"An effect of the disease, along with the sensitivity to light."

Half-truths.

"What about the red eyes?"

"A pigment that reflects the light. Like animals' eyes at night."

Oh, that's good. No confessions forthcoming. So let's do the deed and blow this joint.

Françoise pressed her lips together. She'd give him another chance for the real explanation. "Hardly believable, but clever. Now about the whirling blackness that makes you disappear with your charges?"

He looked away. There was no way to explain that. "What do you want of me?"

Françoise stared at him, his question unlocking a thousand conflicting thoughts. The voice wanted him out of her life permanently. But she wanted to feel his arms around her, hear his heart beat, smell the exotic scent of him, and hear him tell her that he treasured her above all others. She wanted him to kiss her.

You are so far gone, girl. We better get out of here pronto. The weight of the soft bottle in her right hand seemed to triple. *Make him a drink.*

The very fact that she wanted him to kiss her meant the voice was right. She had to leave him now. Tonight. "I don't know what I want," Françoise said in a small voice. "Maybe the truth. Maybe I just want a drink." She turned to the sideboard that held the cut-glass brandy decanter. Out of the corner of her eyes, she saw him lean his elbow on the mantel and put one boot on the andirons in a pose grown familiar over the last days. He stared into the cold firebox. With her back turned, she took the soft purple bottle and pressed on the top. One side flipped up.

"It's time to get you down to the warehouse. The *Maiden Voyage* leaves for England in four days. You'll be on a barge to meet it in three. Jennings will take care of you until then."

"Is that where you keep them? The ones you rescue?"

Time for Eternity

She squeezed.

More. He's not human.

"Yes. There are rooms fitted out behind the back wall."

She poured more into the drink. If the drug could kill him, the voice would not have been after her about using the sword. She glanced behind her, but he was still staring into the grate. He was going to hate her. The next moments would be the last time she saw him. She slid the purple bottle behind a Sevres vase and poured brandy into the glass. It made a big drink. She poured a small one for herself.

Holding her breath, she took the two glasses and turned. He was so beautiful, standing there. And he had been kind to her. More than kind.

Do it. Or I swear to drive you really crazy.

She put her mouth into some kind of smile and held out his glass. "You do good work then." She was going to hate herself for this as much as he would hate her.

He took it. "Never enough. Never. You've seen the prison."

She tried to breathe. He took the glass and downed it in several gulps. "But it has to be done," he continued. "And my condition makes me ideally suited…"

He trailed off, his mouth pressed into a grim line, and shook his head. He set his glass on the mantel. Françoise realized she was trembling. When would it take effect? What would he do if he realized what she'd done?

He took a breath as though to say something else, blinked rapidly a couple of times. His gaze slid to the glass on the mantel and then to Françoise. His eyes hardened. He looked around the room. She could see his eyes were swimming. He caught sight of the soft purple bottle peeking from behind the vase on the sideboard and pushed past her.

"You little fool," he whispered. "Where did you get laudanum in this strength?" His steps slowed. He practically fell against the sideboard as he grabbed for the bottle, his eyes questioning. "What…?"

And then his eyes rolled back in his head and he

slumped to the floor. The soft purple bottle slid from his loosened grasp. What had she done? Françoise ran to him and knelt.

He's not dead. He just swallowed enough morphine to take down an elephant, that's all.

What did the voice know? She felt for the pulse in his throat under his cravat. It beat back at her, slow and steady. Françoise sighed in relief. He wasn't dead. Now she could go, on to whatever life of shame and regret was left to her.

The other who shared her body was startled by that thought. *You won't regret this.*

"Yes I will," Françoise whispered. Tumult sounded in the hall. Raised voices, many feet. Françoise stood, heart in her mouth. "All my life."

"Where is he, man?"

"Do you want to end up with a haircut from Madame G?"

"We'll find him anyway."

The clatter grew closer. Françoise looked to the figure of Avignon, sprawled on the carpet, both parts of her dismayed. Before she could do more, the door burst open and the little man she had grown to hate strode through the door, booted soldiers in his wake. At the sight of Henri, unconscious, he stopped. His gaze swept over Françoise, around the room, then back to Henri. Then a smile crept across his mouth.

"Well, well." He crossed the carpet and pushed at Henri's rib cage with one foot. Henri' chest rose and fell. "I've never seen Foucault drunk. And he certainly wasn't drunk when he was with you at the Conciergerie tonight, freeing prisoners."

So they knew it was Henri. This was bad. Worse, they connected her to his actions.

If I hadn't stopped you touching him, he would have taken you to a garret to give you his blood. He wouldn't have been home when these assholes arrived. This is new territory.

Françoise felt her blush increase. Such language! And what did the voice mean about Henri giving her his blood?

Madame Croûte pushed in behind the soldiers, who had

Time for Eternity

ranged themselves around the perimeter of the library. "He's not dead, is he?"

Robespierre shook his head, a puzzled look on his face. "But he's unconscious."

"Good. I'd hate to lose the chance to question him." Her eyes were avaricious.

Françoise could see Gaston and Jean in the hallway. Gaston was wringing his hands.

Robespierre walked over to where the opaque purple bottle lay and bent to pick it up. He sniffed at it and drew back in distaste.

Madame Croute snatched it from him and sniffed. "Laudanum? Not...quite."

"Probably related." Robespierre turned to Françoise. "Perhaps I misjudged you. When we saw you there, we knew for certain it was he who was committing these criminal acts against the Republic. We considered you an accomplice. But you weren't in on it with him, were you? You went to confirm your own suspicions then acted on what you saw. You have done the people's business tonight." They thought she'd drugged Henri to turn him over to the Committee of Public Safety? Worse, they were only here because her presence had betrayed him.

"How does he do it?" Robespierre asked.

She had to keep herself out of prison if she was to help Henri. She couldn't leave him in these straits. "I...I've no idea." That, at least, was the truth. "I saw only what your guards saw."

The voice sighed. *You're not going to leave him, even if they let you go.*

Robespierre frowned. "They say he just disappears. Some illusion, surely."

What, no mention of red eyes and whirling blackness? Maybe no one wants to tell him.

Madame Croûte knelt beside Henri. "This one is slippery. We must take extra precautions. I want him chained, alone, in plain sight of guards at all times. Strip him to make sure he has no weapons on him." She caressed the line of his jaw. "Don't feel you have to be gentle. I'll be by to question him."

"Do you feel that rigorous questioning is a woman's work, my dear?" Robespierre asked.

He really knows jack about her, doesn't he? Françoise had a dreadful sinking feeling in her stomach.

Madame Croûte only smiled. "I'll have what you need from him. The only pity is that we'll have to wait until the drug wears off before he can feel anything." She turned the strange opaque bottle in her hands, squeezed it, and gave a little gasp when the material rebounded to its original shape. "What is this thing? Witchcraft?" She narrowed her eyes at Françoise.

"Avignon imported it. A new kind of bottle," she lied without thinking.

They'll have him in the Place de Revolution in the end. That's what happened last time according to Donna. Maybe the guillotine is the best answer. The voice didn't sound sure, though. *He can't infect you if he's dead.*

What happened last time? What did that mean? *Guillotine is the best answer to anything? Who is mad now?* Françoise thought back. If the voice could hear her thoughts, she didn't need to say it aloud. *They are going to torture him to find out where he hides the prisoners. He doesn't deserve that. If she breaks him, the families don't deserve what will happen to them either. And I'm not going to let Henri get his head cut off.*

The voice was silent at that. Maybe it hadn't heard her after all.

"You have done your work well, my child." Robespierre smiled kindly. How could he smile like that when he was going to allow his dreadful mistress to torture Henri? "You have the gratitude of the Revolutionary Council." The soldiers dragged Henri's body past Gaston and Jean. She had betrayed him!

Mother Mary, forgive me. She wasn't sure which one of them thought that.

Madame Croûte stared after Henri. "Would you like to

238

Time for Eternity

see me break him, child?" She glanced to Françoise. Her expression was remote, serene, as though she weren't really present in the room anymore. "The process is quite...exciting. Or would you rather wait for the guillotine?"

Françoise felt her knees buckle. *Sacredieu,* what had she done? She looked from one to the other of them, then out to Gaston, who was glaring at her. Jean looked only confused. Madame Croûte raised her brows, encouraging.

"I'll wait." Françoise wasn't sure whose voice had managed to answer.

Seventeen

Françoise stood with Gaston and Jean watching the front door close. Outside the clatter of boots, the clop of hooves, and the shouts slowly diminished. She felt full and completely empty at the same time.

"Why," Gaston asked as they stared at the door. "After all his kindness to you?"

Françoise felt the tears roll down her cheeks. "I never meant this to happen." That much was true. She couldn't say that a voice inside her that might actually be a part of her had wanted to kill him. She should never have let the voice talk her into even drugging him. If only she'd been stronger! "I couldn't let him give me carte blanche, either here or in England. I couldn't be anywhere around him…" Because he'd infect her with his disease. That was it, wasn't it? Or was it that Madame Vercheroux had said so clearly that he would never love her? She couldn't say that either. "For reasons I can't explain. And then I realized he might be helping those families who were facing the guillotine and that we never really knew him, any of us, because he wasn't just the wicked duc who gambled and dallied with married women, but a man of principle who risked his life for others. And if that was true he wouldn't *let* me go even if I managed to escape, he'd find me to try to save me from my decisions." The words were tumbling out. "When I went to the prison to see for myself if it was him, and what that would tell me about who he was, I didn't know my very presence would condemn him. I never meant him to be captured. I meant to give him the drug so he would hate me for it, and not come after me."

Suddenly her knees *wouldn't* hold her anymore. She sank to the floor, heaving sobs that caught in her throat. Gaston bent and patted her back.

"There, there, *petite*. We will find a way to free him."

240

Time for Eternity

She looked up at him and saw he didn't believe that. He and Jean exchanged looks. They were wondering what would become of them with their employer tortured and executed.

"I didn't mean for them to take him," she repeated, as much to herself as to them.

"Well, we have some time. They will not torture him until the drug wears off." Gaston's brows drew together in thought. "Perhaps the general could put in a word for him…

That sounded so tenuous.

But it might be all they had. "I'll ask him personally," she said. She wondered why the voice, so intent on getting her away from Henri a few moments ago, was now silent as she made plans to gain his release. Perhaps it was shamed by the fact that they had delivered him to the tender mercies of Madame Croûte. She certainly was.

*****

Henri managed to raise his eyelids. It seemed a monumental effort. Darkness was punctuated by coronas of light. He couldn't seem to move his limbs. Something was scraping at him. He couldn't tell what it was. Dull red surrounded him. Was his Companion turning the world red? No. Only parts were red. Cuffs, collars. Uniforms. Voices echoed. He couldn't understand them. Were they shouting at him, or did it just seem that way?

His hands were above his head. They were pulling on him. Dragging him across stones. That was what was scraped. He didn't feel it though. Everything was far away. Laughter echoed, deep and masculine, around him, distorted into something hellish.

She had done this. Drugged him. The one sure way to subdue his Companion. She must know what he was after all. And was so appalled that she betrayed him. That was the only thing that hurt him through his haze. They bumped him up some stairs. A horrible clanking sounded, a screech of rusted metal. They dumped him on the stones. Then they were tearing at his clothes. More laughter. They pushed and prodded him as they stripped him, turning him this way and that. Pulling on his boots. The voices turned angry. Fighting over his clothes.

He felt cold iron. He rolled his head to watch them lock heavy shackles on wrists that seemed to belong to someone else. He heard a thud and couldn't breathe for a moment. They were kicking him. But it didn't hurt. Cold iron on his ankles. He couldn't raise his head to look. Chains clanked, metal on metal. The sound echoed in his brain. They hauled him up to standing. He hung from his wrists, his arms stretched wide. His head lolled forward, his hair cascading over his chest, escaped from its queue. They grabbed his ankles, pulled them apart.

One yanked his head up by his hair. The soldier's face was grotesque, the nose out of all proportion, the lips stretched impossibly wide in a grin. He was saying something Henri couldn't understand. He felt the punches in the gut, dully. Shouts came from somewhere, and laughter. The soldier spat in his face.

They went away. Henri hung there, trying to hold on to consciousness.

But he couldn't.

*****

Françoise paced her room, unable to sleep in spite of the fact that it was nearly four in the morning. How soon could she call upon the general? Ten of the clock? Six hours. But they wouldn't torture him until after the drugs had worn off. How long would that take? And they were going to torture him before they sent him to the guillotine. There was time. *Dear God, please don't let me have killed him.*

She sat, quite suddenly, in a chair she was passing. The moon shone in through her windows, open to catch any hint of a breeze in the July heat that held the city in an odiferous embrace. Her thoughts were a jumble of exhausted fragments.

Maybe I could sneak in with another of those bottles and drug his guards, she thought. Implausible and suicidal. Where was the bossy voice now when she needed some

242

direction? "You've been remarkably silent," she whispered.

I'm thinking.

"I hope you're thinking of a way to set him free. You say he's a monster, but he's not."

Hello-o-o. Red eyes. Whirling blackness? The voice had a very strange way of talking.

"Hello-o-o, yourself. His actions aren't those of a monster."

You...you may be right... I never knew that about him the first time.

"A man's soul makes him a monster, not whatever..." She swallowed. "Whatever he can do that other men can't. Madame LaFleur said I had to look beyond the surface."

Advice I didn't hear the first time around... That's one reason I'm thinking.

Which brought up another point. One Françoise could no longer avoid. She had never asked because she was afraid she didn't want to know the answer.

"Who are you?" she whispered.

You wouldn't believe me if I told you. The voice sounded as exhausted as she was. Or maybe it was world-weary, a state long past exhaustion.

"Why do I feel as though I've done everything, seen everything, before? That began when I started hearing you."

Françoise searched her mind, but nothing answered her. "Well, I'm going to help him," she said. "And don't you try any tricks with headaches. The only thing you'll do is drive me to throw myself off the Pont Neuf. And then where would you be?"

I'm thinking about that too.

*****

Henri squeezed his eyes more tightly shut, then opened them. He was still muzzy-headed, but it wasn't as bad as before. He raised his head. Pain sent waves of nausea through him. He swallowed, trying to control his stomach. At least that meant the drugs were wearing off. He breathed in the stench of… prison: body odor, old damp stone, urine, blood.

Blinking, he tried to focus on the cell around him. He was shackled, naked, in the middle of the cell by long and very heavy chains that went through rings in the low ceiling and were fastened to more rings bolted into the stone on either side of the cell and well out of reach. Blood drooled at his wrists from the rough edges on the shackles. The drug was still retarding his healing. That was bad. If anybody with an open wound touched his blood, they'd be dead in hours. He looked down. His ankles were locked to two rings set in the floor. He was spread-eagled. Effective restraint if he were an ordinary man. It wouldn't hold him, once the drug was out of his system. Until then he was trapped.

Torchlight flickered in the corridor, though outside the sun was high. A guard paced outside the cell. No, two, with hands on the pommels of their swords. A third guard stood in shadows directly across from the cell, two pistols, fully cocked, laid against his shoulders. The metalwork gleamed in the torchlight.

Companion! He called the organism that was his other half just to see if it could answer yet. His blood stirred sluggishly. Not nearly enough to give him strength to pull those rings out of the walls or to translocate. But he could feel again. His head hurt like the devil. He had some broken ribs. Breathing hurt, anyway.

Françoise had drugged him. The thought hurt more than his ribs or his head. Was she really in league with Robespierre and his hell-spawned lover? He'd be out of here soon. But that would be bad, somehow. He needed a plan. He couldn't think…

His head sank slowly onto his chest.

*****

Sometime later, he woke again. The sun had set. Someone was opening the cell door.

"Bring that over here." It was a woman's voice.

Uncultured. Croûte. Her shape was silhouetted against the light of the torches the guards held high. They brought in a metal bowl of glowing coals, held by two wooden handles, and set it on a tripod. Another guard brought in a small folding table. He set it up near the brazier and laid out a box with knives that gleamed like silver crescent moons.

Croûte let her gaze travel over his body, lingering on the genitals hanging between his splayed thighs, then walked around him slowly. "My, my. You are quite a specimen. Aristos take care of their bodies. It will be a pleasure to work with you." She touched his buttocks.

Henri gritted his teeth. He tried calling to his Companion. A slow roll of pressure slid down his veins, but the world did not go red. There would be no escape from this woman for a few more hours. So he must stand whatever she did. It would be pain, that was all. Maybe even dulled by the remaining drug in his veins. He would live through it. He always did. In the end he wouldn't even have scars as reminders.

Croûte came round to his front again. She bent and hefted his balls, displaying his penis. He had never felt so vulnerable. "Impressive. Perhaps there is a way you can avoid my ministrations, at least for a while."

"Not likely," he grunted.

"You disappoint me. Well, perhaps you'll change your mind. In the meantime, I'm going to ask you questions." She smiled as though they were at tea and not about to do a dance of pain. "I do hope you won't answer immediately." She examined the open box that held the knives. She selected a curved specimen that looked as if it came from northern Africa. "I want to know where you've hidden the criminals." She stepped up to him, holding the knife. It caught the torchlight and glinted a fiery red.

"Prepare for more disappointment," he rasped.

Her smile spread. "You refuse to answer? Oh, that won't disappoint me at all." She made a cut across his chest over the nipple. He flinched away. Blood welled immediately.

Susan Squires

She might not be able to kill him, but if she caused enough damage fast enough, she could weaken him. Which might delay escape even longer.

"At least we know you can feel."

"More than you can, bitch."

Anger suffused her face with a rush of blood.

*****

Marta felt the rage inside her roll like a water serpent, lazy and powerful. This creature with his handsome face and his sneering mouth was like all aristos. But now she held the upper hand. And she could make him pay for what he was and what his brother nobles had done.

"You think you're better than me, don't you?" She shoved her blade into his shoulder. It sank into his flesh. So satisfying. He grunted. Blood welled. He wasn't such a proud devil now, then, was he? "Well, let me tell you, *Citizen.* You and your kind have had your turn." She stepped back, fury almost blinding her. All she could see was his face, and then it morphed into another handsome face. "I had the Duc of Berry's bastard when I was fifteen. He raped me one night when he was drunk and didn't even recognize me the next night when he came to the stables to collect his horse. To him I was just a disposable cunt to be used and forgotten." Did she hate him more for raping her, or for not remembering it?

She stepped in and shoved the knife into his loins near his right hip. The resistance of the flesh was heavenly. It almost dulled the pain in her gut. In her empty womb...

*****

The cry that bounced off the ceiling in the tiny room was her own. She knew that. Under the eaves in the servants' quarters. No midwife, only Nelly, the simple girl who swept out the kitchens to attend to her swollen belly. The screams that tore at her were half for the pain and half for the hatred of the handsome face that had got her here and of the laughter from

Time for Eternity

the fine sots who had taunted her all these months for her growing belly even as they threw her down in the hay and shoved their cocks into her. Let them rot in hell for what they'd done! Bringing a baby that looked like one of them into the world was the last thing she wanted. The pain took her, and tore at her. She felt like she was splitting apart.

"Here it come, Marta." Nelly was excited.

"Noooooo!" she shrieked. But it was too late for resistance. The baby slid out between her thighs, a bloody bundle still connected to her by a slimy cord, into Nelly's waiting arms.

"He's beautiful, he is, Marta."

But all she felt was empty. There was a hole in her middle that would never be filled.

*****

She shook her head to clear it. She didn't want to remember that time. But maybe taking her revenge would make her forget. She pulled the knife from his hip. The bastard felt that, now didn't he? His breathing was ragged, and the torches caught a sheen of sweat on his body. A deep satisfaction rolled through her.

"It wasn't the last time one of them took me," she said. Her voice was remarkably calm. "The daughter of a groom spends a lot of time on her back in the hay. When they got tired of using their cocks they sometimes used broom handles and pistol barrels." She hadn't even known what that would mean, except for the pain. "And that baby—every time I saw it, it reminded me of those aristocratic bastards." That had been the worst of it...

*****

It wouldn't shut up. It just cried all the time, wailed and wanted and wailed some more. "Let me pull at your tits. Clean the shit off my backside. I'm cold. I'm hot." It was always

Susan Squires

something the thing wanted. And it wasn't hers.

It was theirs, all of them. It had the black hair of the Duc of Berry, and a little pinched face. How was she supposed to love a thing like that? Her father said it was a judgment on her that it looked so pinched and frail. He was always telling her to feed it. But her nipples were sore from it pulling. It seemed to have a hard time getting milk. Maybe because she didn't want to nurse it. She didn't want it to have any more of her than it had got already.

She sat, sometimes, down at the millpond at dusk when the birds rose in swirls over the water. She laid the bundle on the ground and tried to let the water soothe her.

But it cried. It always cried. She couldn't sleep. She couldn't get any peace. Not even at the pond at dusk. The thing looked like the damned Duc of Berry. That was the problem.

It was getting darker. The pond was still and calm. She couldn't see that it looked like the damned duc. That was good. But she could hear the thing wail. It would never stop shrieking.

Unless she made it stop shrieking.

She could. She could make it be quiet. She picked it up, hating it. Hating how it had swelled her belly, and how people had laughed or whispered, and how the other rutting aristos had plowed her with anything to hand because her belly was an advertisement for her willingness whether she was willing or not.

She rocked back and forth on the bench by the pond in the growing darkness, and all the while the thing wailed.

She couldn't stand it. She shouldn't have to stand it. The whole thing was not her fault, it was theirs, all of them. And then it was all so clear. She picked up the bundle and she walked into the water until the cold of it crept up to her cunt and then she leaned over and held the bundle under the water until it stopped shrieking. It was so easy. Why hadn't she done it sooner? And then she walked back out of the water, and went home to blessed silence.

*****

Marta breathed slowly, feeling the relief as she had felt it then. She realized she'd been talking all the time the memories took her, telling the Duc d'Avignon why he had to suffer. Now his face had a guarded expression, wariness over the pity in his eyes. Damn him. He was in no position to pity her.

She walked around the man whose black hair was so like the Duc of Berry's. But the Duc of Avignon was naked, and chained and spread-eagled, waiting for her to make him pay for being who he was. She pulled the blade across his buttocks. So satisfying. But there was more. He must know the real reason he must suffer. She would tell him.

*****

Avignon blinked in horror. She had killed her own baby because it reminded her of the man who had raped her. Or maybe it reminded her of all the men who had raped her. The world was cruel. Men were cruel and women too. He understood her pain. He pitied her. But he could not forgive her cruelty, not just to him, but to the many she betrayed to the guillotine only for being of the class she blamed for her pain. He would get no mercy from her. He hissed as he felt the blade slice across his thigh. She moaned in satisfaction.

"A girl like I was has nothing to call her own—no one who cared about her," Croûte whispered in his ear. "I got to thinking that a baby is the only thing a woman *can* have of her own. The only thing that's safe to love. So I decided I wanted a baby after all. One I got by design, not from some bastard noble who took me whether I wanted him or not. So I found a stable lad I rather fancied. He didn't fancy me, but I knew how to get round that. A man will stick his cock in any likely hole. I let him fuck me and fuck me for nearly a year, because I wanted a baby from that nice little cock of his. Something *I* used *him* to make." She laughed. It was high and it went on too long. Finally she sobered, gasping. "Wouldn't you know? Those aristo bastards had ruined me for making babies, so the doctor said, and I'd killed the only one I'd ever have." She wiped her eyes with her arm, and left it across her face for a moment.

The guards had turned to stone behind her. They stared ahead, seeing nothing, and he was willing to bet if they could have closed their ears they would have.

"So I had nothing. But then the Revolution came along, and I found a way to get back my own," she said, taking her arm away and throwing her head back. "The aristos are paying for what they did to me. My legacy won't be anything as insignificant as a baby. I'm going to leave a whole new world, one where aristocrats can't be cruel to citizens just as good as they are. Wealth will be redistributed. Everyone will be equal."

Croûte was naïve. The world was the world. "You've not changed anything. There will always be hierarchy. You are the new aristocrat, more equal than others, torturing people, killing them, just because you can."

She laughed and shook her head, the laugh more normal this time. "For the greater good, not for my personal enjoyment."

"You aren't enjoying this? I can smell your cream. You want to rub yourself as you torture me. You're sick, Croûte."

He thought that would make her angry again. But she shrugged. "I get pleasure from righting the wrongs your kind has been committing for centuries. What better way to combine pleasure and the greater good? That's not sick. It's justice."

"You have become what you hate most. I've seen it before." A thousand, thousand times before. "You don't want to change the world. You just want your share."

"I leave the philosophy to my little lawyer." She held up her knife to the light. Blood dripped on her hand. "Now, let's start the questions again."

*****

Françoise hurried down the Rue de Rivoli toward the Conciergerie, eyes filled with tears of frustration. She'd been to three of the men she'd met at Henri's soirée Wednesday, including the young poet who had so admired her. No one would do anything for Henri. They feared the committee too much. Robespierre had imprisoned Henri. Now nothing would save him. They told her so repeatedly. The impoverished vicomte advised her to emigrate. The general, in creaking stays, offered her carte blanche on the spot since she would need a new protector. Slapping him for his impertinence probably did not further her cause.

All that time wasted and she was no nearer to freeing Henri. She had to see him. Maybe he'd have an idea how she could help him. Gaston had given her fat roulades of gold coins to bribe the guards. He had wanted to come with her, but she convinced him he mustn't be seen to support his former employer. The household's only chance was to portray the duc as a vile master who had taken advantage of them.

Thinking what they might be doing to Henri had her frantic. Had the drug worn off? Or maybe he had already escaped in a whirl of darkness and she was worrying for nothing.

He can't draw his power until the drug is out of his system.

"I'm not speaking to you," she whispered, pushing through the late afternoon as it turned into evening. She should never have acquiesced even to drugging him. Still, the voice seemed to know a lot about Henri. "Can the drug wear off enough for him to feel what they are doing to him, and yet he can't draw his power?" That would be the worst of all worlds.

Maybe. A pause. *Probably.*

Françoise began to run.

At the guardhouse, there was the usual long line of supplicants. She fought her way to the front, over loud protests and pointed elbows. She waved to the young guard with the lank hair and luxuriant mustachios who had already been the recipient of her largesse.

"Oh, ho." He grinned. "Come a-visiting, my sweet?" He pulled her from the line.

She palmed an entire roulade and let him see it. "Henri

Foucault, Duc d'Avignon."

The guard's eyes widened. He looked around to be sure that his fellows were engaged in playing piquet. "That visit, it would be dangerous, mademoiselle."

"And therefore worth the exorbitant price I am willing to pay."

The guard's eyes darted around the vestibule and the little stone courtyard that contained the guardhouse. He nodded brusquely. She handed him the roulade. He stared at her from head to toe. "Have you brought anything you should not have?" Before she could answer, he chuckled, pocketing the roulade. "What matter? He could not hide anything you brought him. But the guards at the cell, they will need encouragement as well." He raised his brows.

She nodded. It was dangerous to let him know she had more money on her. But what else could she do?

He motioned her toward the corridor leaving the vestibule. "Come with me."

Françoise hurried after him, practically running to keep up with his long strides. They wound their way into the bowels of the old palace, past the teeming cells noisy with sobbing women, crying children, and the supplications of those nearest the bars. One cell was totally dark and quiet except for low moaning and wet coughing. It smelled like putrefaction. She tugged on the guard's coat "What is that cell?"

He chuffed a bitter laugh. "Those won't live to visit Madame G. Infected wounds, bad lungs—they're dead already except in name. A quick end would be a kindness."

She stared over her shoulder as she hurried forward. Pray to God, Henri never had to be put in that cell. And she found herself glad that Henri had gotten out Monsieur Navarre and his son Emile. She had no idea where they were at this moment. But it had to be better than this vile place. She almost ran into the guard's outstretched arm. He had stopped stock-still.

"Shhhhh," he hissed. Ahead she heard the tromp of feet, some masculine laughter. The guard pulled her into a side corridor they had passed a few feet back. She expected him to wait until the guards passed and venture out. But instead he hurried down the narrower hallway, lined with smaller cells on either side. She followed him down two sets of stairs, ever deeper. Her courage started to fail. Was the guard just taking her to some remote spot to rob and rape her?

The corridor no longer held any cells. Only stones that dripped and sweated. For all she knew they could be under the Seine. How many prisoners had screamed over the years in this prison? She'd heard that Ravaillac had been tortured to death here for assassinating Henri IV in 1610. The walls seemed to ooze with pain absorbed over centuries.

At last they came to a long, straight corridor. Around the broad shoulders of her guide, she saw that a room widened out, almost like a cave. It was lighted by torches. Men in blue uniforms splashed with red cuffs and lapels crisscrossed in front of the heavy iron grate of a cell.

"Well, my fellow *hommes d'affaires*," her guard announced as he strode into the room. "Allow me to introduce a lady who will change the month of July for you." He turned and swept an arm toward Françoise, who lurked in the shadows of the corridor.

She took a breath. All three men stopped where they were and turned toward her.

What are you waiting for? This is what you wanted.

She fumbled in her reticule and broke two roulades inside as she stepped into the room, her gaze drifting toward the cell. She saw a form in the shadows, pale, hanging in chains, its dark head drooping on its chest.

She swallowed. She dared not think about Henri. "Gentlemen." She nodded greetings.

"You'll get us sacked or worse, Ravelle," one of the older guards said. The others looked either stricken or uncertain.

"Ahhh, you are a coward, Orteaux." He beckoned to Françoise and pointed to her reticule. She took out a handful of coins and held them so they glistened in the torchlight.

"Just a visit."

Susan Squires

The guards' expressions ranged from relief to avarice. Françoise counted out ten coins and held them out. One of the younger guards, with a complexion composed mainly of pustules between wisps of beard, grabbed for the gold. She snatched back her hand. "Alone." She had to see Henri alone. The guards looked dubious. She grimaced. "Where would I go?" She chanced a glance to the shadowy cell. "Where would he go?" She held out the hand with the gold again.

It was Orteaux she had to convince. He was chewing his lip. He glanced to the glittering coins, a year's salary. He nodded. He obviously hated himself for it, but he nodded. The guard with the pustules snatched the gold from her hand and strode to the corridor.

"We'll be near," Orteaux warned as he took the next handful of coins. He went to unlock the heavy chain that bound the barred door to the grated front of the cell.

She poured the last handful into the third guard's hands. "You too," she said to her guide.

When they had all slipped down the corridor and she heard their excited speculation on what each would buy with his bribe, she turned to the cell. Her heart thumped in her chest. Henri hung in chains, spread-eagled, naked. He had not raised his head through all her negotiations.

As she reached out to pull open the heavy door, her hand shook. He wasn't dead. They would have told her that. She could just make out his pale form, marked with darker streaks. The muscles in his shoulders and arms bulged even though the chains stretched his limbs. His taut abdomen narrowed to the rib of muscle that girdled his hips and cradled his genitals.

He won't die from a little torture. The voice's words might be callous, but she could feel the fear of what they would see in the cell trembling in it.

"Courage," she whispered half to herself, half to the voice. She jerked on the door. It squealed in protest. It was so heavy she could barely pull it open.

As she walked into the cell, her eyes grew accustomed to the dimness. She clapped her hand over her mouth to stifle a

254

Time for Eternity

cry, lest she bring the guards running. Blood leaked from dozens of wounds on his body. Chest, belly, shoulders, biceps, thighs—someone had placed careful cuts about four inches long everywhere, even on his groin next to his genitals. Between the cuts were dark burn marks and the discoloration of bruises. Henri raised his head. His face was grotesque. One eye was closed entirely, the other just a slit. Blood leaked from what was surely a broken nose. His lips were swollen and split, the skin over his cheekbones, too.

She rushed forward. "Henri," she whispered. "Oh, Henri, what have they done?" Her hands hovered around his face.

Don't touch him! He's bleeding.

"What you planned, I expect." The voice was thick and slurred.

Of course he thought that. "No, no. You don't understand. I just wanted..."

But there was no excuse for what she'd done. She couldn't bring herself to make one.

"Have you come to gloat?"

"No!" She paced away. "I tried all day to get the men who were at the house on Wednesday to help you." She whirled to face him.

A broken chuckle escaped him, sounding like a wheeze. "I'm sure that went well."

"It didn't. The cowards."

"Why are you here, Françoise?" The words were difficult for him to form.

"I...I had to tell you...how sorry I am. I never meant for this to happen. I only wanted to leave you because..." What could she say?

"What had I done to you?"

"Nothing," she practically wailed. "Nothing but kindness. But a part of me... A part of me thought you would make me into a monster. With your blood. I know that sounds mad. I had dreams... About the bottles. And there was a sword. I was supposed to use it. And when I almost got your blood in my scrape, the voice inside me started saying that even though I had escapted that once, you would infect me sooner or later. I got a headache so bad I couldn't think if I didn't do what the voice wanted. But I wouldn't kill you. So then the voice said that if I gave you the drug, and ran away, you'd hate me and wouldn't come after me." She sputtered to a stop. All this talk of voices…what must he think?

"How were you to kill me?" he whispered, staring at her with one eye that burned.

She squeezed her eyes shut. "I don't know why it had to be that particular way. It made me want to vomit. Maybe it was all this talk of the guillotine…"

"Say it."

She sucked in a breath and held it. "Decapitation," she whispered.

"You know what I am," he slurred. It was an accusation. "I knew it."

"But I don't. I don't know," she wailed. "This voice inside me…" Where was the voice? Why was it silent? Perhaps it was waiting, waiting to see what Henri would say. "It knows."

"It is too horrible for you to accept." His speech was laborious. "But you know about the blood, how to subdue me, kill me. You *know* what I am. That's why you gave me to them."

"I swear I didn't know they were coming. I only wanted to get away before something terrible happened that changed me forever."

"You were right. Go," he slurred. "Find Jennings. He'll take you to England."

"I won't leave you to be tortured."

"I'll heal when the drugs wear off. When they see that they'll be too frightened to come into the cell to torment me."

"Draw your darkness, then, and go."

"I don't want to get out. I must keep them occupied with me until the ship is ready in Le Havre. No one is safe until that ship is away. Just until Monday evening."

"That's three more days." Her stomach turned. He was

Time for Eternity

still trying to save those he had helped escape. "Send the… the cargo on the barge tonight" The guards might be listening.

"If the ship isn't ready to sail when the barge gets to Le Havre, the cargo will just be picked up and returned."

"Won't they be watching any barges, and your warehouse?"

He looked distressed at that. He hung his head. "I'll think of something. Go to Jennings."

He's right. You've got to go.

She stopped. "I'm not leaving Paris until I know you're free." Her voice shook.

She saw him gather his strength. "Can't you admit to yourself what I am? I'm vampire." The word vibrated in the dank air of the cell. "I suck human blood. I control minds and translocate. Do you understand? You were right. I'm a monster."

Vampire? Something that sucked human blood? The very definition of a monster…

Hate to say I told you so.

The cell receded around her. Only Henri was real. And his presence filled the cell to overflowing. Vampire. "Why didn't you tell me?" she breathed to the voice, to Henri.

Henri grimaced painfully. "Humans have an… aversion to my kind."

You think? The voice was bitter. *And you, girlfriend, would never have believed me.*

Françoise could only stand and shake. Shocking as it might be, she couldn't deny the truth of it. The sensitivity to sunlight. The healing. He probably turned into a bat and spirited the prisoners away. "Do you drink their blood, the prisoners?" Her voice sounded callous, distant.

He turned his battered face away. "No."

"Then who do you kill to get what you need?"

"I don't kill." He still wouldn't look at her. "I take a cup from someone different every fortnight. It doesn't harm them." His voice was getting clearer. Was that true?

Yes. The voice was grudging. *But that doesn't change*

Susan Squires

that he sucks their blood.

Françoise looked at Henri, his body so battered, and guilt washed over her. She had caused this. He might be a monster, but he was still Henri. How could he keep them from torturing him if he wouldn't disappear? She peered at him in the dim light. Was that cut across his left breast sealing itself? His broken nose straightened, slowly. "How do you do that?"

"My infection is a parasite that has…unusual properties. It rebuilds its host."

"Are you…immortal?" The words hung in the air between them.

"Except for decapitation." His eye opened a little as the swelling drained. He looked more human, more like Henri. But he wasn't human. How had she ever even hoped he might love her? And she had, she realized in embarrassment. Why, he might have lived for…

Five hundred years.

Françoise's thoughts ricocheted around her brain. She put her hand over her mouth to keep herself from whimpering.

He saw her reaction and sagged in his chains, even as other cuts slowly sealed themselves. "Just go," he whispered. "Jennings will keep you safe. Forget the world holds creatures such as I am."

"How can I go, knowing what they will be doing to you?"

"I'll be fine. And what do you care? I'm only a monster."

Tears welled. She swallowed, unable to respond.

"Guards!" he shouted hoarsely. The clatter of boots sounded immediately. She felt their presence behind her. "Escort the lady out."

He was so used to giving orders, his certainty was as infectious as his blood. Footsteps sounded behind her. A hand took her elbow and turned her to the door. Tears were falling now.

Just go… The thought was only a whisper in her mind. The weight of the Conciergerie's grim stones settled on her shoulders as she followed the guard to the world above.

Eighteen

Françoise walked back to the Place Royale, her feet proceeding independent of thought. Henri was vampire. Anyone would call a vampire who sucked human blood a monster. Anyone sane. Henri wanted to frighten her with the name for what he was. Yet she still believed what she had told the voice. It was by one's actions that man and monster were measured. And by that scale, Henri was a good man.

And no matter what he was, he shouldn't be locked in the Conciergerie and tortured by that vicious woman. The very thought made her want to tear her hair. She had no faith that the Croûte woman who had hurt him so wouldn't hurt him again. Could he disappear? Would he?

You can't save him. Your only hope is to escape with the prisoners. If you stay here and by some chance he escapes, then you're back to leaving him or killing him, or getting infected and becoming just like him. Not attractive alternatives.

But how could the prisoners get on the barge if Henri's warehouse was being watched? And what of the servants at number sixteen? If they were left behind they might bear the brunt of Robespierre's wrath. She couldn't allow that. She'd come to care for them.

But what could she do? What could she do about any of it?

Across the park, Françoise saw several *sans-culottes* loitering in clear view of number sixteen. She stopped and melted into the deep shadows of an elm tree where the fading light angled off its trunk. The mob was watching Henri's house. Oh, this was bad.

"You're so fond of giving orders," she whispered to the voice. "What do you suggest?" A young man, passing, gave her an odd look. Talking to herself in the park. Oh, dear.

Susan Squires

I don't know jack anymore. From the point that you didn't get infected when Henri broke the glass, my experience seems almost irrelevant.

She didn't know who this Jack was, but it didn't matter. What was the voice talking about? "Enough of all this mystery. I can't think straight about helping Henri or the families he rescued or Henri's servants either if I can't control my own mind. Either I'm going to go mad right here, or you're going to tell me who you are and why you are inside me. Which is it?"

I'm afraid I'd blow your little mind.

She had a vision of an exploding head. There was a lot of blood involved. "I don't care."

I don't know what to do. The voice sounded suddenly tentative. *If I tell you everything, will I still exist? Maybe now that you're not infected I never lived more than a single lifetime. There is no Frankie, only Françoise.*

"You're afraid you'll...die?" Françoise skipped over the part about more than one lifetime. The voice was called Frankie and she was afraid she'd die.

Maybe I'll never have been. That's a more complete annihilation. All I wanted to do was come back and change the way things turned out. But I don't like being so weak I can barely pull open Henri's cell door. I hate not being able to smell, and see and taste and feel the way I used to. It's all so...dull. Is being just...you my destiny?

"Who are you?" Françoise was truly frightened now.

You don't even recognize me. The voice was depressed. *I thought I'd be the same person, just without the...monster part. But maybe that made me who I am. If I give that up...will I like being so stupidly optimistic and vulnerable?*

"Well!" Françoise harrumphed. "I'm the one with the body. And you can't control me. Headaches will just end me in an asylum or floating in the Seine. And then where would you be? Dead for sure. So I'm in charge." Was that true? She pushed on. She couldn't afford not to be in charge with everyone around her in trouble and no one to help them. "Stand and deliver."

Silence.

Time for Eternity

She searched for leverage in what the voice had implied. "If I'm your destiny then maybe you are mine. Maybe we need each other, Frankie, at least right now. Things are dire."

We're in a jam, all right. Along with a lot of other people like the people he rescued and his staff. I don't know what happened to them the first time around. I didn't know what he was doing. I was feeling sorry for myself in a garret on the Right Bank while...maybe while they were guillotining Henri. That's how he died. I thought maybe it was my drugs that let them kill him, but the first time around I wasn't involved, and you didn't have any drugs because there was no me to bring them back. So I don't know how they killed him.

Dear God! Henri... No. One thing at a time. "You'd better start telling me just what you mean by all this talk about the first time around," Françoise whispered. "We have to work together if we're going to change the fact that the prisoners can't escape with everyone watching them, and Henri may be guillotined, and I might...turn into a vampire. Take a chance." And then she stopped. There was nothing more she could say and they both knew it.

Emotion rolled deep inside her, her own fear, and the fear and uncertainty that came from this person named Frankie as well. They could feel each other.

She closed her eyes.

There was a slow exhale, whether her own or the voice's she didn't know. She slid down the tree trunk and sat at its base. Now. Now she would know.

*****

She was standing in the Hall of Mirrors at Versailles again. The mirrors were dim and smoky in the darkness across the room. A shadowy figure was reflected there. It began to run forward and she picked up her skirts and ran too. As they neared each other, she saw that the figure had her face, just as it had in her other dream. But it was dressed scandalously in

Susan Squires

tight leather breeches that went all the way to the ankle, heeled boots, and the veriest scrap of clinging bodice with a knitted silver net pulled over it. One could see every curve of her body. Her eyes were lined with kohl and her lashes thickened though she wore no white powder or patches.

And then they collided, melting into one another. The mirror melted away, the grand room spun round.

*****

Françoise gasped and clutched her head as the room in the vision disappeared and was replaced by cascading scenes complete with drenching emotions. A garret, Henri leaning over her, forcing her to drink his blood. Sickness. Being alone and afraid. Realizing what she was. Vampire. Strong. A monster. The period of crying and not getting up from the bed. Her first taste of blood. The revulsion when she killed those from whom she drank, the guilt. The first attempt at suicide. The knowledge that she couldn't end it, but was doomed to live the life she'd been handed forever. Learning to take less blood more frequently, so she didn't have to kill.

The images started coming faster, whole lives-full of memories. The melee of Paris greeting a triumphant Napoleon. The ship to the Americas. Living alone in cabins in various woods. Civilization encroaching on her again and again. Industry belching smoke. The horror of war again and again. Moving on, always moving on before anyone could find her, know her, love her. An endless string of places and faceless people arching up their necks for her to drink. And through all, the despair, even as it died down to glowing coals, beneath it the self-hatred. The dreams of killing Henri before he could infect her.

The images started to slow. A city of hills by the ocean, all sleek and strange. Glass glowed. Buildings were impossibly tall and featureless. A tavern with a glowing 0 with a tiny 2 hanging onto its hip above the door. She floated inside and there she was, talking to a beautiful woman. She knew what had been said, who the woman was. Donna. The excitement of believing that she might have a chance to come back and change everything consumed her. Then there was the pretty girl in the bookshop confirming that the book about the time machine had been written by Leonardo da Vinci. Rome. Florence. Il Duomo. The Baptistery. The gleaming machine. And Versailles.

The machine was at Versailles, and it had brought her back to now.

Frankie was Françoise herself. Only a Françoise who had been infected by Henri, abandoned by him—whether that was his fault or not—and who had learned to hate herself so much she was willing to kill Henri to prevent him making her a vampire.

She opened her eyes. The Place Royale seemed strange or maybe a little quaint. "Sorry I didn't recognize you," she said.

Silence.

"Are you there?" What if revealing herself *had* killed Frankie? Panic choked her throat. She needed Frankie to help Henri, and Gaston and Jean and Pierre and the families...

Yeah. I'm here. Which may mean that we're going to get infected by Henri no matter what we do. That's the only way there is a Frankie.

Françoise felt Frankie's horror at that as if it were her own. Which it was, in a strange way. "We've still got to save him, Frankie." She stood, still leaning against the trunk of the elm tree. She understood now what Frankie meant by "in a jam." They surely were in a jam. "Jennings." Maybe Jennings could help them.

A long pause. Frankie was deciding.

"We'll sort out the part about getting infected later. But we can't stand by and do nothing about what's happening around us."

I'm with you.

"Maybe forever. Might be dull for you. As you said— no special powers."

Maybe not. Maybe I'll just disappear if there's no

Susan Squires

longer a chance to get infected. The whole thing is a little wild, huh?

Not how she would have put it. But she understood what Frankie meant. "At least I'm not insane." She started back across the park, toward the river. Time to go to the warehouse.

Wait. If they've posted guards, you'll need a reason to get inside.

Françoise chewed her lip. Very well. A tray of food for Jennings. From a pretty young girl. She started back to the house. Pierre would provide.

Nineteen

Madame Croûte lifted her skirts in distaste as she came into the cell. "This floor is filthy. Wash down the stones twice a day," she commanded. At the shock in the guards' eyes, she snapped, "Not for him, idiots. For me. I refuse to dirty my shoes."

Henri was feeling better, at least physically. The drug was almost out of his system. His wounds had nearly healed. He could probably muster enough power to transport away. But the minute he did that, this despicable woman and Robespierre would descend on the warehouse and number sixteen, and tear them apart looking for him. People would get arrested, killed. Even Françoise, God forbid. They might find the prisoners behind the back wall of the warehouse. Or they might burn it down and almost a hundred people with it. He had to keep this creature focused on him until the barge could take the prisoners and Françoise down the Seine to Le Havre and safety. He wasn't quite sure just how to do that, short of letting her torture him. And he was not about to give her the satisfaction.

And then there was the problem of how to get the prisoners out He always loaded the escapees onto his barge in specially made crates right under everyone's noses. But Françoise was right. They'd be watching the warehouse and his barges. They must realize that was how he was spiriting the families out of the country. Only the drug had kept him from seeing the problem.

The depression that had dogged him since Françoise left settled on his shoulders. She'd been appalled at what he was, of course. She might not have intentionally betrayed him, but she'd wanted to escape him enough to drug him even before she could acknowledge to herself that she knew what he was. Now that she knew, she hated him, just like Cerise de Haviland four hundred years ago in Alcaise. He'd made sure of that. What choice had he? Françoise was in danger every minute she stayed in Paris. She should never have come to visit him, for God's sake. He only hoped all her talk of hearing voices didn't mean her mind was fragile. She'd grow strong again once she wasn't faced with the horror of a vampire in her life. She must. She was young. As for him, one way or another, the work he'd used to stave off madness was about to end. If he got this shipment of prisoners out, it would be the last. Had he made a difference? Perhaps it had all been pointless in the face of the evil the world seemed to spawn.

As Croûte sauntered over to him her eyes widened. "So you weren't lying," she remarked to the guards around her. "He does heal." They were setting up the brazier and the table with her implements arrayed on it. They had entered reluctantly, keeping nervous eyes on Henri.

He just stared at her. Let's see if she had the courage to torture him now that he was something she couldn't explain in her rationalistic world. She ran a hand over his chest, marked only by the faint pink of new skin.

The woman looked up into his face, speculating. She wasn't yet afraid of him. He healed—what of that? That wasn't a threat to her. Or maybe she did not comprehend anything beyond her small view of nature.

She touched his back where she had cut him during her last session. He could practically hear her thinking. She cupped his buttock as she said to the soldiers, "Send troops to search his residence for more of the drug the girl used on him. It was in a kind of soft lilac bottle." Even if there was more, they couldn't force it on him now. But the fact that she was calling for reinforcements showed that she was realizing she might not comprehend exactly what was going on here. A guard clicked his heels and nodded to acknowledge the order, turning crisply to stride out of the cell.

"In the spirit of scientific experimentation…" She held her hand out to the side, her gaze never leaving his face. "Knife," she barked. The big guard who had beat him senseless the last time put the handle of her favorite curved blade into her

Time for Eternity

palm. "Let's just see for ourselves." He'd let her have one cut. Let's see if she retreated when it healed. He flinched as she drew the blade across his left pectoral, leaving a deep cut. Fine Stoic he was. She motioned to the guard. "Hold that torch over here." She stepped back, staring intently at his chest. He could feel the wound begin to seal itself. Not as quickly as once it would have, but enough to be perceptible.

"Blessed mother Mary preserve us," one of the guards muttered.

Madame Croûte only grinned, though invoking Catholic saints was technically against the law. "A useful talent. That means you can heal whatever I choose to do to you. That will prolong our game, perhaps indefinitely."

Damnation. How could he keep her focused on him and not on Françoise and the others if she wasn't even frightened of him?

"But wait!" She seemed to consider. "Can you disappear?" She shook her head. "I think not, or you would have done it. Still, that last guard died swearing it was true."

Yet again he was the cause of death. But his was not the only blame here. This woman was evil. A plan began to form. Could he compel her to leave those he loved alone? Maybe with frequent renewals of the compulsion. And maybe if she knew he was nearby, and had to find him, that would keep her focused on him.

Let's play a little hide-and-seek. He let his eyes go red.

She stepped back, visibly shocked.

"Like what you see?" he murmured. He captured her gaze and watched her go slack. "You won't hurt Mademoiselle Suchet or any of my staff. You will not touch my property. Now," he added conversationally as he released her, "I'll be taking another family out. See if you can find me." *Companion!* The whirling darkness rose around his knees from the stones. Not as fast as he liked, but the effect was not lost on Croûte and the guards. Their eyes were wide. "I'll be joining you here later for another visit. Shall we say, an hour?" And he winked out of sight.

"I need a tray of food, Gaston," Françoise said, hurrying through to the kitchen.

"How is he?" Gaston trailed in her wake. He didn't have to say whom he was talking about. "Did you find him well?"

"Not good." She set her mouth. She wouldn't tell Gaston how bad it was. Or that Henri was a vampire. Or about the prisoners concealed in the warehouse. Or how much danger he and the other residents of number sixteen were really in. "Have the gendarmes been here?"

"Not yet. The mob is milling about in the park."

She glanced back at him. He knew his danger, then. "Don't tell them I have been here."

Gaston reached out and grabbed her shoulder. "Don't do anything foolish, mademoiselle. You must wait. Three days. It will all be over in three days."

She searched his face. Gaston knew about the prisoners hidden in the warehouse.

"They're watching the warehouse. He can't get them out."

Gaston looked perplexed.

"Besides, he can't last three days."

Gaston paled, but he gathered himself. "He is strong."

Did Gaston know how strong? "We can't let him suffer." She watched Gaston blanch further. "We have to hurry things along somehow."

Gaston straightened his shoulders. "What can I do?"

"I don't know."

Yes you do.

Frankie, as always, was right. "Wait. You can get the household out before the mob attacks. Is there somewhere you can go?"

"Calais. I have a cousin there."

She nodded. "Now, how can we get the servants out of the house?"

Time for Eternity

Gaston tapped his finger against his prim mustache, thinking. "I shall send them on errands one by one."

"They will be followed."

"Ahhh, but the market is crowded. One could lose oneself. Annette to Fanchon, the groom to the ironmonger, another to the saddler... I see how it can be done."

"Appoint a meeting place outside the city."

Gaston smiled. "And me, I go to the warehouse with you."

"No, no, my friend." She took his shoulders. "The staff depends on you for leadership. Their safety is in your hands."

"What about his grace?" Gaston was frowning again.

"His grace can escape when he knows everyone else is safe." Gaston didn't need to know how. "I will be sure he knows that all is well with you...and with everyone at the warehouse."

He got a mulish look about his mouth. She raised her brows in challenge. Gaston sighed. *"Oui,* mademoiselle. I shall do my part."

She smiled and patted his shoulders. "Now, go."

*****

Franchise hurried up the quay toward the warehouse with her covered tray. The sky was that peculiar greenish blue that would shortly deepen into twilight. It must be after seven. Torches were being lighted up and down the street. To her right, the Seine, a miasma of effluvia from a large and dirty city, rolled sullenly beyond the stone wall that lined the Quai Henri IV.

Two guards were posted at the warehouse. Several others lounged against the stone wall.

I told you so.

She swallowed once and hurried forward with her tray just as a whole marching troop of soldiers rounded the corner and spread out along the quay.

Uh-oh.

Susan Squires

Dreadful.

The only way any crates will get out of this warehouse is if the army takes them out.

Françoise stopped in mid-step. She sucked in a breath. "You're a genius, Frankie," she whispered under her breath. She could feel Frankie turning over the idea as well.

Mais bien sur. Françoise could practically feel Frankie grin. She hurried forward.

"Please, good messieurs, may I pass to take Monsieur Jennings his supper?"

"Locked up tight, he is." The older of the two guards had a paunch bursting two buttons on his uniform. That was quite an achievement in these troubled times when food was scarce. From inside the warehouse she heard the faint pounding of hammers and the creak of wood.

"Well, well, what have we here?" The man with a saber scar on his right cheek lifted the white linen cloth that covered her tray. "Cassoulet," he murmured reverently.

"Oui. Prepared by Pierre Dufond, the chef of the Duc d'Avignon himself. And bread of course, fresh from the oven." The guard lifted the lid of the other brown glazed dish. "Haricot verts. With fresh butter and almonds."

The guards looked as though they might drool onto the tray.

"One man can't eat all that," the heavy one said.

She glanced over her shoulder. Other guards were strolling across the street. "Enough to share with you two, but perhaps not for everyone." The two guards frowned at their compatriots. "I shall take the smaller pot of cassoulet and half a loaf, and give you the rest as a.. gratuity for opening the door."

"Done," said Saber Scar.

The heavyset one pulled one of the great wooden doors open. "Don't even think you're getting any of our due," he said to the two lounging up.

"Share and share, ye know," one of the newcomers said. The conversation took a decidedly belligerent turn.

Françoise bent, took her bowl and loaf, and slipped

Time for Eternity

inside while their attention was on keeping what they thought they had coerced from her.

Inside, the warehouse was dark. As when she had been here before with Avignon, crates and barrels loomed in the shadows. The smell of tar and brandy and dust was everywhere. Ahead, several pools of light illuminated the desk she remembered from the night Madame LaFleur had died. Three men in their shirtsleeves were knocking together crates.

Jennings looked up from where he was directing some others to bring bundled stacks of planks from the back. "Mademoiselle! What brings you here?" He hurried forward.

"You know they are watching the house and this place, don't you?"

He nodded. "Yes," he said, glancing back at the crates, worried. Then he took the tray from her with a question in his eyes.

"Pierre's cassoulet. My pretext for coming. Most went for a bribe to the guards." As he set it on the desk she decided she had no time to be roundabout "I know about the special cargo you have behind the back wall. He told me.

Jennings looked wary.

"They'll be watching any barges, and they'd open any crates and barrels you tried to load." He'd thought of that. She could see it in his eyes. He was building crates for human cargo because it was the only thing he knew to do. "The only way these crates are getting out of this warehouse is if the army takes them out."

"And how will we arrange that?" His disbelief was obvious.

"I think Avignon can arrange it."

He frowned. "He's in a cell in the Coneiergerie."

"But he has a frequent visitor. Madame Croûte. Who, if she thinks about it, would want the contents of this warehouse very much, especially since she is bent on killing the goose that lays these golden eggs. This will be the last clutch."

"You've seen him?"

She nodded, her mouth grim. "He's trying to hold out

until the ship arrives in Le Havre and the barge can get down the Seine. But it won't serve." She didn't want to dwell on why not.

The English had more restraint than the French, and while Gaston had asked about Henri, Jennings did not. "But once she has the crates, they'll be under as tight a guard as they are here."

Françoise smiled. "But then she'll have no reason to guard this empty warehouse."

Jennings's eyes widened. "So we don't move them in the crates at all?"

"They'll be on the lookout for Avignon's barges. Can you find another boat?"

Jennings frowned again. "Several skiffs would be better. Draw less attention. Maybe we can meet up with the *Maiden Voyage* in the Channel. If we get to Le Havre before it arrives." He'd gotten a gleam in his eye. "We'll break through the wall to the warehouse just to the south, bring them out there. But there are a lot of people behind that wall."

"Can you get them into the boats without anyone noticing?"

"We'll have to." He shrugged. He shot her a sharp look. "Any way to get Avignon out?"

"I'll take care of that. Just you mind your cargo." She looked around. It was strange to think there were people crammed in behind that back brick wall, silent and fearful.

She shot him a smile she hoped was confident "Time for me to go." She glanced to the cassoulet. "Enjoy your dinner."

*****

I thought that went rather well.

Françoise was hurrying down the quay toward the Conciergerie on the north end of the Ile de la Cité. "If he can get boats on such short notice. If Robespierre does not arrest him. If he can get them out without anyone noticing…too many ifs."

Time for Eternity

My, aren't we Little Miss Sunshine? What a glass-half-empty kind of girl.

Françoise knew what she meant, surprisingly, perhaps because she now shared experience with Frankie. "I am more optimistic than you are," she protested. "You never saw the good in Henri. You still think I should kill him or abandon him if he escapes. That is not a 'Miss Sunshine' girl either."

Because that may be the only way to prevent becoming like him.

"Was it so horrible?"

You know how lonely it was.

"You didn't *let* yourself be close to anyone."

Whoa. Bad me. Just because they'd fear me if they knew what I was. And don't forget that they'd age and die, and hate me either for abandoning them or because I didn't age with them ... How shallow of me to let that stand in the way of a relationship.

Françoise tried another tack. "But you weren't horrible, and neither is Henri."

I killed people.

"Not after you knew how to take less blood more frequently."

That was his fault. He left me there, not knowing anything. Frankie's distress was palpable.

"You said yourself there's a real possibility he couldn't come to you. Donna said he was guillotined about this time."

The thought of the guillotine shot through both of them and revulsion shuddered up from someplace so ancient and elemental that it would not be suppressed.

"How could they guillotine a vampire?" they thought together.

Donna said they could do it if he was injured too badly, or if his strength was sapped by being burned in the sunlight. I don't know how it happened the first time.

"But we know one way they might be able to do it now. They could drug him with the drugs you brought back."

God forgive me.

Susan Squires

Françoise turned. They had to get back to the house and pour those bottles out before the drug could be used on Henri. *Hurry.*

*****

Françoise slipped behind a tree in the Place Royale park. She wanted to cry but Frankie wouldn't let her. Gendarmes swarmed in front of number sixteen. Their torches lit the night. How many servants had gotten out? Now she couldn't even approach to find out.

They'll find the morphine in the shampoo bottles.

It made sense. It was the path of time when Henri had been guillotined trying to come true, even though somehow Frankie had bent time enough that Henri hadn't made Françoise vampire the way it had happened before.

Maybe we can't change the part where he dies.

"Well, we are certainly going to try," Françoise breathed. There wasn't much time. Françoise slid through the night with all the practice of Frankie's two hundred years of experience. Only when she reached the other end of the park did she start to run.

*****

Henri shimmered into the cell again. The warehouse had one more family of four. It had been a joy to take them out under the nose of Madame Croûte, though it had taken almost all his strength to transport four times in one night. But he had seen all the troops around the warehouse. What good to get them there when there was no way to get them out? He hadn't even seen Jennings, just deposited the children behind the wall and gone back for the parents before the guards or Croûte could realize what had happened.

No guards loitered outside his cell now. No point when it was supposed to be empty. They'd be back soon. It had been nearly an hour. He just hoped his compulsion on Croûte worked on a mind that was so bent. But she'd be back too in a few moments and he could give her a refresher course.

What he wanted was Françoise. One touch. That would sustain him.

But he didn't want that. He wanted her out of Paris. Out of his life. Out of danger.

He heard steps down the hall. Several. Voices. Guards. Was Croûte back so soon? She would be very angry now that she knew another family had escaped.

Dread warred with relief as he saw Françoise appear. With her halo of golden curls flaring with light from the torches, she looked like an angel.

She hurried in then turned on the guards who had accompanied her. "Go. You promised."

They looked shocked that he was inside the locked cell, though free of his manacles. "Your funeral, Mademoiselle. That brute is not human." One of them opened the cell as the other held loaded pistols on Henri. "Croûte will be back any minute. Either he gets you or she will." They locked her in with him.

Françoise stood, coiled, as the footsteps strode away, then flung herself forward, stopping only inches from his chest. "Oh, Henri, are you all right?" She scanned his body.

"I'm well," he said. Better for seeing her. But she shouldn't be here. "I told you to go to Jennings." He wanted to hold her. But he held himself rigid instead.

She moved a lock of hair away from his face. Her touch was gentle. "I've been to Jennings. That's why I came. We don't have much time, Henri. They are searching the house. I'm not sure Gaston got all the staff out."

"Looking for the drug." He smiled grimly. "She can't make me take it. I hope she can't really torture my staff. I used my power on her mind. But I'm not certain of that."

She glanced behind her to be sure the guards weren't lurking. Then she moved in and stood on tiptoe to whisper. 'The only way your cargo will leave the warehouse is if they stop guarding it. She'll want all that lace and brandy and salt, won't she?"

275

Susan Squires

He blinked at her.

"If she takes all your goods, why guard the warehouse?"

The girl had a plan. And it was not a bad plan.

"Only you can plant the idea in her little avaricious brain. Jennings is getting skiffs ready. He'll take them out through the warehouse next door after the goods are gone. It's risky."

"Better than nothing. If the families get out, I'll see to my staff. There are fewer of them…

At that moment the murmurs of the guards down the hall stopped. Boot heels clicked.

"What are you doing out here?" Croûte's voice accosting the guards.

Damnation. There were few choices. He couldn't let the Croûte woman find Françoise here. He grabbed her and drew her into his naked body.

"Why guard an empty cell?" The guards were trying to delay Croûte. That was good.

"Don't be afraid. And try not to scream."

Companion! The power welled up his veins like slow sludge. But the room went red. He had enough. Barely. He called for more. As he held Françoise, a feeling of rightness enveloped him. Where to go? The answer surprised him. Dare he? The whirling darkness was already at their knees. Françoise looked up at him with frightened blue eyes. She was biting her lip. It might just stop the scream.

"Good girl." He smiled in reassurance and thought about the boudoir he knew so well.

The room went black. Françoise emitted a gurgling sound of suppressed pain.

Red wallpaper flocked with fleur-de-lis popped into life around them. "Are you all right?" he whispered, as she turned in his arms. He saw her gather herself. She nodded.

"I knew what to expect."

Of course she couldn't have known that. He glanced around. Marianne Vercheroux had turned on the little upholstered stool that sat before her dressing table and was peering into the corner. He had chosen a shadowed area near

276

Time for Eternity

the dressing room, as though they might have just walked in instead of appearing in a whirl of darkness. There was little explanation he could offer for the fact that he was naked.

"Marianne, you must take care of her until I can come for her." He pushed Françoise into the center of the room. "A day, no more."

"Henri?" Marianne stood, wide-eyed. "How did you get in? What…what's happened…?"

"No time, Marianne. I must get back. I have a job to do. Just keep her safe, will you?"

He felt for the dressing room door behind him. Françoise turned those big eyes on him. They were so wise and sad, it startled him. He glanced to Marianne Vercheroux. He willed her to do as he asked but he dared not use his power. He had need of every drop he had. She lifted her brows, then sighed, sad, accepting. She nodded. Henri allowed himself a half-smile as he shut the dressing room door. Before it could even click shut the blackness whirled up around him.

*****

Françoise stared after the closing door. She wanted to run to him, to tell him not to go back there. What if Madame Croute had the drug? Could that woman give it to him against his will? Henri thought not. But he might be wrong. And then she could send him to the guillotine.

He knew that. But he would not leave those families in the lurch. And she herself had given him a task. Her eyes filled.

Frankie said nothing, but Françoise could feel that she was frightened for him too. Together they turned to Madame Vercheroux. Why had Henri brought her here? Hiding with his spurned lover was not a choice that immediately sprang to mind.

The woman looked…resigned. "Why, you ask yourself? Because he knows I am a romantic, under it all. And I will not thwart true love, even if it comes at my own expense."

"He doesn't love me." How it hurt to say that. "You

Susan Squires

told me yourself he doesn't love."

The woman's smile was sad. "Did I say that? Perhaps I did."

Françoise looked over her shoulder. The buzz of electric aliveness was already gone.

Madame Vercheroux turned back to her mirror and wiped away a speck of something from the edge of her eye. "La," she said lightly, "but how lucky my Deirdre had a cold in the chest tonight. I cannot bear another to handle my *maquillage* or I would have had a dresser with me even now." She glanced in the mirror to Françoise. "I am asking myself how he will get through the streets unnoticed when he is stark naked. But he will manage, just as he managed escaping to bring you here." She looked up sharply. "Was his carriage seen?"

Françoise thought quickly. "No, we came in a hired hack. I covered him with my cloak."

Madame Vercheroux swallowed. "Why he would want to go back there I cannot think. But that is where he is going, isn't it?"

Françoise nodded. A woman who cared this much for Henri, even if he didn't love her, would know that Henri wouldn't be thinking of his own escape.

"Very well. You will stay here tonight in this room. I will go out as planned. I must be seen or my absence will be noted."

True. Madame Vercheroux caused a stir wherever she went. Françoise looked around at the four walls of Madame's boudoir and wondered if she would still be sane by morning.

Madame got up and patted her hand. "He will be all right. He always is."

But Françoise could see the worry in her eyes.

Twenty

Henri shimmered into the cell at the Conciergerie in one corner. The guards were blocking the cell door bars, trying to keep Madame Croûte from seeing inside, where they would think Françoise still stood. He blew out the torch to his left that shed light in his corner even before the whirling darkness had drained away. She peered around the guards' broad shoulders. "Is he here?"

Henri leaned against the stone, his arms crossed over his chest, one ankle crossed over the other, as though he hadn't a care in the world. "I'm here."

The guards turned to stare, giving Madame Croûte her opening. She pushed past them. "Open this door at once." The guards took in the fact that they had locked a girl in with him, a girl who was now nowhere in evidence, though the door was still securely locked. No guard made a move, and Madame Croûte did not protest when she saw Henri unchained.

The big guard crossed himself. If Madame Croûte saw the gesture, she made no comment. Her eyes narrowed. She carried a basket. More knives? Acid? His stomach rolled. It didn't matter. She wouldn't have the courage to come inside now.

"Why did you bother to return?"

Henri smiled, slowly. "I suppose just to see the look on your face." He pushed off the wall and strolled across the cell. The remaining guards pressed themselves against the far wall and reached for their weapons. "I am rather disappointed in you, Croûte. So fixated on getting answers from me you know I'll never give you. You have another opportunity. One that will ensure you never experience again what that girl of fifteen endured. I'm surprised you didn't think of it immediately."

She didn't want to ask him what the opportunity was.

Susan Squires

She clenched her thin lips. He pushed a shackle and watched it swing at the end of the chain. He caught a strange scent mingled with the soldiers' sweat and the urine and blood in his cell, and of course, the pervasive smell of old stone. He knew that scent, but he couldn't place it.

"What opportunity?" The words seemed torn from her.

He smiled and shrugged, pushed the shackle again. "Well, no matter what happens here, I'm done with my role as the official... procurer of difficult items."

Her brows drew together. She didn't want to admit she hadn't thought of that.

"So that lace you're wearing? The brandy your little lawyer likes so much? All over now." He watched her digest it. "Except what's in the warehouse." He paced to the other side of the cell, and leaned again on the wall. "You could burn it. Or let the mob have it, I expect. Distribute the wealth and all. Or..."

The calculation began behind her eyes.

"The profit is one hundred percent when one didn't pay for the goods in the first place. Enough for security all one's days... He paused, as if considering. "Or keep some for personal use and sell the rest. Of course one would have to cart it to a safe place before the Revolutionary Council confiscates it."

She was looking at him, but she wasn't seeing him. "Difficult. There's the matter of the soldiers guarding it for Robespierre..."

Croûte's eyes focused again. "I can take care of that," she snapped. A small smile played about her mouth. "Obviously you know by now who pulls the strings behind the little lawyer." She cocked her head on one side. "And lest you make others' mistake and think I'm stupid, I know your ploy. You're trying to keep me busy until your ship arrives in Le Havre and you can get your prisoners to it."

Henri kept his face still through centuries of practice, though he dared not breathe.

"But perhaps you don't know that we have your cook and your majordomo, right here in this very prison. We haven't

Time for Eternity

yet found the girl, but we will."

Damn. Was her mind so chaotic that he couldn't compel her? "Did you not understand my instructions?"

"I did. And somehow you can compel minds with your red eyes. But I had already issued the order, and no one compels the mob. They're looking for your ward even now. So I trust you'll be here when I return?"

"I'll be here." At least the rest of the household had escaped. He could only hope she wasn't smart enough to look for Françoise at the house of his last lover.

She wouldn't have the courage to enter the cell again. He'd be spared the knives. He'd know when the warehouse was empty of crates because she'd be back to gloat. He must put his faith in Jennings to get his charges away. He'd give Jennings enough time. Then he'd find Pierre and Gaston. He'd get them down to the quai along with Françoise.

"Until we meet again." Croûte turned on her heel and left with her basket still on her arm, taking that elusive scent with her.

*****

It was near morning. Françoise paced the red-flocked boudoir like a caged bear. How many hours?

Seven. Stop pacing. You'll wear yourself out.

Seven. That was time enough to have emptied the warehouse. Had Jennings been able to procure skiffs? Was the warehouse still guarded?

"I should be helping Jennings."

He told you to stay here.

"Since when are you taking Henri's part?" She retrieved her cloak from the tiny, round-backed chair upholstered in gold brocade. "I thought someone who has lived for two hundred years with strength and supernatural powers would have a lot more courage."

I'm old enough to know that things never work out well. Frankie's tone was defensive. *And I'm the one who's trying to*

Susan Squires

do something about our situation.

"By killing Henri?" Françoise snorted. "It's a good thing one of us is young enough to believe in him or we'd botch our second time around more thoroughly than the first."

I didn't botch the first time around. I was made vampire and abandoned, remember?

"Had it ever occurred to you that if you had gone to help Henri, instead of automatically assuming that he'd abandoned you, with all your new powers you might have been able to save him from the guillotine?" Françoise swirled her shawl around her shoulders.

Frankie was silent. Françoise could feel the shock that her statement had caused though. And well it should. Fear wound itself around her own spine. Henri had been killed in that other life. And Frankie might not want to stop that happening.

But Françoise did.

And Frankie would know it.

"We'll sort this out later," she whispered, going to the window. She opened the casement and peered out. Madame Vercheroux's boudoir looked out on a tiny garden under a pergola covered with an old and gnarled wisteria vine. She might just be able to reach it with her toes if she let herself hang from the sill. She took a breath. Well. What were her choices? She couldn't get out past Madame Vercheroux's servants without causing a stir. And she didn't want to get Madame in trouble for having helped her.

Being so weak really sucks.

Françoise picked up her skirts.

*****

Henri paced his cell, ignoring the guards who cowered in the shadowy corridor, their taunting and bravura gone. Where was Croûte? Hadn't enough time passed for her to empty the warehouse?

Maybe if he waited for her return, it would be too late. Maybe she had already found the families and they needed his protection. If there was anything he could do to protect them. Or maybe she had found Françoise. But if he transported out too soon... His brain couldn't help replaying all the possibilities in a tattoo of probable failure.

You'd think that in a life of five hundred years, he would have learned patience.

Maybe what was bothering him was the fact that he didn't have all his eggs in a basket he could protect. Maybe he should find Gaston and Pierre, get Françoise. He had power enough for only one or two more transports tonight. He should go for Gaston and Pierre first, since he couldn't get them out any other way. If he used up his power on them, he'd have to take Françoise across town physically and hope to avoid the mob. Not great odds.

It always ended badly. Always. He got some out, but there were so many more he couldn't save. The world devolved into the chaos of stupidity at every turn. His years weighed upon him, along with the coming despair of living without Françoise.

Françoise. She had a plan to get the families out. What an act of faith in possibilities that was. He couldn't let her plan fail. He had to draw on a little of her faith and get to it. Dawn was an hour or two away. Jennings had to get the prisoners out tonight.

So there was no time for patience. He must go, no matter the odds. Relief washed through him. He might not win through, but his course was clear. He had to try. He drew his power about himself like a cloak. The world went red. He was for Pierre and Gaston. But first...

Two of the guards were physically shaking. The metal of pistol barrels and sword and scabbard clattered against each other. He swept his gaze across them, capturing their will. "You," he said to the biggest of them, a strapping lad with a luxuriant mustache. "Strip and hand your clothes through the bars."

*****

Susan Squires

"Monsieur Jennings," Françoise whispered fiercely at the gaping door of Henri's warehouse. "Are you here?" A faint sound of irregular thumping and crashing came from the back. She peered into the darkness. The entire floor of the giant building was empty, except for the detritus of broken crates and barrels, and Monsieur Jennings's desk, made small now by the open sweep of space around it.

She stepped inside. Far away in the corner to her right, she saw four or five figures, Jennings and several of his men in shirtsleeves and one or two dressed in torn and dirty lace and satin. The fathers of the families. Monsieur Navarre grinned at her, and saluted, his eyes no longer sad, before he turned back to his task. She had never realty believed the families were here in the warehouse, but now she could see a piece of the rear wall in jagged brick pattern had been swung open like a door. When it was shut it would leave no sign of what it was. But open, she could hear a baby wail, and low female voices.

The men took turns in twos swinging large, heavy-headed hammers at a section of the side wall. The others hauled away the bricks and mortar.

Jennings looked up. "Mademoiselle Suchet, what are you doing here?"

"I've come to help. Do you have boats?"

"Aye. Tied up two docks down. Enough, I think." He sounded a bit doubtful. He glanced to the door and strode across to shut it. "Was that open when you came?"

She nodded. "I saw no one in the street but a scruffy urchin. No soldiers."

Jennings sighed in relief. "Well, Croute took the bait."

"Looks like she took everything."

A large section of the wall collapsed. The men pushed through grimly. "Get on to the next wall," Jennings ordered in French. He turned to Françoise. "The warehouse two over has stairs down that go under the street from inside the building to where the boats are tied. Less chance of this little parade being seen."

"What can I do?" Françoise asked.

Time for Eternity

"Look confident and go to the women. They'll have to keep the children quiet when we start to move." Françoise nodded and turned to leave.

Why does he do it?

Good question. She turned back. "You are *Anglais.* These people are nothing to you. Why do you risk anything for them?"

Jennings's hatchet face grew grim. Then he managed a shrug. "What are they to Avignon, just because he's French? Every other Frenchman looks the other way. Maybe the right question is, what is Avignon to me? And that's a long story, miss. Let's just say he done something for me once when no one else would lift a finger to help me and mine."

Henri seems to inspire fanatic loyalty in spite of his nature.

Françoise nodded. "Something to think about," she said to both Jennings and Frankie, and hurried back to the open brick doorway.

One boat was away, another half filled with women in big skirts, their panniers torn out to make extra room, children in ragged dresses and grimy short pants, babes in arms, and worried, dour fathers. Three more rocked at their moorings, empty. The first boat was only a shadow, the creak of oars lost as it moved downstream. Dawn was coming soon. Jennings handed a woman who once had been heavy down onto the ladder to the rocking boat below. Now her skin sagged about her chin, sallow from prison.

"Give my best to the 'Dark Lord.' " She must mean Henri. Did she know what he was? But of course, they all did. He had used red eyes and whirling darkness to rescue them.

Monsieur Navarre handed her child down to her and reached for the next woman's hand.

"Will he be coming with us?" The woman held a toddler's hand. "He has been so kind."

"I do not know, Madame," Navarre said.

"I shall pray for his safety," the woman said, scooping up her child with one hand and her skirts in the other.

Susan Squires

"I only hope we can repay his kindness," a young girl of about fourteen said, as she helped her mother into the boat. "He read us stories for an hour every night." She blushed. "The little ones enjoyed it."

Henri had visited them every night?

"And to have his personal chef prepare our meals," Navarre said. "That was the outside of enough."

"He could shush my Charles when no one could quiet him. And here I was afraid at any moment he'd spit up on his grace's silks." This woman cuddled a curly-headed child not yet two.

"Plays a mean game of piquet," another man said as he hurried the next woman into the boat. "I think he let us win, though."

Jennings chuckled. "Well, you wouldn't have accepted money direct, would you? It's his way." He gestured to two men. "You two take the oars and this one's full."

They practically revere him. Frankie was stunned.

It was hard to imagine Henri dandling little Charles on his knee. He'd done it all to reassure them. All the women were secretly in love with him. All the men admired him. Even though they knew what he was. That was…interesting.

The prisoners and several of Jennings's men took up oars and the second boat slid out into the darkness. Françoise looked up to see the next group of people hurry down the steps that came out under the level of the stone streets above to the wooden docks that jutted out thirty feet across the muddy banks to where the sluggish, smelly water rolled through the city. Barges creaked in the darkness of the deeper water beyond, some weighted down with cargo, and others moored for use by bathers, though why anyone would want to bathe in waters that floated corpses and garbage, night filth and the runoff from the slaughterhouses, Françoise couldn't say. It was especially foul in July when the water level was low.

They moved down to where the next boat rocked. Françoise hurried the women down the steps. A little boy asked, "Where are we going?" in a plaintive voice that echoed with frightening clarity in the predawn air. His mother shushed him. The city would be stirring soon. They didn't have much time.

"We better start loading two boats at once," Jennings said *sotto voce* to Navarre. "Go bring the next group out." Navarre nodded and took off up the wooden dock at a run. Emile watched him with big eyes. But he didn't cry. Perhaps even he felt the tension in the air. "You, there, get that rope ladder. They won't like it, but we're running out of time."

Out of the shadows under the steps up to the street above, Henri stumbled, burdened with something heavy over his shoulder. Beside him, Gaston sank to his knees with a gasp. Françoise had never been so relieved in her life.

More families poured from the doorway and streamed past Henri toward the boats.

"Henri," she whispered, running toward him. He was dressed like a soldier in the blue of the Revolution, a sword swinging at his hip. His dark mane spread across his shoulders. His face was lined and tired-looking.

Relief washed his expression. Then he frowned. He strode forward, not setting down his burden. "Can't you follow orders? You might have been taken."

"I wasn't." The burden was Pierre. "Oh, dear. Is he alive?"

"Yes. He has a head injury thanks to the mob." He gave a curt nod to Jennings, who had hurried up behind her. "Can you get these two into a boat?"

"Aye. We're already riding a little low. We might as well ride lower." He motioned to one of his men, who took the groaning Pierre from Henri.

"And Mademoiselle Suchet, of course," Henri said, to Jennings, not to her.

"Of course."

"What about you?" She couldn't help that it sounded like an accusation. Behind her a third boat pushed off the dock and shushed away into the river.

At that moment she heard a noise above them on the street. The noise of many people. The urchin she had seen earlier peered over the stone wall. A glow made him stand out in stark silhouette. Françoise stood riveted, as she and Frankie both realized what that innocent urchin might really mean. Jennings looked over his shoulder from his place directing the disposition of the ladder. Henri turned.

The dirty child pointed at them. Shouts echoed into the lightening darkness. Behind him the glow resolved itself into torches, and a crowd appeared. A shouting, angry crowd.

Henri swiveled to survey the boats and the refugees. They were still climbing down into two of the remaining three boats. Jennings looked grim.

"Shall we push off with what we've got?" he asked.

Françoise saw Henri purposefully let the tension out of his shoulders. He pulled his sword. "I'll hold them off until you can get everyone away."

He turned toward the crowd. It had already grown.

"You can't!" Françoise pleaded, taking his arm. "You'll be killed."

He won't. But they both knew that in some other version of this experience, Henri had been guillotined. What had Donna said? Enough damage or sunlight Françoise glanced to the lightening sky. Was this the beginning of that dreadful end?

"Take her to the boat, Jennings." He didn't look at her. He just stood there, his sword limp in his hand.

Jennings pulled her away. Françoise looked up at him, aghast. "You're not going to let him sacrifice himself, are you?"

Henri took off at an easy lope toward the wooden steps up to the street.

"It's him or all of them, miss," Jennings said, just as though he weren't wrestling her toward the boats with a big hand on each of her elbows. "He made his choice a long time ago."

"Henri!" she cried.

He took the steps two at a time, sword now at the ready. She recognized the uniform of the *sans-culottes* as men poured down the stairs, shouting and crying for blood.

Time for Eternity

Jennings practically pushed her over the side of the dock and into Gaston's waiting arms. Narvarre swung down, with Emile in one arm and settled the child on a bench. Families poured into the other boats.

"I have to go to him!" She struggled toward the ladder. The boat tipped precariously.

"He wouldn't want that," Gaston whispered to her.

Jennings cast off the lines then swung down the ladder. "To your oars, lads." Three of his men and two of the tattered aristocratic fathers, including Narvarre, sat down at the oarlocks. Jennings took the remaining oar and pushed the boat away from the dock. "And do you think we can put our backs into it?"

Françoise stood in the center of the boat as it turned slowly out into the current. Henri advanced up the stairway, thrusting and tossing adversaries over the railing. She turned as the boat turned so that she could see the tableaux of terrible courage. Gaston pulled her down to sit Henri had made it to the top. Maybe...

She saw the first knife thrust home, just above his kidneys as the crowd engulfed him. Cudgels rose and fell.

He can survive this.

But both she and Frankie knew it was likely he would not. Françoise might have avoided becoming vampire, but Henri was on a path to the Place de Revolution. The boat found the sluggish current and the oars began to send it downstream in earnest. She was dimly aware of the other boats at her back gliding downstream with them.

The scene on the quay began to recede. Henri was still standing. She saw his sword gleam red in the light from the torches. Men still fell over the stone balustrade as he dispatched them. But they were on him now like ants engulfing a larger prey, stinging. She saw him stagger. Sabers flashed now into the torchlight.

Then she couldn't see him anymore, only the ragged crowd. The whole was like a painting, small and unreal, a step removed from the pain and the anguish that drifted on the air.

Susan Squires

She hardly realized she was trembling until Gaston put his arm around her, and then the tears that had been coursing down her cheeks turned into sobs. She buried her head in Gaston's shoulder and cried into his coat that smelled of prison.

He made soothing sounds. She looked up and saw him dash away a tear. They sat, looking back, long after they could no longer see the scene on the docks. The boats passed under the Pont Neuf, pulling downstream hard, past the stark walls of the Conciergerie. The refugees were silent as they passed the scene of their former suffering.

"He was a good man," Gaston muttered.

Even Frankie had to agree.

Twenty-one

The blows stopped. That was strange. The sun was rising, somewhere. The gray of dawn had lightened into a bloodied glow. Appropriate, since he was lying in a pool of his own blood. The scent of blood was almost overwhelming. He rolled his head. The crowd had parted. He hardly felt the pain of a last sword thrust. He was distant from himself, removed.

There it was—that strange smell again. He sucked in a breath. He was still able to do that. It was the smell of the drug Françoise had given him in his brandy.

Above him, he saw Croûte's face appear, distorted, as though it were seen through a magnifying glass.

"Well, well." The voice echoed horribly. "You got them out. For now. We will still catch them. We are everywhere. Your sacrifice was for nothing."

She knelt beside him and pulled aside his coat "You might heal even this. But you won't escape." She uncapped the soft bottle and pulled his jaw open. He couldn't resist. Maybe he didn't want to resist. It was over now. No purpose to his life. Everyone he ever cared for gone. Perhaps Croûte would do for him what he could not do for himself. End it.

End. That sounded peaceful. Though he would have to face the guillotine to gain peace.

She poured a good portion of the bottle down his throat.

*****

Françoise woke slowly. She was hot. She cracked her eyes and shaded them with her hand against the glare.

"Are you awake, *ma petite?*"

Gaston. She nodded and sat up. She'd been cradled in his lap.

Susan Squires

"Good, for it is my turn at the oars." He whipped a handkerchief from his coat pocket, miraculously white. "Perhaps you could soak this in the water, and give Pierre some comfort?"

Françoise nodded. Her eyes felt like scratchy, dry pebbles. Gaston relieved one of the older aristocrats at the oars.

"I'm hungry," a little girl wailed.

"Soon, *ma chérie,"* her mother whispered with frightened eyes.

Françoise looked around. They were moving through the countryside northwest of Paris, among the barges. There were other boats, but their own, heavily loaded craft looked conspicuous. Who would not realize they were fleeing?

She got up and knelt beside Pierre, who was sitting up, but looked gray. "How are you, my kitchen wizard?" she whispered. His limpid brown eyes held despair. He shook his head slowly. She dipped the handkerchief over the side in water noticeably less foul than in the city. The river was bigger here too, having taken on several tributaries on its way to the coast north. "Jennings will get us away."

"Who will appreciate my magnificence? No one had so discerning a palate as his grace."

Françoise had trouble breathing for a moment. She could not answer him, but instead wrung out the cloth and dabbed at his head.

Jennings pulled at his oar. He looked exhausted. She gave her handkerchief to Pierre and crawled over several people to get near him. She raised her brows in inquiry.

"What?" he gasped, bending his back and reaching forward.

"We are rather conspicuous."

"Avignon's barge should be coming upriver somewhere between here and Rouen. Closer to Montes-la-Jolie if we're lucky."

"Is that the plan?"

He nodded, pulling at the oar. "We'll take the barge to Le Havre. If we're lucky the *Maiden Voyage* will just be coming in. If not, we pull out into the Channel. We'll find her.

And then it's to England." He said the word reverently.

She sighed. For him England meant life. She had the worst feeling that what meant life to her was on the way to the guillotine. The drugs she'd brought back from her future were a means to his end, if the wounds he sustained and the sunlight were not. And there seemed to be nothing she could do about it. The path of history was like a river, flowing inexorably back into its course. She crawled to the back of the boat and sat in the stern, looking back toward Paris.

Well, you got your way, Frankie, she thought. *We aren't vampire. And if Henri's dead, he can't ever make you vampire. So why doesn't that feel good?*

I don't know.

Maybe because a good man died. One I love. You never loved him like that, did you?

I thought I did. Frankie was pensive. *But it was just infatuation with the wicked duc. I never really knew him. Not like you do. You were right. When I thought I was abandoned... I automatically blamed him.*

So why do you think I looked for the real Henri this time around? Something was niggling at Françoise's brain.

Maybe it took both of us together to see the truth. My experience and your... your optimism.

Françoise chuffed a bitter laugh. *A kind word for naïveté. I'm not optimistic now.* A weight settled on her, doubly heavy because it settled on Frankie too. Her future had changed and yet it hadn't. She was going to be just as disappointed, as cynical as Frankie. She'd just achieve it in a single lifetime.

Wait.

She sucked in a breath. *Frankie, you're still here.*

I know what you're going to say. It's just one of these time-travel-conundrums. If Robert Heinlein couldn't figure it out, I sure can't.

Françoise pulled herself up, thinking hard. *No, you said it yourself. Frankie, you only exist if I am made vampire. If I die in a single lifetime, there is no you. So it's still possible that Henri makes me vampire.*

Susan Squires

Silence.

I'll take that as an affirmative. Which means he's not dead yet. Françoise inhaled and felt a power over her own destiny fill her lungs. *We could still save him.*

No, no, no, no, no. We are not going back there. You can't risk being made vampire.

What's so bad about it? He doesn't kill people to get blood. You didn't either, once you understood how to do it. And you didn't do anything with your powers because you were frightened and you hated yourself. But Henri helped people with his powers.

A drop in the bucket.

Better than no drop at all. Look around you. What would the world be like if these hundred people had died?

Probably better off, Frankie grumbled.

Françoise stared pointedly at Emile, his thumb in his mouth, being cradled by Christophe Navarre.

Okay, okay. The world isn't ever better off beheading children.

Ex*actly. Or as you would* say... *Bingo.*

You're going back to try to save him, aren't you? Frankie seemed disgusted but resigned.

But that was a problem, wasn't it? Françoise swallowed. *But how to get off the boat? I don't swim.*

A silence ensued. Françoise could feel Frankie holding something back. At last Françoise heard Frankie's muttered, *I do. I swim.*

Françoise let certainty wash through her. That was her answer. Gaston and Jennings would try to stop her. But when night fell, she could slip over the side. She still had coins from the roulades she had used to bribe the guards in the pockets tied inside her skirts. She'd hire a carriage. She might not be in time. But how could she not try?

Like you're going to break into the Conciergerie. She's drugged him. He was wounded. You'll never get him out.

I'll think about that later.

You'll get made vampire and I'll have come back here for nothing. Talk about bitter.

294

Time for Eternity

If he isn't guillotined, maybe things turn out differently. Maybe you have lifetimes of love with him. Maybe you're happy.

Frankie snorted. *You heard Marianne Vercheroux. He doesn't love women. Especially not twenty-one-year-old almost virgins.*

Françoise swallowed. Henri didn't love her. It didn't matter. *You must make a stand somewhere,* she thought to Frankie. And that was it, wasn't it? You must try to get what you wanted. And Françoise wanted Henri alive. No matter the cost. No matter if he loved her.

She loved him and that was all she had for certain. How far she had come from her girlish infatuation with the wicked duc. If she had ever guessed that the wicked duc was actually vampire, she would have run screaming from Paris. If she had guessed that he was a good man, she would have been equally shocked. But there it was. He was both a monster and a good man, and "wicked duc" didn't come close to compassing the depth, the complexity of him. It was that complexity she had fallen in love with. She hadn't even known what love was when she had mooned over her delightfully forbidden next-door neighbor. Now her love would go unrequited, and maybe she'd be vampire. Would she end up bitter and jaded like Frankie?

No, she wouldn't. This was her choice. That made all the difference.

Looks like you'll be stuck with me, Françoise thought.

They call that multiple personalities, and it means you're insane.

What's more insane than time travel?

They could kill you, you know.

And worse. Madame Croûte had tortured Henri. "It doesn't matter," she whispered to herself, as much as to Frankie. *I'll hate myself if I don't take this chance. And you of any know what that does to one.*

At least I'm a good swimmer?

Françoise smiled. Frankie had just given in. She could feel Frankie's conflict, her doubt. But there were always

Susan Squires

doubts. One just had to absorb the doubt and...and do what had to be done anyway.

*****

The carriage changed horses at Poissy for the last time. It was near dawn by the time she reached Paris, just twenty-four hours since she'd seen Henri fall under the swords at the quay. Croute could not have sent him to the guillotine the same day. She'd want to toy with him. Françoise held to that. Her clothes were almost dry from her swim in the Seine, but her money was gone. That meant she had only one thing to barter for her entry to the Conciergerie. It was that thought that gave her the idea for how to get Henri out.

Lunatic plan.

"How appropriate for us."

Don't count me in on this one, baby doll. You'll get made vampire somehow, and then...

"Then you don't cease to exist. That's good, isn't it?"

Silence. *Maybe. Maybe not.*

Françoise leaned out the window and asked the driver to let her out by the Quai de l'Horloge at the far end of the Pont Neuf just next to the Conciergerie.

She made her way straight to the gatehouse. No one would expect visitors at this ungodly hour. She was wearing one of Fanchon's creations—a befrogged day dress in blue and black that she knew made her eyes even bluer. It might be the worse for wear, but no one could mistake its line, the drape of the fabric, the costly braid, or the expensive brooch that looked like a military medal. It would do. A huge iron grate had been lowered in the stone archway in front of the gatehouse. She leaned up against it. *"Alors,"* she called. "Is there a man inside?"

A sleepy head poked out of the guardhouse. Thank the Lord, it was the guard whom she had first bribed. He looked around for the source of the call, *"Ici, "* she called. "I am here."

He frowned in recognition. "You again?"

"But yes. With the same purpose."

Time for Eternity

The young man shook his head. "Not this time, sweetling. Croûte's got your...whatever he is...locked up tight, at least until she sends him down to get his hair cut"

Françoise gasped. "He is going to the guillotine? Today?"

"Can't say I'm sorry about that. So no more visits. Regardless of the price."

Don't believe him. They all want what you're going to offer. He'll take you up on it, even if he doesn't intend to deliver his part of the bargain.

Françoise grabbed for what courage she could. "I'm afraid I don't have any money."

Bat your eyelashes, honey. They love that.

Françoise hated herself. She blinked several times. "Is there nothing I can trade for a visit?"

The young man stared at her. Then he cleared his throat and wandered over to the iron grating. "It does get lonely guarding the scum of the earth for the people of France. I ... I could use a little company."

"Surely a hero such as yourself does not lack for company." Françoise laughed.

He leaned against the iron strapping from the other side. His voice was husky. "Well, as you say. But with a demanding job like this, a little comfort is always welcome."

They're all alike, aren't they?

No. They're not. Just some. Be grateful for that. "Well, I could give you...company."

The young guard grinned slowly. He fished out the keys that hung on a ring on his wide leather belt and opened a side door. Françoise smiled at him. The sun was rising. The courtyard of the prison beyond was still in shadow, but it would be filled with sunlight soon. She had to get Henri out before full light. The guard pulled her into his arms. His breath smelled of cheap wine, the kind made with alcohol and red dye, not grapes.

"Oh, monsieur," she protested, turning her head away. "The light—there will be no privacy here." She turned and took

Susan Squires

him by the hand, pulling him through the door and along the stone corridor. The open cells were quiet at this early hour. She glanced over the guard's shoulder. Someone must be awake. She saw a shadow shift inside the cell and another. She reached up and put her hands around the guard's neck. He took her invitation and bent to kiss her hungrily. His wet mouth covered hers. She let his tongue pry open her lips and search her mouth. One hand cupped her bottom through her skirts. She pressed her breasts against him and swabbed his tongue with hers.

Gack. Frankie gagged.

Françoise kissed him as though she was kissing Henri. Which she was, in a way. She let her weight fall against him. He stepped back. Not far enough. She pulled her fichu from her neckline. The dress hardly covered her nipples now.

"*Merde,* but you want it from me, don't you, little bird?"

She nodded even as she pulled him down to kiss him yet again.

"Right here?" he asked, gasping.

"Right now," she murmured into his mouth.

He fumbled with the buttons on his breeches. She rubbed the hard rod beneath the flap even as she kissed him frantically. His erection sprang free.

Are you going to do this?

If I must. She lifted her skirts above her hips. "Brace yourself. You mustn't drop me."

He grinned and stepped back, dragging her with him. Still not far enough. There was nothing for it. All depended on the next moment. She pushed the guard with all her strength. He stumbled back against the bars.

An arm snaked out of the cell and wrapped around the guard's throat. His head jerked back against the bars. His eyes widened in shock. A hand gripped the wrist of the arm across his throat. He opened his mouth to yell for help and Françoise pushed a fistful of her fichu into it. He grabbed her shoulder, his fingers digging into her flesh. Other hands now reached through the bars, pulling at his arms, pinning his legs to the bars. He struggled, but he didn't let her go. His face turned red,

Time for Eternity

then pale, then red again. Revulsion shuddered inside her. Inside the cell there was no sound.

The guard's grip on her shoulder relaxed as he slumped, held upright only by the disembodied arms from inside the cell. The one brawny arm across his throat was pulled even tighter by the hand at its wrist.

"Don't kill him," she whispered, rubbing her shoulder. "We have what we want."

The hands withdrew and the guard slumped to the ground. Françoise knelt quickly and fumbled at his belt for the key ring. The clink of keys seemed to echo against the stone. She looked quickly up and down the corridor. Other hands had appeared on the bars of other cells, waiting. But no guards.

Can't you be quieter?

She froze as she heard voices. They weren't in the corridor though. Maybe the courtyard. She put her finger to her lips so the prisoners could see it and tiptoed around the unconscious body of the guard to the archway that now cast light into the corridor about twenty feet away. Peering around the edge of the wall, she saw a phalanx of guards moving off toward the main gate. They were carrying something inside the square, but she couldn't see what it was. The tramp of boots faded. She heard the main portcullis being raised. There wasn't much time.

It took several tries before she found the right key.

The huge lock snicked loudly and cracked open. It was the work of a moment to take it from the metal clasp.

She opened the door.

The shadows inside moved forward. A man with brawny arms inside his soiled shirt stepped out into the corridor.

"I need a diversion," she said.

The man grinned. *"Pas de problème."*

Françoise put the key ring in his outstretched hand. Then she watched as he went down the line of cells, opening doors. He tossed the keys to others and gestured three or four men into a huddle. Cells opened down the line. Françoise

Susan Squires

grabbed the hand of a middle-aged woman who looked like she had her wits about her.

"Collect the young and the weak and keep them quiet." The woman met her gaze. They both knew that people would be killed today. The woman nodded and gestured to two others.

At the end of the long corridor, a torch showed a figure taking the keys downstairs to a lower level. One of the leaders grabbed the sword from the unconscious guard and half a dozen prisoners went down to the guardhouse.

Françoise waited. The place had to be in chaos before she could make her move.

It didn't take long. A guard somewhere raised a shout. Others came running. The six prisoners came back from the guardhouse with swords and even a pistol or two they tossed to the able-bodied. The corridor had filled with gaunt men, dirty men, but men who knew that their lives and maybe the lives of loved ones depended on this one desperate chance. They surged out into the courtyard, armed or not.

Shouts, screams of pain. As soldiers fell, their weapons changed hands. Prisoners dropped and bled. Guards appeared from everywhere, but the prisoners must have found other keys on other rings, because prisoners began to surge out from every archway.

Françoise shoved through the tide like a fish struggling upstream. She knew her way to Henri's cell. Down the stairwell, and down another, as though she were descending into hell.

Better hope he's in good enough shape to walk out. You'll never be able to carry him.

"Be quiet."

But when she got to the cell, panting, the door was open and the shackles were empty.

Had he escaped with the others? Was he in some other cell? She looked around wildly. But no other cells were near. She stumbled back up the corridor and started to climb stairs.

When she got to the place where the prison break had started, the cells were all empty. The melee still echoed in the courtyard. The young guard was groaning as he tried to sit.

Time for Eternity

She knelt beside him. "Where is he?"

He looked dazed and rubbed his throat where a livid bruise was beginning to form.

"Where is he?" she shouted, shaking his shoulders.

Don't be stupid. Let him answer.

"The devil?" he choked. "They executed him this morning."

Susan Squires

Twenty-two

Nausea threatened to overwhelm Françoise.

You couldn't have stopped it.

Françoise pushed herself up. She couldn't give in to Frankie now. "You're still here. That means he's still alive. It's not too late." She picked up her skirts to run.

She wasn't alone. Prisoners streamed out the gates of the Conciergerie into the Quai de l'Horloge, past the great clock tower and over the Pont Neuf. Escaped prisoners and a few blue-coated soldiers were joined by the hoi polloi racing onto the bridge to see what was happening. Confusion reigned. Some escapees commandeered boats tied to the quays and were setting off downriver. Fights had broken out, it seemed indiscriminately.

Françoise pushed her way single-mindedly toward the Quai des Tuileries, past the grand palace without a king. This was the shortest way to the Place de Revolution. If she were going to find Henri alive, it would be along this route. It seemed the entire city had gone mad in the early morning light. It was only that which gave Françoise hope.

The sunlight will burn him. Françoise could feel Frankie shudder.

She swallowed her own fear and shoved her way through the gathering crowds.

The mob didn't seem to care who was fighting whom, or for what purpose. Whatever they thought was happening, it looked like an excuse for looting. She saw people running, hugging whole hams or baskets of fruit to their chests like babies. This was the result when all society began to collapse and people were desperate.

A group of mounted soldiers pushed their horses into the crowd gathered at the garden in front of the palace. She hoped they wouldn't restore order too soon.

Time for Eternity

A familiar face under a red queue of hair jogged past her, going in the opposite direction. "Jean," she shouted. Could it be? He turned. It was Jean.

"Mademoiselle Suchet," he cried, breaking into a run. "Are you well?"

"I thought you left the city." She wanted to hug him. He shook his head. "I stayed with my brothers hoping the search would die down."

How many siblings does this guy have?

"They're taking Henri to the guillotine."

His expression grew grim. He pulled her around and began marching her away. "I saw him in the tumbrel."

Françoise felt the blood drain from her face. "Did they execute him?"

"Not yet. But when they do it will be a mercy. You can't save him."

She pulled out of his grasp. "Listen to what I tell you," she hissed at him. "You will go to Madame Vercheroux. You will beg, borrow, or steal her carriage, and you will bring it to...to... the churchyard at St. Sulpice. Do you understand?" St. Sulpice was abandoned since the churches had been nationalized.

He looked dumbfounded.

"Do you understand?" she shouted as people streamed around them.

He nodded, shaken.

"Then go." She pushed him in the direction of the Faubourg and began to run.

The Place de Revolution opened up in front of her. People streamed across it. A crowd was bunched around the raised platform with the huge contraption in the northeast corner of the park near the Jardin des Tuileries. The giant frame stuck into the morning air. The blade was up, ready to descend, its gleaming edge a threat. Françoise could feel Frankie's revulsion. That was her Companion shuddering at the threat of the death it tried to avert at all costs. An executioner and several soldiers surveyed the crowds pouring into the square with puzzled expressions. Françoise only glanced at the platform; for there, plunging and snorting in fear, was a horse harnessed to a cart. A tumbrel.

Françoise was already running. There was no driver. A man was trying to steady the horse with a hand on its harness, but he didn't look like he knew what he was doing. It was…it was Robespierre. He must be there to personally see that Henri was executed. His revolting mistress must be here somewhere. Françoise looked around. The bitch herself was over near the guillotine. The crowd of gawkers began to disperse to join in the free-for-all. Françoise couldn't see anything in the back of the cart. No, wait. There was a post just behind the driver's seat and…and something was chained to it.

Don't think about it.

Françoise and Frankie knew what they would do. Robespierre be damned.

Françoise hurried up to the cart. She didn't look in the back, but climbed up into the driver's seat and picked up the reins. The little lawyer was still trying to prevent the horse from bolting and taking Madame Guillotine's prey out of striking range.

"I don't know how to drive a cart," she muttered as she struggled with the reins.

I do.

"Stand away," she ordered Robespierre. "I've got him."

But he looked up and saw who it was. "You can't save him." He wrenched the horse's bridle down and to the right. The horse squealed, but all four feet were on the ground.

"You there," Robespierre yelled. "Help me get this tumbrel to the guillotine."

Two men diverted from their course and started for the cart.

It's now or never, girlfriend.

"The horse will bolt."

So what?

She shook the reins over the horse's back. "Yahhh," she yelled. The horse neighed in fright and pulled the harness from Robespierre's hands as he jerked away. Robespierre lost his footing and fell under the plunging hooves as the horse took off at a gallop. The cartwheels bumped over an inert object. The cart careened away. Françoise's heart leaped into her mouth.

Fast is fine. People will get out of our way. Just gather up the reins a bit.

The crowds did move too. The horse steadied as it felt someone in control. She headed back to the Pont Neuf. It was the closest bridge. The cart clattered across the nine stone arches, past the fighting crowds around the Conciergerie, and headed up into the winding streets on the Left Bank as fast as they could go.

The tumbrel clattered behind the horse's pounding hooves. St. Germain-des-Prés was closer than St. Sulpice, but it had a prison attached to the abbey, and that meant soldiers. She hauled the horse to the right. In the distance she saw the mismatched towers of St. Sulpice. She turned into the churchyard and pulled around to the porch doors. Only when she had climbed down did she allow herself to look in the back of the tumbrel.

It was worse than she imagined. Henri was naked, his flesh swollen and suppurating. He was bloodied from dozens of sword wounds. But the fact that he bled meant he lived. His wrists were locked to the post by heavy manacles. He seemed insensible. That was just as well.

Don't you dare start crying, Françoise. Just get him out of the sun.

Françoise turned to the church. The altar cloth. She could cover him.

No time. Just open the doors and drive the cart inside.

A horse and cart inside a church? Sacrilege? She didn't need Frankie to chastise her for even asking the question. She pulled on the great, carved doors, hoping they hadn't been locked. But they were open as they had always been. She propped them wide with two stones. Then she dragged on the harness and the horse, tired now from his exertions, walked calmly inside.

The nave was cool even in July. The perfect hiding

place. "Mother Mary and Jesus, forgive me if this is a sin," she murmured, crossing herself as she knelt. Even from the far end of the long nave she could see there was no altar cloth, no golden candlesticks, no chalices. The church had been stripped. But the light from the stained-glass windows still painted the dim interior with vibrant color. The church was still alive. And so was Henri. She whirled to the doors and kicked the stones away. They swung shut. The horse stamped, the sound ringing down the nave.

"I don't suppose you know how to pick a lock?" she asked Frankie.

Why would a vampire need to know how to pick locks?

"Then how are we going to get Henri out of those shackles?"

How tough can locks be in 1794?

Françoise unpinned the military medal-looking brooch from her bodice. The pin was about two inches across. She climbed up into the wagon and knelt beside Henri.

Don't think about him. He'll live. Once the drug passes, he can heal this. He can.

Françoise swallowed. She pulled her eyes away from Henri's ruined face and tried to focus on the lock. The dim light was good for Henri, but not ideal for picking locks.

You're supposed to just feel it.

"Right. When I have no idea what I'm doing," Françoise grumbled. At least the horse had calmed. He stood quietly, sides heaving. She poked around in the keyhole for what seemed like forever.

Lift. You're supposed to lift with it. I saw it in The Pink Panther.

The Pink Panther was a movie, and Françoise knew what those were. Shocking. She hadn't really had time to be shocked by Frankie and what Frankie's world was like. She'd make time for that later. "You are always full of such good advice."

I'm more experienced than you.

"An experience you are trying to get rid of, I might note."

Time for Eternity

The mechanism clicked. Françoise opened it gently and laid Henri's arm at his side.

Not bad for a novice.

"Be quiet." She poked her pin inside the second shackle.

Once the locks were open, she tore up her underskirts to make bandages for his wounds and tied them up the best she could. Then she sat down to wait. It seemed hours until she heard a carriage outside.

She hurried to the doors and cracked them open. "In here," she called. "What took you so long?" Jean jumped down. Madame Vercheroux opened the door and stepped into the churchyard.

"Is he alive?" she asked anxiously.

"Madame, what are you doing here?"

"I find that Paris has become intolerable. I believe I am emigrating." She raised her beautiful brows. "You are going to Le Havre, *n'est-ce pas?*" She didn't wait for an answer but returned to her question. "Is he alive?"

"Yes. But he is not a pretty sight."

"Poor Henri." She pushed past Françoise, her satin skirts rustling. They heard the gasp.

Françoise looked back at Jean. "Help me get him into the carriage."

"Should we wait for night?"

"Croûte knows what the sun does to him. She'll expect us to wait. We must move now."

Madame Vercheroux came back out onto the porch of the church. Her face was white. She pressed her hand to her mouth. "Even if he lives…the scars…and he was so beautiful."

Françoise cleared her throat. She couldn't tell Madame that he wouldn't scar. "We will need money to get to Le Havre, not only for the journey, but there may be bribes… Henri can't help us …"

Madame Vercheroux waved a hand dismissively. "I never travel with less than five thousand francs. I brought some clothes for you and for Henri as well as mine." She gestured to

Susan Squires

the trunks strapped to the carriage.

"You've been to the house?"

"Of course not. The place has been ransacked. Everything stolen or destroyed." She shook her head, sighing. "But what I have should fit him well enough, and I contrived for you."

Madame Vercheroux had another lover, even though she still loved Henri.

Figures. Frankie sounded disgusted.

Françoise took a breath. "Jean, take the horse and cart out where someone can find them. They will not lack an owner long."

In moments they were away. The crowd outside the carriage shouted and jostled against it. It was only a matter of time until they grabbed the doors, pulled the occupants out and tore them apart. Henri lay on the floor at their feet covered with a traveling rug. Madame Vercheroux and Françoise had spread their skirts out wide to conceal him. Françoise peeked through the drawn blinds, feeling helpless. Jean was apparently trying to make his way toward the main road to Versailles. That was good. They were tracing the river on the Rue de Grenelle, through the mansions of the Faubourg St Germain. The crowds must be looting the luxurious houses, empty or not. She leaned out. Jean struggled with the horses as people pushed and shoved around them.

"Into a side street," she shouted.

"I'm trying, mademoiselle," he yelled back.

"Beasts!" a woman shrieked over the roar of the crowd. Ahead, the mob surged up the steps of a particularly beautiful house from the last century and through the doors of carved wood. The sound of breaking glass was echoed again and again as paving stones found windows. A woman on the stairs looked on, her hands to her face in horror. "Traitors!"

It was Madame Croûte.

Croûte lived in the Faubourg? That was the refuge of the last remnants of the aristocracy. And the crowd knew it. The roar of outrage from the ragged men and women in their ill-fitted clothes made of coarse cloth and red revolutionary

308

Time for Eternity

caps felt like the growl of an animal.

A heavy rococo cabinet sailed out of an upstairs window and the crowd scurried to avoid its impact. Madame Croûte shrieked in protest, but fear bloomed in her face. Now she faced the rage of the mob instead of directed it. As the crowd surged around her and into the house, Jean urged the horse forward. People converged on the house from all directions with angry shouts. The first blow to Madame Croûte was landed by a brawny man with sleeves rolled up above his elbows. Fragments of the crowd's protests wove themselves into a litany of betrayal, their rage focused on the woman who only seemed to share their ideals.

Françoise sat back as the carriage pulled away, unable to watch a crowd turn into a killing beast for a second time, even if she had no sympathy for its victim.

*****

Françoise sat with Henri's head in her lap in the rocking carriage. Across from her, Madame Vercheroux dozed. The blinds were pulled against the late afternoon sun. It had taken hours to get out of the city. They stopped, in spite of Françoise's protests, for a dinner at an inn, losing nearly two hours as Madame refreshed herself.

Now the sun was setting, washing the countryside in a golden light.

The morphine must be wearing off. Henri rolled his head and groaned from time to time. How she hated that he had to be in pain before he could heal.

He's healing too slowly. After all he's been through, his Companion is exhausted.

Françoise knew what she meant. Henri needed blood. She swallowed around a lump in her throat as he opened his eyes. They clouded in pain. His breathing grew labored.

"How...how are you?" she asked.

Now that's a stupid question if I ever heard one.

"You came back for me?" His voice was a hoarse

whisper. "You shouldn't have taken the chance." He glanced over at Madame Vercheroux.

"She came for you too. We're in her carriage on the way to Le Havre."

He blinked against the pain and shook his head ever so slightly. "The *Maiden Voyage* will have lifted anchor by the time you get there."

She hadn't thought of that. Of course they would be away as soon as Jennings arrived with his charges. Jennings thought Henri was dead.

"I'm a liability. Leave me at Versailles. Book passage on the first vessel crossing the Channel at Le Havre."

Versailles. Actually, that wasn't a bad idea. No one would think of looking for him there, whereas Robespierre would send straightaway to Le Havre. If he was still alive after she had run him down. Had she killed the little lawyer? Is that what killing felt like?

I don't feel guilty at all about that one.

No. Françoise wasn't even sure he was dead. She resolved not to feel guilty. It had been Robespierre or Henri. She'd choose Henri every time.

And I have unfinished business at Versailles, one way or another. Do it.

Françoise leaned forward, pulled open the window shade a hair. "Jean! Jean, pull in at Versailles. The palace."

"What? What?" Madame Vercheroux snorted, coming to herself.

"Jean will take you on to Le Havre. Henri needs time to recover."

"Henri! Henri, you are alive." Madame Vercheroux leaned forward. "I cannot see you in this dark coach. Let me raise the window shades."

"No!" Françoise and Henri said together.

"The light is what burned him so badly," Françoise said. "He has a . . . condition."

"I won't leave you like this," Madame Vercheroux insisted.

But in the end she did. Henri gathered himself and said

no captain would take on an injured man obviously running from the authorities. He promised to follow them to England. Françoise let him believe she'd be going with Madame. It was easier than arguing.

They bribed the old caretaker, Brendal, who remembered them from their previous visit, and he and Jean carried Henri up to the king's bedroom. They unloaded one of the trunks from the carriage. When he was tucked in, Françoise went down to see Madame off.

"You stay with him?" Madame asked. She didn't seem surprised.

Françoise nodded. "As long as he'll let me."

"I told you not to give your heart." Madame shook her head.

Double standard. She gave him hers.

Françoise said, "One cannot choose where to give one's heart. If it is broken, so be it."

Madame sighed. "I was once as young as you."

Françoise smiled. "You have no idea how old I am. Or how old I feel. Be careful."

"They won't stop us. They are glad to be rid of my kind."

"They would love to take your five thousand francs and the carriage," Françoise warned.

Madame pulled on her gloves. "I will have given the carriage in trade for passage before morning. Do you think I will like England? One hates to think of ending in Austria."

"You will be the center of attention wherever you go, Madame." She leaned in to kiss the older woman. "Thank you for everything."

"Fau," Madame said, giving Françoise brisk kisses on both cheeks. "I was tired of France." Her eyes grew soft. "Take care of him." And with a wave of her hand she was gone.

*****

Henri opened his eyes on darkness as the pain crashed

over him. Why was it taking him so long to heal? Someone was in the darkness with him. He turned his head.

Françoise sat in a chair beside the great bed. Where was he? Ahhh. Versailles. He recognized the brocade on poor dead Louis's bed. He and Françoise had made love in this bed.

"Why aren't you on your way to Le Havre?" It was night. He could feel it.

"I couldn't leave you to Brendal and his wife. They'd know how badly you were hurt, and see the healing."

They'd know him for a monster, as she did.

"The healing doesn't seem to be going that well," she continued as she stood and adjusted the sheets that covered him.

"Just...slow. I'm weak."

She chewed her lip. "I know what you need."

The pain made it hard to think. She...she was opening the throat on her white nightdress. His Companion stirred sluggishly in his veins as it felt the blood beating in the artery in her throat. "Leave me," he rasped. Who knew what he might do in his current state?

She shook her head slowly and smiled. He could see her pulse in the hollow of her neck. "It's safest if you do it. But if you can't raise your Companion, I'll cut my wrist."

How did she know about the Companion? It throbbed at him, needing. It had just enough power to run out his canines. He ripped his gaze from her throat and turned his head away. He couldn't take her blood. She pushed herself up to sit beside him on the bed. He could smell the soft scent of lavender soap. She turned his bead toward her. Down the neck of her nightdress her breasts swung free. She smiled so tenderly at him, and bent to kiss him.

His Companion growled. He could feel his canines slide out. She kissed his lips, running her tongue along his canines then baring her neck. Damn her! And he was weak and in pain and he couldn't think. Her throat was white. Her pulse throbbed until it was all he could hear.

"Go on," she said. "I won't let you take too much."

How would she know what was too much? How did she

Time for Eternity

know any of this?

In the end the decision wasn't his. His Companion took her up on the offer. One minute he was kissing her neck, feeling the warmth of her flesh on his lips, and the next moment he had sunk his canines into her carotid artery and was sucking rhythmically. The first taste of her pure, young blood in his mouth and he forgot everything but the pull against her flesh and the warm liquid sustenance that tasted of copper, tangy and sweet at once. She lay beside him and held his head to her throat, making soothing sounds that turned to little moans of satisfaction.

It was he who pulled away in spite of her promises. "Enough," he gasped, licking his lips as his canines retracted.

She laid him back down. "That will make a difference soon."

Already he felt himself swooning back into the darkness. How did she *know* that?

Twenty-three

Françoise eased Henri into the brocade dressing gown. He was naked, his marvelous body pristine. All trace of Madame Croûte's desecration was gone, though he still had some stiffness in shoulder and hip. Frankie might have seen herself heal many times over the centuries, but it had never been wounds like this, and the whole was wondrous to Françoise. Being this close to him, she could feel the slow throb of his vibrations. He was still weaker than was his wont. But his body had the same effect on her it always had. She glanced to the bed where they had made such ecstatic love. Had that been only a week ago? It now seemed like another life, one she could never recapture.

Françoise pulled a chair up to the window that looked out onto the night. "Would you like to sit up for a while? Brendal brought us some wine and a nice Camembert from the village."

"I'm to be let out of bed? Hallelujah. My gaoler relents." He sat carefully in the chair as she hovered over him. He looked up at her with a softness in his eyes that startled her. "I don't mean that. I don't deserve the kindness you have shown me."

He...he never looked at me like that. Frankie sounded a little stunned. *When we were here a week ago... I saw that expression, but I didn't recognize it for what it was...*

"What did I do? I read to you, fed you a couple of times, and watched you sleep."

He blinked slowly, considering her. "You know very well it was more than that."

Françoise felt herself blush remembering how...sensual giving him her blood had been. "I did what I could." She poured herself wine. She had to redirect this conversation. "Brendel says the Revolutionary Council sent Robespierre to the guillotine without even a trial this morning. They blamed him for the mass escape from the Conciergerie. Croûte fell to the mob."

"The Revolution is cannibalizing itself." He sounded sad.

Ding, dong, the witch is dead. Both of them.

"You fought the Revolution. I wouldn't think you'd be sorry it's disintegrating."

"Man at his worst is always a sorry sight. You might be surprised to know I voted to establish the National Assembly. Something had to be done about the priesthood and the aristocracy. Just not this. Our country may be torn apart for good."

She was surprised in one way and in another not surprised at all. She wanted to comfort him. On impulse she said, "It will rise from the ashes with the help of a little soldier who becomes emperor."

He looked at her strangely. He almost said something, but thought better of it.

They looked out the windows, a gulf between them that made it hard for Françoise to breathe. Night spread out over the gardens. The rabble was gone again, the detritus from their picnics blown across the grass and into the hedges by a summer wind. Beyond the formal gardens the water rushed, silent from this distance, at the Fountain of Apollo. Françoise and Frankie stared out at it, standing beside his chair while Henri sipped his wine.

There's a grotto in a grove somewhere out there. Leonardo's machine is there, if it hasn't already returned to the twenty-first century.

"Françoise," Henri began. She wasn't used to hear him sound anything but masterful or indolent, though that indolence she now knew was a pose. She looked down to see him toying with his glass. "I hardly know how to say this to you. I have no right."

She made her tone light. "What right don't you have after saving me from the mob and the tender mercies of

Susan Squires

Robespierre?"

He looked up and searched her face as though his life depended on it. She saw his Adam's apple slide up and down his throat as he swallowed. Dear Lord, but he made her throb. But now that she knew the man beneath that beautiful face was more than beautiful. It was…dear to her. *You should be reminding me of what Madame Vercheroux said about him,* she thought to Frankie. *He never engages his heart and he will break mine.*

But Frankie was suddenly silent.

He looked down at his wine again. "It has occurred to me that there is one way that you could look so young and yet display that…world-weary experience I've seen. Yet I can hardly credit it…" Again he raised his face to hers. "How do you know about the Companion? How did you know to give me blood and what it could do for me?"

She couldn't tell him that! She managed a laugh. "What vampire doesn't need blood?"

He clenched his lips, his eyes challenging her.

Tell him.

He'll think I'm mad. Françoise chewed her lip, frowning.

Trust me. Tell him.

"If I was vampire you'd feel my electric energy and I'd smell of cinnamon and ambergris as you do," she said to buy time. Of course she had also just demonstrated once again that she knew more than any human should about vampires.

If you want to continue any kind of a relationship with him, he needs to know the truth about you. About us. Show him the machine, if it's still there. That will make him believe you.

Still, he looked his question.

Frankie was right. She took a breath. "Are you up to a walk? I'll show you the truth."

He examined her face, then put away his questions. He nodded and rose. She took his hand as they went down the stairs. It might be the last time she touched him. No words passed between them. She lit the lamp sitting on the table in the grand foyer and took it with her. Through the front doors and down the steps into the gravel drive, she drew him across the gardens and the vast lawns toward the Grotto of Apollo. It was up a little rise, surrounded by trees. The two statues of Apollo's horses were placed strategically on the hillside. The central piece of Apollo himself and his six nymphs sat in the mouth of the man-made cave above them. They struggled up the rise and Françoise realized how weak Henri still was. Frankie trembled in excitement within her. She paused in front of the gleaming marble and looked back at Henri. "Suspend some disbelief here."

He stood beside her, peering into the cave behind the statue. "I'll try."

She squeezed around behind the statues and started into the cave. The lantern flickered and steadied. She held it high.

A gleam of bronze answered her light.

It's still here.

Françoise walked forward as she heard Henri gasp. Leonardo's wonderful machine loomed over her. Françoise stood in awe, no matter that she had seen it in her vision of Frankie's experience. Huge jewels winked in the light from the lantern.

"My God," Henri said. "What is it?"

Françoise turned. "It is a time machine built by Leonardo da Vinci, for a friend of his named Donna di Poliziano. Do you know of him?"

"Of course." He paused. "But I know Donnatella well. She never mentioned…

"She doesn't find it until 1821. She used it to go back and make Jergan vampire."

"But she and Jergan have been together since the death of Caligula in Rome."

"In one possible version of events they were not. She regretted it." She took a breath. "And in one possible version of events you made me vampire at the moment you broke that glass in the library. I was infected through a scrape." She raised her hand where a scab still graced the pad of her palm under her thumb. He paled. "You abandoned me after three days, or

Susan Squires

so I thought, and I lived the best I could, thinking I was a monster—"

Knowing I was a monster, Frankie interrupted.

"I didn't know…anything about what I was. When the craving for blood got so bad I thought I'd go insane, I killed for what I needed. At least at first. And I hated myself for it. I was almost killed by a vampire just because I was made, not born to it, so I shunned other vampires. Always I dreamed of coming back to change what happened to me. I called myself Frankie and was working in a…tavern when I met Donna. She gave me directions to Leonardo's machine." She gathered her courage. She had to tell him all; how small she was, how selfish. "I came back in time to kill you, Henri, thinking that was the only sure way to prevent you infecting me." She was not proud of that. Even Frankie seemed subdued. "I'd been in an auto accident once and the emergency room gave me morphine before I could heal, so I knew what it could do to a vampire's powers. I brought bottles of morphine and…and a sword." Her voice shook slightly. "And the reason I seem both young and old is probably because Frankie now lives inside this body with me. I guess we couldn't both exist physically in the same time. She merged into me. I control the body. But she's in here with me." She tapped her head.

He looked doubtful. But then he stared at the machine. His doubt changed character. Now he was wondering what this machine could be, and how she could know about vampires, if not the way she claimed.

"I know what Frankie knows, about vampires and what will happen in the future. That's how I know that Napoleon will make France great again at great cost. His legacy will be the Napoleonic Code of law though. It will protect the people, yet save the mob from itself."

She let him consider that for a moment. He tore his questing eyes from hers and took the lantern to walk around the machine. The jewels winked white and red and green and blue, their facets sending scintillating lights around the cavern. "How does it work?" he asked.

"I've no idea. I only know that it takes a vampire to

power it."

He reached out and touched a massive gear, looking up at the rococo intricacies of the many interlocking gears above. "I would not have abandoned you. Not in any version of events." He turned to look at her. "And if you were vampire and lived, I did not. It takes about three days of infusions of a vampire's blood to give you immunity to the Companion. If you don't get it, you'd die. I stayed with you for three days at the least. You might not remember those days. One is delirious until the Companion makes peace with its new body. And making vampires is forbidden, so I must have cared about you...very much...to have tried to save you at all."

She managed a shrug. "I didn't know that. Frankie avoided vampires. She knows only what her own experience taught her. She doesn't do that thing you do to disappear, and she doesn't control minds, at least not normally." But inside she was fixated on the words, "I did not abandon you."

He ignored what she just said. "Do you believe me?" His eyes were burning in their intensity. "I didn't abandon you."

She rolled her lips together under her teeth, as if that would give her more control over the situation. "Donna said you were guillotined."

"Not this time."

"I don't know. Maybe you still will make me vampire, and maybe you'll still be guillotined. Because it seems awfully difficult to change things. Robespierre died on exactly the day the history books two hundred years hence said he did, though there was no mention of the prison break." That was only one of the things that had been torturing her over the long hours at Henri's bedside.

Henri's eyes fixed on her. She couldn't move. "If I'm guillotined, you'd only have accomplished what you came back to do. Operation successful." He paused. "You must have hated me very much."

Françoise closed her eyes. "I didn't know you. Not really. I never looked hard enough to see that you were more than just the handsome, wicked duc." She opened them. "But of course, I was just a naïve girl of twenty-one. Maybe I didn't know how to really...see a person.

He raised his chin. "And now you aren't just that girl. And I am caught."

"Caught?"

Caught. Listen to him.

Françoise had almost forgotten about Frankie, what with all this talking about her in the third person as though she weren't a part of Françoise now.

"Do you still hate me?"

She shook her head, convulsively.

Henri broke the look that stretched taut between them. "Do you want to go back to your own century?" He glanced to the machine. "I'll power it for you as soon as I'm able."

"Frankie is comfortable in that time, but would I be at home there? Because maybe if I'm not made vampire, then...then Frankie will never have existed. Will I go forward only to have all Frankie's experience ripped from me? I'd be alone and lost in a world I don't understand." She stared at the machine.

Even as it faded. The whole thing just slowly disappeared, making a sound that seemed to suck the air from the grotto. Françoise put her hands over her ears. Henri stepped back a pace and drew Françoise into his arms. Then the machine popped back to clarity.

"Merde. What was that?" he asked.

"Uh... uh ... well, Leonardo wrote that the machine wouldn't stay back in time forever. It would revert to the time it came from."

He set the lantern on the sand and took her by the shoulders. "Then there isn't much time. Do you want me to try to draw my power and pull that lever to send you forward?"

She looked up at him, her eyes searching his face. But it was to Frankie that she thought, *Should we go? I don't know what will happen to you if we go, or if we don't.*

Frankie sounded wistful. *I don't know either. But you can't leave this time. Not now.*

Time for Eternity

Françoise couldn't speak. She shook her head to answer Henri. Her eyes filled. Sound filled the cave again. She and Henri turned to see the machine fading. It blinked back to clarity briefly and then it faded inexorably until it was... gone.

Françoise sucked in a breath. *Frankie?*

Still here. Frankie sounded relieved, but a film of tristesse covered the relief.

Henri turned Françoise into him. Her mind was spinning. Now she was here. With Henri.

But not for long. Her heart felt full to bursting. He could never love her. He'd lived for centuries, having liaisons with the like of Madame Vercheroux just so he'd never have to really love a woman, leaving broken hearts in his wake. For who could not love a man like Henri?

Stop thinking and listen. Give him a chance to muster the courage.

*****

Henri took her in his arms, pulling her against his chest. He kissed the top of her head. Lord, could he believe what he'd just seen? The irony of it... A vampire who didn't believe that the cleverest man in history could make a machine that came through time. And Françoise, his marvelous Françoise, was stranded between two times, between two lives, between two versions of events, and struggling to make sense of it all alone. "I'm sorry. This must be hard for you." Reluctantly, be held her away from him and mustered a smile. "Your life will be very different this time. I shall set you up in England with a sizable fortune. You will have your pick of reverent beaux and live to be society's *grande dame.* The wisdom you have acquired from...from Frankie will ensure that you are beloved by all your family for generations to come."

She blinked. But she said nothing.

"I only hope you will not despise me for being the monster you so hated in yourself, and let me come to visit you on occasion." Damnation, had his voice cracked? He cleared his throat. She mustn't know what it took to say that. "I shall be Oncle Henri to all your children." He picked up the lantern and turned to the cave entrance. Was that conversational enough? It had nearly killed him to produce that insouciant tone, in spite of all the practice he'd had. He held out a hand. "Let's go back to the palace."

*****

He wanted to be an uncle to her children? Françoise wanted to jerk her hand from his.

Why don't you? You aren't going to let him get away with that, are you?

Get away with what? Françoise thought.

Lying to you about loving you. He really loves you. Love for all time, loves you.

If he really loved me...

If he really loved you he'd say he wants to make you vampire when you just told him you thought vampires were monsters and that being one ruined your life? Think again.

I... I don't want to be vampire, Françoise protested. *No one wants that.*

Like hell. Now you're the one lying. You've been toying with it for days. You don't think he's a monster.

Of course not. They were coming down on to the lawns along the grand canal.

Then you wouldn't mind being like him. Tell him, for God's sake, before it's too late. Don't live a second life of regret. Don't become me.

There's no chance he loves me enough to spend a hundred lifetimes with me.

He never looked at me the way he looks at you. He cared for me enough to save me when I was infected. But he loves you. Enough to give you up to make you happy, knowing it will destroy him. The noise of the fountain of Apollo cascaded around them.

I think what he loves is the you in me, Frankie.

Well, there's one sure way to nail that down.

Time for Eternity

Françoise stopped, jerking her hand from Henri's. The one way to ensure that Frankie stayed around was…

Henri turned to her in surprise.

Now or never, girlfriend.

*****

The girl was standing there, practically shaking. What was wrong? Was she afraid of him after all this time? He was afraid, afraid to say anything lest he push her over some edge he couldn't quite see. But she just stood there, trembling. "Françoise," he finally said, louder than he wanted over the cascade of the fountain. "You're safe. You're just a normal woman now who can have a normal life. A good life."

"I don't think you're a monster," she blurted. She stopped to take two breaths and then said, "I don't even think I was a monster. I lived a life of regret for nothing."

She didn't despise him for being vampire? She knew his inmost secret and she…

"I love you." She sounded as though she were drowning, or had just run a mile. Her beautiful breasts heaved beneath her fichu.

She loved him? In spite of what she knew? Impossible. And yet, she had something within her that knew everything, or almost everything. She had walked in his shoes. He forcibly tamped down hope. "There is no life for us together," he said, as gently as he could. "Human and vampire doesn't work. One ages and dies and one does not. That makes both bitter."

"So you don't love me?" She lifted her chin in that charming, pugnacious way he adored.

If he had an ounce of courage he would break her heart right here and now instead of breaking it over years a piece at a time. He closed his eyes.

"Don't!" she gasped. "Don't even bother to deny it. It would only be your generous nature getting the better of you because you don't want to hurt me. But Frankie says you never looked at her the way you look at me, and if I don't push for what I want, the whole thing will just go sour again and I'll be left with nothing. So I'm going to tell you, Henri Foucault, just once and then I'll never say it again. I love you and I think you love me too, maybe not for what I was the first time round, but for what I am now, and if we don't push for what we want, we have only ourselves to blame for getting less."

Henri wasn't certain he could find his voice. "What do you want?" he asked. His words were so quiet they were lost in the roar of the cascade behind him, but he did not doubt she would know what he was saying.

"Make me vampire."

She didn't know what that meant. She couldn't.

But she did. She, of anyone, knew what she was asking for.

He had to warn her anyway. "You will tire of me. Eternity is a long time." And he always abandoned his relationships because he was afraid of being abandoned. As his mother had abandoned him. The irony of him creating the very situation he was most afraid of, just so he could be in control, washed over him. There was no question that he would gladly spend his centuries with her. But did he have the courage to risk that she would tire of him?

"This from a man who has left a string of broken hearts across France for centuries? I'm the one taking the chance here."

His next words would decide his fate. He knew that. It was one of those moments where you truly did not know what words would come out when you opened your mouth. "You are not taking a chance."

They stood, facing each other like combatants for a single moment more, before he took her in his arms thinking that perhaps he would burst, or burst out laughing, or maybe sob with fear and relief and joy.

He swung her into his arms. "We need somewhere quiet," he growled into her ear.

Twenty-four

Henri laid her on the high bed in the king's bedchamber almost reverently. She could feel Frankie smiling inside her. This was going to be it. She was going to travel down a road she knew and yet that would be wholly new, one she embraced this time, not one she was dragged down kicking and screaming. Henri, beautiful and good Henri, who had struggled so against the darkness in his life, was gazing down at her with something in his eyes that Frankie recognized, and that Françoise was coming to believe in too.

"Sick for three days," he warned her.

"Will you stop with the warnings?" Where had that come from? She sounded like Frankie. She cleared her throat "I mean that I want this."

He ran his hands through her curls, his brows tightening in doubt.

"I am not an innocent. Who knows better than I what I'm getting into?" She deliberately smoothed his brow. "And I don't want to be infected by a cut, or palm to palm like swearing we're blood brothers. You're going to love me, Henri Foucault, and you are going to press your lovely lips to my throat as you run out your canines and sink them into my carotid, and when you've tasted my blood, I want to taste yours."

He raised his brows. A smile was almost discernible at the corners of his mouth, but he couldn't keep it from lighting his eyes. "You're very decisive."

"It's about time."

He feigned a mournful expression. "An eternity with a shrewish wife. I shall become a shadow of myself. The wicked duc tamed at last."

"You have been acting the wicked duc the whole time. I

Susan Squires

feel cheated at such a sham." She smiled slyly up at him. "But perhaps you can play the wicked duc just one more time?"

This time he did grin. There were no two ways about it. He went to the dressing table in the corner and got something, she couldn't tell what. He put it in the drawer of the night table. Before she could ask what he was doing, he pulled the fichu from her gown and tossed it to the floor. Then rubbed his hands over the tops of her breasts. She arched her back. "Shall we get you out of these clothes, mademoiselle?"

It took two of them the better part of a quarter of an hour to get naked together.

One thing about the twenty-first century is that their clothes are easier to shed.

Be quiet, Frankie, and enjoy what you missed the first time around.

Henri lay beside her on top of the red brocade embroidered in gold. Then he got up. "Too scratchy. This must be perfect."

He picked her up in one arm, reminding her how strong he was, and pulled back the coverlet to reveal the sheets. He laid her down and crawled up beside her. His body was as beautiful as it had been before, but now there was some added poignancy about it, as if its beauty were all the more precious for having been violated. He kissed her, his lips as soft as his body was not, his tongue moist and intimate in her mouth. How different from the guard she'd kissed. She ran her hands over his chest, feeling his nipples peak under her touch.

He growled in response and bent his head to her nipple. Dear God, but that was sweet. Sensation shot to her loins. She throbbed, helpless with longing for what was to come. He sucked first one breast and then the other, first gently and then with coming passion, just as he would soon be sucking at her neck again. The very thought of how sensual an experience it was to give him her blood made her writhe under him. That provoked another growl and she could feel his throbbing erection along her hip. She reached for it as he kissed her throat. She arched her neck, inviting him, but he was only moving from breast to mouth and so finished the journey by

326

Time for Eternity

thrusting his tongue between her teeth, exploring, savoring.

She ran one hand over the muscles in his back as she slid her other up his shaft. The head of his member was exuding a little moisture and she spread it with her thumb. That made him catch his breath. Where had she learned to do that?

From me. And I'll lend you some vocabulary. They're called "cocks."

Good. I can give him more pleasure. She clasped his cock and stroked up and down.

"God, Françoise, you'll draw me."

"Then get to it, wicked duc."

He needed no more invitation. She spread her legs and he slid his finger between her nether lips. She knew he would find her slick and ready. He positioned himself over her on one arm, and held his cock at her entrance. She moved her hands down his back to cup his lovely buttocks. They looked into each other's eyes as his buttocks bunched under her hands and he thrust slowly inside her. She breathed in as fully as she could and exhaled in satisfaction as she was filled. Slowly he began to move.

This was what she had wanted. Not just sexual excitement but the closeness, moving as one, the tenderness giving way to passion. This was what Frankie had missed for all those years.

He laid himself down over her, his hair hanging over his bulky shoulders. The weight of him was so satisfying. "Françoise," he murmured. "I love you." It was a simple declaration. Not flowery. But direct and heartfelt. His vibrations ramped up. Did he have enough power to draw his canines, weak as he still was?

Doesn't feel weak to me, Frankie noted, chuffing a laugh.

Sure enough, the scrape of canines along her neck said he was doing fine. She opened her eyes so she could see the burgundy red of his. Someday hers would glow like that. She smiled at him when she felt his hesitation. "Do it, wicked duc." She arched her neck and turned her head.

Susan Squires

His teeth sank into her artery. The prick of rose thorns—hardly more. They withdrew. Then the rhythmic sucking began that matched the mutual thrust of their hips. She had never felt so much a part of another. Her blood pumped through her artery into the soft pull of his lips even as the fever built in her loins. He pumped inside her until she was close, so close to ecstasy…

He stopped, stock-still.

"What?" she asked. Was he having doubts?

He gave her throat one final lick. "Turnabout is fair play," he whispered. He slid out of her. Her womb grasped at him in disappointment. He rolled over until he could open the drawer of the night table and got something out. She couldn't see what was in his closed fist. Then he sat up against the headboard. His cock was still amazingly stiff.

Oh, yeah. That's a great idea.

She crawled into his lap. He lifted her hips as if she weighed nothing. It was up to her to position him then he lowered her onto his shaft. Yesssss. That was what she wanted. He drew her forward and licked her neck. She must be drooling blood. She could feel the hum of satisfaction that was his Companion. Even now her blood had made his vibrations ramp up the scale. He felt more alive. She had done that for him.

He helped her move up and down along his shaft. The pressure that had eased ramped up again. She moaned as she bounced. The thing she craved would be coming soon.

It was then that he flipped open the little paring knife for nails he had in his hand. How endearing that he had hidden it from her, thinking not to frighten her. She wasn't frightened. He held her eyes as he cut his chest right over his left nipple. She bent her head even as she started moving on his cock again. He thrust up to meet her.

Blood welled from the cut. This was the moment.

"There is no going back," he warned.

She lifted her head to glare at him in mock severity. "Didn't I say no more warnings?"

She licked across the cut. The blood was thick, viscous, sensual. It tasted o f . . . something metallic. It tasted alive. Was

Time for Eternity

that the Companion swimming in his veins?

He held her tight, covering her curls with kisses as she licked, and they moved together in increasing urgency. The feeling of taking his blood just as she was about to take his seed pushed her over some edge and she lifted her head, arching her back and pressing her breasts into his bleeding chest as she clenched around his cock in mind-engulfing ecstasy. On and on the orgasm rolled. He kept thrusting against her to prolong it until finally she gasped. Had she been holding her breath? The feeling had already begun to ebb when he finally let himself climax. He grunted against her breasts as his cock pulsed inside her.

They stayed, pressed together, his cock still inside her, for a long time. She ran her fingers through his hair, holding his head to her. He kissed her breasts, smeared with his blood.

At last they sucked in huge mutual breaths and broke apart. When she looked down at him, a tender smile on her mouth, he looked so doubtful that she had to laugh.

"I wanted this, Henri."

"And I have wanted this too much to have it be right. I'm still not sure you know what you've sacrificed."

"Frankie knows what being vampire is. It was she who prodded me to fight for what I wanted. She's the only reason I had the courage to tell you I loved you."

"She is an optimist. That rarely works out well."

Françoise blinked. "No she isn't. She is embittered and cynical. Optimism is naïve. That's what she always says I am."

"But encouraging you to push for what you wanted required a leap of faith. What better definition of an optimist?" He must have seen her stunned look. "Maybe Françoise contributed enough naïveté for Frankie to be optimistic, just for once."

Had she? Had she contributed anything to Frankie? *Frankie?*

Bingo, girlfriend. But the voice was faint.

Frankie? Was Frankie fading like the time machine? *Don't leave me, Frankie! Now that I'm vampire, you exist. You*

Susan Squires

can stay. I need *you, Frankie.*

But Henri doesn't abandon you, probably for longer than a hundred lifetimes. So there is no bitter Frankie anymore...

She trailed off. "Frankie, no!"

"What is it?" Henri tensed under her. "What's happening?"

I'm ceasing to exist. I feel it.

You can't. Henri won't love me if I'm just a naive young girl. He loves you, Frankie, not me. You said yourself he never looked at you the way he looks at us together.

She felt Frankie soften, faintly. *But I'm inside you now because you experienced me for these brief days. You will be my immortality.*

If you don't exist, you won't come back to this time, and then I'll never see Henri for what he is, and you'll never give me the courage to want to be vampire...

Too...complicated, girlfriend. Leave that to Arthur C. What has happened, happened. Time just moves on.

I can't live without you, Frankie.

No. She heard the whisper, so faint within her it was hardly there. *You can't live without him. You have as much of me as there is for me to give. It will be enough...*

Frankie!

But there was no answer.

"Françoise. Françoise! Are you all right?" Henri held her head between his hands.

Tears welled. "She's gone. She's gone and I can't be what you love without her."

"It's all right, Françoise." He smoothed her hair. He pulled her to his chest, but she pulled back. His worry showed in his face.

"She said she didn't exist anymore because we stay together for a hundred lifetimes and there would be no bitter Frankie."

"You don't feel her inside you anymore?"

"Bingo."

"What?"

Time for Eternity

Françoise blinked. About five times. "That's...that's something she always said. It means, roughly, you have said something correct."

He raised his eyebrows. They stared at each other for a long moment.

"Maybe she isn't entirely gone. You think?" Françoise heard something subtly different in the way she chose her words. Maybe it was the cadence.

Henri smiled. "Perhaps not."

Françoise felt a little ripple inside her of something...faint She smiled. Tears spilled over her cheeks. "I'm glad," she whispered aloud. "I grew to like you, girlfriend."

"Maybe she grew to like herself."

Françoise put her arms around his neck and kissed his forehead, fiercely. She was feeling light-headed. "You're a wise man, Henri Foucault." She started to shiver.

He lifted her off his lap and swung her into his arms. "Let's get you under the covers. Rough three days ahead. But I'll be here to give you my blood."

She was really shaking now. "B-better be longer than three d-days this time, buddy." Buddy? Where had that come from?

"Quite a bit longer." Henri pulled the duvet up around her. "Frankie was wrong. With luck, it will be more than a hundred lifetimes." He bent and kissed her forehead.

"M-maybe."

"That's all we can expect, my love. Our chance. Frankie had the courage to try to change her lot She gave us something lost to us the first time round. Can we have less courage?" He smiled at her. "Maybe we'll find a way to use what we are to mean something to the world. There are other places where people need help besides France, you know."

The man was a hero, not a wicked duc. And she loved him from someplace inside that was closest to who she was, maybe even closest to God.

She grinned even as her teeth chattered. She was going

to be vampire. She was going to have the powers Frankie missed. She was going to love this man forever. Donna di Poliziano had been right. She'd found what she really wanted and claimed it.

"We do what we can, guy. We do what we can."

Epilogue

"Do you think it will still be there?" Frankie worried as Henri guided the sleek black BMW rental car down the steep hill of California Street into the part of San Francisco known as Cow Hollow. The lights of the city were just coming on. "I mean, what if she's sold it? Or what if...if I never gave it to her because Donna never gave it to me, because in this version of time I was never bitter and didn't need to go back?"

"Calm down, *ma petite,*" Henri said. "It does no good to twist your hair like that."

Frankie jerked her hand away from her curls. She glanced at Henri. He smiled. How she loved that smile.

"And stop chewing your lip?"

She took a breath and tried her best to scowl at him. It was always hard to scowl at Henri. "You know as well as I do how important.. no, how *dangerous* that book could be. What if someone uses it for their own purposes?"

"If she's sold it, we'll track it down and buy it. And the other argument is circular. You know that. It will either be there or it won't."

Bingo. Henri was right, of course.

"I might remind you that *you* used it for your own purposes and things seem to have turned out well." His eyes were laughing at her. But she knew it was love that made them laugh.

"There. There's the shop." Miraculously, a parking spot waited for them right in front. In San Francisco, no less. Vampire luck to the rescue again. On the whole she liked being vampire, strong and alive as she had never felt before Henri had given his gift of blood. She had to admit she was eager for one of their number, Julien Davinoff, to finally produce a successful synthetic blood. If anyone could do it, Julien could. But it didn't matter. She would never let the inconvenience of needing blood every couple of weeks stand in the way of the life she had built with Henri. She was so lucky, in so many ways.

She watched his face as he eased the Beamer into the parking space. He was tired. He'd just flown in from Somalia the night before. He'd had to get his team out of that hellhole before it all collapsed and their risked lives turned into lives lost. Doctors Without Borders was Henri's current effort to make the world a better place. She loved him for that.

ROSSANO'S RARE BOOKS was painted in gilt over the window of the little shop. Under those words a single pedestal stand displayed a great book that looked like one of those old dictionaries a foot thick. Light glowed from within, but Frankie couldn't see anyone inside.

Henri reached over and took her hand. "You're holding your breath."

She let it out. "Okay, let's go." She didn't wait for him to open her door. But he made it to the door of the shop ahead of her and pushed it open. A bell tinkled as they entered.

The familiar head of red hair poked out from a door in the back. "Be right with you."

Frankie scanned the shop frantically but she didn't see Leonardo's book. Henri took her hand. She breathed.

Of course not. No one would keep something so valuable on display. The bookshop was crammed from floor to ceiling with leather-spined books of every shape and size. Comfortable chairs and a sofa sat on an oriental carpet in cones of soft light cast by several reading lamps.

The woman she remembered hurried out from the back, looking distraught. She was a lovely thing, well upholstered like her chairs with winsome curves and a perfect translucent complexion that went with the wavy mass of red hair. She stopped dead when she saw Frankie. "It's you!"

"Uh, yes." Suddenly, Frankie didn't know what to say. At least the woman recognized her. That meant that she had been in the shop. And she had left the book here.

Time for Eternity

"I've been looking for you for the last week." Suddenly she peered at Frankie. Her eyes slid to Henri. She looked a little stunned. Frankie was used to it. Women always looked stunned when they first met Henri. She tore her eyes away and back to Frankie. "You look...different."

Frankie patted her hair self-consciously. She no longer had the original Frankie's spikes. "Where are my manners? Lucy Rossano, this is Henri Foucault."

Ms. Rossano nodded to Henri. "A pleasure, Mr. Foucault Am I to credit you for the change I see in Ms. Suchet?" She glanced back to Frankie. "She looks so much...softer."

"I like to think so," Henri murmured. It was left to Frankie to blush.

"Never mind that," Frankie said. "I've come about the book. You have it?"

"That's why I've been trying to find you. No one had heard of you at the address you gave."

"I've been...away. Do-you-have-the-book?" Frankie spoke each syllable slowly.

Lucy Rosanno ran her hands through the thick mass of her hair. "Yes. Yes, of course. But someone has made an offer on it And...and I don't know what to do."

"You haven't sold it?" Frankie and Henri both said it at once.

"No, no. At least not yet. But...but they offered...they offered a million dollars."

Frankie and Henri glanced at each other. The book was easily wroth that. And more. An original by Leonardo da Vinci? A million was low if she sold it at auction.

"We'd be willing to match whatever you're offered," Henri said calmly.

Ms. Rosanno looked at him like he'd grown another eye. Her mouth worked but she didn't manage to bring forth any sound. If anything, Henri's offer seemed to leave her even more distressed. Her pale complexion alternately flushed and went dead white.

Susan Squires

Frankie began to get the oddest feeling; a tingling right at the edge of her mind. "Why ...why were you looking for me?"

Ms. Rosanno's clear green eyes searched her face. "At first I just thought I should share the price with you. You just left it here, you know. You didn't ask anything for it. I thought it wasn't right that I should get a million dollars and you get nothing at all."

"And a f t e r ...?" Frankie asked, because there was definitely something else going on here. Frankie could feel it.

"I started to dream about the book. And I couldn't bear the thought of selling it at all. I started thinking about it every waking moment. And I wondered...how you could give it up like that...just leave it here and not look back?"

Because for me, it had already done its work. Now where had those thoughts come from?

"Is...is it cursed or something?" the young woman asked. "I mean, were you trying to pass it on to get rid of it?"

And it all became clear to Frankie. She knew what she must do. She smiled, and she knew the smile was reassuring because it felt true and right. "No. No, I had already used it to make me happy, and I was finished with it."

Ms. Rossano's eyes got big. "You do look happy," she whispered.

Frankie stepped forward and took the girl's hands in her own. "Don't sell the book. You don't want to sell it, do you?"

The girl's eyes filled. She shook her head.

"Do you need money?" Henri asked. "A million dollars is a lot of money."

The girl gave a jerky laugh. "Who doesn't need a million dollars? The shop..." She looked around. "It's hard."

Henri looked to Frankie. "We're meeting Donna and Jergan at Ozone tonight after the opera. They know everyone who is anybody in the arts in this city. I'm sure they know collectors who would like to browse your collection."

"Keep the book," Frankie said, looking into those clear green eyes. "You're meant to have it, just as I was." She turned to Henri.

Time for Eternity

"Time to go?" he asked her. She nodded. Henri took one of his cards from the inside breast pocket of his Armani suit, and handed it to the little bookseller. "If ever I can be of service, don't hesitate to call."

And they left. Frankie relaxed. She needn't worry now.

"What happened to all the anxiety?" Henri clicked the key fob and the car chirped as it unlocked itself and turned on the lights. The fog was coming in and the air felt thick and damp.

"The book isn't dangerous, at least in her hands."

"True. She can't power the machine. She's human." He opened the door for her. She watched him walk around the front of the car. He opened the door and slid in behind the wheel. "She doesn't even know the machine is under the Baptistery in Florence. She'd need a crane to lift the stone that leads to the crypts."

"It doesn't matter. She'll use it. The book's meant to be hers. I felt it."

Henri smiled and turned the key. The engine caught with a purr. "So...you're thinking this book is a supernatural object?"

Frankie laughed. "Leonardo was artist and scientist together and that made him half magician. That book describes a machine half science and half art. Maybe the book itself has been transformed into a sacred object. Sacred objects have a will of their own, you know."

"You're making this up, aren't you? Just so I'll think you know what you're doing?"

She chuckled. He always knew. "Maybe."

"Maybe," he echoed. She didn't know whether he was talking about her making things up, or the truth of what she'd said. She didn't know herself. She leaned across the armrest between them. She missed bench seats in cars. Henri put his arm around her.

"Let's go have a drink at Ozone," she said.

"That's where all this started."

"And it's been quite an adventure. Living with you is

Susan Squires

always an adventure."

She pulled her head from his shoulder. "This from a man who led the Resistance in Marseilles? Dodging the Nazis every day? Captured and tortured and I couldn't find you for weeks? And I won't even mention risking your life to save the Dalai Lama, or that time—"

"See what I put up with?" Henri raised his eyes to the roof of the car. "This is what comes of living with one woman for two hundred-plus years. They know everything." He lowered his eyes, though, and they were soft—the look she'd come to treasure. He kissed her forehead silently, letting his lips linger there. Then he glanced at the clock.

"We have hours before we have to meet Donna and Jergan. And we have that lovely penthouse suite at the Fairmont with that huge bed."

"With clean sheets."

"They might have put chocolates on the pillows."

"You could order champagne."

"Done."

About Susan Squires

Susan Squires is a *New York Times* bestselling author known for breaking the rules of romance writing. She has published seventeen books with Dorchester and St. Martin's Press. Her contemporary Magic Series is independently published with six novels and a novella. Whatever her time period or subject, some element of the paranormal always creeps in to her work. She has been a finalist in the Romance Writers of America Rita Contest, and won numerous regional and national awards, including the Holt Medallion, the Golden Heart, and the Book Buyers' Best award, as well as garnered several Reviewer's Choice awards from RT Book Reviews and starred reviews from *Publisher's Weekly*. *Publisher's Weekly* named *Body Electric* one of the year's ten most influential mass market books and *One with the Shadows,* the fifth in her Companion Series, a Best Book of the Year.

Susan has a Masters in English literature from UCLA and once toiled as an executive for a Fortune 500 company. Now she lives at the beach in Southern California with her husband, Harry, a writer of supernatural thrillers, and two very active Belgian Sheepdogs, who like to help her write by putting their chins on the keyboarddddddddddddddddddddddddddd.

Follow Susan on Twitter, like her Facebook page at AuthorSusanSquires or check out her website at http://www.susansquires.com .

Susan Squires

Coming soon: *Twist in Time*. Here's a sample:

One

It was okay to be a little obsessive, Lucy Rossano told herself, trying to breathe. Perfectly normal. She clutched the shoulder bag that contained the book to her chest. It was the most valuable book she'd ever acquired in the eight years she'd been dealing in rare books. So of course she couldn't bring herself to sell it, no matter the price, or donate it to a museum, or even lock it in the safe at the store. It was by frickin' Leonardo DaVinci. Who wouldn't want to carry it around all the time?

And sleep with it.

"I can't *believe* you have a book that shows a picture of the very machine I'm working on." Brad could hardly contain his excitement. He pushed past the guard's desk at the Super Collider Lab. "Hey, Wally. Just in for a quick check on the power levels."

The guard's eyes widened. "Uh, okay, Dr. Steadman." His stare shifted to Lucy. She could feel him registering the really red hair. It was the only reason anyone ever noticed her.

"Oh. Uh, Lucy's my...my new research assistant. Lucy, why don't you sign in?"

Lucy moved to the loose-leaf binder as in a dream. This couldn't be happening. Brad was wrong. Maybe the whole thing was wishful thinking on his part. Right. Wishful thinking—*Brad*? Practical, sub-atomic-particle-expert Brad? He'd been her father's research assistant at Stanford. Wishful thinking wasn't in his gene pool. She signed her name. The guard passed her a visitors' tag. She clipped it to her black knit jacket. Her hand shook.

"You sure work all hours, Dr. Steadman," Wally said, waving them through.

Brad grabbed her hand and practically dragged her

Time for Eternity

through two double doors. When the doors were safely shut, he said, "And you showed it to me only hours after I'd had a breakthrough in powering the thing. What a coincidence!"

Yeah. Just a coincidence. But she'd had the book for months now and hadn't told a soul. So why had she felt so… so *compelled* to show her friend Brad the book today of all days? The urge had haunted her at the Exploratorium. It should have been just like any other visit. She and Brad went to the Exploratorium every few months since her father died. He was trying to interest her in the hands-on exhibits meant for children. He thought she'd be happier if she went back to school and got a degree in some kind of science, preferably particle science so they could work together. Like that was going to happen. Her doctorate meant nothing to him, both because it was in Comparative Literature and the fact that it was from Berkeley, not Stanford.

Still, she liked the Exploratorium, as much for the picnics they always had at the Palace of Fine Arts next door as anything else. The classic, semi-ruin built for the 1918 Pan-American Fair held a strange attraction for her. Today the place was all torn up because the city of San Francisco was retrofitting it to withstand earthquakes. But the mysterious basement they'd uncovered below the Rotunda floor only seemed to make the attraction stronger. Why had it been built? Why was it empty? In the middle of her speculation, the urge to show Brad the book began to feel like she'd ordered Thai food extra hot—a burning sensation she couldn't control. Finally, as the November fog rolled in through the Golden Gate and down the colonnade, she'd pulled out the book and let Brad page through it in the overhead light of the car.

Now, here they were, hurrying down the long corridor of the Super Collider Lab to see…what? An impossibility.

"I *knew* this was important, no matter what Casey said." Brad had been under a lot of pressure since some guy from the government had come in to supervise his project. "He doesn't give me the respect I deserve." Brad glanced back to her. "Just like someone else I could name."

Susan Squires

Lucy mustered up a smile. Brad was a strange mixture of rampant ego and insecurity. It was kind of nice to have a friend who needed you as much as you needed him. And she had been needy after her father died. "You know I think you're brilliant."

Brad's eyes darkened. He set his lips. "Yeah. You think I'm smart. That's why you bother to hang around with me."

That was only part of it. They did have good conversations. But she also hung with Brad because he'd known her father. Now that she was alone in the world, Brad was a kind of connection to him. And Brad had been a friend indeed, helping her with the funeral, arranging to sell her father's boat so she could keep the store going. "You know it's more than that."

A little glimmer of something flashed in his brown eyes. "I know."

That was puzzling. But so was this whole thing puzzling. When Brad saw the picture of the machine in Leonardo's wonderful book, he freaked out. He said the machine actually existed. The Italian government found it under Il Duomo cathedral in Florence and asked Stanford's Super Collider lab to find a way to power it. No one knew what the machine actually did.

Except Lucy. Leonardo's book told her.

It was supposed to be a time machine.

Therefore it wasn't real. She couldn't be hurrying down some corridor of a lab in the hills of twenty-first century San Mateo County to see a time machine built in 1508. Impossible.

But that's not what her bones were telling her. She'd always known that Leonardo's treatise, which had such a hold on her, was no ordinary book.

It had all started with a girl named Frankie Suchet.

*****

"I've got a book I want authenticated," the beautiful young woman said. Her blond hair was spiked out and tipped with coal black. Her blue eyes glowed in translucent skin. She

Time for Eternity

was lean and boyish, dressed in tight leather pants and a skimpy sweater that showed her flat belly. Just the kind of body Lucy always wanted to have. "Professor Lambeth over at Berkeley said you could do the job." *The woman began unwrapping a brown paper package tied with string.*

"Don't you want to know how much I charge?" *Lucy asked, taken aback by the girl's abrupt demeanor.*

"Charge what you want. I need to know if it's real." *Her voice was hard.*

Lucy sighed. It would be some diary found in an attic trunk, worth no more than its sentimental value. That's what usually walked in her door. The bookstore was just creaking by, yielding just enough income to hold body and soul together. She'd charge the woman a hundred bucks just to make the service seem worthwhile and tell her the bad news.

The large book revealed on her counter had a beautiful tooled leather binding. Who would do something so expensive for a diary? The style was almost High Renaissance, with scenes of angels swirling up toward a radiant cloud. Lucy ran her hand over it. Not stamped. You could clearly see the mark of the awl in several places.

There was no title page, only a dedication…in archaic Italian.

"For Contessa Donnatella Margherita Luchella di Poliziano, from her friend Leonardo DaVinci. I dedicate to you my greatest work."

A chill ran down her spine. It couldn't be. Get hold of yourself. *A fraud. The writing was certain proof. She turned a page. Her eyes scanned the note.*

"What you see before you is a time machine."

Right. Somebody was trying to put one over on the academic community. They'd probably go for it, hook, line and sinker, too. Who didn't want to believe that Leonardo DaVinci had built a time machine? She scanned again. Something about only the Contessa having enough power to make the machine

Susan Squires

run....

"You are asking yourself how it works. If you care to read the journal, you will know. But if you are in haste, know this, time is not a river but a vortex, and with enough power a man can jump into another part of the swirl.

So, my dear Contessa, pull the lever. Think of the moment you want to be in as you leap into the maelstrom. You will end in the moment you imagine.

Be warned: the machine will go with you but it cannot stay long in another time. To return, you must use it again before it disappears. I do not know how long it can stay. I do not know what will happen if you make it back to the time you are in now, or what will happen if you don't. I give you only the means to change your destiny, or perhaps all of our destinies. Use it if you will."

But the book wasn't Leonardo's. She'd known it from the first words of the dedication. Leonardo didn't write that way. Then she turned the page.

My God.

The writing of the central text was done from right to left. Each letter was written backwards. It would read correctly in a mirror. Exactly how Leonardo wrote his notebooks—why, no one knew for certain. Diagrams, calculations in the margins, long batches of text that would take many hours to translate...it all looked amazingly authentic. And on the final pages, there was an intricate picture of a machine with incredibly complex interlocking gears.

"What do you think?"

Lucy looked up at the girl. The look in those blue eyes was cynical, but only on the surface, underneath there was a terrible, wrenching...hope.

Lucy managed a shrug. "Well, if it's fake, it's one hell of a fake. The paper is made from macerated rags rolled out in a

Time for Eternity
press. The writing is in the manner of Leonardo. There's a
chance it's real. I'll know in a couple of days."

*****

Frankie Suchet had left her name and address. The book had been real, of course. But that wasn't the strangest part of it in some ways. When Lucy had told her, three days later, the girl had taken a gigantic breath and said: "Well, that's it then." And she had turned around and made for the door.

"Don't you want to take the book with you?" Lucy had called after her.

The woman had turned in the doorway. "You keep it. I have what I need from it."

And she'd walked out.

That was the last Lucy had seen of her for five months. And then one day, she walked in through the shop door, accompanied by the most drop-dead gorgeous man Lucy had ever seen. At least Lucy *thought* it was Frankie Suchet. She had to look twice. Gone was the spiky hair, the air of cynicism...

"It's you! I've been looking for you." Lucy's eyes slid to the guy. She tore her eyes away and back to Frankie. "You look... different."

The girl ran her hands through her hair self-consciously. "Where are my manners? Lucy Rossano, this is Henri Foucault." She pronounced it in the French manner. Ahn-ree Foo-coh.

Lucy nodded to the guy and felt herself blushing like every other woman probably did when confronted with that man. "A pleasure, Monsieur Foucault. Am I to credit you for the change I see in Ms. Suchet?" Lucy glanced to Frankie. The soft expression was the real change.

"I like to think so," the hunk murmured.

Frankie's blush joined Lucy's. "Never mind that. I've come about the book."

"That's why I've been trying to find you. No one heard of you at the address you gave."

"I've been...away. Do-you-have-the-book?" Frankie

spoke each syllable slowly.

Lucy realized she was staring at the couple. She ran her hands through the thick mass of her hair. "Yes. Yes, of course. But someone has made an offer on it. A…a million dollars. I couldn't sell it, of course, because it really belongs to you."

The couple glanced at each other. "Nonsense. It's yours. But we'll match whatever you're offered," Foucault said.

Lucy's mouth worked but she couldn't manage any sound. She couldn't sell it to the woman who had given it to her. She wanted to say she'd just give it back. But that would mean giving it up.

Frankie leaned over the counter, blue eyes burning. "There's more to it, isn't there?"

Lucy felt trapped. But this woman would know about the book if anyone did. And Lucy needed to know. "I've started to dream about the book. I think about it every waking moment. Is…is it cursed or something? I mean, the way you just left it here when it was so valuable—were you passing it on to get rid of it?"

Frankie smiled. Suddenly she seemed sure of herself. "No, I had already decided to use the knowledge it contained to make me happy. I had all it could give me."

"You do look happy," Lucy whispered.

Henri looked to Frankie then spoke to Lucy. "If you're short of money, we know some influential people in the arts in San Francisco. We'll spread the word about your shop."

"Keep the book." Frankie looked into Lucy's eyes. "You're meant to have it just as I was."

*****

And they left her a treasure. Sometimes she wished they hadn't. The book had hold of her, no matter how much she pretended she wasn't obsessed. She'd begun to make up fantastic stories about Frankie Suchet using the machine to make herself happy and what that might mean. She'd day-dreamed about using the machine as if it really existed. Because ever since her father died, Lucy had been drifting, waiting for…something. She wanted what Frankie Suchet had.

Time for Eternity

Certainty? Happiness? She wanted that. She wanted her life transformed into something meaningful, even though she didn't know what that meaning would be.

And now the whole sequence of events seemed like destiny. The feeling was overpowering. The book had been left to her. Frankie believed it was meant for her somehow. The Italian government sent the machine to America to give it power. Her friend Brad was assigned to the project. Too many coincidences. The book and the machine were coming together with power only the Super Collider lab could provide.

And they would be used.

Tonight.

Maybe it wouldn't work. This could all still be some elaborate hoax.

But Lucy no longer believed that. This was destiny. Her destiny.

*****

A guy with a ramrod straight military bearing and a brush cut stepped out of an office directly into Lucy and Brad's path. She could practically feel Brad cringe. The guy had an intense look about him.

"Colonel Casey, just the man I wanted to see." Brad wasn't an imposing man, maybe five nine or ten, lean from being a runner. He dressed precisely in pressed chinos and Bruno Magli loafers, maybe too precisely. He wasn't God's gift to women. But he and Lucy had their common looks in common. She wasn't God's gift to men. Maybe that drew them together—a lifetime of being everyone's second choice. There was no way Brad was fit to stand up to Casey.

"I heard you made a breakthrough, Steadman. About time. Though what this retro bunch of gears is supposed to do is beyond me." His eyes never left Lucy's face. They were the palest blue she'd ever seen. Even though his hair was blond they seemed unnatural. "Trying to impress your girl with a government project that requires special clearance?" The sneer

Susan Squires

in his voice was evident. "Not smart, Steadman."

"As a matter of fact," here Brad cleared his throat, "Miss Rossano is my research assistant. I've located a book about the origin of the machine and its purpose."

Lucy tried to relax. This guy would never let the machine be used, destiny or not, by some girl he didn't know. She was off the hook. She had no desire to succumb to some fate over which she had no control, regardless of the feeling in the pit of her stomach.

"Okay. Give me the book. I'll take a look. *You* wait in the lobby, Miss Rossano."

Like hell. She wasn't giving up her book. She leaned forward and stuck out her hand. "That's *Dr.* Rossano. Nice to meet someone else who reads sixteenth century Italian."

Casey stared at her. Boy, if reptiles had blue eyes... He didn't take her offered hand. He shot a disgusted glance to Brad. Then he gestured down the hall.

She saw Brad swallow as he led the way. Casey fell in behind them.

Brad opened a door at the end of a long hall. Lucy had memorized each detail of the diagram in Leonardo's book. But that didn't prepare her for the sheer size and weight of the machine standing on a platform across the lab. It gleamed faintly in the tiny work lights that still left shadows in the cavernous lab. The whole experience was like the first time she'd seen Rodin's *The Thinker* in the sculpture garden at the Norton Simon Museum. Everybody knew what it looked like from pictures in countless art books. But that never prepared you. It was that dense occupation of space that gave it emotional resonance.

The giant, brass gears towering above her, immensely heavy, made her catch her breath and struggle for air. The gems that studded the wheels coruscated with emerald green, ruby red and the blue of sapphires as big as your fist. Where had Leonardo gotten such jewels? A fortune winked from among the interlocking wheels, none bigger than the huge diamond that formed the knob of a control stick. Everything looked just as it was in the book, except for the lunchbox-sized metal box

Time for Eternity

bolted to the frame just under the largest wheel.

Could this medieval machine really send someone to another time? On the face of it, it was ridiculous. Yet if anyone could build a time machine surely it would be Leonardo DaVinci. Half scientist, half artist, in some ways he was more than either—a magician, perhaps. Was it that possibility that had fueled her obsession?

Both the colonel and Brad watched for her reaction. She thought Brad might explode with excitement. "It's Leonardo's machine, all right." She couldn't help that her eyes filled.

"DaVinci?" Casey's voice was sharp.

Lucy nodded. She could hardly see his light eyes in the dim room.

She saw Brad tried to calm himself. He cleared his throat. "If the book is right this machine could be more important than you've been thinking, Colonel." Was Brad excited only to prove himself to Casey? Maybe.

Casey's hard eyes reassessed her. "And *you*, Dr. Rossano, know what it is."

She nodded slowly. Well, at least he'd never believe her. "Yeah. It's a time machine."

"A time machine," Casey snorted. "Right. Are you crazy, Steadman?"

"No, you've got to see the book, Colonel," Brad protested. He hurried to a long table that faced the machine and switched on a small work light. "Luce, bring the book and show him."

Lucy hefted her bag off her shoulder. The book wouldn't help a military guy believe. Huge girders loomed in the ceiling far above her. The place had that peculiar sterile environment that left only a faint metallic odor. She pulled out the book and spread it open. Casey leaned over it. Lucy pointed. "Leonardo's signature." She flipped pages to show the diagrams on assembly, key notes in the margins, mathematical equations. Then she flipped to the full drawing. Casey drew in a breath. She paged back. "Here's where he says that time is a vortex. And here…he says the jewels focus the power."

Susan Squires

"How do I know that's what it says?" Casey asked softly, his eyes darting over the text.

"You can check it with another expert in archaic Italian." There. That would buy time. She could feel the machine looming above her, heavy with…with purpose. That was bad.

"How do you select a time? There are no dials or settings we could see."

Lucy smiled. This would seal their disbelief. "It says in the book that you pull the handle, and just think about the time you want to be in."

Casey blinked once and chuffed a disgusted laugh. "Oh, great. I get the really good assignments."

"Okay. I know it sounds a little out there," Brad admitted. "That's why we've got to try it. If we've spent a lot of someone's money powering a machine that doesn't do anything, better to know that now. If it's a hoax all the Italians have is a fortune in tourist dollars when they put it on display in the Ufizzi. But if it's not then we've got something *everybody* is going to want."

Lucy was dismayed at Casey's look of speculation. He couldn't be considering powering up the machine, could he?

"And then this wasn't such a crappy assignment after all," Brad continued. "In fact, you can probably name your next one." Brad really struck a chord with that. Casey thought he'd drawn a crappy assignment and he was now thinking how nice it would be to come up with something incredible no one ever expected. "So why don't we test it out? Right here. Tonight."

No, no, no. Definitely not. Lucy looked around wildly. The machine seemed to be vibrating in satisfaction. "Wouldn't…wouldn't that be bad scientific method? You should do a….a controlled experiment." Brad was always talking about controlled experiments.

"Well, we've got a problem," Brad said, his eyes on Casey. "We can't go to my boss, or your boss, and tell them we've got a time machine. We'd be laughed out of the office."

"Well, yeah," Casey said, dripping sarcasm. "I guess we would."

Time for Eternity

"Unless we had proof. Come on, Casey." Brad was on a roll. Sure of himself. "You want prestige and power. If it works, you're in like Flynn. A time machine built by Leonardo DaVinci and powered by our project?" It must have killed him to share the credit for the project.

Lucy could see that Casey was becoming convinced. He'd gotten that speculative look, in spades. "Your little lunchbox over there works?"

"Of course it works," Brad said through gritted teeth. "We successfully moved the gears today using a fraction of the power it's capable of."

"Could you go to the future?" Casey stared at the machine, even though he was addressing Lucy. He was caught by the possibilities. He would be the one to use the machine tonight. Maybe that was okay. But it didn't feel right. She shook herself mentally. What was she thinking? She had to get out of here or something... momentous would happen.

But she answered anyway. "I don't know. Leonardo was more interested in understanding the past. I guess if time is really a vortex you could go either way."

Casey continued to stare. "What if you can't power up the machine again once you're there?" Oh, yeah. She'd been through that possibility in her mind a thousand times.

"According to Leonardo, the machine can't stay in another time forever. It's too much pressure on the flow of time. It'll snap back to where it came from with you or without you."

"If he knows what he's talking about. And if he doesn't?"

She took a breath. "You get stuck there, along with your machine." There. That should make them think twice about using it.

Brad looked desperate. He wanted the project to succeed that much. "Look," he said. "There's always risk. Somebody has to be first. Sam Yeager had to go up and fly fast even though nobody knew what would happen when you broke the sound barrier. John Glenn had to go up in Apollo.

Sometime, somebody just has to do it."

Casey peered at the illustration in the book then straightened. "I agree." He turned to Lucy. "How about her?"

Both Brad and Lucy were stunned. "She isn't even part of the team," Brad sputtered.

"She's perfect. She's obviously read this book a hundred times. She knows how it's supposed to work." Here Casey looked at Brad. "And we have plausible deniability. We were doing tests and she pulled the handle while our backs were turned." He'd gone through all the permutations in his mind. One. It didn't work. Nothing lost. Two. It did work and she went back and returned. He won big. Three. She went back and only the machine returned. He won. He didn't care about her. Four. She went back and neither she nor the machine returned. That was bad. They'd have to admit that she hoodwinked them. But it was one in four. Odds were with Casey. *Really* with Casey with how big the odds were that it wouldn't work in the first place.

Lucy felt the lab almost tremble with intent. Brad's face was a comical combination of eagerness and guilt. He wanted so badly to try the machine. Badly enough to risk her life? Apparently. "Brad?"

He took a long breath. Fear flashed across his face before he pulled down a mask over both the fear and the eagerness. "You'll be okay, Lucy."

So that was it. He did want it that bad, but he didn't have the courage to use it himself. Casey looked at her. Brad looked at her.

It all came down to this moment. The months of obsession, the feeling of her life being without purpose, stale and tasteless since her father died, her fascination with how happy Frankie Suchet had been. If she walked out now, what would she be walking out *to?* She had nothing out there. A successful business, maybe even wildly successful since Frankie and Henri had directed all their friends to frequent her shop, but it didn't *mean* anything to her. She had no friends except a crazy old loon of a landlord and Brad, and Brad didn't look to be a great friend right now. She had nothing but her obsession with the book. And if she walked out, they'd never let her take the book with her. That left…nothing. Her life beyond the walls of this lab had not a shred of magic in it. But here, in this sterile place, magic hung in the air, delivered across time by a magician named DaVinci.

A thrill of… expectation made it hard for Lucy to breathe. How long since she had had expectations of life? A feeling of rightness washed over her. Everything was about to change, and that was as it should be. Her breathing calmed. "Okay." She turned to the machine. "Rev up your lunchbox, Brad."

Brad looked back at Casey. Casey nodded. Brad took a breath and turned to the machine. "Get me more light," he called over his shoulder.

"Nix. That'd attract attention," Casey snapped. He turned off the light on the table. "Only the work lights."

Brad knelt in front of the machine without further protest.

"Let me watch you," Lucy said, leaning over him. "I'll have to start it up myself to make it back." She watched him flipping lighted switches and murmured the pattern to herself. "Blue, then the two whites from left to right, and then the red."

The machine began to hum. Vibrations just at the edge of her awareness filled the room. She steadied her breathing. She was going to do this. How…miraculous was that? The right feeling pushed her fear behind some kind of curtain in her mind. She knew all the things that could happen. She could get stuck in the past. She'd probably be burned as a witch. A red-haired witch. It was an insane risk. She just didn't care anymore. All this was meant to happen. "Okay, to you two it will probably seem if as only a moment has elapsed before I reappear." She closed the book, tucked it into her bag and slung the bag on her shoulder. "Let's get this show on the road."

"You should leave the book here." Brad was trying to sound like Casey. Not.

"Hey, I'm not going back to who-knows-when without my references."

Susan Squires

"Let her take it," Casey said. "Does us no good if the thing doesn't work." He nodded to her. There was respect in his eyes.

"I'll go back far enough that they'll be in awe of me and my machine." She was wearing the outfit she'd worn to the Exploratorium, a flippy knit skirt and matching slinky jacket over a green shell, and ballet slipper flats.

"Better pick summer time." Casey said, echoing her thoughts. "Hate to see you ruin those shoes in snow." Was Casey kidding? How did you know with a guy like that?

"You got it."

"Give her all your change," Casey ordered Brad. "Just in case she's there long enough to need to buy food and lodging. Silver is good." They each piled a handful of coins into her bag.

"I won't be there long. I'm going to figure out where I am, grab something to bring back with me as proof and high-tail it back here." Was that true? She stepped up under the machine in front of the lever topped by that impossibly huge diamond.

Brad knelt by the lunch box again. "After you do the switch sequence push this chrome button here, and that will start the power." It was a rounded pad you pressed with your palm.

She nodded and put both hands over the diamond knob. Brad slapped the button. The power hum passed out of hearing range, but she could feel it in her chest and throat. She pulled the lever down. No gears moved. The feeling of power in the air made it difficult to breathe. At last the big gear in the central portion of the machine creaked.

God, it was going to happen! She had to think of a time period. The small gears began to spin, faster and faster. Shakespearean England? Fin de siècle France? She spoke French pretty well. The gears whirred until they were only a blur. She couldn't decide! A white glow filled the room. She thought Brad was shouting, or maybe it was Casey. She couldn't make out the words.

What she really wanted was to go back to a time when

Time for Eternity

magic was possible. Any time, it didn't matter—a time when people believed in magic and it transformed their lives.

The gears seemed to stop, time hung suspended. Oh, no! Did Brad's lunchbox not provide enough power? Or was Leonardo's design flawed? The glow was cut by a hundred beams of light, colored like the jewels. They crisscrossed the ceiling, illuminating the girders above. What was happening here? She felt that possibility of magic she'd imagined receding. A sense of loss suffused her....

Then everything happened impossibly fast. The sensation of time slowing changed in an instant to a feeling of being flung forward like a slingshot, and everything was a blur and she was screaming, only she couldn't hear herself scream....

Susan Squires

Made in the USA
Monee, IL
14 February 2021